BEFORE

WE WERE

INNOCENT

Also by Ella Berman

The Comeback

BEFORE
WE WERE
INNOCENT

ELLA BERMAN

BERKLEY

New York

BERKLEY
An imprint of Penguin Random House LLC
penguinrandomhouse.com

Copyright © 2023 by Ella Berman

Library of Congress Cataloging-in-Publication Data

Names: Berman, Ella, author.
Title: Before we were innocent / Ella Berman.
Description: New York : Berkley, [2023]
Identifiers: LCCN 2022032629 (print) | LCCN 2022032630 (ebook) |
ISBN 9780593099544 (hardcover) | ISBN 9780593099568 (ebook)
Subjects: LCGFT: Novels.
Classification: LCC PR3102.E753 B44 2023 (print) | LCC PR3102.E753 (ebook) |
DDC 823/.92—dc23
LC record available at https://lccn.loc.gov/2022032629
LC ebook record available at https://lccn.loc.gov/2022032630

Printed in the United States of America
1st Printing

Book design by Daniel Brount

*To my own fierce friendships—some of which have lasted,
some of which are lost. I think of you all often.*

BEFORE
WE WERE
INNOCENT

ONE

2018

I KNOW IT'S HER FROM the moment I hear the knock at my door. After ten years, with no warning, somehow, I still know.

Over the years, I've begun to think of Joni only in photographs— reassuringly flat shots of her golden arm slung over my shoulders, eyes knowing, grin wolfish, face tanned and inscrutable, maybe careless in the wrong light. Now that she is inches away, I remember the full animality of our friendship. The clamminess of her skin as we slept side by side, matching leg hairs dusting our thighs; the keloid scar just above her left temple; the viscous blood that would trickle from her nose often and without any warning, although usually when she was being her worst self, as if her body wanted so badly to remind us that she was human.

Joni's short hair is wet, slicked back, and her lips are swollen in the flickering porch light. I remember that she used to chew her bottom lip when she was feeling vulnerable, and I never mentioned it because it felt like a waste of this rare insight I'd been given.

Now I can see that her mouth looks painful, red raw where she's torn at it.

Joni doesn't attempt to hide her shock at my own appearance in return, and I stand rigidly as she takes me in—hair hanging limply to my waist, faded T-shirt thrown over flannel pajama shorts, pale skin that has seen less sun in five years than it used to in one summer. From afar, I've kept abreast of Joni's transformation from scrappy, magnetic teenager to overgroomed media rent-a-personality, but this is the first time she's seen me outside of my teenage state, probably seared as indelibly into her mind as it is my own (hip popped, pink tongue sticking out of lips coated in MAC's Rapturous).

"Jesus, Bess," she says finally. "You're a little fucking young to retire to the desert, aren't you?"

As Joni's openers go, it could have been a lot worse, but I still feel my perspective shift. I wonder if she can already sense the stifling flatness of life next to the Salton Sea—a wasteland or a kingdom, depending on how you ended up here.

"I need your help," Joni says next.

I think of the ghost between us. The three of us sticky with sweat, sunburned bodies loose from cheap beer as we danced to our favorite song underneath a palm leaf canopy, or lying on our stomachs on a hotel bed, dirty soles of our feet in the air, as Joni and I competed over who could shock Evangeline into laughing first. Then, inevitably—the unnatural angle of Ev's neck under the skinniest moon I've ever seen. Ten summers that have felt like ten seconds and ten lifetimes all at once.

When Joni takes a step toward me, I move away and she pretends not to notice, just like how I pretend not to notice that her hand is shaking as she plays with the button of her white linen shirt. I think about the last time we were together and the cruel things we both said, knowing they could never be undone. I think about everything I lost while Joni elevated our shared existence, upgrading her life like a company car. I think about the end of that summer and feel the shame trickle down the back of my neck. There are ten thousand reasons why I shouldn't let Joni Le Bon inside my house tonight, but still, I take a step backward.

"Follow me," I say.

TWO

2018

I LEAD JONI INTO THE kitchen, walking carefully around the saguaro cactus that shoots through the center of my house like a missile, causing the tiles around it to crack and cave. When I look down, I realize I'm wearing the humiliating pair of bunny slippers my ex-boyfriend Ivan gave me as a birthday present, and I wonder if I can slip them off before Joni notices.

"You are aware you have a strikingly phallic cactus," she says, more at ease now, "in the middle of your house."

"I had noticed," I say as I open the fridge. "Do you want some water?"

Joni frowns. "I'd prefer wine."

I rifle through the cupboard under the sink, coming up with a bottle of California chardonnay that Ivan must have bought before he decided I was unsalvageable. It has to be a shitty bottle for him to have left it behind, considering he unscrewed all the halogen lightbulbs on his way out.

I pour two glasses, watching as Joni takes in the surroundings— the slate gray blinds pulled down; the peeling shiplap walls and mismatched furniture; the stark print of sunflowers hanging on the wall above the TV, an image so bland that my brother once asked if it came with the frame. If I see a flicker of approval on Joni's face, I think I know why—my home is the diametric opposite of the Calabasas McMansions we both grew up in, with their acute angles and surfaces designed so that you can never quite escape your own reflection, because why would you want to when you've spent thousands of dollars on tweakments to not only maintain but *elevate* your own face?

"You live here alone," Joni says.

"Does that surprise you?" I ask, leaning against the cabinet, waiting for her to tell me what she wants from me. Nine years ago, I spent my dead grandmother's inheritance on this cabin beneath the San Jacinto Mountains precisely because of its isolation—so that people from my past wouldn't just show up one day because they were "in the area."

"Are you off the grid?" she says instead. "Are you generating energy from compost or something?"

"Joni."

"I'm just trying to understand," she says.

"Why are you here?"

Joni nods and takes another sip of wine.

"It's my fiancée," she says. "Willa."

"Your fiancée," I repeat, even though I already know that "Willa" is Willa Bailey, semifamous influencer and activist—information I have gleaned from Joni's Instagram account, which I follow from an anonymous burner profile: @pizzancacti23. I can already picture Willa's face in my mind as clearly as I can any celebrity's—wide easy smile and thick, expressive brows that tend to cave inward when she talks, like the Sad Sam dog I kept stuffed down the side of my bed for the duration of my teenage years—but I would never give Joni the satisfaction of knowing it.

"Trouble in paradise?" I ask.

"I guess you could put it that way," Joni says carefully, and it throws me. Is Joni careful now? Does she deliberate over each perfect word instead of letting them fly out of her mouth like a swarm of wasps?

I watch as she bites down on her lip, hard.

"A few weeks ago, Willa found out that I slept with someone else," she says after a long pause. "And, while I promised her it was a one-night thing, it wasn't exactly as simple as that . . ."

"You're still cheating on her," I say.

"I didn't say that," Joni snaps back like a snake before she catches herself, smiling a little.

"I may have been keeping a door open that I should have closed," she says, and I don't know why I'm surprised at how little she's changed.

"But, earlier tonight, Willa found a . . . photo that this person, Zoey, sent me, and I knew that it had to stop. So, I drove over to Zoey's apartment and I ended it. For real this time."

I stare at her, still unsure exactly what she wants from me. The Joni I knew always owned her choices unequivocally; *surely* she doesn't need me to tell her that she's a good person, that Willa probably doesn't deserve better, that she's only human despite all the praise and fervor and adulation claiming otherwise in the years since we were friends.

"The thing is, Willa thinks I came straight here," Joni says. "To give her some space."

"And why would she believe that?"

"Because every time I was with Zoey, Willa thought I was with you," Joni says levelly. "I told her we were planning something to mark the tenth anniversary. A celebration of Evangeline's life, since we obviously didn't make it to her funeral."

I swallow, wishing I hadn't asked, because what would a celebration of Ev's life even look like now? The only people we could invite would be other ghosts from our past—people Evangeline would also have been destined to outgrow and forget existed had she made it past her nineteenth birthday; people who had never really known her anyway, not like we had.

"But, Bess. If Willa finds out I lied to her, it won't be good."

"It won't be good," I repeat. "Because . . . ?"

"*Because* I have the biggest month of my career coming up," Joni says. "*Because* everything I've ever done has been building toward this moment, my book release, and for someone who has built a career on radical honesty and authenticity, this secret *liaison* isn't exactly a great look for me."

Everything I've ever done. Funny how this book, this pinnacle of Joni's career, happens to land on the ten-year-anniversary summer of the incident that made her infamous, I think, fighting a swell of resentment. Her MO is self-help, only Joni never calls it that. In her posts, it's always *self-growth* and *personal development*, as if it's never too late to overhaul your disappointing personality.

"Not because you love Willa, though," I say. "What, did you just get bored of her?"

Joni glares at me.

"Bess, I don't want to go into the minutiae of my relationship with you right now, I'm just asking for your help."

For a split second, I am blindsided that, once again, Joni has built a life worth lying for to protect.

"You haven't actually told me what you want me to do," I say, even though by this point, I already know.

"If anyone asks, I left my house around six and got here at nine p.m.," Joni says slowly, scanning the kitchen and landing on the dirty pan still sitting on my stovetop, a telltale strand of anemic spaghetti hanging over the edge. "You made pasta, and then we sat in the kitchen drinking this bottle of wine and catching up about the past. It's three hours, Bess. What difference does it make to your life?"

I think of all the ways I could say no to Joni. I could tell her how horrified I am that she would ask me this—that after ten years, I would be the person she canvasses to lie for her, even after everything we've been through. I could remind her of how badly she'd betrayed me the last time we saw each other, how much we'd wanted to hurt each other back then and how stunningly we succeeded. I could tell her about my life as it is now—how I've worked to tread lightly, to leave little trace of myself, to forget all the things we did and didn't do, constructing a new identity based on my actions rather than my instincts, and how Joni turning up and asking for this will disrupt everything all over again because I didn't leave space for anyone else in my life, but least of all her.

"Why did you do it?" I ask quietly, and Joni's eyes flash with fury.

"You're not listening to me," she says, speaking slowly as if I'm being willfully stupid. "I would have thought that you, more than anyone, wouldn't question me."

I swallow a rising lump at the back of my throat.

The problem is, Joni has always known who I am. And that's exactly why she's back.

THREE

2018

IN THE MORNING, JONI is poised and collected, already showered as she deftly works the imposing coffee machine my parents insisted on sending me, eyebrows groomed, smile impenetrable. I stand by the breakfast counter and, when she places a bowl of cereal in front of me, I try to appreciate being waited on, even if it is just dry shredded wheat from someone who has gone our entire adult lives without wanting to see me until now.

"Is everything okay today?" I ask.

"Okay?"

"With Willa," I say, eyeing her curiously.

"Oh." Joni tucks her dark hair behind her ear. "I'm not sure. I left my phone at home."

I stare at her for a moment longer. "You can use mine if you want."

Joni waves her hand at me and searches for something in the fridge.

"I have half-and-half under the sink," I say. "If that's what you're looking for."

Joni winces and closes the fridge.

"I'm sorry for asking you to help me after . . . everything," she says, widening her eyes at me. The mannerism is so odd, so decidedly un-Joni-like, that I instinctively narrow my own eyes back at her.

"How have you been, anyway?" I ask. "Apart from this."

"What a tragically *quotidian* question," Joni says as she studies the use-by date on a bottle of Advil before tossing it into the trash. "You realize I haven't seen you in nearly a decade?"

And whose fault is that? I think.

"Fine," I say. "How's your mom?"

"If you find out, do let me know," Joni says, without missing a beat. "Last I heard, she was in Dubai. She still doesn't believe in the internet."

As she's talking, I take a seat in the low fishing chair I keep set up for the rare occasions my own parents visit from wherever they are in the world. Their visits are generally fraught, and we all avoid referencing life before 2008, unless my brother, Steven, is there, because he has all the tact and confidence of a Southern California real estate agent despite working in software engineering, and he never seems to notice when my parents go pale or when my smile has been pasted on my face for so long that my lips are cracked. Every time they leave, they invariably try to replace every freestanding item in my home, and I invariably have to send it all back.

I open my laptop and sign in to the complaints interface of the dating app I moderate: 5oulm8s. It's 6:05 a.m., an hour before I'd usually start, but I want to make it clear to Joni that I'm not going to mold my entire day around her just because she's been back in my life for all of six hours. Now seems as good a time as any to start sifting through the darkest dregs of online behavior—the private interactions on a dating app notorious for its hookup culture.

"Is this your work uniform?" Joni asks. I look down at my gray leggings, already sagging at the knees, and the oversized green

5oulm8s hoodie I received when I first joined the team nearly eight years ago.

"I am both wearing this and working, yes . . ."

"I mean, your whole vibe," Joni says. "This is a deliberate choice?"

"I work from home," I snap. "And you were hardly looking like Gisele yourself last night."

Joni grins at me, her mouth as wide and knowing as it was the day I met her. I feel a small sense of relief that the Joni I once knew is still in there somewhere, underneath all that taut and glossy skin and motivational messaging, until I wonder whether she is hoping for the same, if she will try to coax out the old Bess, the one I've taught to yield and be good and expect little.

"We were always so envious of your hair," Joni says now, the subtext being that nobody would be envious of anything about me right now. As she talks, she reaches out and takes a clump of my hair in her hands, the split ends nearly translucent in the morning sunlight.

"It's just dead skin, Joni," I say, and Joni raises her eyebrows slightly, as if someone else were here to log her dissatisfaction with my answer.

"Have you spoken to Theo recently?" she asks casually.

"Not for years," I say. Joni nods like she had expected that answer, which begs the question of why she asked it in the first place.

"So, what's Zoey like?" I ask.

"Touché," Joni says, and it feels like it's one for one now, an eye for an eye, and maybe we can stop poking each other to find the places we're still tender.

"Joni, as thrilling as it has been to see you, I do actually need to start work," I say.

"What do you do?"

"I'm a moderator for 5oulm8s. The dating app."

I brace myself for Joni to bring up the gaping divergence between my current job and my childhood dream of moving to New York and becoming the next Patti Smith, but she just runs the back of her hand across her lips.

"Soul mates," she repeats. "You know, I tell my followers not to be bound by concepts like *soul mates* or *destiny*. Those labels are just designed to imprison you, to make you feel so grateful you never stop to question anything."

"Hmmm," I say, thinking of the videos I've watched of the masses of followers who show up at Joni's speaking engagements—women who fill sprawling ballrooms and marquees in places like Palos Verdes and Great Neck carrying Le Bon Babes–branded tote bags as they work up the courage to leave their husbands and take what they truly deserve, and who shout back her snappy catchphrases with the unselfconscious abandon of the newly converted. And it has become something of a cult—Joni has one of the top weekly podcasts in the country, where she coaches anonymous callers through a crisis; a YouTube channel on which she interviews other women in media about their tool kits for emotional resilience; and a further side hustle as a keynote speaker. She is also a regular on the daytime TV circuit, doling out advice on bouncing back from adversity, seemingly working double time after any sort of national crisis. She's worked ferociously to use what happened to us to her advantage, and her success is further proof of her dogma—the idea that through determination and sheer grit alone you can all but guarantee your own happiness.

"I want someone to be with me because they wake up each morning and *choose* me," Joni continues. "Not because of some ridiculous myth that we found each other because we were destined to do so, as if to drift apart would then amount to some massive universal failure as well as a personal one."

"*From Blocked to Unlocked,*" I say, quoting the title of her book, mostly to shut her up. "*Choose your way to happiness.*"

Joni glances at me quickly, a small smile appearing on her face.

"So you keep track of my career," she says.

"You're hard to miss," I say. "Is that a regular slot on *The Morning Hour,* or do they just cart you out after a national tragedy to offer up pithy platitudes and toxic positivity?"

"You may well laugh, but those pithy platitudes paid off my mortgage," Joni says. "Or, I should say, those national tragedies did."

"Did you ever do a test to find out if you're an actual psychopath?" I ask.

"I asked my therapist once."

"And what did they say?"

"She said I probably wasn't," Joni says. "Or she might have said possibly."

"That's a big difference," I say.

Joni grins at me.

"Okay, Joni," I say. "I have to focus on work now."

"I haven't seen you in years, and you can't even have breakfast with me?"

"Unfortunately, I don't have access to the same mine of refrigerator magnet quotes you seem to have plundered," I say instead, realizing as I do how easy it is to fall back into our old rhythm, the well-rehearsed patter of saying a lot without saying anything at all. "So I had to find an actual job."

Joni is quiet for a moment.

"I know it's weird, me turning up here after however long, but doesn't it mean something that, after all this time, you're the person I came to first?"

"Maybe your new friends are just worse liars than I am," I say.

"I came here because there isn't anyone else in the world I trust as much as I trust you," Joni says softly.

I swallow, keeping my eyes trained on the laptop even as my heart jumps in my chest at her words. *A throwback,* I tell myself. A former version of myself still desperate to be needed by sixteen-year-old Joni with her fierce wit and her monogrammed lime green iPod Nano.

"And maybe something good can come out of this whole shit show," she says.

I raise my eyebrows at her.

"You," she says as she slips her oversized Gucci sunglasses over her eyes. "You and me."

I watch as she finally moves across the room to leave, unpredictable as ever. When she reaches the door, Joni turns back around to appraise me one final time.

"It's the difference of a matter of hours. Can you do it for me, Bess?"

As she's talking, I think I see a flash of the Joni I once believed existed underneath her jagged confidence—my loyal, vulnerable friend who would always strike first but only ever to protect us. The one who would have done anything for me, and who once proved it in the worst possible way.

And, after a moment, I nod.

FOUR

2018

ONCE JONI HAS LEFT, I throw myself into the day's work, tearing through the first few complaints quickly. With each case, I have the option of only three responses—ignore, block, or warn. There is a definitive list of circumstances and behaviors that warrant an instant block (unsolicited nudes, transphobia or any hate speech, soliciting and general phishing for ca$h), and these are the holy grail of cases as they take up the least time, leaving little room for interpretation. Complaints that result in a warning are generally more nuanced situations that could be interpreted in various ways, and they can take a little longer to unpack. I open a complaint where a female user has accused a male user of standing her up at their arranged meeting spot, and I skim through their messages, the last of which was an exchange of phone numbers a few days earlier. In this case, since the users were no longer interacting within the app, there's only one action I can take. I click *ignore* and continue to the next complaint. I swipe through some more cases, blocking a user five thousand miles away for unleashing a flurry of misogynistic language that would have once made me flinch but now registers only as being blessedly simple to resolve. *Block*. Then another dick pic sent after a user didn't respond for a few hours—this one red and wet at the tip, belligerent-looking. *Block*.

When I first started working for 5oulm8s, I used to spend hours on each individual case, searching for the absolute truth, as if anything is ever that binary. Every decision felt vital—what if I blocked someone who didn't deserve it? Or, even worse, what if I ignored a complaint about a real predator who went on to hurt someone? It has taken me a while to grow a thicker skin and to understand that I am being paid per resolved case, not per hour. Now I speed through each complaint, my decisions as swift and instinctive as they are considered in my own life. Going with my gut seems to work—I'm the most consistent moderator working on the app, not to mention the longest serving, but the irony that I'm the one doling out such swift and unsubstantiated judgments isn't lost on me.

Thanks, team! All active complaints have been resolved!

I feel vaguely panicked when I read the pop-up message, even though I know the well of complaints will be replenished once the hour is over, a time when most users have a free lunch hour to fill and work colleagues to avoid, not to mention that the other side of the world will be waking soon and reframing their late-night interactions in the stark morning light. I lean back on my chair and stare up at the lightbulb above my head.

Can you do it for me, Bess?

I grab some cash from the drawer under the TV before making my way out of the house. As the desert unfolds around me in every direction, I think of how daunting it felt when I first arrived here, buying a home for myself in a place where I knew nobody, back when I didn't know how long I'd have to punish myself for. How, once I'd made the decision to leave everything I knew behind, I had envisaged myself curling up on the porch each night with a glass of wine as I read alone in the dying light. Maybe a Maggie Smith anthology or some Plath, depending on how hopeful I was feeling, how much of a cliché I felt like becoming. A life of scarcity and solitude, but still a Hollywood version without any of the grit or mundanity of real life—realizing too late that I've forgotten to buy toilet paper for the third day in a row; accidentally sleeping through to dusk without anyone else on earth noticing; the quiet humiliation of being the only person around to turn off the lights I turned on hours earlier.

I drive with the windows down, letting the breeze sail between the blistering sun and my skin. I'm waiting at the lone set of traffic lights when a man walks past my car, carrying a large, panting mutt in his arms. We nod at one another, his wrinkled face folding into a quick smile, eyes hooded and sad. Once I've safely pulled away, I allow myself to wonder whether he seemed lonely and if I should have asked if he needed anything.

The town center consists of a liquor store, a taqueria that is rarely open, and a gas station. Three sunburned men stand outside the liquor store, drinking cans of cheap beer as they hungrily eye each passerby. The youngest, topless and sunburned, grins lasciviously as I approach, and although my instinct is to meet his eye defiantly, to walk right through him until he has to step aside, I force myself to cross the street instead. I've taught myself to be smaller like this—less reckless than I was made.

———

The gas station attendant, Ryan, smiles when I enter the brightly lit store. Ryan is tall and good-humored, and, when I first moved in, he told me that he was only working in the family business to make enough money so that he could move far, far away from his siblings. That was nine years ago, and in that time I've come to understand that the family business, this gas station, is also possibly a drug front, judging by the constant stream of faceless people I see slipping out the back entrance whenever I drive past at night.

When I walk toward the grocery section, Ryan grimaces, warning me to keep away, and on closer inspection I can see that the oranges are dusty with mold, the tomatoes already rotten from the heat. I pick up a few packets of instant ramen instead and drop them onto the counter.

"Good day?" Ryan says, wiping the back of his hand across the wispy hairs on his upper lip.

"Same same," I say, and he laughs.

"It's always 'same same' with you," he says, and I smile at him as if to say that *same same* is all I ever wished for.

—————

Once the water has boiled, I ease the noodles into the saucepan and watch as they begin to soften. While I'm waiting, Joni's voice fills my mind once again, so unlike her smooth podcast voice, which has a barely contained creamy smugness to it, as if she alone has been chosen to understand the secret to true happiness.

Can you do it for me, Bess?

I swallow a forkful of noodles, and then I turn on a local country music station in an effort to drown out Joni's voice in my head. I've spent the past ten years trying to forget what happened, only for her to walk back into my life as if no time has passed at all. The problem is, with a history as complicated as ours, I have a feeling one simple favor won't be the end of it.

I open the 5oulm8s app interface. There are 3,827 new complaints since I logged off. When I first started, I used to lament the fact that there was no way of contacting the complainant or, for that matter, the user being complained about—no dialog box into which I could justify my decision, apportion some blame, or impart any advice. Now it is a comfort to me. Whatever the details of the complaint, however convoluted or heinous the story, there are only ever three possible outcomes: ignore, block, or warn.

FIVE

2008

THE TRIP WAS A graduation present from Evangeline's parents to her, or rather, to all of us. A ten-week stay at the Aetoses' family home in Tinos, a Greek island in the Cyclades, all expenses covered, including first-class flights.

My parents were horrified when I told them about it, as if it were just one more way that living in Calabasas was bound to ruin me and my brother, Steven, who was two years younger. Since moving to California from England, my parents had frequently described our requests and decisions (me trying out for the cheerleading squad, Steven matter-of-factly requesting a German car or nothing) as being "one step too far," as if it wasn't their fault that we were even there in the first place. They meant one step too far in testing their inherent values, the values they had once believed they would instill in us too, but they almost always gave up in the end. Our priorities may have been warped, but our parents were the ones who had made strangers out of us by depositing us in the heart of this new world.

I was fifteen when we arrived in Calabasas, a strange Disney-like enclave made up of immaculate gated communities and un-equivocally desirable public schools. My family had uprooted from the suburbs of Sussex after my mom was tapped to take over the economics department at Pepperdine University. I still remember her bewildered face as she showed us around the McMansion the university had found for us, and the exact moment I understood that for miles around us, all that existed were more gated cul-de-sacs just like ours, all filled with comedically large houses and the same marble fountains and clinical front lawns and teenagers driving luxury cars with personalized plates. "The public school is *really* good," she kept repeating every time we entered yet another sterile room in the house, and it instantly became a family mantra, one that we'd throw out whenever we were taken aback by some local quirk, something we didn't understand. "The public school is *really* good" is what I said when we were asked to move tables in the middle of our first Christmas Eve dinner, chopsticks only just buried into plates of noodles, because we were disrupting an otherwise clean shot on a soon-to-be infamous reality TV show.

Once we arrived and understood that everything we thought we knew about the world and our peers was now void, my brother and I figured that either we could stumble around under the dazzling sunshine like my parents did, equal parts bewildered and bemused, as if they still couldn't quite work out how they'd ended up there, or we could start over, immersing ourselves in this new culture like nothing had come before.

At first assimilating involved effort—observing our new classmates closely, all of whom seemed to implicitly know when to be impressed and when to be bored by the unfamiliar trappings of excess around us, as well as knowing what to wear to a *kickback* and what to wear to a *party*, and how the difference between those two things could sometimes be a festival-quality sound system or a thirty-thousand-dollar arch made of real, tie-dyed roses. I was often a beat behind my classmates, missing the pop culture references and movie quotes and song lyrics that seemed to be ingrained within the brains of these Southern California natives, and which always served to remind me how different I was in the least rectifiable of ways—all these tiny holes in my knowledge that somehow amounted to something infinitely more significant. I felt myself retreating as I became an observer, a student of the nuances of this strange subculture.

Until I met Joni. We were in the same biology class, and I had noticed her immediately, predominantly because she seemed popular, maybe even slightly feared, despite the fact that she eschewed the Calabasas High uniform I had quickly adopted like it was part of the curriculum—low-rise jeans and a skinny tank, oversized sunglasses, and as many necklaces as our parents would buy us. Joni, on the other hand, had a vintage fringed leather jacket that you could smell from five feet away whenever it rained, and she wore it with baggy jeans and a rotation of faded T-shirts she'd cropped herself, all with slogans like O'CONNELL FAMILY REUNION '98 or CAMP RAMAH IN THE ROCKIES. Her blunt hair grazed her angular chin, and her dark brown eyes were set above high cheekbones. When she spoke, you could see the glint of metal from her tongue piercing.

From the start, I heard the rumors about Joni's temper—a preschool expulsion for scratching a girl so hard it left a scar on her cheek; a soccer team ban after she broke the record for the most fouls committed in a single game; how, in fourth grade, Joni had allegedly fractured a kid's nose at his own birthday party because he'd dared to laugh at her bowling shoes. I didn't know if these stories were all true, but I always listened a little more closely when I heard her name.

———

The first time I spoke to Joni was during cheer tryouts. I had already noticed her standing on the sidelines with Evangeline, wearing a black T-shirt that read WILL FIGHT FOR BEER in orange fuzzy letters across her chest, and I could feel her eyes on me as I stood in the field. At one point, I felt something graze my bare shoulder, and when I looked down, I saw a tampon lying at my feet. I glanced over at Joni and she raised her eyebrows, as if to say, *Really?* I turned my attention back to the soft-spoken senior who was lecturing us earnestly about how the life lessons we could learn on the squad would transfer to real life, but already I was seeing it all through Joni's withering gaze, a habit I would soon find impossible to shake. I began to feel mortified that I was even standing on the field, trying out for the role of some idealized version of myself I'd never become, with all these other girls just desperate to find another label, another shortcut with which to identify ourselves—daughter, dog lover, *cheerleader*.

Once the speech was over, I debated whether or not to follow the stream of girls heading to put down their names, and the captain noticed my hesitance. "Get over there, bitch," she said enthusiastically, and I took all of three seconds to think about it before loping right off the field in the tiny PINK shorts I'd begged my mom to buy me just three days earlier.

"Temporary insanity, right?" Joni asked, grinning as I handed her back the tampon. "Did you skip lunch or something?"

"Must have been the meth I took with breakfast," I said, surprising myself and evidently Joni, who let out a shock of laughter. After that, she introduced me to Evangeline, whom I'd registered before only as someone who made surprisingly thoughtful points about books I assumed had already been bled dry of any signs of life in our shared English class, as well as being quite startlingly pretty when you bothered to look at her, which I almost hadn't on account of her otherwise slightly bland manner.

We all climbed into Evangeline's car, a cherry red G-Wagon, and went to the beach instead. There, as the sun beat down on us and brazen seagulls edged ever closer, I learned that Ev and Joni had been best friends since seventh grade, after Ev transferred over from her showy private school in Chatsworth because she was being bullied. At first, I couldn't quite comprehend how they'd bonded—Joni was fierce and coiled, each observation sharp and unpredictable as a bayonet, while Evangeline was more placid in temperament, babyish even, with her goofy smile and colorful crochet crop top and her blanket of pecan brown hair. She turned out to be one of the most lusted-after girls in our high school, and I thought at first that she was the type of girl guys decided to fall in love with because her goodness reflected well on them, but that wasn't quite right. She was more complicated than that.

That first afternoon, I felt intimidated by Joni's confidence and envious of the way Evangeline didn't feel compelled to wade into everything, shouting her opinions like the rest of us in the hopes they might define her, and over time I understood that this was how it worked, that they balanced each other out. Evangeline never judged when Joni and I smoked weed, or drank until we peed ourselves laughing, or hammed up our sexual exploits to make each other shriek, and, in return, we were fiercely protective of Ev, never making as much fun of her as she sometimes deserved with her blind spots and almost willful naïveté.

Over the next year, we became close in a way I could never have anticipated, but that's not to say that it was effortless. Instead, I felt a conflicting pressure to keep up with them while always deferring to their longer, closer friendship, at the same time as I worked to create a groove for myself as the natural bridge between them. Even though I understood that they'd chosen me, I never felt entirely safe in the knowledge of *why*, and, as a result, I often tried to overcompensate with exaggerated tales of my old life in

England that I thought might impress them but instead compelled Joni to raise an eyebrow, or Ev to kindly change the subject.

However fraught it could be, my attempt to assimilate with them felt substantially less daunting than trying to assimilate with an entire shifting student body, and by the end of that next summer, we had all brought our own cultural touchpoints into our shared canon: littering our sentences with the odd syrupy French word thanks to Joni's bilingualism (*Merci, mon ange,* I'd say when Joni passed me the bong); obsessing over every scene in Ev's favorite book, *Valley of the Dolls*; and dressing up as the Heathers for Halloween after I stayed up all night making a PowerPoint presentation about why it was inarguably more iconic than their longstanding costume tradition of the Virgin Suicides. I took the rumors of Joni's latent violence with a pinch of salt, since other than the odd poke or sharp pull of my hair if she wanted my attention, I was yet to witness it firsthand.

Soon, my family became uncomfortable reminders of how much I'd changed, and I felt wary around them, like if I relaxed for even a moment, there was the possibility that the old, unacceptable version of me would inadvertently step out of this human suit I'd created from nothing but sheer will. My parents eyed me with interest, like a stranger they'd invited into their own home, but I always figured that I'd return to them one day, maybe after college, or just once everything didn't feel quite so *critical* anymore. I promised myself I would be good again.

After Evangeline's death, I told my parents not to come to Greece. I knew that seeing them there, stumbling around foreign surroundings all over again, might be the thing to break me. I didn't think it would be long until I could return to California, and, for some reason, they listened to me. By the time they arrived in Greece, it was too late—Joni and I had already been reduced to sound bites from strangers constructed from the bones of our very worst behavior. We had become caricatures not only of ourselves but of every parent's nightmare come to life. We were ruthless. We were sex-crazed. We were killers. And to my own parents? I was a stranger all over again.

We had all assumed that losing Evangeline would be the hardest part. We were all wrong.

SIX

2018

O N THURSDAY NIGHT, JONI calls to tell me that Willa is gone.

"Gone," I repeat, flinching at Joni's choice of word and the slew of memories it elicits. *Evangeline's gone. Gone too soon, gone to a better place*, and any of the other hollow euphemisms I had to grit my teeth and tolerate in the brutal year following our best friend's death.

"Not actually gone," Joni says now, her voice filled with barely concealed irritation. "But she's not here."

"Okay," I say, swallowing. "Where is she?"

"I wouldn't know," Joni says. "She's unreachable."

I freeze, the phone pressed to my ear.

"Joni . . ."

"She's just attention-seeking, Bess. These fucking zillennials, they can't handle not being the center of the universe at any given moment. I swear she'll be back within the week."

"How do you know?" I ask, trying to keep my voice level.

"Because my darling fiancée has done this to me before, *multiple* times after a fight."

"So why are you even telling me?"

"I'm telling you because Willa's parents are now involved, and obviously they're only too happy to blame this most recent escapade on me. They haven't liked me since Willa dropped out of USC to focus on her activism, but what they fail to understand is that Willa is *actually* protesting against her lobster-roll, sorority-legacy, Verbier-vacationing upbringing, and that it has very little to do with me. I eat at Nobu three times a week and my house costs nearly twelve hundred dollars a month just to run, for God's sake. I'm hardly the poster child for sustainability."

I pause, waiting for the other shoe to drop.

"So," Joni says eventually. "I might need you to extend our white lie a little."

"You want me to lie to Willa's parents for you?" I ask.

"It will just make my life a lot easier if you stick to our original story," Joni says. "This is so fucking typical, I can't even tell you. I'm about to have the biggest work month of my life and Willa pulls this shit."

I pull my cardigan closer around me, a familiar sense of dread threading through my veins.

"Joni," I say slowly. "I don't know how I feel about covering for you when you don't actually know *where* Willa's gone . . ."

There is a silence while Joni processes my words, and I think about also asking if she suspected Willa was going to pull her disappearing act when she came to my house three nights earlier, but I can't quite find the words to accuse her of this. I wonder what it would take for Joni to throw our past back in my face; whether her scars really have healed or if her sacrifice will always be there, simmering just below the surface.

"Look, Willa's parents, the media, all the assholes who are jealous of my success because I'm a woman, and a queer one at that, they're going to use this—this moral *miscalculation* of mine—to destroy everything I've built," Joni says furiously. "And I would have thought that you might know better than anyone how it feels to be miscast."

Miscast, I think. Like an inadequate actor floundering onstage. From where I'm standing, the problem was never that we were miscast; it was that we were exposed.

"This obviously complicates things, but I'll need you to cover me for another week, *max*," Joni says. "Just until Willa has made her point."

"And what point is that?"

"That she's the one in control."

I pause because I can't imagine Joni not being in control of any aspect of her life, and the thought disturbs me more than anything else she's said.

"And Zoey?" I ask. "She's aware of all this?"

"Zoey's *my* problem," Joni snaps.

"Have you even told the police that Willa's missing?"

"Have you been listening to me?" Joni says, her voice tight with something I can't identify. "If this gets out, it will blow up just because of who I am, and that's both the last thing I need right now and exactly what Willa wants to happen."

Joni says *who I am,* but we both know she means *who we are.* A knot forms in my stomach, and now I'm thinking not of Willa but of the photographers who tracked our every move from the moment we landed in LAX from Athens; the wheedling reporters who pretended to be on our side until they felt compelled to mention our strange behavior after Evangeline died; the miles of newspaper inches taken over with a postmortem of not only that one night but our entire dumb teenage lives leading up to it— thousands of careless texts and emails and snide yearbook quotes wedged alongside our classmates' overwrought accounts of the most mundane interactions recast in a sinister new light; the creepy offers of support from a certain type of stranger on the internet; the cruel and scathing commentary from every other faceless stranger on the internet; and then, worst of all, the subtle shift I saw in both my parents' faces, as if in the time I'd been gone they had both been crushed and reconstructed so carefully that only I was cursed to notice and understand all over again that it was my fault nothing would ever be the same.

"Trust me, Bess," Joni says. "Everything's going to be okay."

I don't hear from Joni for a few days, a fact that bothers me more than I want it to, mostly because I understand that she will be playing it like this on purpose. Joni will know that her reappearance in my life has only made it feel all the more empty now that she's gone, just like she'll know that I now check my phone for news of Willa half a dozen times before I've even logged on to work. Most of all, Joni will know that I'm questioning whether the predictability of a life without her is still preferable to one with her, even with the threat of chaos she brings, and it's this fact alone that stops me from calling the number I find scrawled on the dishwasher manual next to my fridge, the familiarity of her pretentious French sevens nearly winding me.

One night in bed, I load up an old YouTube video of Joni on my phone. She's addressing a crowd from the stage of an anonymous conference room in downtown San Diego. It was filmed a couple of years ago (before she discovered her trademark ivory jumpsuits), and Joni wears a green velvet suit as she scans the crowd with purpose, as if she has endeavored to make eye contact with every single audience member before she utters so much as a word.

"You all know what happened when I was eighteen," Joni starts, her voice more honeyed than I've ever heard it in real life. "You read about me at the time; you probably judged me. Maybe you even hated me. But that's not why you're here today."

Joni holds the audience's awe like a newborn baby.

"You're here because of what happened next. You're here because you witnessed me taking the worst thing that had ever happened to me, the injustice, the shame, the *grief*, and you watched me transform it into something so magical, so brilliant, that you almost didn't believe I was the same person you first saw, all those years ago."

On-screen, Joni pauses, her eyes shimmering under the stage lights. "But I'm not special."

The audience is silent, absorbing every word as if she were delivering a sermon.

"I am just like you."

Joni lets the words resonate before she starts pacing, her posture near perfect as she crosses the stage.

"The only difference between us right now is one choice. One simple choice I made when I saw not only how the world expected me to behave but who they wanted me to *be*. So I made the choice to become who I wanted to be instead. Not only did I refuse to be defined by my past for a moment longer, but I refused to be defined by any other human in my life, whether that was a stranger behind a computer screen or my own mother. And now I'm here, standing in front of you, asking you to make that same choice. People in your life will want to shame you, to keep you in your old habits and dysfunctions because you're easier to predict that way. They'll want to keep you trapped on autopilot, an eternal victim of your own trauma, because you're easier to *control* that way. But I want to tell you that we deserve so much more. Say it with me—we deserve *more*."

I pause the video, the frame stuck on a close-up of Joni's face, flushed with the thrill of believing her own hype, and I wonder if the fury that once lived inside her is still lurking somewhere. I remember now why I stopped watching her videos, choosing to track her progress instead via her Instagram page, where I can at least read her grandiose captions and claims in my own voice, flattening them with varying levels of skepticism, to paper over the fact that I am still a bystander in my own life. Joni moved so quickly to secure her status as the keeper of our shared story that I never stood a chance.

I open Instagram next, searching for Willa's account. I scan her grid as if she might have left a clue as to her whereabouts, but it remains uncharacteristically dormant. Up until a week ago, Willa was posting daily, speaking out on a range of issues, from climate change to trans rights to corporate tax evasion, as well as posting sponcon in her role as "brand ambassador" for a millennial makeup line and an ethically sourced mineral water company. The two most recent posts are bright and poppy shots of Willa's twenty-third birthday taken by a famous fashion photographer solely so they could be shared and fawned over on their socials—Joni grinning as she presents Willa with a five-tiered rainbow cake, topped with a single sparkler; Willa, heavenly in a white dress as she slots one of her birthday presents, a signed early Nikki Giovanni anthology, into her sun-soaked bookshelf, her new, glittering engagement ring pulling focus. Photos designed solely to make you regret every decision that has led you to your own sorry existence.

Afterward, I google Willa's name. When nothing new comes back, I feel reassured, somehow, to know that nobody else seems worried about her either.

SEVEN

2018

I OPEN THE DOOR THE following afternoon expecting to find Joni but facing two detectives from the Los Angeles County Sheriff's Department instead. I stand blinking in the stark sunlight for a moment before pasting a smile on my face. It feels both shocking and inevitable that this is happening, that I am calmly inviting these two strangers into my home and offering them a cup of coffee in the 105-degree heat.

The detectives, a male and female, visibly sweltering in their beige LASD uniforms, decline a drink and take a seat instead on the sofa Joni had slept on one week earlier, before introducing themselves to me as Detectives Frost and Jenkins. I take a seat on the fishing chair opposite them, my back already slick with sweat.

"Elizabeth Winter, huh," Detective Frost says, in a thoughtful way that makes me think she must have already recognized my name, because surely nobody would make the connection between my current state and the defiant, shameless girl from that final summer. I can feel my heart rate pick up even as I maintain a mask of amiability, as if I have no history with conversations just like this one—questions that seem innocent on the surface but are riddled with hooks sharp enough to gut you at the earliest opportunity.

"Bess," I say. "I've always gone by Bess."

"Do you know Willa Bailey?" Jenkins asks, his flat tone giving little away. He has thin lips and a worryingly uneven mole on his chin. I shake my head: *No, I do not.*

"What's this about?" I ask.

"Willa's parents have notified us that she hasn't been in touch with them for coming on a week now," he says, before adding, "We've been assured this is out of character," as if to justify his presence in my home.

The fact that Joni didn't even think to warn me the police are involved should tell me everything I need to know: Joni believes that by simply reappearing in my life and bestowing her sparkling presence on me once again, she has done enough to secure my loyalty toward her. I feel sick with the effort of trying to resist the pull of her, even when she's nowhere near me.

"A week," I repeat. "And they're only just getting in touch?"

"There seems to have been some confusion," Frost says. "Between her partner and her family as to where exactly she was supposed to be during this time."

I pretend to be transfixed by a loose plastic screw in the leg of the fishing chair.

"I'm sorry, I don't know Willa personally," I say, shaking my head again slowly. "I wish I could help you."

"And how long have you known Ms. Le Bon?"

I pause, pretending to count. "Thirteen years in September."

Detective Frost raises her pale eyebrows and makes a note in her pad. I wonder if she views it as an achievement to have preserved a childhood friendship for so long, or whether she's acknowledging our shared history and that this is no normal friendship. I stiffen as

I remember the leaked topless photos that made the rounds online, or the viciously cavalier messages I sent to Joni and Ev after I had sex for the first time, soon to be printed in newspapers across the world.

"When did you last see Ms. Le Bon?"

"She stayed over last week. Monday night."

"That's May seventh?"

I nod as Detective Jenkins makes a note this time.

"What time did she arrive?"

I swallow, thinking not of Joni or Willa but of Evangeline, of how she used to clench her hands into fists whenever we made her lie for us. I try to shake the feeling that I'm in a lucid dream, that I might open my eyes in a moment to find that none of this is real and Joni never came back for me at all.

"Are you worried?" I ask. "About Willa, I mean."

"Please answer the question, Ms. Winter."

Both detectives are staring at me now with growing interest, and I know this could all end here if I just tell the truth. I've already lived a lifetime without Joni; what's another one? My mouth is bone-dry as I work out what to say next. And then—"Joni got here around eight or nine. Or actually . . . closer to nine."

A split in time. *Irreversible.* But isn't that what I wanted? I remember Joni's face on the beach in Mykonos the night Evangeline died, her eyes drilling into mine as she held my face in both her hands.

"And this is normal for you?" Detective Jenkins asks, a light snark to his voice. "A weekday slumber party?"

I frown at him and Detective Frost quickly qualifies her partner's words. "Everything seemed fine? It was just a regular night for you both?"

"Well, I don't know if I'd say that," I say, my mind reeling at the thought of what I've done. Then, reluctantly, because they're still watching me closely: "We were planning a tribute for a friend who . . . we lost ten years ago in July."

The two detectives exchange a look.

"Right," Frost says gently. "Well, we'll let you know if we have any follow-up questions."

At this point, Jenkins stands up and thanks me before he heads toward the door, perhaps already mentally moving on to the next interview, the next alibi he needs to check in order to keep Willa's hysterical family at bay. The thought that this is over and soon they will both leave panics me because it means I will be left alone to think about what I've done and, even worse, why.

"When was she last seen?" I blurt out, and Frost glances at her colleague, who is already opening the screen door to the porch.

"We're trying to find that out," she says as she hands me her card. *Anastasia Frost, Homicide Bureau.* She sounds like she should be a harpist at a New York conservatory, not trudging around a forgotten corner of Imperial County, I think, before the word *homicide* registers.

Noticing my discomfort, Detective Frost puts her hand on my arm.

"Right now, this is a missing persons investigation," she says reassuringly, and I tell myself that she wouldn't be acting so kindly toward me if she had any reason to doubt my story.

"Does she do this a lot? Willa, I mean?" I say, as we walk toward the door. "Does she disappear a lot?"

Detective Frost glances above my doorframe as if to check for a security camera and, once again, I'm relieved not to have any close neighbors peering through curtains or pretending to take their dog for its sixth walk of the day just so they can get a better view of the action.

"Not as far as we know," she tells me, leaning in close enough that I can see the fine dusting of hairs on her upper lip. "Not according to her parents. But parents aren't always the best judge of things like this."

My heart is pounding as I wave goodbye to them on the porch, forcing an appropriately concerned smile as they drive away, and then I eat a microwave burrito while watching a game show in which contestants have the duration of the show to teach their old dog a new trick. After much hysteria, one woman has almost got her dog to fling himself on his back after she uses her hand to gesture pulling a trigger, but he can't seem to hold it for long enough before jumping back up for his treat, pink tongue glistening. Even as I follow the ups and downs of it, I know that I'm just pretending everything is still the same. Somehow, I already understand that, once again, my life has been irreparably carved into before and after, and while I want to be furious at Joni for making me do this, I also know that I'm the one who sat opposite those two detectives and chose to lie to them.

And I'm also the one who feels more alive than I have in years.

———————

Later that night, I wake fighting an insatiable thirst. As if in a trance, I throw a pair of jeans over my pajamas and drive myself to the dive bar a few towns over. I've been here twice before, always like this: furtive, unplanned visits once the rest of the world is asleep and the fierce longing in my body makes me feel sick with its intensity. It's a common meet-up venue for the more covert local users of the 5oulm8s app—an anonymous cavern in which they can connect and dissipate in a matter of hours, leaving little trace. Most of the patrons are too high even to remember to drink, too focused on dancing and meeting someone who might take them home or maybe just to a bathroom stall, and the bar area is empty as I order drink after drink. The black ceiling drips with condensation as I down tequila sodas and watch the swaths of anonymous bodies dancing, heads tossed back and eyes closed as hands creep down bare skin and mouths brush against necks. When I'm drunk enough (drunker than I've been in a long time), I join them, closing my own eyes as the music rips through my bones, a clinging sweat coating my upper lip.

When the bar finally closes, I make out with a twenty-year-old in a faded baseball cap while I wait for my cab, pretending not to hear him when he asks for my name halfway through. His kisses are rough, wanting, and we are both breathless by the time my Uber finally pulls up. He slips his hand around my waist, trying to hold on to me, and I feel a nauseating kick of longing in the pit of my stomach as I pull away. As the car jerks away down the street, I touch the fingerprint-marked window and wonder if he will send a stranger a photo of his penis as he lies in bed later.

It's four a.m. when I get home, and I catch my reflection in the bathroom mirror.

You are a liar, I tell myself, rolling the word over in my mouth. *You were a liar then and you're a liar now.*

In the mirror, my long hair is wild, matted to my neck with dry sweat, and my wide-set blue eyes (by all accounts "unsettling," "calculating" eyes) are bloodshot, and my vest is damp and stained with drinks and a stranger's urgent handprints. I test out a small smile, my teeth white and neat, and then I break into a bigger one, eyes narrowed, lips peeled back until you can see almost every tooth. And, just like that, I know that Joni has done what she always does—she has coaxed the darkness out of me. Joni is a reminder of both the girl I once was and the woman I once thought I would become, and right now, with the memory of a stranger's hands on my skin and tequila racing through my veins, I think that may not be such a bad thing.

I text the number Joni left, three words only.

I did it.

EIGHT

2008

M Y PARENTS COULDN'T FATHOM how a trip halfway across the world could cost them nothing. Even
though we had lived in Calabasas for almost three years by then,
they still didn't understand how it all worked. That to most of these
people (although not the ones like us, who were there only circum-
stantially, on borrowed time—but the Calabasas *lifers*), money was
the most dispensable thing in their world. It was the thing that
made their lives easier, not harder, and the thing they used to get
whatever result they wanted, either by doling it out or taking it
away. So, to me, it made perfect sense that Evangeline would have
me and Joni accompany her on her voyage of self-discovery, as it
meant that neither of her parents would have to entertain her—*we*
were the performing monkeys and bodyguards, all in one.

Evangeline was the oldest out of the three of us (by two months),
but there was something naïve about her—some guilelessness that
was equal parts admirable and irritating because nobody else could
get away with being as sincere as she often was, and part of what
allowed her to be so pure was that we were always there to give
her something to resist against. Evangeline would frequently be

horrified by the things Joni and I said, some throwaway remark or bitchy aside, and we would both overcompensate, instinctively papering over the cracks of our shame by pushing it even further until Evangeline clamped her hands over her tiny shell-like ears to block us out. I always figured that Joni and I were so callous because she was so soft, but perhaps it was the other way around.

Evangeline was also the wealthiest, at least forty times over—her father, Stavros, a conspicuously absent oil baron; her Danish mother, Freya, a former model who watched TV from her cream Alaskan king bed most afternoons, propped up on multiple pillows like she was in a hospice. I always knew that there was something missing in Ev's homelife, but the damage never felt quite tangible enough to address—her mom was always around, after all, physically if not emotionally, plus Ev and her brother, Theo, technically had access to anything they ever wanted: box seats at any concert, private jets available to whisk their friends to join them on birthday weekends in the Caribbean, the unspoken prospect of any job they wanted after college. It was predominantly because of this unruly wealth, the type that is hard to see past, that I never questioned Ev's homelife, even though I always felt a pressing need to get out of the Aetoses' silent house almost as soon as I'd arrived, and Joni and I privately referred to it as *the mausoleum* when we were being assholes.

Joni was more interesting to look at than I was, with her short black hair and Angelina Jolie lips, and she definitely ranked higher than me on the family wealth scale (her mother was a prolific cosmetic surgeon from Tokyo who had met Joni's dad, a Parisian rhinoplasty expert, at a conference in London), but Joni would say she slid down to meet me by virtue of the fact that she was openly gay in a time and place where this wasn't the norm, and a little odd. Joni had one frank, unapologetic mode of existing that could be disconcerting, and a way of processing things that meant she wanted to slice straight through to the subtext of any conversation, whether you were aware of it or not. I loved Joni almost from the moment I met her, but in the way you might love an adopted feral cat that more often than not makes your life hell—I always understood that aligning myself with her perhaps hadn't been my best choice.

The Aetoses' house in Tinos had been Stavros's grandmother's home, and the family had summered there every year for the first decade of Evangeline's life. As the kids got older, their interests and needs changed—Ev went to a fancy gymnastics camp one summer while her beloved Theo learned to surf in Costa Rica, then the next summer Theo joined a friend on safari in South Africa while Evangeline went to Paris with their nanny. The Tinos house had been neglected, becoming little more than a fond childhood memory for the family, when Stavros announced his intention to sell the land. In true Evangeline fashion, the thought of losing something she had once loved drove her insane, and she became entirely fixated on proving to her father that the house *was* wanted, that she alone would make sure it was appreciated and restored and loved as much as it had once been. She decided that it would be the perfect location for our last summer together before we went off to our separate colleges (I had got into NYU, Ev was following her brother to Brown, and Joni was going to Berkeley), even though we'd never expressed any interest in going, and secretly I'd have much preferred a summer in the Aetoses' Greenwich Village town house, or their villa in Lake Como, or even a forgettable week in Cabo along with the rest of our classmates.

We'd been planning the trip for nearly three months when Stavros's sixtieth birthday party rolled around at the start of May.

He'd already celebrated his own existence on a superyacht in Turks and Caicos, as well as in New York and Paris (photos splashed across the pages of the *National Enquirer* and *Page Six* due to the omnipresence of a certain Victoria's Secret angel by his side), but this was an occasion for his family, ostensibly to keep up appearances for the kids. The party was held in a grand marquee on the lush rolling grounds of the Eagle Hills house, and Dido sang a few songs while Freya and Stavros Aetos watched from an opulent love seat directly below the stage, unflinching under the gaze of their four-hundred-plus guests. Theo and Evangeline sat on either side of their parents, and I spent most of the show staring at the back of Theo's perfect neck, willing him to turn around and notice me.

When the music was over, Stavros got up onstage and made a brief speech (laced with a string of quips about offshore bank accounts and his wife spending his children's inheritance on parties like this one) while Freya sat stiffly in a white feathery Marchesa gown that made her seem even less substantial than usual. I didn't see her and Stavros interact at all, unless it was to pose for a photo, when she would allow him to drape his arm around her fragile frame, and Evangeline and Theo would both appear like magnets, baring their glittering teeth for the camera before walking off together to confer about something in the corner, fending off well-wishers and people trying to ingratiate themselves in a way that was both polite and unyielding at the same time. They were dressed similarly, in the type of simple, tailored clothes that neither of them favored in everyday life: Theo in a pair of cream chinos and a white shirt, his golden brown hair styled in a wave over his forehead; and Evangeline in a short cream silk dress with a looping bow at her neck and gold sandals, her hair loose down her back. When they were together, there was an indisputable aura around them that Evangeline lacked when she was alone—an air of tragedy that set them apart from everyone else, perhaps because we could all see just how self-absorbed, how *useless*, these parents were, and how it was left to the kids to manage them. It meant that Ev felt unreachable to me and Joni that day, like she was a different girl altogether from the one we knew, and I wondered whether this version of herself was a mask or if it was the other way around.

When Joni and I approached Freya later, champagne tingling through our veins, she stared at us vaguely, her eyes glossy and unfocused. Up close her skin was the texture of a moth's wings.

"Thank you for having us," I said. "It's a beautiful party."

Freya looked around the tent, as if for the first time. "Is it?"

I could see Evangeline watching us from the other side of the marquee, her face stitched with concern as Theo slipped his hand into hers, and I felt envious of their closeness.

"I'm sure my husband has appreciated your presence," Freya said, as if she had no clue who we were, despite having met us both hundreds of times before. "But if you'll excuse me . . ."

"We're so looking forward to Tinos," I said, hoping to jog her memory mainly because I knew how humiliated Evangeline would be if she knew.

"Tinos," Freya repeated, the word so strange sounding in her mouth that I questioned whether I had got it right at all.

"We're going for the summer, with Evangeline," Joni said. "To your house."

"Oh yes," Freya said, something passing across her face for half a second—a flicker of life, dissolving once again into a dull vagueness. "Evangeline never was very good at letting things go."

On our way home, I asked Joni if her own parents were okay with her going away for the entire summer before college, and she glared at me witheringly.

"I think they'll survive," she said, before biting a chunk out of her bottom lip.

A few days later, my mom told me that Joni's dad had walked out on them three weeks earlier, moving back to Paris with an aesthetician he'd met at another convention, this one in Las Vegas. Joni's mom had found a cleverly placed credential lanyard in his pile of washing and had swiftly thrown a Baccarat glass paperweight at his head, resulting in thirty-six stitches, a potential skin graft, and an abrupt end to their twenty-year marriage.

Joni never spoke a word of French again.

My own parents eventually agreed to the trip, as I knew they would, but they insisted on paying for my flight to Athens themselves. They said they didn't feel comfortable letting the Aetoses cover everything, which just meant that Joni and Ev now had to fly economy too. I knew my parents thought they were doing the right thing, but I wanted to scream at them that Evangeline's parents wouldn't have given the extra five thousand dollars for my fare a second thought, perhaps wouldn't have even known about it. I wondered whether Evangeline and Joni had discussed the situation and decided not to mention it to me, even in jest, and the thought was even more humiliating than knowing that neither of my friends would have considered flying anything other than first class before they met me.

My mom drove me to LAX herself in our family Prius as NPR played quietly through the car speakers. Occasionally we'd pass the ridiculous black limousine driving Joni and Evangeline, and I would pretend not to see them as they wound down the windows, giggling and waving as envy slithered through me, and my mom asked me for the fortieth time whether I'd remembered to pack Tylenol and antihistamines.

When we pulled up at the curb outside the terminal, I was alarmed to find that my mom was crying, her eyes milky and tender behind her glasses as she swiped at them.

"Oh, God. What's wrong?" I asked, my hand already on the door handle. When the automatic doors opened, I could see that Joni and Evangeline were already in the check-in line, and I hoped this wouldn't be a sign of the summer ahead, that I wouldn't always be rushing to catch up to them like a snotty younger sibling nobody wanted there.

"I don't know," my mom said, swiping at her eyes before correcting herself. "This is a big deal, Bess. The first trip without us? This is actually a pretty big deal."

After a moment, I put my arms around her and hugged her, and I think I wished then that she'd take it all back, that my mom would say *of course* she'd only been joking when she said I could go away without her. That there was no way in hell I was mature enough to fly across the world with these two girls she hardly knew, that, in lots of ways, *I* hardly knew unless you counted knowing exactly what shade of pink someone's tongue is, or how long they could wear Crest Whitestrips before their teeth started to hurt, or how many people they wanted to fuck before college. Instead, we could turn around and drive home, and we'd make guacamole and watch a movie we'd already seen thirty times, and maybe we'd go camping for a few days like we used to, before Steven and I had had to readjust to our new reality, reassessing our priorities and our lives that had little space for ordinary, loving parents and bike rides around canyons or playing on the swing my dad spent months installing in the backyard even though we were both already too old for it.

My mom pulled back and gently wiped at my cheeks, which were embarrassingly streaked with tears too.

"I love you," she said, and I laughed a little to defuse the situation. I thought of Evangeline's mom, distant and fragile in bed, her eyes tracking the brilliantly rendered characters on her fifty-six-inch TV, and of Joni's mom, her own face as smooth as a boiled egg as she looked at me appraisingly the first time I met her, before benignly telling me that my full cheeks made me the perfect candidate for buccal fat removal.

"I love you too, Mom," I said.

NINE

2018

I WAKE UP TO A loud hammering at my front door and Joni calling my name. I check my phone for the time—7:10 a.m. Joni must have left her home in Malibu as soon as she got my text. I stand up with a splitting headache and not nearly enough sleep to adequately arm myself against our shared history, already regretful of the choices that led me to this moment.

When I open the door, Joni is waiting in a pair of white jeans and a blue linen shirt. She waves a ziplock bag filled with grayish powder at me and smiles winningly as the blazing sunlight assaults my eyes.

"Cordyceps," Joni says by way of explanation, just before she pushes past me and makes her way through to the kitchen.

"Excuse me?" I stare after her.

"It's an adaptogen," she explains as she opens my fridge and takes out a carton of orange juice. As she talks, a flash of "Joni Le Bon" comes through—the charismatic, striking multihyphenate who is just as confident sharing her unfounded opinions as facts online as she is ranting about the gendered politics of shame on a talk show. "Ayurvedic? It's the only thing for depression. You still look like shit—this desert is uninhabitable, I swear to God."

While she's talking, Joni casually pours the juice into a glass before stirring in a significant amount of powder with a pen she finds on the counter, and I watch it all in disbelief.

"Unless, of course, your intention is to slowly rot alone," Joni says, glancing up at me then, absorbing everything from my unwashed hair to my stained vest through narrowed eyes. "In which case, forget the Cordyceps and go off."

Is she being fucking serious?

"Joni," I say slowly. "You're just not going to explain why I had to lie to the *police* for you?"

Joni rolls her eyes as if I'm being dramatic.

"Thank you for doing that," she says. "But truly, it's only a temporary thing."

A lightning bolt of pain shoots down my left temple, landing in my jaw.

"Do you think you need to tell the truth?" I ask quietly. "If Willa is actually missing, this is surely bigger than any argument you may have had."

"If I change my story now, it will just distract them from finding her, which, I'm sure I don't have to point out, is in none of our interests now."

A tug of panic, deep in the pit of my stomach.

"I'm also interested as to when you, of all people, fostered this inflated sense of trust in the capabilities of the police."

"Joni," I say, my tone a warning shot.

"Look, they already searched the house," Joni says casually. "And I answered a few questions."

I swallow another wave of tequila-laced dread.

"Do you . . ." I trail off before trying again. "Do you have a lawyer?"

"Come on, Bess," Joni says. "Lighten up. I *promise* you Willa will be back in the next few days, and this conversation and all the other ones like it will be rendered entirely meaningless. It's a tragic waste of both our energy."

"Where does she usually go?" I ask. "In the past when she's done this."

"Rehab in Utah, her aunt's house in Beacon Hill, a horse ranch in Wyoming," Joni says, reeling off the locations. "Tulum, once. It doesn't matter where, as long as I don't know. It's a power move."

I pretend I don't understand what it would be like to be so desperate that you walk out of your own life.

"You know it would be easy for the cops to find out where you were that night if they wanted to," I say. "They can check your cell phone location."

"I told you I didn't have my phone," Joni says. "Plus, I think that whole cell tower system is fairly flawed."

"Well, someone would have noticed your car," I say, even though it's a black Range Rover and noticeable only in its ubiquity.

"Look, it's never going to get to that point," Joni says. "Trust me."

"Have Willa's parents heard anything?"

"I was the one who told them. They had no clue Willa had even left until I called."

"So nobody's heard *anything*? It's been over a week now, Joni."

"I'm acutely aware of that, *Bess*, but I also have too much other shit to worry about with my book release next month," Joni says coolly. "Trust me, she knows what she's doing."

"Did you already know?" I ask then, steeling myself against her reaction. "When you came over that night. Did you know that Willa would do this and that you'd need me to cover for you?"

"How would I have known that?" Joni asks, looking at me strangely, and it's a relief when I decide to believe her.

"So you didn't come over to thank me, but you came over to . . . ?"

"The Cordyceps," Joni says.

"You drove here from Malibu before sunrise to drop me a bag of mushroom powder," I say, and Joni smiles again, her perfect, sharp teeth sparkling even in the dim light of my kitchen.

"You know where I live?"

"Okay," I say, opening my laptop. "I have to start work now."

Joni studies me for a moment, and I can tell that there's something else on her mind.

"Bess . . ." she says. "Do you want to talk about the last time we saw each other?"

"Are you going to apologize for what you did?" I ask, not lifting my eyes from the screen.

When Joni doesn't answer, I flick my eyes over her.

"Then I don't think we have anything to talk about."

After a moment, Joni pushes the bag of powder across the counter toward me.

"Trust me," she says, looking around the room one last time. "Cordyceps. It's the only cure for . . . for whatever the fuck this is."

Joni walks out, leaving me staring after her.

My brother emails me moments after Joni's departure, and, with a sinking feeling, I remember that we have our biannual coffee this week. Over the past five years, he has insisted on letting me know every time he has a meeting in Palm Springs so that I can drive up to meet him at some ridiculously overpriced brunch spot where we plow valiantly through an hour in each other's company, presumably so we can both promise our parents that we tried. I figure that at least this time our meeting will serve as a momentary distraction from Joni's chaotic reappearance in my life, or, more specifically, the fact that I clearly left the fucking door wide open for her.

I email Steven back, telling him that ten a.m. at the Ace Hotel works fine for me, and to make sure he doesn't stay up too late

51

slobbering over some nineteen-year-old model at a Hollywood club tonight.

He still uses the account he set up when we were teenagers, back when you could still get a name like BradPittsGoatee@APG.com.

———————————

Once I've sent the email, I search to see if there's any news of Willa. Still nothing.

My browser hovers over the search bar, and I can't help but think how easy it would be to just surrender and type Evangeline's name into it. I can already imagine the pages of results that would appear to remind me of what I already know, that whatever we do now, nobody will ever forget what happened, and our history will always be out there, waiting to be reignited, reinterpreted, wielded against us at the earliest opportunity. Joni has rebuilt her life on facing this fact head-on, refusing to forget, while I have done the opposite. My entire adult life has been built on the merits of restraint, of treading so lightly that I leave no trace of myself.

On Instagram, Joni posts a photograph of herself holding up a copy of her book and smiling serenely.

One month to go! Thanks for all the support, you truly wild creatures. Viva my Le Bon Babes 🖤

TEN

2008

THE GOD IN CHARGE of flight seating assignments must have been a teenager once too, because my seat for the first (and longest) leg of the journey was in the middle, right between Evangeline and Joni. It meant that I had to be included in every conversation they had, and if Evangeline spoke particularly quietly, I could repeat it so that Joni could hear. I still felt unsettled from running up to join them in the check-in line only to find that they had already taken what seemed like three hundred photos on Ev's pink digital camera during the car journey. They had even looked vaguely surprised to see me, as if they had forgotten I was coming on the trip, and I was reminded once again that they had been a perfectly happy, perfectly self-contained duo before they ever met me.

I could also tell that Joni didn't love that I had been the one who had known my way around the airport terminal, having flown to and from the UK multiple times over the past couple of years. I pointed out the best bookstore and magazine kiosk, and steered

Joni away from ordering a burrito at the place that had once (maybe) given Steven a particularly humiliating bout of food poisoning on a flight back to England. She wasn't used to me being the native in any situation, alien as LA culture still was to me much of the time, and I think she was hoping I wouldn't be able to sustain this superiority for the whole summer just by dint of the fact that we would be in my home territory of Europe. She needn't have worried— the gray mundanity of the suburbs of Sussex I grew up in was as similar to Tinos as Calabasas was to the moon, or Bushwick.

We hate-watched the *Sex and the City* movie together in full, and then Joni got up to use the bathroom. Evangeline put her hand on my arm and I slipped one earbud out.

"Are you excited?" she asked, and I nodded.

"Thanks so much again, Ev," I said. "It's so generous of your parents."

Evangeline frowned, and I realized it hadn't been what she wanted from me at all.

"I can't fucking wait," I added.

"Well, I've already explained this to Joni, but I don't know if she totally got it. I don't want you to be freaked out by the house— it's been in my dad's family for generations, so it's not what any of us are used to, but that's exactly why my family has always loved it. It's all rickety, with wood rot and, like, actual holes in the wall that you can look right through to the outside," she said, smiling as she recalled its flaws fondly. "Because a lot of it is made from stone. So we'll kind of be slumming it, but at least it's real, you know? Like charming squalor. We can play cards, read books, swim in the sea every day. I think this summer is going to be pretty special."

I never quite knew how to respond when Evangeline was sincere like this. More often than not it made me want to shake her, but sometimes I could feel a rush of scalding envy that she had everything in the world a girl could want and also somehow got to keep her innocence longer than the rest of us too.

"Cool, cool, cards are great and everything," I said, weaving my sun-bleached hair into a loose braid over my shoulder. "But are there any local hotties you can introduce me to? I'm thinking a young fisherman with a haunted past and a cabin filled with poetry books."

My tone was flippant, but I was being deadly serious. I'd had sex for the first time a year earlier with a senior at a party in Eagle Hills, and I'd found it to be an entirely uncomfortable experience. While I'd thought I wanted it at the time, in a carnal, frantic way that made me feel ashamed to remember, the act of sex had left me feeling (like most things did) lonely, as if I were fundamentally different from everyone else. It was a cycle I repeated over and over again with my next quasi boyfriend, Ben, whom I'd slept with ten or so times before breaking it off to leave for Greece. Ben had made me beg for it, and yet I still felt unfulfilled at the end, like it was some failure of mine that sex hadn't turned into this magical thing that made people wild enough to write songs about or kill each other over. I told myself that it was a privilege to feel empowered enough to choose my own sexual partners and not be judged for my own desire, but it didn't always feel like that. Still, I'd been promised that sexual liberation was a *good* thing, and, in my mind, there was no alternative but to persevere until it felt like it.

"I guess there's a few guys our age," Ev said, after a pause. "But their English won't be great. And I don't know about your Greek . . ."

"Oh, you know me, Ev, I'm extremely goal-oriented. I'll be fluent by the end of the summer," I said, opening the copy of *Us Weekly* I'd bought at Hudson News. There were two pages filled with various female celebrities posing in beautiful gowns, and, when Joni sat back down, we went through comparing each one in heats until we each ended up with our winner. I ended up with Keira Knightley in a strapless purple pleated dress, while Joni and Evangeline went for Rihanna in a neon yellow Giambattista Valli gown, which I instantly realized was indeed the better option, but by then it was too late to change my mind.

"Did I tell you that Theo might be coming?" Evangeline asked casually as she flicked over the page I was still scanning. I paused, forcing myself to read a headline before responding.

"Oh yeah? For how long?"

"A week max, don't worry."

Joni leaned across me then, grinning. "I don't think Bess was worried."

I felt my cheeks burn hot, but Ev ignored Joni. It was the quality I admired most in her, this ability to absorb only what she wanted to, as if she could create her own reality that way.

"He's moving around Europe with a few friends from college, but I don't think Tinos is exactly what they had in mind when they booked the trip. It's more like a numbers game thing."

"Meaning?" Joni asked, and I realized I was holding my breath.

"Meaning they're trying to sleep with a girl in every city they visit."

"Wow," Joni said. "Men just love to remind you at any opportunity how heinous they are, huh?"

I could feel Ev bristle beside me, so I gave Joni a warning dig in the ribs. She instantly pinched me back so hard it brought tears to my eyes.

"I've already told him under no circumstances is he allowed to stay for longer than a week," Ev said, effectively closing the subject. "He's my favorite person in the world, but I don't want his fratty friends ruining our trip."

I felt a heady mix of adrenaline and disappointment, but I tried to curb it. Theo had already left for college when I arrived in Calabasas, and was about to start his final year at Brown, but I'd met him maybe eight, nine times at various charity or familial events that called for his presence, and he always made my stomach drop, with his golden dimples and easy self-possession. His general good-naturedness felt almost subversive under the circumstances, when their mom was so useless and their dad so distracted, and it seemed to me that Theo was the antithesis of the disposable guys I half-heartedly hooked up with in LA—he was confident without being arrogant, assured but not entitled, responsible but not a buzzkill. It wasn't even that he was particularly witty or smart himself, rather his palpable confidence felt generous, *contagious*, as if he somehow elevated everyone around him. I found that I couldn't help but be my best self in Theo's presence, mostly because it was what he expected from us all.

Every time I saw him, I got the impression that he could be into me too, but I never told anyone, not even when we bumped into him at Coachella and he pulled me through a body of strangers to get a better view of Arctic Monkeys because I'd once mentioned that I liked them, or the time I'd been flirting with his friend at the Roosevelt and, in a gesture that was both humiliatingly brotherly and insanely hot, Theo had casually reached out and tucked a loose strand of my hair behind my ear while I was in midsentence. Once, when we were hanging out at the beach by Point Dume, a soccer ball Theo and his friends had been kicking around found its way to me and I kicked it back, the ball miraculously soaring through the air in a perfect semicircle before landing right at Theo's feet. He grinned at me in a way that made my insides melt, before shouting, "All *right*, Ronaldo!" Afterward, I had quizzed Steven so relentlessly about the soccer star that he bought me tickets to an LA Galaxy home game for my next birthday.

I guarded these interactions in my mind fiercely, little dream-like scenes I could recall whenever someone I hooked up with didn't call or text, or if I felt particularly uninteresting compared to Evangeline's charm or Joni's charisma. How I felt about Theo wasn't the only secret I kept from my friends, but it was potentially the biggest one, and instinctively I knew that Ev would feel territorial over one or both of us at first, and that Joni would tease me mercilessly about my feelings while messing with the easy rapport Theo and I had built over the past couple of years.

I held the knowledge of Theo's stay like a protective shield around me, and it didn't even bother me when I got back from the restroom to find that Joni had moved into my seat, her head pressed back against the leather headrest and her eyes fluttering, as if she'd fallen clean asleep in the two minutes I'd been gone.

Later, witnesses at LAX would remember seeing the three of us around the terminal. They'd mention how Evangeline was even more beautiful in the flesh, her skin even more glowing, her eyes the color of honey, and a cashier would recall how Evangeline had wanted a burrito but I had refused to let her get it. There was no way of clearing any of it up, of explaining that the reason I was so bossy and domineering was precisely that it was so unusual, and that it was actually *Joni* who had wanted the burrito anyway, not Evangeline, who would never have dreamed of eating anything so robust. I was powerless against these lies and half-truths, this string of small but potent snapshots of our friendship and every-day examples of the power I held over my sweet, angelic friend, which would then form an unrecognizable portrait not only of our friendship but of who I was at my core. Because who would care what their friend ate if they weren't playing some sort of sick game?

The single father sitting in front of Ev on the plane would go on to describe me as boy crazy, which was one of the nicer terms used to describe me in that period. It was worse in a way, because it meant that I would always feel a perverse sense of indebtedness toward him.

ELEVEN

2018

I WALK INTO THE DINER at the Ace Hotel to meet my charming, frustratingly uncomplicated younger brother for the first time in nine months. The barman moves around the coffee machine to get a better look at me as I pass, and I resist the urge to hiss at him. I wonder if he recognizes me, or whether something about my particular type of scruffiness belies my tragedy in a way that the other patrons' doesn't, with their ripped jeans and geometric tattoos and casual mimosa orders.

Steven is sitting at a russet booth wearing a gray T-shirt bearing the logo of his local coffee shop, his reddish hair longer than usual and curling around his ears. When he stands up, I can see that his features have softened since I saw him last, maybe from gaining a little weight, but that it only makes him seem more substantial than before. Less decorative.

"Hey, Bess," he says as he gestures at the bench opposite him. I sit down and my brother pushes a can of Calidad beer and an iced glass across the shiny table toward me. I stare at it, unsure of why he assumed this would be my beverage of choice at 10:55 a.m.

"It's happy hour in England," he says, holding his glass up to clink mine. "Bottoms up."

"Cheers," I say, and, when he smiles, I can see that his eyes are a little bloodshot. I wonder now if his weight gain is alcohol-related, and if it is, whether it's my fault, and I'm thinking suddenly that this was a terrible idea and I'm wondering how long I have to stay for it to be deemed if not an entirely *successful* encounter, then at least not a disastrous one.

"How's it going, baby brother?" I ask cautiously.

"Good," he says, nodding. "I'm actually doing really good."

Steven puts his head to one side and studies me, and I brace myself for whatever it is he's about to say, but it seems like he changes his mind, because then he just drums his fingers on the tabletop.

"How's work?" he asks eventually. "Any particularly gnarly stories recently?"

"No stories," I say, glancing down at my phone. "But I do have some stunning photos I can show you."

"No way," Steven says. "No dick pics before lunch at least."

I smile back at him, wondering if I need to ask when exactly he started drinking before lunch.

"Have you spoken to Mom and Dad recently?" he asks.

"Not for a little while," I say. "They're in Barcelona, right?"

My parents, after moving us across the world, decided to get the hell out of California as soon as my brother graduated from high school, my mom taking up various visiting professor posts at universities across the world. In the past five years alone, I can remember them being in Singapore, Toronto, and Berlin, my parents assimilating to each new culture in a way they never could in Los Angeles.

"Can you imagine how Mom is pronouncing *paella* right now?" I ask, smiling. "I'm not sad to be missing that."

Steven lets out a snort of laughter.

"I thought maybe they'd already told you my news," he says, and then signals to the server. "Two more beers. And a breakfast bagel, egg white only, thanks. Bess?"

"I'll have the same," I say, shutting the menu. Then: "Don't you have a meeting this afternoon?"

"They canceled on me," Steven says after a slight pause. "But I think I'm just going to get a room and crash here tonight anyway, as I have a bunch of calls with the Sydney office later."

"That's shitty they gave such short notice," I say. "Don't they know how important you are? Youngest ever middle-class white man promoted to senior management at Konnect, wasn't it?"

"Well, they actually told me yesterday," Steven says lightly. "So not too bad. But I appreciate your outrage on my behalf."

"So why did you come out here, then?" I ask, confused.

"To see you, Bess," Steven says, and I feel a crack in my chest. "Come on."

"Sorry," I say quietly, but it gets lost somewhere under the excited cheer of a neighboring bachelorette party who have finally received their mimosas.

By our fourth or fifth beer, both Steven and I have loosened up immeasurably. It's more than I'd usually drink, but I'm with my brother and I feel unexpectedly relaxed, so I allow myself to sink into the feeling of relative numbness, of my limbs turning slowly to butter, until I'm barely thinking about the thousands of 5oulm8s cases that are getting raised and then resolved without my knowledge, or about Joni sitting in an empty house in Malibu waiting for Willa to come home, or the fact that, somewhere in a police station in Los Angeles, my words are being written out and committed to public record, another indelible half-truth fettered to my name.

The lunch crowd has cleared out, and Steven and I share a cigarette we bummed off our server by the fire pit outside. On the other side of the gate, hotel guests splash around in the pool, filming themselves lounging atop large inflatable floats shaped like rainbows and cacti.

"You know, you never actually told me your news," I say. "You said you had news!"

"Oh yeah," Steven says, looking proud of himself. "Bess, I'm getting married."

"What?" I say, staring at him. "Are you sure?"

"Pretty sure," he mumbles, embarrassed now.

"Congratulations," I say, nodding. "Wow, that's really great."

"Her name's Nova," he says. "I'd really like you to meet her."

"Is she the one who finally convinced you to stop threading your eyebrows?"

Steven groans. "Oh man, you knew?"

"*Everyone* knew," I say, and we both laugh, and then Steven takes the cigarette from me. He exhales in a way that makes me think he doesn't usually smoke either and that we both just looked at each other and remembered crouching down together next to the barbecue and passing a cigarette between us because we figured that's what we were supposed to do.

"Do you know who turned up on my doorstep last week?" I ask then, hesitant because it isn't something I would ever usually reference, but particularly not to someone who was *there* through it all, who has his own memories and scars. Steven shakes his head, waiting.

"Joni," I say, and when he doesn't say anything, I add, "Joni Bonnier. Le Bon."

"I knew who you meant," Steven says quietly. "What did she want?"

"Nothing exactly," I say, sensing a shift in Steven's mood. "I just thought it was strange that she came back after all these years."

Steven nods, his expression heavier now, as if I'm testing the limits of his infamous good nature.

"You know that Nova was in the same year at USC as Willa," Steven says next, and, despite the alcohol, a warning signal goes off inside me.

"I wasn't aware that Nova existed until about five minutes ago," I say tightly. "So no, I didn't know that."

"They weren't close, but they had some mutual friends," Steven says.

I don't know how to respond, so I just shrug.

"I heard that Joni didn't get in touch with Willa's parents until she'd been missing for four days," Steven says.

"Joni says Willa does this a lot," I say. "She thought she was coming back."

Steven stares at me, shaking his head.

"Why are you so interested in this?" I ask. "I never had you down as an ambulance chaser. You certainly didn't seem to care so much when it was me in the back of one. Metaphorically speaking."

"Come on, Bess," Steven says, and I already feel guilty for breaking the first rule of our family code.

"Look, neither of us actually knows Willa, so maybe we should trust Joni's judgment on this," I say, sounding markedly more confident than I feel. "She says Willa will be home within the week."

Steven looks like he doesn't believe me, but he doesn't try to fight me on it either.

"Whatever happens, I think you're better off without Joni in your life," he says. "She's a vampire. Always has been."

I feel a snap of defensiveness.

"I don't know if that's fair."

"What was that saying Dad used to love? If it looks like a duck, swims like a duck, and quacks like a duck, then it's probably a duck?" he says, not seeming to notice when I balk at his words. My dad had abruptly stopped using that expression after my summer in Greece, when we learned how it can be used against you.

"Look, you could never see it with Joni," he says. "But everyone knew she had this ruthlessness except for you."

"I knew her better than any of you, though," I say. "She wasn't *ruthless*, she just didn't fit in with anyone who thought Calabasas was the coolest place on earth."

Steven absorbs my unkindness with little more than a shrug.

"So, you really don't think she knows where Willa is?" he says finally.

"I have to think not," I say.

"That's a weird way of putting it, Bess," Steven says. "Why do you *have* to think anything?"

"Because I know what it's like to have people assume they know everything about you," I say flatly. The cigarette has nearly burned down to the end, but I still take another drag.

"So that's the real reason you wanted to meet?" I ask eventually. "To ask me about Joni? Well, you can report back to your future wife that I know nothing, if that makes your life easier. And hey, look at that—you didn't even have to pay for a hotel room."

Steven watches me for a moment, his face unreadable.

"That's not why I came," he says. "Fuck, Bess. You really don't make it easy, you know?"

I want to ask him exactly what I don't make easy, but we both know what he means. I don't make it easy to love me.

"Do you know who I see sometimes?" he asks after a while, his voice softer than before.

After a moment, I shake my head.

"Theo Aetos."

I feel a shift deep in my bones, and all I can do is frown down at the ground.

"Yeah," Steven says. "He comes up to the city for work every couple months."

"Oh," I finally say. "That's weird he calls you."

Steven shrugs. "It is a little weird because we were never friends—he was, what, five years older than me? He'd already left for college when we moved to Calabasas, right? I don't know, maybe he likes seeing people that knew his sister or something. It's not, like, the *easiest* hang, but he's a good guy, always asks after you."

"And what do you tell him?" I ask quietly.

"Well, I kind of figured that you would be in touch with him if you wanted to be, you know? So I keep it vague," Steven says. "Anyway, talking about Joni made me think of him."

"I see that," I say, and then I change the subject.

———————

Later, when the sky is bruised and dusky, the palm trees black against it, Steven will insist on ordering me a taxi so that he can watch my journey home on the app. I'm secretly touched by the gesture, and I feel a tenderness toward him that surprises me with its force.

"Bro, I live nearly two hundred miles away from you most of the time, and I'm still here, right?" I say, and Steven studies me like he's really thinking about the question.

"Just about," he says, nodding. "Just about."

TWELVE

2008

THE AETOSES' TINOS HOUSE was, as Evangeline had warned, not in the least what Joni and I had been expecting. Their LA house, in the most prestigious gated community in Eagle Hills, was more of a compound than a home: a colossal mock chateau with three further guesthouses, two tennis courts, a small golf course, and a marble swimming pool. Inside the main house were a steam room and sauna, an indoor pool next to a cinema room, and, naturally, a true-to-scale replica of Studio 54 in the basement. Joni and I always found the basement the most intriguing part, not because of any interest we had in the club (which felt like something people our parents' age only ever referenced to convince us that they had been young and wild once too) but because we couldn't imagine Freya ever venturing far enough out of her bedroom to have even seen it. Evangeline's father, Stavros, was barely ever home, and everyone assumed he had at least one other family in another part of the world, or perhaps even on the next block.

The house in Tinos was different. It was rough around the edges to say the least—an old stone fortress (older than anything we'd ever seen in LA), built in a beautiful olive grove on top of a cliff, hidden from the road by rows of cypress trees. We were unable to access our sarcasm for once as we wordlessly took in the goats roaming around the grounds and the way the sunlight filtered through the old lace curtains in the kitchen, any cynicism firmly cast aside for the next few hours as we explored the house. Its flaws—the roving damp patches and peeling paint, the unfashionable antiques, the general sense of *oldness*, the possibility of ghosts in the air— made it seem all the more romantic to us, isolated as it was on the cliffs above the ocean. We sat on the roof of the house and watched the sun set that night, the scent of thyme in the air, and I felt like I'd already matured five years by being somewhere new, without the safety net of my family. It felt like magic.

Our first few days in Tinos were idyllic. We threw on swimsuits each morning, followed by a layer of tanning oil, before Joni and I diligently followed Evangeline to whatever local treasure she wanted to share with us, her eyes glowing and mouth set in a proud smile as she showed us around the island she'd loved so much as a child. We piled into the dusty red Fiat the Aetoses kept as their "runaround" car, and Ev drove us down dirt tracks to tavernas on the beach or in the hills, where we were waited on by grinning servers who already knew her name and asked after her family, places with laminated menus and twinkling lights that served whole fresh fish with clear eyes amid mounds of tzatziki and creamy taramasalata. We were given complimentary bottle after bottle of local wine, as well as a steady stream of licoricey ouzo, which we made our way through slowly as we lounged around, knowing we had the whole summer ahead of us to get drunk and what felt like the rest of our lives to lose track of ourselves.

Tinos itself was a peaceful island—rustic and pious, with most of the culture revolving around its beautiful yellow and white

Greek Orthodox monastery. In hushed tones, Evangeline told us that, come August 15, thousands of Christians would make the pilgrimage to the island for the Assumption of the Virgin Mary, to touch the church's holy icon, Panagia Evangelistria, a portrait of a beatific Mary kneeling with her head bent in prayer. Ev said that we would gather to watch the pilgrims make the journey to the church in the punishing heat, many of them crawling on their hands and knees from the moment they reached the island. Joni and I appreciated the commitment to drama, and we both managed to resist making any inappropriate innuendos while inside the church, which was something of a miracle in itself.

Joni and I had been ravaged by mosquitoes on our first night, so from then on we would lather on layers of mosquito repellent, rolling and then spraying it on our sunburned flesh until it stung, and then we'd eat slow, wine-soaked dinners (always cooked by Ev, with a cursory turn chopping onions or rinsing rice from Joni and me) on the farmhouse-style table outside the kitchen, talking at candlelight not about our futures but about our past—shared stories of triumphs at school, or often-repeated declamations about what we had thought when we first saw each other. (*A glorious Anglo-Saxon warrior! A statuesque goddess!* Joni would say about me, even though I'd explained to her repeatedly that my family were neither German nor even particularly English.)

On our fourth night, Joni opened up about her situation at home, a situation I'd carefully avoided mentioning even to Ev, for fear of it looking like I was talking behind Joni's back. But at one a.m., over a bottle of retsina from Ev's dad's wine cellar, Joni told us that her dad had left the family home two days before her eighteenth birthday. I remembered that we'd gone to our favorite stretch of beach in Malibu with around twenty other kids to celebrate only the day after, and the thought that Joni had been wrestling with this secret even while she was passing around a bong and sitting on my shoulders in the ocean made me ache for her, even though I knew she'd hate for me to show it or do anything at all beyond mirroring her own blistering anger.

Joni's father had taken her to Nobu to tell her, and when he'd shown her photos of his new partner, Joni had made a quip about how *ironique* it was that he'd left the family for a woman who closely resembled her mom's second face, or was it her third (Joni couldn't remember, there had been so many), and then when she'd finally mustered up the courage to ask if it was because she was a lesbian, having come out to her parents when she was fifteen, her dad had just stared at her blankly like he'd forgotten the conversation had ever taken place, in a way that served to remind Joni just how insignificant a cog she was in his life, an altogether humbling blow when she needed it the least.

Evangeline observed Joni quietly, and it was only once Joni had finished, her jokes finally drying up to make way for something darker, that Ev started to speak. "Theo told me something a few years ago," she said slowly. "He said that some people believe we choose our parents before we're born, because they have something to teach us. And that doesn't always look how you think it will, and it won't always be a lesson taught intentionally by them, or even in good faith, but whatever we do learn is necessary for our souls to progress."

We were all silent for a moment. Even though the theory sounded like something you told yourself to make up for the fact that you were burdened with shitty, selfish parents, the fact that Theo had thought to say it gave it an extra layer of poignancy, so I tried it out on myself for size, wondering what my parents might have to teach me beyond the obvious. Compared to Joni and Ev, I knew I was glaringly, almost humiliatingly, lucky with my draw, but that night I found a way around it by envying the others for the option of diminished responsibility. Maybe being able to blame my deficiencies, the unsettling feeling that there was something inherently wrong with me, on my parents would have been easier.

"That is just the most . . . insane bullshit I've ever heard," Joni said then, shaking her head. "You think I'd have deliberately chosen those two ignoramuses for my parents? What was my soul so desperate to learn, the perfect ratio of body dysmorphia to anorexia? No, for some entirely inexplicable reason, my parents not only chose each other, but they also chose to have *me*, presumably the result of either some drunken accident or an ill-advised bet, and now my dad has beaten the system by kindly *unchoosing* to have me."

I could sense Joni's vulnerability through the practiced carelessness of her tone, and, for just a second, I thought I understood her. I thought I understood that the rest of it was all bravado, and that at her lowest moments, when she woke up at four a.m. and prayed for it to get light so that she might feel like herself again, she believed she was unwanted. Unloved. Maybe even unlovable. Joni thought that her parents had made a mistake in having her and that her dad had dealt with that in the most brutal way possible— by sticking around for just long enough that he could tell himself he'd behaved nobly when he escaped the second she came of age.

"I'm sorry," Evangeline said, putting her hand over Joni's. Instead of moving her hand away or changing the subject, Joni just smiled and closed her eyes.

Moments later, I slapped an opportunistic mosquito on Joni's thigh, and she whacked me back instantly, giving me a thudding dead arm for the next few minutes like only Joni could. Despite the pain, I was relieved that the tension was broken. I didn't like having to feel sorry for Joni, because I understood how much she'd hate it if she knew.

THIRTEEN

2018

HEO, THEO, THEO, FUCKING Theo Aetos. The thought of Theo with my brother, so close that Steven could touch him without ever thinking about it, could slap a hearty hand on his back when their team scores on the TV above the bar, or bump his fist as they're saying goodbye, bare knuckles meeting for a couple of seconds, is unbearable. The thought of Theo asking Steven about me, and somehow Steven understanding that I wouldn't want Theo to know the truth about my life, is crushing. And now the gates have been opened and it's time for me to indulge in my favorite form of self-harm: stalking Theo online.

Theo Aetos, who, far from becoming the session drummer he once dreamed of being, is now the founder of an early stage investment company that specializes in building sustainable and ethical consumer product companies. Theo, on whose sparse Instagram account, too seldom updated to even be set to private, I once found a woman called Sophia (tagged in a high-contrast photo of a German shepherd from a few years back), the fashion journalist he married three years ago in an intimate ceremony at their favorite vineyard in Napa Valley.

Theo and Sophia, who live in the suburbs of Portland and who, while not having kids, have an indeterminate number of rescue dogs and the volunteer work they do at the local food bank to keep them busy and fulfilled. Theo and Sophia's house, deemed worthy of an entire spread in *Vogue* two years back: Sophia looking striking in a floral Vampire's Wife dress but still fighting a losing battle next to Theo just in chinos and a white shirt, with his beautiful broken nose and seaweed green eyes. Theo, in fewer photographs than his wife, probably because he can't seem to shake his expression of mild bemusement, as if he doesn't exactly know how he ended up being photographed by strangers in his tree house–style mansion overlooking Lake Oswego, just so that other strangers would then admire and envy his good fortune. Other shots of the couple at a gallery opening in New York; snippets of gossip about Theo's dating life from years earlier; a few early mentions of Evangeline, soon destined to be referenced only within the context of her brother, as if Theo's "tragic loss in his early twenties" might explain something about him (his work ethic, his philanthropy, his dedication to his wife).

Is there any way I could have handled it all differently? Or was this outcome inevitable, the natural order of things? Maybe I was always destined to be drunk and alone, looking in at Theo's glossy, perfect life from the outside, wondering if I could have changed any of it if I'd just tried harder, been better, not let the shame take hold of me like it did.

I open up the email folder titled "MISC," and there they all are, suspended in time, waiting for me to answer. Some years are quieter than others, with emails sent only on Ev's birthday or the anniversary of her death, and I think it's because Theo is happy, too lost in the everyday grind of his new existence to live in the past. Other years are agonizingly prolific—the end of each month punctuated with a flurry of emails, always asking the same question of me, over and over again, as urgent as if it were the first time.

Bess—can we talk?????

FOURTEEN

2008

THE NOVELTY OF OUR Tinos life began to wear off in the second week. Yes, the island was paradise and the house was charming, but it was also borderline dilapidated and the standard of living was not what we had come to expect, as spoiled and entitled as we all were. For starters, the plumbing was ancient, if it even existed, and Evangeline instructed us to use the creepy outhouse as our bathroom if we needed to shit, which made every night feel like the opening sequence of a horror movie. The water was also freezing, which made both showers and washing up futile, and the old floorboards could administer monster splinters (obviously none of us had remembered to bring anything as dazzlingly mundane as tweezers). The wind kept us awake at night, and when we woke up, our skin covered in mosquito-bite welts, the swimming pool would be filled with dead insects, wasps still twitching on the surface as we tried to swim. The half-hour walk down a donkey trail to the beach was tolerable, but the climb back up could be savage, canvas bag straps rubbing against our sunburned shoulders as we trekked in silence, often starving and monosyllabic by the time we made it back. Our cell phones didn't work, and there was no TV or internet in the house, and we had to drive twenty miles to a small internet café with two computers if we wanted to check in with our parents. Only Evangeline could drive the run-around car, as it was stick, and Joni and I began to understand we would be entirely at the mercy of Ev and her nostalgia for the next eight weeks. As gentle as she was, Evangeline could also be surprisingly stubborn.

The power dynamic began to shift, and for the first time in our friendship, I didn't feel like the newcomer, the spare part who needed to be grateful for having been included at all. Once she'd shown us all her favorite spots on the island, Ev seemed content to hang around the house, empty mornings and listless afternoons spent waiting by the pool while she cooked some inevitably over-extravagant and unsatisfying meal that we'd have to coo and compliment her over for hours. Joni and I began to feel like we had been misled into accompanying Evangeline on a trip so that she could make a point to her father about loyalty and stability while basking in the golden memories of her unhappy childhood.

"I'm so fucking bored, I'm worried I'm going to eat one of you," Joni announced as she threw her towel down next to mine. A few scattered grains of sand landed on my oily thigh, and they only clung on harder when I tried to flick them off. I had woken early and slipped down to the isolated cove below the house alone for the first time, and, while it had felt thrilling in theory, it was more than a little eerie being alone on the empty beach.

"Are you sure you're not just hungry?" I asked, leaning back on my elbows. "I never thought I'd miss my dad's cooking, but jesus fucking christ, I'm *starved*."

"I'm starved of attention is what I am," Joni said. "There's got to be *one* other lesbian in this godforsaken place, right? Sappho, wasn't she *Greek?*"

"I think so," I said, unsure. "Was she a poet?"

"I don't need her to be a poet," Joni said scathingly. "I just need her to not be you or Evangeline."

"Well, I've heard that every island has a lesbian," I said, testing it out because I still never knew exactly how to participate when Joni joked about her sexuality. "But I've also yet to see evidence of anyone under fifty living here."

"Didn't Ev say she knew people here? Like, our age? I thought there were going to be more bars and stuff."

"I think the issue is that we're in the middle of nowhere, and it's not like there's a ton of taxis, so someone would have to drive. You know Evangeline isn't going to drink and drive, and neither of us can work that car," I said, pleased that I got to be the translator for once, the one trying to explain Ev to Joni. It felt like a natural position for me, given that I often secretly measured myself on the same spectrum—Ev at one end, Joni at the other.

"Ughhhh," Joni said as she stood up again, dusting yet more sand onto me. "She's literally holding us hostage. Do you think there's any way we could convince her to leave? Maybe go island-hopping?"

"Honestly, she seems to love it here," I said, feeling guiltily thrilled that Joni and I had found this new cause, this extra link between us.

"We could always go without her," she said.

"Maybe," I said carefully. "But I don't know how my parents would feel about it."

"Whatever. You're all talk, Bess," Joni said, and I tried not to let it bother me, even though it was true. If I was being honest with myself, the thought of leaving the island didn't exactly appeal to me either, since I figured that, any day now, Theo could turn up with his friends. I knew the presence of four frat boys probably wouldn't satisfy Joni enough to make her want to stay, but I was holding out hope that they would arrive sooner rather than later. *Surely* Theo wouldn't wait until August to come when he'd have to be back in Providence so soon?

"This is inhumane," Joni announced, tossing her hair over her shoulder.

I knew that it was ridiculous, how trapped we were beginning to feel in a place so beautiful it was almost painful to behold, but I also understood it perfectly. We were eighteen years old, alone for the first time in our lives, burning with power we were desperate to wield and an eagerness to become something other than our parents' daughters, and instead we were trapped for months in a crumbling house on a hill, in the middle of nowhere. It wasn't that we were "sex-crazed," as people would later jump to describe us as, but more that we could feel the time slipping away from us viscerally. Time to learn how to get out of our own heads for long enough to enjoy sex, yes, but also time to experience everything we possibly could and to already know what kind of women we wanted to be *before* we had to buckle down and focus on our studies or our careers or on finding the person we wanted to be with forever. We knew that we were supposed to want more than our mothers had, but we didn't know what that meant yet. Instead, everything felt urgent, like we were clawing through molasses to join a race everyone else had started without us.

Along with the two guys I'd slept with back in LA, I'd also done clumsy hand and mouth stuff with three more, and Joni had been with six girls total, only one of whom I'd ever met. We kept track of these partners in a running list on our Facebook messages, sending each other a few flippant notes about each encounter to make each other laugh. Keeping track like this, as cruel as some of our comments were, alleviated some of the pressure bound up in those first few years of sexual activity—pressure that could both flatten and shatter us when the partner didn't live up to our expectations, or when the experience was even vaguely traumatizing, like a drunk UCLA junior shoving his thick sausage fingers up my vagina like a drill. It was, I thought, a low-stakes form of self-protection—we pretended to care less than them from the moment it was over. And we had the evidence to prove it.

"I don't think I can handle this for the whole summer," Joni warned me that day at the beach. "We would have been better off staying in Calabasas."

Joni stalked toward the ocean and I watched as she didn't break stride, not even when the water crashed into her chest, soaking her black swimsuit. I understood that she couldn't flinch because she knew I was watching.

———

Despite Joni's disappointment with me, something was breached that day at the beach, and Joni and I started to sneak into each other's rooms at night to complain about how hungry we were, how just because Evangeline's mother had given her a disordered attitude toward eating, like suppressing your appetite was something to be celebrated (as if a bowl of yogurt and honey was enough to sustain us until dinnertime), it didn't mean *we* had to be starved all day too. We weren't even drinking as much as we'd hoped— occasionally Evangeline would open a bottle of wine from her father's collection, but then she'd get huffy when we drank it too quickly, when we forgot to let it breathe because we were more interested in getting drunk. We began to notice that Evangeline weaponized her wealth too, quietly asserting the final decision over what in the shopping cart was worth buying or scrapping, or which tavernas she deemed acceptable to stop at for lunch, or when she wanted to drive to the market to buy beaded anklets or sandalwood incense, when we'd assumed it would be a democracy. She could be snobby too, sending back plates of calamari or gemista without an ounce of embarrassment or, if we ever insisted on going to a particular restaurant we'd spotted that she didn't know, looking pointedly in the other direction when the check came so that Joni and I were forced to scramble around for change to cover her share. It wasn't necessarily her fault—she'd been taught to expect the world to yield for her, after all—but we still felt misled: Ev had always seemed too aware of the trappings of privilege to behave like an entitled brat, but we realized now that, much like her father, on some level Ev believed we were in Tinos not as individual beings with our own needs and requirements but to make her life easier.

When Evangeline drove us to town, Joni and I would open the windows and complain about how hot it was, how dusty the roads were, how uncomfortable it was when the shop owners stared at us, anything to show her that this wasn't the trip we had planned. It felt satisfying, siding with Joni like this, as I'd always been a little intimidated by her, and it was a relief to no longer be courting approval from Evangeline, who was so firmly in her own world that she rarely doled it out. It made us both wonder why we'd tried so hard before.

FIFTEEN

2018

FOR THE FIRST TIME in years, I am unable to focus on work. I start late after picking up my car from the Ace Hotel, and my brain feels syrupy, my instincts muffled somehow. My fifth case of the day is a user with an IP address in South Carolina who has been using the photo of a sorority girl in Savannah, Georgia, to solicit male nudes. I feel strangely sorry for this person who didn't feel like their real self was enough, whose other active account reveals him to be an older, reluctant-looking man, and I linger over the case for too long before giving him a warning. When the case disappears, I feel pissed at myself because I know it should have been a straight block.

Less than an hour later, I stand and stretch, announcing aloud that I'm going to get some lunch. My words hang in the air as I shuffle around looking for my keys, and I wonder again if I should get a cat, or maybe a rabbit, mainly to make moments like this feel less embarrassing. The idea of a pet soothes me somewhat, until I remember that the coyotes would inevitably get to it.

Ryan is behind the counter at the gas station, peeling price stickers off a sheet and applying them to boxes of Colgate. His phone is pressed between his ear and his shoulder, but he waves at me, watching as I circle the store.

When I get to the counter, he murmurs something into the phone and hangs up. I push the loaf of bread, mayonnaise, and a can of tuna toward him.

"Let me guess . . . duck à l'orange?" he asks, and I smile at him even though I feel mildly humiliated.

"You know, some guy came in here earlier looking for you," he says as he checks the date on the tuna. I think first of my brother, even though of course he would come to my cabin, not here, if anything had happened to our parents.

"Really?" I ask. "Are you sure he was looking for me?"

"Yeah." Ryan nods. "But I didn't tell him where you lived."

He says it proudly, as if not sharing someone's home address with a stranger isn't the bare minimum involved in existing, an opening clause of our shared social contract, and I feel a thrum of anger.

"I think it was a reporter," Ryan says. "From the questions he was asking."

"Okay," I say, now looking pointedly at the groceries between us.

"You know, I never thought you did it," he says then, and when I look up, I can see that his eyes are ravenous.

"I knew who you were the first time you came in," he continues. "But trust me, I know bad people. And I knew that someone who looked like you, someone who came from where you did, couldn't kill someone."

As he talks, I think of all the other men too: the ones I'd tried to date in the years following Evangeline's death, yes, but also the strangers I'd just tried to buy a fucking book from or attempted to move past in the Gelson's dry goods aisle. Men who were always at pains to tell me that they were feminists too and allies, and that they'd read any of the hundreds of op-eds written about us at the time, and they weren't scared of me because they could tell I had good intentions and a gentle soul, as if that were always a compliment. Men who thought they were doing me a favor every time they mentioned it before I did, as if it were a sign of their generosity, their mercy.

Ryan is still staring at me, perhaps waiting for me to thank him again, and I wonder now if he's seen the grainy photos from my short-lived MySpace account—the ones where fifteen-year-old Joni and I swept our hair across our foreheads and posed in lacy push-up bras, lips pouting, dense false eyelashes grazing our eyebrows as we stared into the lens of her family computer; the ones where we looked like we were the type of girls who chased danger so that we'd finally have a reason to justify the deep sadness we felt, some way of escaping our bland upper-middle-class existence.

"Did he say what he wanted?" I whisper, and Ryan thinks about it for a moment.

"I don't believe he did, no," he says. "But I saw the other girl on the news, so I figured."

I stand there nodding even as terror climbs through every cell in my body. And that's when I understand that this will only end once Willa learns what I have been forced to reckon with time and time again: *You can never truly disappear.*

At home, I turn on the local news network. At the end of the hourly update, a photo of Willa fills the screen. I recognize the shot from her Instagram page—a portrait of her throwing her head back and laughing in Lake Tahoe. Underneath are the words APPEAL FOR INFORMATION ABOUT MISSING LOCAL WOMAN.

"Los Angeles police are appealing for any information about the whereabouts of this twenty-three-year-old woman, Willa Bailey, who has been missing for ten days. She was last seen by a neighbor on the deck of her Malibu home on May seventh, just after seven p.m. She's five feet six inches tall with pink hair and brown eyes, and anyone with any information is asked to call the Los Angeles County Sheriff's Department."

I watch as a photo of Joni flashes up next, a press shot from a keynote speaking engagement where her magnetism and vivacity ooze out of each perfectly tight pore, and I have the brief and disturbing thought that if it were me who had lost someone, a partner or family member, they would inevitably use a photo of me from that summer in Greece.

"Willa's partner, famed podcaster and personality Joni Le Bon, acquitted of any involvement in the death of Evangeline Daphne Aetos in Greece nearly ten years ago, is yet to make a statement on her disappearance. We will update the story as it unfolds."

I open a beer and try to quell the panic rising inside me. When I see the same car drive past three times, slowing as it passes my house, I close the blinds and turn out the lights. Moments later, the porch creaks and I leap behind the sofa, gripped by a sickening panic. I think of my family and what it would do to them to have our lives ripped back apart along the same badly restitched seams all because somehow, after all these years, Joni has exposed me again.

Only that's not quite right . . .

I'm the one who exposed myself.

When the afternoon shadows start climbing the walls around

me and I can't bear to be alone any longer, I call the only person in the world who could understand.

The car Joni sends is black and sleek, with tinted windows and blue LED lights in the footwell. I run my fingers across the cool leather, and it takes me a moment to remember when I was last in a car like this.

It was winding up the hills of Greece, just before Evangeline died.

SIXTEEN

2008

AFTER FIVE WEEKS IN the Tinos house, halfway through our stay, Joni and I were at breaking point. Evangeline had become more stubborn than ever, complaining that she wasn't getting enough sleep because Joni and I stayed up too late, turning up in the doorway of whichever room we were in, sleep mask pushed up on her head as she whined about the acoustics in the house. She'd wake up at six a.m. and bang around until we were forced to emerge too, bleary-eyed and sleep-deprived as she talked brightly about what she had planned for the day, and it had begun to feel like she was trying to control which hours we were conscious, as well as everything else. By this point, even Joni and I were barely talking to each other after Joni accused me of hogging the computer on one of our rare trips into town, but when the front door flung open at nine one Sunday night (during our 675,882nd game of Scrabble), it was my hand she reached for.

"Please don't get up," Theo said, grinning as he surveyed the scene in front of him. "This is a charming portrait."

We sat frozen on the floor as what felt like an indeterminate number of college-age guys piled into the stone room, and it felt like the world had opened up again, even though none of us would ever give them the satisfaction of knowing that. After a moment, Evangeline jumped up and threw herself into her brother's arms. Theo hugged her back for a long time, and I wondered if even Ev wasn't having as much fun as she let on. It didn't matter, because from the moment the four of them arrived, Ev, Joni, and I instinctively transformed into heightened versions of ourselves. Or perhaps we just remembered who we were—three smart, college-bound young women who were entirely self-sufficient *thank you very much* and having the time of our lives in paradise, because how could we not?

As Ev and Theo caught up in the kitchen, preparing the food that the guys had picked up on their drive over (frozen pizzas—how unbelievably *boyish* and *American* of them), Joni and I showed the others around the house, staking claim to all the things we'd once despised, to make us sound brave and rugged—"The rats are actually kind of cute. It's the *snakes* you need to worry about."

We ate dinner outside, and the first mouthful of pizza felt miraculous, the cheese oily and familiar. Evangeline had insisted on us eating local and fresh, and Joni and I would take turns naming restaurants we missed at night ("Katsu-ya. The original one. Your turn."), but I hadn't realized how much I'd been yearning for a carb coma to remind me of home.

Theo and his friends from Brown, Zack, Bardo, and Robbie, seemed as thrilled to see us as we were them, and we all stayed up until four a.m. that night, cracking into Stavros's wine collection—dusting off bottles of red that Evangeline didn't even complain nobody was letting breathe for long enough. The atmosphere crackled with jokes and self-admiration and hope, and I caught Theo staring at me no less than seven times. The first time I caught him he looked away instantly, the second time he shrugged blithely, and from then on we just smiled at each other across the table. Evangeline fell asleep sitting up with her chin resting in her hand, and Joni was the one who finally called it.

When we stood up to leave, Theo touched my waist lightly, his fingers landing on the bare skin between my jean shorts and cropped T-shirt for less than a second.

"Wait here," he said. "I actually got you something in London."

I held my breath even as I told myself not to expect too much.

When Theo came back, he was grinning. He pressed a balled-up garment into my hands and, when I held it up, I saw that Theo had bought me a red soccer jersey with the name RONALDO on the back. I felt stunned that he'd thought of me even when he was nowhere near me.

"Shit," I said, unable to reach anything else for a moment. "Thank you."

"I saw it and thought of you," Theo said, and then he made a whooshing noise and arched his hand through the air, as if he were following the trajectory of the ball I'd kicked that day on the beach.

"It was a lucky kick," I said, even though I knew that hadn't been it at all. It was because Theo made people better than they were.

As I lay in bed later, the dawn chorus already warming up, I felt as if my entire body was alight. And if I had to relive one moment for the rest of my life, it would still be that night: the sense of hope, of infinite possibility, of tomorrow promising to be even better than today.

I woke up at around ten a.m. with a clawing headache and a dry mouth, unable to sleep longer for fear of missing anything. What if everyone had been up for hours before me? Bardo and Joni had been talking about going down to the beach for sunrise—what if they'd all just waited until I'd fallen asleep, and then snuck down?

What if being together in the water at sunrise was so brilliant, so perfect, that it was all any of them would talk about for the remainder of their stay? I felt sick at the thought of all the ways I might have already missed out, but when I got downstairs all I found was Bardo and Robbie sleeping in threadbare boxer shorts, snoring on opposite ends of the L-shaped sofa. Nearly breathless with relief, I sailed past them and into the kitchen, where I found Evangeline slicing lemons.

"Morning," I said.

"Hey," she replied, without looking at me.

I sat down at the kitchen table, waiting for her to comment on the beautiful weather; or how she'd dreamed about Mr. Maxim, our cute*ish* algebra teacher; or any of the things she'd usually say to fill a silence like this.

"God, I'm tired," I said. "Do you need any help?"

"Cutting lemons?" she said. "I think I'm good."

I paused, unsure of how to proceed. Theo's arrival obviously meant that it was more important than ever that Ev was on my side, however unreasonable I thought she'd been over the past month. I didn't think he'd necessarily ask for either her opinion or her approval explicitly, but they were close, and I knew that negative feedback wasn't exactly going to make things any easier.

"Umm, well, I just wanted to say that I'm sorry if things got a little tense for a while," I said stiffly. I'd apologized after fights with Steven and my parents in the past, but I'd never had to do it to a friend before. I had thought we were all in a race to prove who cared the least, and I felt irritable that Evangeline was milking it like this now that she had backup. It seemed unsporting, and not in the current spirit of things at all. Still, I took a deep breath and continued: "This has been such a *great* trip, Ev, like, so great, and I'm grateful for—"

"You're *so* transparent," Evangeline said, her back still turned to me. "Do you know that about yourself? So, so embarrassingly transparent."

It was the meanest thing she'd ever said to me. Perhaps the meanest thing anyone had ever said to me, given how smart I thought I was and how true it could have been. I understood then how cruel Joni and I must have been to her, in that insidious, incremental way that is almost worse because she couldn't have confronted us about it without seeming petty or babyish. I had brought Ev down to my level, forced her to be unkind, and I wasn't sure how to fix it, so instead I just watched as she carried on slicing lemons before placing them into oil on a baking tray. She walked over to the fridge and pulled out a large raw chicken, which she slathered in olive oil with her hands. I swallowed hard, the sight of the jiggling, dimpled skin instantly bringing out the depths of my hangover. When I couldn't bear it anymore, I pushed my chair back and ran to the bathroom to vomit.

―――――――――

Once everyone else had woken up to the smell of lemon-and-garlic-roasted chicken wafting up the stairs, I returned to the fold, stretching and pretending I'd woken up with them too. I watched Evangeline closely, noting how she had pulled her hair back into a perfect messy bun, a few loose strands tucked behind her ears; how she insisted we all sit for lunch exactly where we'd happened to sit the previous night (me on the opposite end of the table from Theo, naturally); how she kept on the frilly yellow apron even while we ate; and how she grabbed her digital camera and insisted on taking a group photo in which we all sat around the table with glasses of wine and plates of chicken and salad, a bunch of children pretending to be adults. As she monopolized her brother's attention, I felt a sort of bitterness toward her that was different from how I'd felt even a few hours earlier, as if she was trying harder than ever to be perceived as selfless and helpful to make me feel worse, even though I knew that this was just how she was, how she had always been. I deliberately ignored Theo to show her just how untransparent, how stunningly *opaque*, I could be when I wanted.

Later, as we were all walking down to the beach, I would pull Joni aside and try to tell her about what had happened in the kitchen.

"Can you believe she'd say something like that?" I said, and by this point I was furious. "What did she even mean?"

"She probably just didn't want things to be weird," Joni said, shrugging me off. "Lighten up, Bess. Not everything's always about you."

Joni skipped ahead to catch up with Bardo, who she'd clearly decided was the fun one and the person she might be able to convince to ditch the other guys to go island-hopping with her, because I'd never shown any signs that I was actually serious about it, but I knew he was only fun because Joni had chosen him. She had coaxed the wildness out of him, and I wondered if she knew the effect she had on all of us. As I struggled to be included—smiling and laughing as Joni's and Bardo's dares for each other grew more outlandish and they swam so far out that we could no longer even spot their bobbing heads; pretending not to notice when Theo hugged Evangeline after she went pale and covered her face with her hands—I realized how fragile these alliances were, how adding just one extra element could make the whole thing collapse in front of your eyes.

SEVENTEEN

2018

JONI'S HOUSE IS SPECTACULAR. An architectural touchstone—a mid-century crested-wave-inspired gem, built from glass and copper and perched over a strip of Malibu coastline that is destined to be devoured by the ocean in our lifetime; the kind of home that implies the owner might even be deserving of their wealth because they have a healthy attitude toward losing it. Either that or the surveyor fucked up.

Joni reaches a hand around the door and pulls me inside. I follow her into a sprawling open-plan room with 180 degrees of floor-to-ceiling windows revealing only the ocean, and a ceiling that follows the curved structure of the roof above. The overall effect is that we're in a gaping spaceship, hovering somewhere above the rest of the world. While Joni's place is flanked by other (less remarkable) beach houses on the same prestigious street, it has been constructed in such a way that the only other houses visible from the window must be ten, twenty miles down the coast. As I lean against the doorframe, I have the uncomfortable realization that it would be easy to lose perspective here.

Joni doesn't seem as tense as I might have expected, straight-backed and poised as ever in a cream cashmere loungewear set, with sharply manicured taupe nails. When I look at her, I can almost convince myself that this is a good idea, that I needed to get out of the desert anyway, with its thick and cloying heat and the flying ants that lodge themselves so snugly in my hair that I only find them once they're circling the drain of my shower.

"Was anyone out there?" Joni asks, and I shake my head. I'd seen a neighbor walking a Doberman with a thick string of drool hanging from his gums, but no other cars in the road, and no camera lenses peeping out from behind the many succulents lining the affluent street.

Joni nods, perhaps remembering how adept I'd once been at spotting a camera or stalker a mile away, and we look at each other for a moment, both unsure of where to start.

"I feel like I can't catch my breath," she says. "Let's go outside."

I follow her out the back of the house, trying not to notice that there isn't a single photo of Willa on the walls.

———

"Why did you involve me in this?" I ask, once we're out on the deck—a glowing white haven with a frosted glass balustrade and a metal stepladder leading straight down to the beach below. I lean against the warm glass with my back to the sunset, arms folded across my chest.

"I didn't know this would happen," Joni says. "I swear."

"But you knew I had to say yes," I say.

"No," Joni says slowly. "I didn't know that."

I stare at her, and, for once, she is the first to look away.

"I had no idea she would take it this far, Bess."

"What time did you leave here for Zoey's?" I ask.

Joni narrows her eyes at me in response, as if I'm the one ruining everything.

"This neighbor," I say, "who saw Willa on the deck when, according to my lie, you would have already left for my house. Did you know he'd seen her?"

"I saw them talking before I left," Joni says levelly.

"And how do you know he didn't see you?"

"He was in the water," Joni says. "Willa called down to him to ask about the surf, because we planned to go out together."

I feel a chill at her words.

"You went paddleboarding?" I ask.

"We didn't, no," Joni says. "Because then Willa found the photo of Zoey on my phone, and I left."

Zoey, I think. The faceless woman who started everything, lurking just off-screen.

"And you're still not worried about Willa."

"I know her, Bess," Joni says. "I know how her mind works."

"Why didn't you mention the paddleboarding to me at the time?" I ask, and Joni bites her bottom lip.

"Because I didn't think I needed to justify myself to you, of all people."

"It isn't going to take long for them to make the connection to Greece," I say quietly.

"I know," Joni says then. "I know that."

We stare at each other for a moment, the waves crashing below us the only sound, and I know that the more I think about it, the more sense it could all make, if I just choose to believe her. Joni's entire alibi may hinge on me confirming she was at my house three hours before she actually turned up, but we both know firsthand how little difference there is between lies and the truth, how either can be distorted at any point to fit someone else's agenda. The only question that actually matters is whether or not I trust Joni.

"I've had to cancel my publicity tour for the book," she says after a moment. "They're talking about delaying the release until

she comes back. Apparently the optics aren't great. Missing fiancée, dead best friend, et cetera."

"Joni, surely even you can understand how strange it would
look to promote your book while Willa's missing, regardless of
how seriously you want to take it."

"You still care about how things look," Joni says, her eyes drilling into mine. "Above anything."

I feel her words like a tiger bite, and Joni reaches out a hand to
touch my arm.

"I'm not trying to be cruel. I'm just trying to work out what
happened to you," she says. "You've made yourself so small."

A knot forms in my chest at her words. *How could I not?*

"But, Bess? How I am, what I've become, it's not necessarily a
good thing," she says, as if she's reading my mind. "That's what
I'm starting to realize."

I think she's about to say more, but then she just shrugs and
picks at a loose thread of cashmere on her top. I half want Joni to
unleash her guts and vitriol onto me because then at least I'd have
a clue what was happening inside her mind. This prickliness, this
clunkiness as she changes tack and adapts, is unfamiliar to me from
Joni. Evangeline held parts of herself back because she was naturally shy, and my insecurities sometimes made me cagey, but Joni
was never like this. Her intentions were always reassuringly close
to the surface—she never could resist the truth, often in the form
of a sharply worded insult that you felt deep in your bones. I always thought that Joni had been so unaffected by what happened
to us that she had, after all, turned it into something positive—a
future, a career for herself—but now I wonder whether she has always been hiding more than I thought.

"Tell me about her," I say, and Joni frowns at me. "Maybe if
you tell me about her, we can figure out where she is, or at the very
least, why she's doing this."

A wave hits the glass barrier, spray cascading over the top and landing at our feet.

"You should know better than most that not everything can be solved. Sometimes your entire fucking life catches on fire for no reason other than to remind you of how fragile it all is. How little control we have over any of it," Joni says flatly.

"That isn't very Joni Le Bon of you," I say. "Don't let anyone catch you saying that."

Joni smiles at me then and it makes me feel sad. "Sorry to disappoint you, Bess."

Afterward, they combed through every crevice of our lives, both physical and electronic. They found the notes Joni and I had passed under each other's bedroom doors in the Tinos house. The ones where we called Evangeline *the Evangelist*, making her out to be some sort of crusading zealot who was so riddled with guilt over her privilege that she had decided to lock us up to teach us the value of abstinence and simplicity. We planned our jailbreak in minute detail to make each other laugh. A particularly incriminating one I had sent to Joni:

> *You tie her up in the cellar next to that truly spectacular wine collection we're forbidden to touch, and I'll block the door. Then we'll choose a goat each and ride into town, high from that most heady combination of Châteauneuf-du-Pape and true liberté. I've heard whispers of a ferry to Mykonos scheduled for 2065, and I'm happy to wait for it if you are. Yours faithfully, Bestiality.*

The notes were on notepaper monogrammed with Stavros Aetos's initials, written in pens paid for by his money. We never thought to burn them, never dreamed they'd one day be printed not only in local Greek papers but also in *The Sun* in London and the *New York Post* even closer to home, to be discussed on talk shows across the world as examples of the decaying morals of teenagers today.

A British tabloid hacked into my emails and retrieved a note I'd sent my brother in those first few listless weeks. They couldn't have known how guilty I felt that I'd left him for the entire summer before I was about to leave him all over again for good when I moved to New York. The email consisted of a few lines I quickly typed out to make him laugh before it was Evangeline's turn to use the computer:

I think I might be in purgatory. They at least let you drink in hell, right?

One more note from Joni to me, a few weeks before Ev's death:

Let's wait until she's asleep and go midnight swimming. We can plot our escape and howl under the full moon, like the true heathens we are.

We sounded frivolous at best, mercenary at worst, and maybe we were. But show me an eighteen-year-old saint, and I'll show you a liar.

EIGHTEEN

2008

I AVOIDED THEO FOR THE next few days, wanting to prove to myself as much as to Evangeline that she was wrong. The energy level dropped slightly after that first night, but it was still a different universe from the one Ev, Joni, and I had navigated before the boys' arrival. On the surface, Evangeline was civil with me, laughing at my jokes and even putting sunscreen on my back when I asked, but she also seemed to go out of her way to ensure that we were never alone together, so I couldn't get a true read on how she was feeling toward me. She seemed to be completely normal with Joni, on the other hand, sitting on her lap for nearly an hour one evening by the pool, staying there even while Joni had some of the spliff Robbie handed her. I hoped she didn't notice that I had started brushing my hair every morning so that it fell over my shoulders like a glossy cape, and that I was now wearing my black bikini with the uncomfortable underwire, covering up in jean shorts only when goose bumps skated across my thighs.

On Saturday night, Evangeline grilled three red mullets to serve with a mezze platter of freshly made dips. She had woken early and driven to the market to pick up the ingredients, and the colorful spread felt both ostentatious and solicitous to me, since the only appropriate reactions were awe and gratitude. I remember wondering for the first time whether Ev was as insecure and hungry for attention as the rest of us, but where Joni was loud and brash, and I was primed and calculated, Ev just hid it behind acts of servitude and got to disguise it as selflessness.

We all stood around to admire the food as Joni lit the large citronella candles at either end of the table.

"Guys, don't stand on ceremony," Evangeline said, pointing to the chairs. "Let's eat."

I went to take my usual seat against the ivy that covered one of the walls of the house, but Theo called my name.

"Come sit here," he said, pointing to the seat next to him at the head of the table. Ev's seat.

"Theo," Ev said, frowning. "Don't be a dick."

"Ev, come on, it's ridiculous," Theo said. "I want to sit next to Bess. This isn't just your house."

The rest of us froze, looking anywhere but at either Theo or Ev. I couldn't even feel thrilled that Theo had made such a public declaration of my specialness—I was too mortified as I waited for Ev to respond. She looked between the two of us, her eyes glowing in the dying light.

"Whatever," she said. "I just thought it would be fun."

She moved to sit next to Joni, her fingers clamped tightly around her wineglass.

"It was fun, Ev," I said quietly, but I don't think she heard me.

———

For the three hours we were sitting at the table, I had the full, brilliant Theo Aetos experience. He told me stories about college, about how he'd tried out for the crew team thinking it couldn't be that hard because he'd been sailing a few times with his dad, but that he'd had to drop his oars after ten minutes to vomit over the side of the boat from exertion. He told me about how his mom had been when they were younger, when his dad was around more, and how she used to sing Fleetwood Mac songs at the top of her lungs when she drove them home from school. He told me that he'd never been in love, but that one day he could see himself settling down with some beautiful overachiever who would ideally outearn and outshine him in every way, and that while he loved drumming, he didn't want to be in a band, he wanted to be a session musician instead because he'd seen how his dad still traveled the world, and it was cool and everything but he'd rather make a stable home for himself and his future family while still doing the thing he loved. Everything he said was like a master class on how to make someone feel special, like you can trust them, but I don't think he knew what he was doing. His attention was so unconditional, and he was so open, so self-effacing, that I started to relax a little, started to tell him a couple of stories in return, even when they didn't paint me in the best light.

"You're faking it?" he asked at one point, his lips pulling back into a grin.

"Shhh," I said, kicking him softly underneath the table with my bare foot. "Not faking exactly. It's just more of a . . . choice than it used to be."

I was talking about my English accent, how I could feel it slipping away from me recently, softening and distorting, first in inflection and then in the way my mouth moved to create the sounds, so that I felt like I was constantly fighting against something, and even now, speaking to him, I had to make an effort to pronounce things the way I always had, the way my parents had taught me. What I didn't tell him was that the extra step between thinking and talking made me feel even more like a fraud, an imposter, but not as much as yielding to a new accent altogether might have.

"I like your accent," Theo said. "But you'd still be hot with-out it."

I smiled and tossed my hair, sneaking a peak at him when he leaned over to move the terra-cotta bowl of olives closer to us. His tanned skin was glowing in the candlelight, and I thought he was the most beautiful person I'd ever seen. More beautiful than Ev, even, now that I knew her beauty was hiding her desire to be needed. I looked at her then and found her watching me, her eyes nar-rowed. I held up my wineglass to her, and she still just stared back.

Later, I carried a pile of dirty dishes from the table into the kitchen. The boys never made any move to clear up after dinner, and even though it was starting to annoy me that it meant it fell to us to do it, as if we were expected to pick up after them just by virtue of the fact of being female, that night I barely noticed. If anything, I was eager to show Theo how domesticated I also was, barefoot and tanned in a tiny white dress with my hair tumbling down my back—how I may not have been the session drummer heir to a billion-dollar oil empire who still planned on marrying up, but that I too contained *multitudes*.

Ev was washing up some forks for dessert, her hands in bright yellow dishwashing gloves, and I watched in the window reflec-tion as she blew a strand of hair off her sticky forehead. I wasn't sure if she knew I was there until she spoke, her voice loud and clear even though her back was still to me.

"*No*," she said simply.

"Excuse me?" I asked, holding the plates in midair over the table where I had been about to dump them. Ev turned off the tap and slowly took her gloves off before turning around to face me. Her expression was unreadable, her eyes landing on me like a but-terfly on a blade of grass.

"If you're asking my permission to fuck my brother, I'm saying no," Ev said slowly, and the blow of the word *fuck* coming out of her mouth stunned me so much that, at first, I didn't comprehend what she was saying. When I understood, I felt a sickening wave of shame that I disguised instantly with outrage.

"Are you saying I'm not good enough for him?" I asked.

Evangeline studied me for a moment.

"That's the thing," she said. "It's actually irrelevant whether or not I think you're good enough for Theo, because nothing's ever going to happen. Not how you think, anyway. And honestly? I could be as shitty a friend as you are and let you chase after him for the rest of the trip, or I could just tell you the truth right now."

As she spoke, her mouth twisted in a way that wasn't entirely unfamiliar to me, that was more an extension of her regular expression than a distortion, and I understood then that this version of Evangeline, this *shadow*, had possibly been lurking below the surface that entire summer, perhaps our whole friendship, just waiting to be invoked.

"You're embarrassing yourself, Bess," Ev said coolly, and then she calmly went back to the washing up while I stood there, swimming in shock. When she didn't look at me again, I threw the dishes down onto the table and stormed back outside, my hands trembling. Joni raised her eyebrows at me as I sat down, but I was too angry to do anything but shake my head.

Evangeline eventually came out with a platter of broken shards of meringue for dessert, a smile pasted on her face. I refused to eat any, clenching my jaw as I tried not to cry.

"Hey," Theo said softly to me. "You okay?"

I nodded wordlessly.

"Do you want to go for a walk?" Joni called across the table. "Bess, let's go for a walk."

My cheeks turned hot, but still I just sat, paralyzed by my fury at having been both seen and dismissed in the exact same moment.

"I feel like a walk," Theo said then. "I'll go with Bess."

Joni glanced quickly at Evangeline, who ignored us as she doled out a spoonful of gloopy strawberries mixed with cream onto Bardo's suspended plate.

I slipped my feet back into my Keds, then stood up to join Theo, who was now waiting to lead me away from the group. My blind fury was eased only slightly by the prospect of this solo walk, particularly for how much it would be riling Evangeline up, although she'd no doubt disguise it under layers of syrupy naïveté or perhaps even victimhood, now that the boys were around to want to rescue her. How entitled for her to believe she could control everything in her life, including me. How dare she have tried to humiliate me like that, implying I was insane for ever thinking I was good enough for her perfect brother. It just compounded what I'd learned about Evangeline over the past five weeks, how, despite her angelic act, she was as entitled as the worst of them. And that was the crux of it, wasn't it? That was how the rot of that level of wealth really manifested. Somewhere deep inside, Evangeline still believed that everyone in her charmed life could be bought. She still believed that we could be maneuvered and shuffled at whim, because we only ever existed as extensions of herself.

I silently stewed as Theo led me around the grounds of the house, passing the rows of fragrant olive and cypress trees and snaking bougainvillea to a soundtrack of crickets. He didn't ask what had happened and I could never have told him, but after a while the methodical sensation of walking together, Theo's hand occasionally brushing mine, began to soothe me. As I became more aware of Theo's steady, grounded presence beside me, I realized that it could have felt odd to be walking in silence after the almost magical quality of our conversation throughout dinner, but after weeks of experiencing every possible type of silence with the girls (passive-aggressive, sulky, loaded, starvation-induced), I knew the difference between when silence was concealing something and when it was building to something, and I felt a thrum of anticipation deep in my stomach at the thought that it could be the latter.

When we reached the lemon tree at the edge of the Aetoses' land, we both stopped. The sky was black behind faltering stars, and I pretended to search for a lemon ripe enough to bring back to the house.

"We're leaving tomorrow," Theo said, watching me as he leaned against the trunk of the tree. "I haven't told Ev yet, but there's a surfing competition in Newquay that Robbie and Bardo have been talking about since we left LA."

"Oh," I said, unable to hide the disappointment from my voice. I thought I heard Theo smile behind me.

"Oh," he repeated softly, then he reached out and took my hand. When I turned around, he took my face in his hands, and I stopped breathing.

"Oh," he said again, before he leaned down to kiss me.

Oh.

"We should get back," I said, when it was already later. Much later. Then: "Ev will be worrying."

NINETEEN

2018

JONI MAKES ME AN adaptogen and pineapple smoothie for my first breakfast at her house. As I watch her move around the kitchen, a look of concentration on her face, I think that she is probably a good person to live with, a good person to be loved by, even though neither comes naturally to her. I wonder if Willa would agree.

"There are reporters outside," Joni says as she presses the glass jug against the ice dispenser on her fridge. "So we need to keep the front shutters closed and stick to the back of the house until they lose interest."

I glance over to the front windows and notice an inch of sunlight streaming through where a shutter hasn't quite locked into place. A shiver runs through me as I move toward it, remembering how it felt to have my every move watched and dissected, even once I was locked safely back inside the gates of my Calabasas community. At the time, I was grateful for the privileges I'd always taken for granted, but even back then I understood that it couldn't be that way forever.

Before I close the shutter, I peek outside. Sure enough, four or five photographers are now gathered at the end of Joni's driveway, somehow looking entirely perfunctory and threatening at the same time. I snap it closed.

"Are you going to talk to them?" I ask, once I'm back in the kitchen.

Joni shakes her head.

"Fuck them," she says as she pours out my smoothie—suspiciously green with chunks of pineapple that make my mouth itch just looking at it. "They can wait as long as they want, but they're not going to get anything from me. My publicist told me that the further I go while Willa's still missing, the more backlash I'll get. Honestly, I have to hand it to her—it's pretty impressive how she's holding me hostage, even when she's nowhere near me."

Despite her bright tone, Joni's face folds into itself with fury.

"I guess there's worse places to be stuck than Malibu," I say, reminding myself instantly of my mom trying to deflect from anything too bleak—trying to stifle the tangle of emotions that might overwhelm us the moment we gave them space to breathe. "The light is beautiful."

"You know better than most how little that means when you lack the freedom to leave," Joni fires back, before walking over to the doors that open out onto the deck. I follow her outside, where the sea mist has cleared to reveal a stretch of painfully hopeful blue sky.

"Have you heard any more from the police?" I ask.

"Nothing of any significance," she says. "They seem to be debating how seriously to take it all."

"Because she's done this before," I say, and Joni nods.

Then: "Her friends are holding a vigil tonight on Malibu Pier. Hashtag pray4Willa, et cetera."

I feel a thud in my stomach. Did our school friends once hold a vigil for Evangeline? Did they print copies of her yearbook photo and hold candles, crying over her wasted beauty, her unrivaled kindness, how unfair it was that she was gone and we were still here?

"Are you going?"

"No," Joni says. "Like I said, I'm not leaving the house unless I have to."

I nod, somewhat relieved to hear that she isn't trying to go to Pilates or dinner at Little Beach House, or wherever else she secretly feels entitled to be. Unlike Joni, I have worked hard to keep a low profile, and, at this point, I am only recognizable as an extension of Joni, as opposed to the other way around.

"I fucking miss being in the water," Joni says, and as she's talking, I notice something I missed yesterday—two paddleboards mounted on the exterior of the house. One pink and silver, one yellow and black, with two oars leaning against the wall next to them.

"Did you go out often?" I ask, gesturing at them.

"Every day," Joni says softly. "Hers is the pink one."

I want to ask if Zoey likes the ocean too, or if she fears it like I've learned to. In my mind, Zoey has become almost mythical—a creature so special, so different from us all, that Joni was prepared to risk everything for her, but Joni looks so crushed that I swallow my words. In the end, I just say, "I'm surprised you don't still go. If you really don't care what anyone thinks."

Without looking at me, Joni walks back inside the house, and, after a moment, I follow her. When we were kids, Joni was always more open, more surface level than I was—a natural by-product of her unflinching honesty—but now her energy is brittle, as if she would be both impossible to pry open and more than capable of snapping if I try too hard. This change in her is interesting to me, not least because of how incompatible it is with the central tenet of Joni's doctrine: the idea that shame can only survive in the darkness. It makes me wonder if she's in more pain than she'd ever know how to tell me.

Joni sinks down onto the sofa and puts her bare feet up on the bamboo coffee table, and I take a seat in the white armchair opposite her. After a stretch of silence, Joni points the remote at the TV, flicking through channels before landing on an episode of *Seinfeld*.

"Are you ready to talk about her yet?" I ask softly, and Joni turns to me then, her eyes flashing so furiously that my stomach drops. (*The exact same eyes as when we were kids,* I remind myself. *Eyes the color of root beer.*)

Then, to my surprise, Joni nods, her eyes tracking mine carefully as she mutes the TV.

"Fine," she says casually. "I'll start."

Now that the moment has arrived, I remember how unprepared I am for any sort of emotional outpouring or display of vulnerability from anyone, but particularly Joni. I wonder if she'll cry out for Willa, and how I might comfort her if she does. *Ginger!* I imagine saying in the same confident tone she adopts. *The absolute only cure for a missing fiancée.*

"Do you remember how she used to accidentally steal our memories? Like, I'd burn my mouth drinking coffee too quickly, and the next day she would insist that her tongue hurt."

My heart sinks when I understand that Joni is talking about Evangeline. I open my mouth to stop her, but Joni is warming up, as if she's coming back to life, and all I can do is watch, stunned that she hasn't been pretending all this time, that she really can just talk about our dead friend like this, at a moment's notice and without pain or regret.

"Or the time you got period blood on that yellow chair in the library, and Ev told *you* the same story a year later, thinking it had been her."

I'd forgotten that either of those things had happened, but I paste a smile on my face, nodding along. Against my will, an image of Evangeline pops into my mind, emerging from the dark blue water of her swimming pool, hair shimmering in the sunlight as she sang along to "Hey There Delilah," or something equally twee that only she could get away with admitting she actually liked.

"And if we pointed out that she'd done it again, she'd get so pissed and flat-out deny it," Joni laughs. "Honestly, I don't think she ever meant to do it. I think she felt things so strongly that even our stories and experiences became part of her. And she couldn't handle anyone thinking she was lying about it because it felt real to her."

"That sounds like Ev," I say woodenly as Joni gets up and walks into the kitchen area. I watch as she takes something from the shelf next to the fridge: a photo frame that had been turned away, that I had assumed was a photo of Willa, but now that Joni shows it to me I can see is a photo of the three of us, taken using a self-timer in our first week in Tinos as we ran wild on an empty cove carved into rocks that shimmered like the surface of the moon. I feel numb even as I force a smile.

"Honestly, she was such an idiot," Joni says, gazing fondly down at it. "Like she had this need for total control that was so fucking bonkers and chaotic and endearing, and *still* all anyone wants to say about her is that she was perfect. Like, are you kidding me? This is the girl who hid her brother's passport so that he couldn't go skiing in Italy one winter break because she couldn't bear to be alone."

And now I'm laughing a little too, thinking about the day we found Theo's passport hidden in a copy of *The Handmaid's Tale* on Ev's bookshelf, and how horrified she was to have been caught out as being just as deranged, just as *shady* as Joni and I could be, and how her cheeks had flushed and she hadn't known whether to scream at us or to make a joke about it. When I stop laughing, all I'm left with is a lump, a rock, in the back of my throat that I have to work out how to swallow.

Joni and I lounge on the deck for the rest of the morning, and there are pockets of time where we could be sixteen again, our skin glistening with Hawaiian Tropic instead of La Roche-Posay SPF 50, staring out at the same foaming waves and talking about anything but the stuff that matters. There are other moments when Joni slips into her cultivated personality and talks of raising vibrations, of reparenting one's inner child, but I can't help but wonder how much of this Joni actually believes in herself. I find that she always takes a small but noticeable pause before saying anything "spiritual," and it makes me wonder if, in a strange way, Joni has had to censor her authentic self in order to preserve it. Perhaps Joni developed this new persona as a coping mechanism, protecting herself from disappearing altogether by splitting herself into two distinct versions. I understand that the alternative is worse—slipping away bit by bit, yielding and folding until one day you look in the mirror and don't recognize what you've become. I wonder if Joni ever gets to be her true self these days, or if this constant striving and learning and teaching, this relentless ambition and inability to sit still or be alone, is a result of not wanting to remember. And I wonder which Joni Willa knows.

Later, Joni goes up to the mezzanine to do some work and I fall asleep on the sofa. When I open my eyes, my skin is covered in fine goose bumps and the sea mist is rolling in again.

I stretch and call Joni's name.

When there is no response, I go to look for her. The house, as impressive as it is, is all but engulfed by the expansive great room, leaving little space for much else. The two bedrooms are near the entrance of the house, and the upstairs consists solely of a startlingly white mezzanine office, reachable by a spiral staircase. There are few places to hide, and Joni is nowhere to be found. Unsettled, I return to the kitchen, checking the mass of event invitations and shopping lists on the fridge, as if Joni might have left a clue as to her whereabouts. When nothing stands out, I take a bottle of white wine from the fridge and figure I'll wait up for her to return. I wonder fleetingly if she's snuck out to see Zoey, but I don't want to believe that Joni would put herself, and me, at risk by doing something so stupid when all eyes are already on her. Maybe she decided to go to Willa's vigil after all.

I'm looking for a corkscrew when I discover a drawer that was once probably the "everything" drawer, the one filled with old keys and tangled headphones and phone chargers, but that is now wedged with photographs. I take out a stack, riffling through them as I lean against the island. Every photo is of Willa, her skin glowing, eyes often closed as she is caught in motion, dancing or laughing to reveal a row of large white teeth, dimples hollowed, head flung back, and I can feel her life force emanating through each one. I wonder if some of these were once on the wall or fridge, and whether they have become too painful, too vibrant for Joni to do anything with but stuff them into a drawer until Willa comes back.

One photograph in particular stands out for me, and it's precisely because Willa isn't moving, isn't flashing her beautiful smile at the camera. Instead, she wears a wet suit on the beach, squinting at whoever is behind the lens as she holds a paddleboard over her hip, her engagement ring catching sharply in the sun. For once she seems unwilling to pose for the photo, and her face is furrowed with impatience, perhaps to get out to the waves, as she glares into the camera. There's an authenticity, a grittiness, to Willa in this photo that catches me off guard, and I slot it within the pages of the book I've been pretending to read for two years—a nonfiction book on emotional resilience my mom picked up for me at an airport.

I walk back to the sofa, balancing my glass of wine and open laptop, and then I type in "Willa Bailey." After scanning through various news articles about her disappearance, I land on Willa's YouTube channel, where she has over a million subscribers. Her videos are either about sustainable beauty products she's found or impassioned calls to action about a cause she's adopted, her eyebrows wriggling with earnestness and outrage. I watch a couple before I find one that's a little different. Willa is filming from the deck of the house I'm currently inside, shooting a school of dolphins as they leap across the ocean. Once they've disappeared into the distance, Willa swivels the camera around and focuses on Joni, who is reading a book in the shade in a pair of marabou-trimmed silk pajamas.

"And this," Willa's voice says. "This is where you find the rarest mammal of all. The Joni, basking in her natural habitat . . ."

Joni looks up, and her face breaks into a genuine grin that makes my stomach hurt. Her face is so filled with love and pride, and I've never seen her look even half as happy as she is here, smiling at Willa on a random day in April. The thought that Joni was cheating on the person who made her look like this makes me feel hopeless.

"No filming me, baby," Joni says, and Willa laughs, a surprising, raspy sound.

"Who are you kidding—" Willa's voice says, and then, above my laptop, the sliding doors open and I slam the laptop shut, guilt firing through me as Joni stands on the deck, her wet body silhouetted against the dark sky.

"Where were you?" I ask, trying to deflect my guilt. "I was worried."

Joni walks toward the fridge in her black wet suit, and I join her as she pours herself a glass of wine. Water is dripping from her hair and creating a pool at her feet, but she doesn't seem to notice.

"I took your advice," she says. "I needed to clear my mind."

"Did it work?"

Joni shakes her head, and, for just a moment, I wonder if she might finally crumble.

"I feel like I'm back there again, Bess," she says quietly.

I nod, understanding that she means back in jail, yes, but also back in that suffocating moment in Greece when we finally understood that we were trapped, and all we could do was stare at each other for the strange, elastic final hours before the police arrived to take us away. Despite everything she's done in the decade since Evangeline's death, all the ways she created and then surpassed her own expectations, Joni is back where we started, waiting to be judged by the world for something she can't control.

"You need to make some sort of public statement," I say. "Even if you think it's bullshit."

"I know," Joni says, sounding young and exhausted as she runs her hand through her hair.

I wonder what she expected by taking so much from the world.

I lie awake in bed for hours, and I can hear Joni moving around the house the entire time. When we were younger, Joni always needed the most sleep out of any of us, often emerging at eleven a.m. when I couldn't sleep past seven, irritatingly bright-eyed and refreshed. She used to boast that she slept eleven hours a night from the day her parents brought her home from the hospital, and I wonder whether this new regimen, these four hours at best she's getting, is a result of her current circumstances or her new persona.

Would Joni even remember the things that used to restore her, or is she so used to putting on a show that she's forgotten?

I unlock my phone and type Joni's name into Google. Before I can even blink, thousands of results appear—news articles from both reputable and fake news outlets. I scroll down, down, down, with my heart in my mouth.

There are photos of Willa and Joni together over the years positioned directly next to footage from tonight's vigil on the pier, where Willa's friends grip elegant white candles and demand the universe deliver her back to them safely, as glossy tears streak their beautiful cheeks. In the background, I can spot the overzealous strangers who have also turned up for the event, the type of people who live for stories like this one, who spend all their time becoming experts in something that doesn't concern them because they want to feel significant for the first time in their otherwise dispensable existences.

While Joni's glaring absence isn't mentioned outright by anyone attending the vigil, it is alluded to over and over again in the rest of the reports. I read on, and, within the first three paragraphs, often before any of Joni's career achievements are mentioned, almost every single piece references what happened in Mykonos. Through my dread, I feel a glint of something uncomfortably close to satisfaction that Joni hasn't outrun the past as well as she'd hoped, that she is still stuck on a loop too, climbing down that same winding path to get away from the Aetoses' stone house that summer.

Using the light of my phone as a guide, I slide the photo of Willa out from the pages of my book, staring at it as if it might hold the clues to what I should do next. As a dull exhaustion blurs my vision, I stare at Willa's unsmiling face until the image distorts. I'm about to snap the book closed when I notice that Willa is wearing her engagement ring, which means the photo must have been taken in the last three months. I frown, wondering why Joni told me that Willa's board was the pink and silver one, currently mounted on the wall at the back of their house, when the board she's holding in the photograph is a deep blue.

I tell myself that I must have misheard, since it would be an odd thing for Joni to lie about.

TWENTY

WHILE THEO AND I spent the rest of the night together, we somehow stopped short of having sex. Every room in the house was occupied, and I got the feeling that Theo didn't want our first time together to be some rushed, gritty encounter just for the sake of it. Even through my disappointment, I liked what this sense of ceremony said about him—or at least what it said about how he felt about *me*, since I was fairly confident that he didn't insist on a one-thousand-thread-count setting for every girl he slept with at college or on his sex tour of Europe. I figured I was probably also more experienced than he assumed, but I didn't quite know how to communicate that I'd have been perfectly happy to fuck him in the back seat of the Aetoses' Fiat without coming across as either pushy or demonic with lust, which was exactly how I felt.

Instead, we lay intertwined on a deck chair by the pool, and I would have done anything he asked if it meant he wouldn't stop kissing me. The gilded black sky was approaching its darkest, but there was no chance I would close my eyes if it meant missing even a second of this night, when all of my adolescent longing had finally found a place to land. I would have felt too exposed if I hadn't seen everything I was feeling reflected right back in Theo's eyes too, hadn't felt it in the way his hands constantly trailed over my skin and in the revealing stories he told me between kisses.

"My dad's ego won't let me work for anyone other than him," he said at one point, after I asked him about his postcollege plans, hoping he'd say he was planning to stay on the East Coast. "But I know there's a part of him that won't respect me if I don't forge my own path, you know? His type of money, the type where he came from nothing and built an empire for himself, it makes strangers out of fathers and sons."

I made a sympathetic noise and batted away the uncharitable thought that there were worse things than having a father who wanted to buy you the world. I thought of Joni's dad, who had walked out of her life in the middle of the night, and figured that at least Stavros always came home in the end.

"I thought you were going to be a drummer, anyway," I said, and he kissed my head.

"Maybe," he said, but his tone was flat, like he already knew it was impossible.

Theo shifted down on the deck chair, and I rested my head on his chest, feeling his heart thump against my temple. The beat was slow and steady, and I wondered if he could feel my own pulse skittering beneath my skin.

"It makes me feel trapped sometimes, how much my sister needs me," he told me next. "It's hard to live up to."

"You're a team," I said, my feelings even toward Ev slightly more benign after my night with her brother. I tried not to think about the cruel twist of her mouth in the kitchen, the cool manner in which she'd assured me I was inferior to her family.

"We've had to be, yeah," Theo said. "And I'd do anything for her, but sometimes the thought of her coming to Brown makes me feel like I can't breathe."

I tilted my face up and kissed his jaw.

"She's stronger than you think," I said, not because either I knew it to be true or she deserved for me to lie but because it seemed like the right thing to say.

When the birds began to chirp, I found myself filled with a deep sadness. I nestled my head into Theo's chest and squeezed my eyes shut as if I could stop time somehow, but the sky kept on lightening ominously around us.

"I'm going to come back," Theo said then, as if he had read my mind.

"What?" I said, angling my head so that I was looking up at him. He smiled down at me, his eyes warm.

"I'm coming back to Tinos," he said slowly. "After Newquay. I want to go to another island, Milos, for the last days of summer. I found this spot a few years back—it's a converted boathouse right on this quiet bay, and the young couple who own it live nearby, and the husband, George, catches fish every day that his wife grills for dinner and hand delivers to the patio, and you can just chill and, like, smoke weed and drink wine and swim in the ocean in the middle of the night, or just do nothing at all and watch the water as time unravels in, like, the most gratifying way. It's kind of my secret spot, and I always thought that if everything gets too much or if the pressure starts weighing on me with my dad or the business, I'll just hide out over there for a while. It's the kind of place where your hardest decisions become clear as water, and you realize that not only do you know exactly what you need to be doing, but you had the answer all along."

As Theo talked, I thought about how similar he was to Evangeline, how uncynical you had to be to be able to talk seriously about time *unraveling* or about decisions becoming *clear as water* before you were even twenty-one, and I resisted the urge to say something witty and self-deprecating that only Joni would have appreciated.

"And, Bess—" Theo started, his mossy eyes meeting mine. "I want you to come with me. I've never taken anyone before, not even Ev, but I really want to show it to you."

I felt my stomach twist as I thought first about how devastated Ev would be if we left her, seconds before I knew that I would still say yes to Theo. I remembered the way Ev had stared through me earlier as if I wasn't even there, and I nodded, brushing my lips against Theo's mouth again to show my consent.

"I would love that," I said softly.

"I'll be back in two weeks," Theo said, lifting my chin with his hand to kiss me again, and it felt like the ground dropped another couple of inches away from my bare feet. "We can tell Ev then."

"Okay," I said, resting my head on his shoulder.

As Theo stroked my hair, I finally allowed myself to fall asleep, now that I knew this didn't have to be the end.

We woke up later to Joni standing above us, arms folded across her chest. I knew it must have been late if even she was awake, and I wondered who else had seen us out there, curled around each other like stray foxes.

"Well, this is unexpected," Joni said dryly. I swallowed, my mouth tacky and dank as Theo grinned at her.

"What's good, Bonnier?" he said, either not knowing Joni well enough to sense her disapproval or not caring.

"You know, you might want to apologize to Ev for last night," she said to me, and I felt a prickle of shame at her tone. She turned her gaze to Theo. "Especially as she found out you guys are leaving today."

Joni smiled, but the subtext was clear—*was it worth it?* She stalked back inside as Theo stretched out next to me and, sensing my shift in mood, gave me a reassuring smile.

"Ev will be fine," he said, yawning slightly as he slung his arm around me and pulled me close.

No, I thought. *She won't be.*

Theo went upstairs to shower, and I walked down the winding path to the beach to clear my head. Once I was in the cool water, I front-crawled out to the strip of rocks Joni and I used as the finish line when we were racing each other, where I bobbed around in the water for a while, hoping the vastness would give some perspective to the shift in my world that felt both permanent and terrifyingly insubstantial at the same time. I swam back underwater, pushing myself even when my lungs felt like they could burst with the pressure. When I finally emerged, I found Evangeline standing on the sand in a lightweight white cotton dress, watching me.

I got out of the water, goose bumps already spreading across my skin, and I wordlessly took the towel she held out to me.

"Are you mad at me?" I asked, acutely aware of how babyish a question it was to ask when I'd spent the night justifying my own decision to hook up with her brother.

Evangeline looked at me, her face as cool and impassive as it had been the night before.

"Why would I be mad at you?" she said.

I licked some salt water from my lips, and then we walked back up the path to the house in silence.

The guys left for the ferry a few hours later, and I didn't get another chance to be alone with Theo. He kissed me goodbye in the same way he kissed Joni, on the cheek, but he also whispered in my ear: "Two weeks, *Ronaldo*."

Ev hugged her brother tightly before he got into the car, and he winked at me over her shoulder as if to say, *See? She's fine.*

I wasn't so sure.

After the guys had left, the grooves of the Land Rover's tires still visible in the dust, the delicate peace we'd established while they were around collapsed once more. Ev was sullen, staring out the window like a seafarer's widow, and Joni scowled at me like I'd single-handedly destroyed the entire trip, as if she hadn't also been heartlessly plotting our escape only five days earlier. She shoved her iPod earphones in and didn't speak to me for the rest of the afternoon.

"Want to play Scrabble?" I suggested tentatively as the night fell, but they both just glared at me.

A little later, once the silence had become unbearable, I tried again: "What does everyone feel like for dinner? I could make pasta?"

Silence as Evangeline stared out the window some more, and Joni pretended to read a book I knew she'd finished weeks before, *Sharp Objects.* "It's about three deranged women doing deranged shit," she had said one night in her room, after slipping me a note saying only: *Ughhhh, she's so smug. Sometimes I wish she'd choke on one of those disgusting sardine bones.*

"Look, Ev, I'm sorry we fought," I said finally, deciding I could afford to be charitable since I'd already won, even if she didn't know it yet.

Ev didn't reply, didn't so much as lift one of her perfect eyebrows. I felt furious that she could just ignore me like that, as if I were worth nothing more than one of the mosquitoes we no longer bothered to swat away from our flesh.

When Joni next went outside to the bathroom, I made sure to intercept her. I grabbed her arm and pushed her back into the outhouse.

"What the fuck," I hissed, pointing to the house.

"Look, she's just hurt, Bess," Joni said wearily. "You hurt her."

"You can see how this is insane, though," I said, but Joni just shrugged.

"She doesn't like change. You know that about her."

Joni walked back into the house to rejoin Evangeline by the window, and I watched them from the outside, the golden light settling over them like a Renaissance tableau.

I counted down the minutes until Theo was due to return.

TWENTY-ONE

2008

L ATER, BARDO WOULD SIT in the cozy studio of a network talk show, and he'd tell the two anchors that Ev cried the whole night before the boys left for England. I watched the clip of him squirming under the hot studio lights as the anchors grilled him about Tinos only once I was back in California, when I already knew that it had made Steven so angry that he punched a hole in his bedroom wall, his fist traveling right through the plaster and only stopping when it hit a pipe, causing two of his knuckles to shatter so badly that he was ruled out of soccer for the entire season.

Bardo was wearing a crisp blue oxford shirt and striped trousers that kept distorting on-screen, and he'd had a haircut that made him look younger and less worldly. He'd spent a large portion of the segment enthusiastically talking about the trip around Europe before the guys came to Tinos (the côte de bœuf they'd eaten in France that practically melted as soon as it hit your mouth; the incredible surf in San Sebastian; the penthouse upgrade in Florence), and the anchors were growing increasingly impatient with this patently overprivileged, unrelatable jerk as they nudged and prodded him toward the good stuff. I felt almost sorry for Bardo, who looked as if he was already regretting his decision to go on the show and talk about something he didn't fully understand.

Eventually, they made it to Greece, and Bardo described the week they spent in the Aetoses' house with us in the same glowing manner—tripping over himself to mention the meals Evangeline cooked and the nights spent drinking under the stars.

"And we've heard that the girls were thrilled to see you," the female anchor said. "Your friend Robbie told his brother that they acted like 'starving cats' when you arrived."

"I don't know about that," Bardo said. "I think we were as excited to see them as they were to see us. We'd all been away from home for a while. Although obviously, after everything that happened, we ended up going home right after England."

"But the girls . . ." the male anchor said sternly. "How was Evangeline?"

Bardo shrugged. "I mean, okay? She was cooking a lot. I guess maybe she seemed a little sad. She cried the night before we left, but that—"

"She cried? Because she didn't want to be left alone with Joni and Bess."

Bardo looked uncomfortable. "I don't think that was it, necessarily. That doesn't sound exactly right to me."

"Well, you tell us what sounds right to you. You were the one who was there, after all." The female anchor smiled at him. "How did the girls seem over the five days you were there?"

"They were fine. They were good," Bardo said, shrugging again. "Like I said—Ev was doing some cooking. We swam in the ocean. We just laughed a whole bunch that week, that's mostly what I remember."

"But there must have been a reason for Evangeline to have been crying at the prospect of you leaving."

"I think maybe it had something to do with Bess," he said.

"Did she seem scared of Bess?"

Bardo was already shaking his head when the anchor jumped back in: "There was clearly already a division between the girls. Joni and Bess on one side, Evangeline on the other."

I watched as Bardo thought about it, trying hard to wrap his still-developing boy-brain around the concept.

"I guess maybe," he said unconvincingly. "Yeah. I guess Evangeline always seemed a little different from the other two."

"In what way?" It was the female anchor again, her eyes trained on Bardo as he took a sip of water.

"I don't want to sound like a . . . like, I don't want to sound like I'm judging anyone. But the other two weren't as . . . I don't know how to say it. They just weren't like Evangeline. Ev had this thing about her like she was better than everyone, but it was never because she thought she was. It was, like, almost exactly because she didn't think it. But we all still knew."

"Did Bess and Joni know? That Ev was special?"

"We *all* knew," Bardo said again, looking miserable. "And it made what happened so much worse."

The anchors glanced at each other, satisfied, as Bardo hunched down in his chair.

"Thank you, Bardo. We'll be back after the break to talk to a local superhero with an important message for all the SoCal kids heading back to school . . ."

TWENTY-TWO

2018

THE MORNING AFTER THE vigil, Steven sends me an email with a link to Joni's publicist's statement on her behalf, and I read it on my laptop while Joni makes us lunch.

> Willa Bailey was last seen on Monday, May 7, 2018, around 7 p.m. outside her Malibu home. My client, Joni Le Bon, asks any witnesses, or anyone with any information whatsoever regarding her whereabouts, however insignificant it may seem, to call Detective Frost at the Los Angeles County Sheriff's Department. To know Willa is to love her, and, along with Willa's family, Ms. Le Bon is hopeful for her safe return. I request that you respect my client's privacy during this difficult time.

In the body of the email, Steven has written only *As heartfelt as ever*, and I know even I can't defend Joni on this one. For someone who has built a career out of radical authenticity above all else, this secondhand statement is hardly satisfying, particularly after her absence from Willa's vigil. I glance up from my laptop just as Joni calmly plunges a knife into the flesh of an heirloom tomato. She's frowning with concentration, and I wonder for the hundredth time this week what she's thinking, and if she's hiding her concern for my sake or her own.

When I check Willa's Instagram, I notice that her follower count has jumped forty thousand and her last post, the birthday one, now has 1,283 comments from friends and strangers praying for her safe return. I close the browser after reading one from a prominent momfluencer asking what exactly Joni is hiding from in her Malibu mansion.

I reply to Steven's email, avoiding his comment about Joni's statement to ask instead if we can get dinner this week. I tell him I want to meet Nova, which is mostly true, but I wish I'd been the kind of person to think of it before I needed something from her too. I hit *send* on the email before I can back out of it, and he replies almost instantly to ask if I'm free tomorrow.

"Lunch is ready," Joni says brightly then, and I shut my laptop to join her at the table.

Joni seems unnaturally serene as she eats, every movement slow and measured. Her calmness is contagious, and I think that I perhaps won't mention the statement to her, but that I should take it as an encouraging sign she isn't entirely reckless when it comes to public approval. I'm about to ask if she's had any news on her book, when Joni reaches across the table for the pepper and, as she moves, the neckline of her billowing jumpsuit shifts to reveal a deep red scratch, starting at the hollow of her neck and ending halfway down her left breast. I can't take my eyes off it for a moment, and when I look back up at my oldest friend's face, she is watching me. I force a smile as Joni readjusts her top, and we both pretend nothing has changed.

"How's book stuff going?" I ask after a long pause, and Joni's eyes skitter across mine before she flashes her sharp teeth at me in a rueful smile.

"I got a request for *The Morning Hour* today via my publicist," she says carefully. "But it wasn't to talk about the book. She asked if I would be comfortable talking about Willa."

"What did you tell her?"

"I told her I'd rather set my pubic hair on fire than let Willa overshadow this publication on top of everything else," Joni says blankly as oil drips from the clementine suspended at the end of her fork. "Although I'm well aware that ship has already sailed."

"It's just a book, Joni," I say quietly. *We've both been through worse.*

Joni puts her fork down on the plate and stares at me.

"It's not 'just' anything to me. I know that you were always the one who was supposed to be a writer, Bess, and that you probably have your own opinions about the things I've done over the years, but did you ever think about how hard I had to work to rewrite my story? To make sure the fucking nightmare that was our lives back then had an ending, as well as just a beginning? This book is the culmination of every single thing I've done or said since the moment Evangeline died. And now it's being overshadowed, destroyed, all because Willa has decided it's the perfect time to make a *fucking* point."

I stare numbly down at my plate.

"Look, you did what you had to do to survive," Joni says, her tone softer now. "But so did I."

There is a heavy silence between us, and then I wordlessly nod my acceptance of her point. I may never understand all the choices she's made to get here, but I'm the only person in the world who knows exactly what she was running from.

Joni's eyelids flutter closed for a moment.

"Someone sent me flowers, and I thought it was Willa," she says when she opens them again. "But then my agent texted me, and I felt embarrassed that I thought she missed me for even a second."

"Did you send each other flowers often?" I ask gently.

"Once she gave me one hundred white tulips," she says after a long pause. "On the day my book deal was announced."

It wasn't one hundred tulips, I think. It was one hundred white roses—I saw the photos on Instagram. Is she misremembering, or is she changing the details to make it less painful to talk about? Joni smiles slightly when I catch her eye, and I look away.

"She was supportive," I say mildly.

"Most of the time."

"And were you . . . could you be yourself with her?" I ask. "Who you are when nobody else is around. Joni Bonnier, not *Joni Le Bon.*"

Joni frowns.

"There was a time when we were deeply in love," she says, but there is something wrong with her tone, and it's like she is reciting an answer she knows I want to hear. I wonder if she's so heartbroken that she can't access her memories or her emotions, and my heart aches for her. I know better than anyone that grief doesn't always work the way you expect it to, let alone in the way that is most palatable.

"I know it's hard to see it now, but you're lucky you found each other," I say, forcing myself to find some words of comfort but still having to stare hard at my plate to even get them out of my mouth. "Whatever reason you had for doing what you did, and whatever reason Willa had for leaving, one day you'll be able to remember the good."

"What, like you've always done?"

I glance up at Joni then, and, before she has time to disguise it, I catch the look of pure fury on her face. *She hates me for making her do this,* I think, and for the first time, I feel a flicker of doubt that lingers long after her face has reassembled into a blank slate.

"Sorry," I say quickly. "Let's talk about something else. I don't want you to feel cornered."

"No need to apologize," Joni says, before adding, "it was actually a relief to talk about her a little."

Joni flashes me a polite smile, and I know then that she's lying to me and just saying what I want to hear, because Joni may be loyal and fiercely protective and cutting and a thousand other things, but she is never polite. If she feels relieved, then it's only because we've already moved on.

"Oh, I meant to tell you that I had my lawyer send someone to check on your cabin," she says airily as she picks up her phone.

"Was everything okay?" I ask.

"The cabin was fine," Joni says, still not looking at me. "But there were three reporters waiting for you."

My stomach sinks like a rock.

"Sorry. I won't be able to relax until I've replied to this email," Joni says then. I watch her type away, her mouth fluttering as she murmurs along with the words she's typing, in exactly the same way that she used to murmur the words of the book she was reading, and I think about inviting her to dinner with Steven and Nova. Then I think better of it.

TWENTY-THREE

2008

EVANGELINE WAS BARELY TALKING to me, and even Joni was acting strangely, so I spent the long days swimming lengths in the pool or walking around the grounds as I waited for Theo's return. In an act of self-preservation, I would never allow myself to think about him until I was alone in bed in the dark, because that way I always had something to look forward to. At night I could let my humiliatingly base imagination go wild, playing out our reunion over and over again, imagining how I might wrap my legs around him as he kissed my neck (because even though I was five foot ten, he was even taller), and all the things we could do in our remaining weeks in Greece after the separation had emboldened us. I already regretted how I'd wasted time pulling away from him after Evangeline called me transparent, and I figured since she was already pissed at me, maybe even irreparably so, what difference did it make? We could be as brazen and disrespectful as we wanted to be, and if Theo didn't feel comfortable fucking me while his sister was only a room away, that was fine—soon we would be on our own island without anyone around to remind me of some fabricated hierarchy of obligations, or to coldly imply I wasn't good enough for him.

My fantasies didn't die with the end of summer either. In just over a month, I'd be at college in New York, and I already knew how often Theo flew back to LA to see Ev and check in on his mom, and New York was that much closer—only an hour's plane journey from Providence. It felt like everything had slotted into place at exactly the right time—any earlier and Theo's summer in Europe would have stretched ominously between us, any later and we'd have already been too settled into the routine of our respective lives on the East Coast. At first, when conjuring up our future together, I couldn't fully shake the natural cynicism I'd inherited from my parents, but I worked around it until even that became integral to the fantasy, as if my guardedness had only ever existed to be dismantled by Theo.

One night, Evangeline went to bed early, and Joni and I found ourselves alone in the kitchen. Joni was sketching a squid in a tuxedo eating calamari in the Aetoses' ancient guest book, and I was staring out the window, trying to imagine what my family were doing at that exact moment, in an effort to not think about Theo for another hour. Steven was probably in the middle of his first drill of soccer camp, already committing 110 percent, as he was prone to saying, and my dad was probably dropping my mom at work with a kiss on her forehead. I felt a pang of loneliness then, and I realized how much I missed them and their inane chatter where almost nothing came at a price.

I sat down at the table opposite Joni and watched her draw for a while. She ignored me as she carefully added a row of pink suckers to the squid's tentacles.

"Don't you want to know what happened?" I finally asked her. "With Theo."

"I think I can guess," Joni said, her voice a disinterested drawl.

"You did everything but fuck and he said you were the most beautiful—no, the most *fascinating* woman he'd ever met."

I felt a rush of embarrassment.

"Then he told you that old Stavros doesn't understand him, but it doesn't matter because Theo's going to make his own way in life," she said, and when I didn't respond, she grinned triumphantly. "Come on, Bess. I know you're not from LA, but it's textbook rich-kid bullshit; they learn it along with the evacuation procedure of their private jets."

"He wasn't playing me," I said.

"Sure he wasn't," Joni said. "Let's just see if he remembers you when he's back at college, or if he suddenly remembers his dressage-champion, ex-Abercrombie-model girlfriend on the flight home."

I felt a helpless twist of fury deep inside me.

"It's fine, guys like Theo are basically a rite of passage for hetero girls," Joni says. "I'm just warning you so you don't waste any time in New York waiting for him to call."

Joni glanced up at me, and when her expression folded into one of treacly pseudo-pity, I wanted to throw my glass at her head.

"I don't have to wait," I said slowly. "Because he's coming back for me here."

Joni raised an eyebrow.

"We're going to Milos for the last two weeks of the summer."

Joni put her pen down and stared at me.

"You can't," she said. "Your parents would never let you."

"My parents are used to hearing from me once a week at this point," I said. "And I'll still make the flight home from Athens. It's whatever."

Joni shook her head, but I could tell she was rattled, by the rash climbing her neck.

"You said you wouldn't come island-hopping with me, but you'll go with him? You can't just *leave* when things get hard," she said, her tone deadly. "That's not how this works. This is the last time we're ever going to be together like this."

"Oh, here she is—Miss Sentimentality," I said. "Where have you been for the last six weeks?"

"You can't leave," she repeated, and I felt exhausted suddenly.

"I haven't made up my mind," I lied. "But you can't tell Ev, okay?"

Joni nodded.

"Swear?" I said.

"Swear."

The following morning, the fifth after Theo's departure, I wandered into the kitchen late enough to find Joni calmly making banana pancakes. Evangeline was reading her book at the table, and I took a seat at the opposite end, the one nearest the window, so that I could at least watch the goats grazing in the field. By this point I hardly even noticed the stifling atmosphere, so I was taken by surprise when Joni hurled the oily frying pan across the kitchen. It hit the stone wall and clattered to the floor, the noise slicing decisively through our silence.

"THIS IS UNTENABLE," Joni screamed at us both from her position by the stove. I glanced quickly at Evangeline, who was also watching with interest. "CAN YOU SEE THAT? I am in actual living hell, and all I can think about is how I could ALREADY be in fucking Berkeley but instead I'm stuck here with you two, and the vibe is literally SUBZERO, basically DYSTOPIAN at this point, and I can't do it anymore. How are you both so selfish?!"

Joni burst into tears then, her face bright and splotchy as fat cartoon tears dripped down her cheeks. My eyes flicked immediately to Evangeline in shock, and her instinct was the same, even if she was the first to look away. She stood up and wrapped her arms around Joni.

"Okay," Ev said soothingly as she stroked Joni's hair. "Okay, baby girl, I'm sorry."

I watched the two of them, unsure of how to proceed. I felt frozen to the spot, unable to muster up any genuine empathy for either Joni or Evangeline for the first time since I'd met them.

"How can we make this better for you?" Ev murmured into Joni's hair.

Joni wiped her eyes and thought about it.

"I want to go to Mykonos," Joni said. "Please. Even for a week. I just want us to have a change of scenery."

Ev angled her head to look at me then, and I shook my head slightly to show her that in this at least, I was on her side, and that we would never leave Tinos if it were up to me. I'd already done the math—if we left tomorrow for a week, we'd be back in eight days minimum, which was one day before Theo's surprise return. It was too close for me already—what if the girls decided they were having such a brilliant time they wanted to stay a few extra days? I could feel my ghost world, my future with Theo, slipping further away by the second. What if Theo took it as a sign that I wasn't interested in him? What if he came and went before we even got back? I figured if that happened, Theo would probably head straight back to Providence from Europe and I would never get the chance to consolidate what we had, to elevate it from one good but pretty wholesome night into something real and adult, something that could shoulder the strain of the extra commitment and all the flights we'd have to take to make it work while we were apart.

Then Evangeline turned her face away from me, and I knew what was going to happen.

"Mykonos, huh?" she said to Joni. "I think we can do that."

"Thank you, thank you, thank you," Joni murmured over and over, while I sat there in shock.

Joni lifted her head slightly so that she was looking at me over Ev's pearly shoulder.

Then she grinned at me.

There was never a question of whether I would go with them or not. I could never allow myself to be the girl who stayed behind, waiting for a guy to show up. And as much as I didn't want to be that girl, I also understood implicitly that Theo wouldn't want me to be that girl, wouldn't want the type of obsessive devotion I was entirely capable of extending to him from the moment he returned, if I let loose and forgot everything I'd learned from books and movies and magazines and my friends. So, I packed my bag along with the other girls that night, and, in the morning, I diligently made us cheese sandwiches to eat on the way. Joni insisted on catching an early ferry that would bring us to Mykonos at 9:35 a.m., and I possibly made it clear that I didn't want to be there, insisting on sitting alone on the top deck for the duration of the journey, salt water stinging my face as I leaned into the feelings of loneliness and injustice I had been cultivating since Joni's waterworks, but I never once said anything about it. Instead, I tried to imagine a world where none of this mattered, where I was floating around New York City with all my smart and talented new friends who were just waiting for me to walk into their lives, but I couldn't picture it anymore. I couldn't picture jumping into a taxi to school because I was late, or taking a creative writing class, and I couldn't even really picture Theo, not properly. I found that I couldn't picture anything beyond these two girls and the next week.

TWENTY-FOUR

2018

N ICE TOP," JONI SAYS, her arms folded across her chest. "Going anywhere good?"

I pause, one hand still on the bedroom door handle. I look down at the objectively uninteresting striped T-shirt I've paired with jeans in an effort to seem like a functioning human when I meet my brother's fiancée, and, even though I know it's ridiculous, I can't help but feel like I've been caught out. I remind myself that if Joni hadn't turned up on my doorstep two weeks ago, I'd still be alone in my cabin in the desert, obliviously scrolling through dick pics. I wonder briefly if Ryan from the gas station is worried about me.

"It's just Gap," I mumble.

"But no 5oulm8s branding," Joni says. "And it isn't ten sizes too big for you. We must celebrate the wins, however insignificant."

I roll my eyes as Joni stands, still smiling at me expectantly as if to brightly remind me of everything I owe her.

"So, where are you going?"

"I forgot to mention that I have dinner plans," I say. "Surprising, I know."

"With who?" she asks.

"Just my brother," I say. "And his fiancée."

"And this dinner is at their house?"

I pause, aware that Joni is angling for an invite, but equally aware that Steven would possibly clothesline me if I were to turn up with Joni in tow tonight. Her presence would also ruin my primary objective, which is to find out more about Willa from someone else who once knew her, however vaguely. The problem is that saying no to Joni has never exactly been a strength of mine.

When I look up, she is waiting for a response, remnants of a smile still frozen on her face.

"It is at their house," I say carefully.

"And how were you planning on getting there?"

"I was actually going to climb down to the beach and get an Uber from a little way down the coast," I say. "To avoid the reporters."

Joni laughs condescendingly as she checks her Cartier watch. "Well, I hope you brought waders. The tide is fully in right now."

The silence hangs heavy between us until I say, "I obviously would have mentioned it, I just didn't think you'd be up to it."

Joni watches me flounder.

"I love Steven," she says. "How could I miss it?"

"Well. We'd obviously love to have you there," I add finally, peeling my lips back into a smile.

Joni studies me and I relax each muscle, my eyes warm and genuine. If she thinks she can catch me out just by looking at me, then she's sorely mistaken. I've been playing this part for so long I can almost convince *myself* of most things. Once a guy I was sleeping with described me in passing as being "shy," and it took me over a day to remember how inaccurate a description that was of me. I've never truly been shy, only wary, only watchful.

"Give me ten minutes to get ready," Joni says. "We can take my neighbor's car."

I message Steven to let him know the change of plan, and he replies only: **Seriously, Bess?**

When Joni comes out, she is wearing a jumpsuit I haven't seen before—this one fitted, the cream silk taut against her skin. She is overdressed for dinner in the Valley with my brother, but I feel senselessly relieved when I see that the scratch on her chest is hidden. She smiles at me, and, after a moment, I find myself smiling back.

TWENTY-FIVE

2008

EVEN THOUGH EVANGELINE HAD agreed to go to Mykonos, she still made us aware of her sacrifice by quietly refusing to pay for her share of our accommodations or travel costs, despite having more cash languishing at the bottom of her Balenciaga handbag than Joni and I had in our entire bank accounts. Ev frowned out at the water when I paid Joni back for my share of the ferry fee, and when I raised my eyebrows at Joni, she just shrugged as if to imply that it suited her just fine. We'd wanted to be in control and now we finally were—it was time to step up.

In Tourlos, Joni led us to a public bus that would drive us past the moored sailboats and sparkling yachts of the port and into the town center, where Joni assured us there were a ton of hotels that would have a room available at the end of July—the height of their busiest season. We had packed swimsuits, minidresses, and embellished sandals, which we carried in backpacks slung over our shoulders as we navigated the cobbled streets, looking for somewhere to stay. The town was conspicuously beautiful—freshly painted whitewashed buildings framed by blue shutters and stairways, each twist and turn leading you to catch a glimpse of the same backdrop of endless ocean and empty blue sky. After the solitude of Tinos, however, the atmosphere in Mykonos felt like a raucous wedding we'd happened upon without necessarily being invited. Groups of glamorous adults gathered in terraces to smoke hookahs or share souvlaki platters, while others spilled out from bars and restaurants after a debrief of last night's escapades over a bottomless brunch. Everywhere I looked, I saw Louis Vuitton or Chanel bags dangling off tanned wrists, and I heard at least ten different languages being spoken in the space of thirty seconds. Everyone seemed older and more self-assured than us, and, instinctively, Ev reached for my hand. After a moment's hesitation, I let her take it.

"I'm sorry," I said softly, and she squeezed my hand.

"Let's just leave it behind us," she said, and, even though she hadn't exactly apologized, the relief still felt like a tonic, however fleeting I knew our truce would be once we were back in Tinos.

Joni marched ahead of us, finally feeling the weight of responsibility that must have plagued Ev from the second our plane landed in Athens. The sun was scorching hot, and there was a distinct lack of accommodation options, every inch of real estate filled instead with bars, restaurants, and tourist shops selling evil eye pendants next to frilly white and blue dresses to match the town's signature aesthetic.

After around forty-five minutes of circling, I realized that we'd ended up exactly where we'd started—a small bay lined with touristy-looking restaurants. I didn't say anything, but I could tell that Joni knew it too, from the sheen of sweat covering her skin as she frowned furiously at the waves lapping against the rocks. She finally stopped a couple walking out of one of the restaurants and asked them something. They pointed back toward the direction of the bus station, and Joni, puce-cheeked, thanked them.

"Apparently there are some spots up here," Joni said stiffly. Ev and I followed her in silence, my quiet schadenfreude at her discomfort growing with every second.

Just before we reached the bus station, we turned up a winding road that led away from the ocean. We walked up the hill for around half a mile, sweat trickling down the backs of our legs as mopeds and quad bikes raged past us, the drivers occasionally shouting and waving. Finally, Joni stopped outside an unassuming white building with no sign.

"Is it a hostel?" Ev asked, looking unsure.

Joni turned to glare at her. "It's a hotel, Evangeline. Sorry it's not the Four Seasons."

Ev shrugged, and we followed Joni inside.

Joni approached the front desk while Ev and I looked around. The reception area was all white, sterile as a dentist's waiting room, and the woman behind the desk wore a white polo shirt, with her dark hair pulled back into a ponytail. It seemed clean, if devoid of any local charm.

"Can we have a room, two double beds, please?" Joni asked.

The woman checked her computer, then looked apologetically at the three of us, red-faced and hungry.

"We have a room available, but it only has one double. Is that okay?"

Joni looked at us uncertainly.

"Fine with me," I said brightly, then I turned to Ev, joking, "Ev loves to sleep on the floor."

In contrast to the blindingly white reception area, the hotel room was dark and moist, with a small window overlooking the parking lot at the back of the hotel. The receptionist had given us extra pillows and blankets so that we could set up a makeshift bed on the floor, since there was no way we could all fit in the double, but we decided not to shotgun it just yet, figuring we'd wait until later to see who was the drunkest and would care the least.

Somehow, the trek to find somewhere to stay had united us, and it was like the miserable spell of the past six weeks in Tinos had been broken. Instead, we lay on our stomachs on the bed, eating peanut M&M's and watching a Greek soap opera, which Joni and I pretended to translate. We were mostly doing it to make Evangeline laugh, but she was drowning us out, absorbed instead in a magazine she'd found on the bedside table.

"This Italian restaurant looks nice," she said, pointing to a photo of an outdoor terrace with twinkling fairy lights strung between trees.

"Nice," Joni repeated incredulously. "Nice?! We don't want nice. We want dirty, dank, sexy, sweaty . . ."

"We want *filth*," I said. "Not 'the spaghetti carbonara is a revelation.'"

Evangeline laughed, swatting at my arm, and I felt a sting of warmth.

"Ohhh, you want filth, huh," Joni said as she flicked through channels on the TV. "I've got you, Bess."

Before we could stop her, Joni had selected a pay-per-view channel and agreed to a room charge for an adult movie called *Mamma's Girl*, which seemed to be about a rich older woman sleeping with a string of twenty-year-old sorority girls.

"You're welcome!" Joni yelled as Ev hit her with a pillow.

"What are they *doing*?" I asked incredulously. The four women on-screen were contorted, body parts impossible to identify or assign to any one human, and they were all screaming with pleasure in their own signature style.

"God knows," Joni said, and we all stared at the TV for a while, open-mouthed. At one point, I snuck a peek at my friends, feeling a crushing sense of relief because maybe it didn't matter that we'd nearly lost our minds in Tinos, or that I'd monopolized Theo's attention, or that we had wanted to hurt each other, because in that moment everything felt normal again, like we were just hanging out after school. It was just me, Ev, and Joni being the best and the worst versions of ourselves for each other, all at once. I remembered something significant then, something I'd forgotten for a while: Evangeline couldn't have been all that perfect, because she'd chosen to be friends with us.

That night we went for dinner at the Italian restaurant Evangeline had found. We shared pizza and wine, and we found ourselves talking about college, the future, for the first time since we'd arrived in Greece. It was as if we had all made an unspoken pact that time would stand still for the summer, and only now that the end was approaching did we feel ready to discuss our individual futures, tentatively at first, and then with abandon.

As I already knew, Evangeline planned to study psychology at Brown (more as a "safety net" than due to any burning desire to actually practice it) before enrolling at a prestigious culinary school in New York. She had known that she wanted to be either a food stylist or critic since she was a kid, and I envied her for her dedication as well as the unlimited resources that meant she could afford to go to a school like Brown for the sake of it, even when it didn't slot into her dreams. Joni, who was going to Berkeley, planned to fly back down to LA regularly to audition for parts as she studied theater and performance. She'd acted in a few productions in high school, and my private opinion was that she was always passable but that she was much better at playing character roles than the more serious stuff that I figured she'd have to focus on in college. When she'd got in, Ev and I had both worried about how she'd fare, and I think Joni sensed this now, because she waved her hand in the air as she cut herself off partway through a sentence. "Mostly I just want to get my head between some insecure theater queen's legs," she told us, as if giving voice to her most precious dreams had already proved too exposing for her.

When the girls asked me again about my plans at NYU, I said vaguely that I was going to try a few things out and see what stuck, even though I already knew that I would major in English and American literature with a minor in creative writing. I wanted to be a writer, even though I hadn't written in years and had certainly never deigned to say the word out loud to anyone but my mom, years ago, for fear of not being able to live up to it. I think my lack of direction disappointed Joni and Ev, but it was better than the alternative, which was for them to feel freaked out that I had been quietly observing them all this time, taking notes for some yet-to-be-written opus I would later spring on them.

"You poor losers," Joni said. "Stuck in the frigid sludge on the East Coast, while I'm living out my Joan Didion dreams."

I exchanged a look with Evangeline and wondered if Joni was jealous that we would be spending the next four years within a few hours of one another, while she would still be in California. It felt strange that we would be the ones leaving Joni behind, but the truth was I couldn't wait to find out who I was all over again, alone in an overflowing city filled with enough dark corners and open spaces that I might finally have the breathing space to figure out what I liked and disliked when I wasn't being scrutinized or judged for it.

At a certain point we all fell silent, the reality of our futures apart finally sinking in in some tangible way. Talking about our plans like this was bittersweet, as if we had only one foot in the present and one foot already out of each other's lives. I noticed that both Ev and I had carefully avoided saying Theo's name at any point, and I wondered if this was a sign of things to come. *Until he comes back for me,* I thought, my excitement now laced with something more complicated.

"Maybe we should write to each other at college," Evangeline said as she scraped an anchovy off a slice of pizza. "Like, actual letters."

"That is such a charming idea in theory," I said. "It's actually *peak* Evangeline, now I think about it. But if you send a BFF love letter to my new dorm, I will drive up to Providence and kill you myself."

"Seconded," Joni said. "Although I actually have another strong contender for Evangeline's Peak. Or EP, as it shall henceforth be known. Remember when she wrote a letter to John Mayer asking him to donate a lock of his hair for that charity auction, and the police turned up at her house two days later?"

"It actually was for charity," Evangeline moaned, but her cheeks were glowing. "I swear."

"Of course it was, sweetie," I said, smiling.

We went back and forth like that over dinner, gently teasing Ev about her goodness, and we all knew that we were trying to make up for the miserable weeks that had preceded it, but also that our friendship worked best when Evangeline was the center of attention, when Joni and I circled her and pried her out of herself. We'd already discovered that we could be too savage when left to our own devices.

After dinner, Joni asked the waiter to recommend a bar to us. "Nirvana Bar," he said, and then, perhaps sensing some self-destructive streak in us, he continued: "Ask for the Viper. It's pure absinthe."

Joni panted like a puppy dog at us when he walked away, and I saw Evangeline stiffen opposite me.

"Please please please please please," Joni said, clapping her hands to punctuate each word.

"Oh, Joni, I'm so tired," Ev said, a whininess already lacing itself through her words. "And I have a blister from all the walking earlier."

Joni frowned, tapped her fingers on the table.

"Come on, Ev," she said, her voice hardening. "I already said I was sorry."

"No, I just mean I'm so tired," Ev said, then she forced a smile. "You guys go. I'm just going to head back to the hotel."

"No," Joni said. "We have to stay together."

Joni stood up, looking between me and Evangeline, whose face was puckered and unhappy. In the end, I took pity on Ev instead of Joni in spite of everything that had happened, or maybe because of it.

"We could always get an early night," I said to Joni. "Day drinks tomorrow?"

Joni knew she was outnumbered, and after a moment she deflated, shrugging.

"You two are so fucking babyish sometimes," she said, but when we walked out of the restaurant, she still linked arms with us.

I always wonder why we chose that night in particular to bathe in the comfort of nostalgia, and it's easy to suffuse the choice with a sense of foreboding that was never there. I've even questioned my memory of it, whether we had that exact conversation that night, in that restaurant, or whether I just want it to have happened so badly that I've tricked myself into believing it. But the truth is that it wasn't that dinner that was out of the ordinary for us—if anything, it was a brief pocket of respite, of normality, within months of chaos: the summer that came before it and everything that came after that night, *those* should have been the outliers. *Those* were the times that ripped us away from our teenage lives and daydreams, never to be returned again—not in the same way, at least. We would all be fundamentally changed in less than forty-eight hours, even though none of us could have known it at the time.

TWENTY-SIX

2018

J
ONI LEADS ME THROUGH her utility room and into the
small garage next to her house. We walk cautiously, as if a
reporter might be hiding around the next corner, and I wonder if
I could have done anything differently or whether I was always
destined to end up exactly here like this, back with Joni.

When we get into the garage, Joni unlocks her Range Rover
and pulls out a black duffel bag from the back. I'm about to protest
that even wading through the ocean seems like a better option than
driving her car through the waiting crowd of reporters, when she
locks it and approaches a discreet door on the opposite wall. I watch
as she enters a security code and then, after she beckons to me, I
wordlessly follow her into a dark, airless passage that feels both
excessively cramped and endless. I'm on the verge of a panic attack
when Joni stops, flicks on a light, and I see that we've walked right
through to her neighbor's garage, which houses a Porsche Cayenne, three glittering Harley-Davidsons, and a Bugatti that looks
as if it's never been touched.

"He's literally never in town," she says as she throws me a black
baseball cap from the bag. "Tax stuff. He asked me to crank the

engines while he was away for a couple weeks, and that was three years ago. The upside is that I can use them whenever I want in return. Even the bikes."

I climb into the passenger seat of the Cayenne, bracing myself for a potential onslaught of camera flashes and microphones thrust against the glass as we drive back past Joni's house. Despite the heavily tinted windows, I still feel exposed, and I squeeze my eyes shut as the automatic garage door opens. After a few seconds during which I hear nothing, no intake of breath from Joni or squeal of wheels as she speeds up to outrun anyone, I open my eyes and turn to look at Joni's house as it retreats in the rear window. All I see is one lone reporter staring after us, wondering what she missed.

When I turn back around, I can feel Joni's eyes on me.

"Must be another story breaking," she says darkly. "Trust me, they'll be back."

I wonder if it could be true that there were three reporters at my cabin, when only one is here.

Steven and Nova live in a ranch house on a cul-de-sac in the northwestern foothills of the Hollywood Hills, in Studio City. There is a looming California oak in their front yard with a swing hanging from it and a birdbath set up on the front porch, and already I'm disoriented because the Steven I always default to in my mind (the one who gets paid far too much and lives in the sky in an angular apartment in Koreatown) would never tolerate this unhealthy level of suburban quaintness.

Joni and I stand side by side as I ring the bell, and I brace myself for my brother's wrath. The door opens, and Steven and Nova stand together, their faces frozen in near-identical smiles.

"Hi, brother," I say, after an awkward pause, and I step forward to kiss his cheek. He tenses up like rigor mortis is setting in when Joni leans in to do the same.

"Nova, this is Bess, Bess, Nova," Steven eventually says, and I smile at Nova, whose fingers are wrapped tightly around Steven's wrist. She gives off a strong Pilates-teacher vibe, with delicate features and ears that poke out of her long hair.

"I'm so thrilled to meet you," she says, and when she talks, I can see that her teeth are as small as Tic Tacs. She turns to Joni next, and her smile tightens as if someone's pulling thread behind her eyes in not quite the right direction. When she doesn't say anything, Joni puts out her hand for Nova to shake.

"Joni."

"I know," Nova says, staring down at Joni's outstretched hand. "I was at college with Willa."

If Joni is surprised by the news, she doesn't act it.

"Ah," she says. "Well, I hope you didn't waste your parents' money studying media arts and practice too."

Nova's face crumples for a second, and when Steven shoots me a look over her head, I realize just how big a mistake I've made bringing Joni here.

Dinner is delicious and everyone is perfectly behaved, except Nova won't look at either Joni or Steven, and my brother is so stressed that he keeps announcing the dishes abruptly at random points in the meal. We share three people's portions of stracciatella atop chickpea pancakes between four, and the only person who seems even slightly at ease is Joni, who blithely asks Steven and Nova all the questions about their engagement that I would never have known to ask in a million years.

"Let's see the ring," she says, reaching across the table to grab

Nova's hand. Nova moves her hand away and then, as if deciding that to do otherwise would be odd, holds it up for us to admire.

"Beautiful," Joni says. "Nice work, Steven. I didn't know you had it in you. What is that—two point three carats?"

Steven coughs and Nova wordlessly passes him a glass of water.

"So, how did you do it?" Joni asks then. "The proposal?"

Nova looks at Steven for the first time all evening.

"Big Sur," he replies tersely. "Sunset. Our favorite beach."

"Did you make sure to ask her dad for permission first?" Joni asks teasingly, and I can see from the way Steven bristles that he did.

"Did you, when you asked Willa to marry you?" Nova asks pointedly.

"I asked both her parents," Joni says. "I mean, they said no, but at least the thought was there."

"Two courses to go," Steven announces loudly, checking his watch, and I pour myself another glass of wine.

When Nova is in the kitchen, I ask Steven about his daily commute to Santa Monica and, after he laughs darkly, I realize that I've automatically reverted to a classic Winter family conversation trope. We've always stuck to transport, work, and food like we're making polite conversation in a beginner's French class: *Qu'est-ce que tu manges, mon frère?*

Nova brings out the main course then, three roasted baby quails that she's pointedly presented on one large platter to highlight that we're one short. Steven quietly hacks away at them with a carving knife and then doles out meat onto each of our plates as I steer the conversation onto work. I figure I can always resort to asking Nova about her quail-roasting technique as a denouement before we leave, to complete the Winter family bingo.

"Joni has a book out next month," I say, filling a particularly rough silence. *"From Blocked to Unlocked."*

Nova snorts.

"It's about . . ." I say, before turning to Joni. "What's it about again?"

"Oh, actually, Bess? I've been meaning to tell you that the release has been put on hold indefinitely," Joni says, her tone unreadable. "Due to unforeseen circumstances."

"Right," I say, looking down at my plate. "Well, I imagine the market is pretty saturated around this time, anyway."

I plow on, establishing that Steven is still happy at Konnect before I move on to Nova, who, it turns out, studied law at USC, not media like Willa. She is now the youngest attorney at a firm specializing in representing women in tech who have suffered workplace discrimination. Joni, not used to being anything but the center of attention, sulks beside me as I struggle to form anything resembling an intelligent question about Nova's work, but Nova humors me, somehow transforming my incoherent mumbling into something interesting and thoughtful before asking me about my job at 5oulm8s, which Steven has clearly already told her about. I'm hesitant until I realize that she seems genuinely interested in the psychology of it all—the power dynamics simmering behind each case.

"It must be hard to trust people once you've seen how they behave when they think nobody's watching," she says.

"I guess there's an element of that," I say lightly as her words resonate with me on a cellular level.

"Bess could be a writer if she wanted," Joni says loudly, cutting across us both and effectively closing the subject. "She's smarter than anyone I know."

"I've always said that," Steven says, and they stare at each other in hostile agreement for a moment.

"I'm not sure this theory is evidence-based," I say lightly, picking up a piece of baby corn with my fingers. "And I'm happy at 5oulm8s, anyway."

"Dessert!" Steven announces. "Tiramisu!"

After dessert, I slip off to the bathroom, a tiny closet under the stairs with a pair of antlers mounted on the dark green wall. The reprieve is much needed, and I sit on the toilet for a while after I've finished peeing, savoring the feeling of finally being alone after a fraught couple of hours trying to keep the conversation if not flowing then at least shallow enough to avoid disaster. I'm slowly drying my hands on a pink towel when the bathroom door opens.

"Oh, sorry," Nova says, backing out.

"It's fine, I'm nearly done," I say.

Nova steps backward as if to wait outside, but I signal for her to stay.

"Can I just ask . . . were you . . . were you and Willa close at USC?" I ask.

Nova pauses, then closes the door behind her so that we're just inches away from each other. She smells like Aveda shampoo and, faintly, of garlic.

"We only overlapped for two semesters before she dropped out to do . . . this," Nova says, gesturing in the direction of the living room and Joni. "But she seemed like an interesting person. She was fire . . . like, she lit up any room she was in, you know? She always seemed to be laughing, and she was almost always in some wild costume, like she'd just stumbled out of Burning Man. And I remember that she had this gang of people who followed her around—like a David Lynchian pied piper or something. Honestly, I never would have thought . . . I guess you never know, but I never would have thought it would end like this for her."

I lean in toward the mirror, swiping a pretend eyelash from my cheek to avoid looking at Nova. I can feel the anger skittering beneath her words.

"Nothing's ended yet," I say, once I've straightened up again. "We really don't know anything."

"We have some mutual friends," Nova says. "And they all agree that while Willa isn't perfect, she would never put her family through this."

Nova's eyes scan my face as if she's searching for something.

"It seems like everyone who knows her is freaking out," Nova says. "Apart from Joni."

I swallow hard, aware that Joni is less than fifteen feet from where we're having this conversation.

"I'm sure she'll resurface soon," I say stiffly. "But I am sorry that your friends are worried."

Nova just stares at me for a moment, and I do feel sorry for her, being so clearly disappointed in me while still having to impress me because she's in love with my brother, but I also know better than most that trusting someone is a choice, and one I had to make a long time ago when it comes to Joni. What else can I say?

I'm making a move to squeeze past her when Nova puts out a hand to stop me.

"It means a lot to Steven that you're here anyway," she says.

"Sure," I say, off-balance but trying to hide it. "I guess I would have expected him to have better things to do, but we all get old one day."

Nova doesn't smile. Instead, she studies me as if she's trying to make a call before she steps out of the bathroom.

"I want to show you something."

Something in the brevity of her tone makes me uneasy, but I still follow her out of the bathroom and up the wooden stairs. Her posture is perfect, and she walks with her hips turned out like a dancer, long hair swaying down her back. When we get to the landing, she opens a nondescript door and turns on the light.

At first, I just think she's showing me Steven's chaotic office—corkboards filled with a giant map and Post-it Notes covered in my brother's familiar handwriting; grainy photocopies of documents next to hand-drawn diagrams—but when I step closer and spot my name on every single printed page, the rest of the room pulls into focus. The Post-it Notes littered around the room aren't filled with zany ideas for Konnect's latest streaming platform but instead make up a meticulous timeline of that night in Mykonos, detailed in Steven's childish scrawl and stuck at various points on a map, presumably to show how it all unraveled. And then there are the evidence photos pinned to the back of the door—the freakish angle of Ev's neck, a pale hand trailing in the water.

"What is this?" I whisper, horrified.

"He's on the forums every Sunday," Nova says softly. "He doesn't even need this room anymore—he's basically memorized the entire case file and transcripts so that he can defend your honor to these faceless assholes on Reddit. I've told him there's no point in engaging with the trolls, but he still does it, every Sunday. Just comes in here and scours the internet for anyone still talking about you so that he can try to convince them of your innocence."

I back out of the room, my eyes stinging with tears, and Nova turns off the light. She doesn't try to make me feel better or pretend it's okay that this is what my younger brother does when he should be smoking ribs in the backyard or watching football with his friends. That this is exactly how I ruined him.

"I just thought you should know," she says. "I think I'd want to."

When we walk back into the kitchen, Joni and Steven are being brutally civil with one another while debating the human rights risks of cybersurveillance, but I can feel both their eyes on me as I pretend to study the cubist portrait of Kurt Cobain on the wall. I can't quite look at either of them.

When Nova tells Steven that she's tired, I take the opportunity to leave, grabbing Joni by the arm and hauling her up from the couch on which she has made herself too comfortable, balancing her half-drunk glass of wine on the arm so that she can gesticulate animatedly. I pinch her skin harder than I need to, and she pulls her arm away from me.

"Everything okay?" she asks, narrowing her eyes as my brother and Nova walk us to the front door, but by this point our collective relief is palpable. I hug them both quickly and then there's a moment when Joni thanks them profusely, like the night was a perfect success, when I wish I could stay here instead of driving back to Malibu with her, but then the front door slams shut and, just like that, it is the two of us left again.

Neither of us talks on the drive home, until—

"So has your brother always hated me?" Joni asks when we're ten minutes from her house, and, despite everything, I let out a snort of laughter.

"Oh, almost violently," I say, and now, somehow, we're both laughing, and, for just a moment, it feels like we're eighteen again, on the edge of everything.

TWENTY-SEVEN

2008

I WAS THE ONE WHO ended up sleeping on the hotel room floor after Ev and Joni formed an unholy alliance—diving onto the bed and refusing to move or even discuss any other formation in a plan they'd clearly hatched earlier. It pissed me off, particularly after I'd stuck up for Evangeline when she wanted to go home, and, after a rough night's sleep, it meant that I had no such loyalties the following day when Joni suggested starting drinking early, going down to the beach bar for "brunch Vipers." I loudly agreed, smiling pointedly at Evangeline as I did.

We dressed in our most prized outfits over swimsuits—a white tank over a neon green mini for Joni, a bronze knit dress for me, with Ev in a broderie anglaise dress and jeweled flat sandals. Our toenails were painted a matching shade of buttercup yellow, and our limbs were tanned and muscular from swimming all summer. I tried to shake the feeling of anticipation fluttering in the pit of my stomach as we left the hotel, my tiny clutch containing only my driver's license, a wad of cash, and some loose Pepto tablets I felt like I was going to need. I told myself that my apprehension was normal and only because I was out of practice on account of being locked up for so long.

The rain-forest-themed beach bar was quiet when we turned up at eleven a.m., and the hostess told us that we could sit at a table for no extra charge until the late afternoon, when everything would pick up and they could charge someone a thousand euros for the same privilege. The bar struck me as tacky, clearly geared toward tourists, but Joni had looked it up on the hotel computer and assured us that it was bound to get as wild as we hoped it to be, which already sounded vaguely ominous.

We chose a table nearest the DJ booth and alternated between sugary cocktails and cheap beer for the first few hours, until soon even Ev was drunk enough to join the snaking line of strangers dancing the conga around the bar. Joni got to talking to a girl from Manchester who she was pretty sure was into her, so Ev and I were left to our own devices for a while. It was the first time we'd been alone since that night in the kitchen in Tinos, and I wondered if I needed to bring up Theo, or whether it would be best to leave it unsaid until we returned to the island to find him there. I knew I was being a coward, but it also didn't feel like it was entirely my responsibility to shoulder alone, particularly since the further away I got from Tinos, the less confident I felt that what we did or didn't have was even worth talking about.

At four o'clock, we were kicked off the table, and we moved between the bar and the dance floor as the music got louder and more intense. Back in LA, Evangeline drank a little, but rarely enough to totally lose control, so while this wasn't the most drunk I'd seen her, it was close. Her eyes were gentle and unfocused from about five p.m., and I remember that, in my own haze, I felt pleased for her since she deserved a moment to loosen up. She was always so in her head, always planning and worrying, trying to control the weather patterns along with everything else, and it was almost a relief to see her like this, her head occasionally drooping to one side until she dragged it back up, aware enough to laugh at herself a little.

Joni's girl had given her the remnants of a wrap of coke. It wasn't enough for a line, so I dipped my finger in what was left and coated my gums with it as she instructed, but Ev pushed Joni's hand away when Joni offered her some. My mouth tasted bitter and rank for the next hour, and I wished I'd declined too, even though I felt marginally less sloppy than before. Coke usually made me feel sketchy, and we all tried to avoid it back home since it was mainly just the messed-up Malibu kids who were into it, wealthy kids whose parents never showed up at their parent-teacher conferences and who would presumably spend the rest of their lives pushing their neglect to its limits.

Just before sunset, with the ocean rippling like molten gold, the familiar opening riff of "Time to Pretend" by MGMT blasted through the speakers. The three of us were instantly drawn to one another like magnets, clutching each other's sweaty hands as we closed our eyes and danced on the fine sand, screaming the lyrics to a song we had blasted a thousand times in a thousand different places but that had never felt as agonizingly perfect as it did in that moment: "I'm feeling rough, I'm feeling raw, I'm in the prime of my life," we yelled, somehow believing that the words were written only for us. It didn't matter what anyone else thought because it was the three of us together and we were young and beautiful, and we could be anything we wanted to be, even the type of girls who brazenly did drugs and danced on tables in ways that would have made our parents cry. It felt serendipitous, like we were meant to be there at that exact moment in time, and the gratitude for that and all the future moments I would know like it bubbled up inside me, and I understood implicitly that Joni and Ev felt the same from the glossy, nostalgic look in their own eyes as we wrapped our arms around each other.

After the song finished, I took myself to the restroom because the high from only seconds earlier had inevitably morphed into something infinitely more melancholic, and I had already felt so homesick for something I could never get back that I'd nearly burst into tears right there on the dance floor. Instead, I sat in a stall for a while as the bass vibrated through my feet, and I forced myself to breathe until the feeling softened into something manageable. When I washed my hands, the restroom attendant handed me a paper towel, and I dropped a euro onto the small plate on the sink top beside her.

I scanned the bar for Joni and Ev, finding them only a few feet from where I'd left them. Joni was leaning in and talking closely to Ev, her arm laced around her waist. Ev nodded as she listened, her eyes tracking mine as I walked toward them. When I got there, they exchanged a look I couldn't read, and then Joni grabbed both our hands and we half-heartedly danced for a little longer to songs that didn't mean as much to us. A while later, Ev slipped outside, and I caught a glimpse of her through the mass of bodies with her phone pressed against her ear.

When she returned, Joni went off to find her girl, leaving Ev and me alone again. I felt slightly like someone had let the air out of the night, like we'd reached its emotional peak and were already winding down, when a group of men came into the bar at around nine p.m. They were older than us, and I could tell that they thought they were a big deal from the way they surveyed the crowd as they walked in, as if they already owned every one of us. They were led to a round table in the center of the room, and instantly bottles of Cristal and Belvedere arrived in sparkler-lit processions, along with an endless stream of long-limbed girls in dresses even shorter than ours. Still, I could see the moment the men spotted

Evangeline, could see two of them talking about her, and something about the way they looked at us made me feel protective of her. By this point the music had changed from extended remixes of pop songs we knew to a disorienting, visceral techno. My head was starting to ache, and I tried to count how many hours we'd been drinking. Too many. I wondered if I could suggest leaving in a way that didn't make me seem like a killjoy or like I was pining for Theo.

Ev leaned in close to me then and said something indecipherable, her breath tickling my ear. I shook my head and pointed to the speaker. *Too loud,* I mouthed, so she took my hand and dragged me away from the crowd, out onto the sand where a few dozen people lounged on fur-covered beanbags, smoking and chatting.

"It was too loud," I repeated needlessly, and we both stared at each other.

"Where's Joni?" Ev asked.

"One guess," I said wryly.

"She shouldn't be able to ditch us just because it's for a girl," Ev said, and it was sort of the bitchiest thing I'd ever heard her say behind anyone's back, not least Joni's. Her voice had the same edge to it that it had the night she laid into me in Tinos, an edge that it didn't normally have, and I wondered if she felt left out, like we'd outgrown her already.

"Are you feeling weird about going off to college?" I asked softly, but Ev just shrugged.

"Not really," she said. "It will be good to have a change of scenery. Change of people."

I nodded.

"And Theo will be there, anyway," Ev said, her voice now too loud, too bitter, for the mellow outdoor setting. A few people turned to look at her, and I felt irritated at Joni for ditching us. Regardless of what Ev had said about leaving it in the past, she was obviously still pissed about what had happened between me and Theo. I tried to empathize, but the truth was I wouldn't have cared even if Ev had fucked my brother and never looked at him again, although obviously she would never have dreamed of doing either of those things. I tried to be generous to us both, telling myself that it could be less about me personally and more what the change in our shared status signified—that soon we would all be going our separate ways, and this summer was the last time we would all be together like this without new friends or partners or exams or jobs to contend with. I told myself that she was just angry because she loved us both, and that she was scared to lose either one of us.

"He seems excited for you to be there with him," I said, even though it wasn't true.

"Of course he is," Ev snapped. "He's my brother."

"Come on, Ev," I said, my patience wearing thin. "What's the big deal?"

"You're acting like you know him better than me," she said. "This is what you always do—you're so insecure that you have to insert yourself between everyone to feel wanted."

I felt instantly stung, perhaps because while I'd never thought about it, I also knew it was probably true.

Evangeline was about to speak again when a man approached us. I'd watched as he'd purposefully weaved his way through bodies on the dance floor before coming to a stop in front of us. He was from the table in the middle of the bar and looked like he was around twenty-seven, twenty-eight, with thick eyebrows and a small scar above his top lip.

"I'm Pierre," he said, with a French accent. "My friends nominated me to invite you to join us for some drinks."

"Oh, really," I said, grateful for the respite from Ev's surliness. "And they sent you over because they think you've got the best shot with us, Pierre?"

"I think it's because I'm sober." Pierre smiled, revealing sharp, gleaming teeth. "And because my English is better than our resident Englishman's, Kevin. Which you'll have a chance to find out if you join us for a drink."

He pointed over to the table, where the men were clinking shot glasses filled with something yellow. When I looked at Ev for confirmation, she just shrugged as if to say she didn't care.

"Sure," I said, following Pierre across the now frenetic bar because at least it meant I didn't have to speak to Evangeline about Theo anymore. I also figured that Pierre being sober meant that we weren't in any immediate danger, although obviously I had nothing concrete to back up this theory.

Pierre led us through the outer layer of girls vying for free drinks, and pointed to a space on the cowskin banquette, gesturing at one of his friends to move over so that we could fit. The music was so loud that we didn't even have to make small talk with these strangers, just had to hold our glasses of vodka cranberry up in a silent cheers every time the moment called for it, and then, what were the chances, Joni returned from the dead and somehow slipped herself between me and Evangeline just in time for more free drinks. Soon, the men were passing around a bag of coke with a tiny metal spoon dipped inside, and Joni and I did a couple of bumps before handing it back. This time I felt it, the jolt back to life as Joni and I climbed up on the table and danced, our hips swinging, hair tossing. "That's it, girl, *werk*," Joni said in my ear, and I threw my head back and laughed. When I looked down, Ev was staring up at us, her face blank and inscrutable.

I think now of all the people in that bar, all the drunk patrons who would later turn into witnesses, experts on the body language of eighteen-year-old girls. "I felt uncomfortable just watching those two," one of the girls who had been hanging around the table (and snorting a line of cocaine from her friend's bare stomach) claimed later. "And you could tell that the dead girl—Evangeline? You could tell that she did too."

———————————

The truth was that Evangeline was too drunk to feel much of anything, but that doesn't excuse any of it. When one of the men told us about a party back at their villa in the hills of Agios Stefanos, we all hesitated. Joni and I were high, and Evangeline was wasted, but after a quick, overwrought conference in the restroom, where Ev didn't look at me once (a conference possibly modeled on the same end-of-high-school movies we'd all devoured and internalized— *this might be the* only *opportunity we'll ever get to go to a party like this together*), we agreed. A few of the other girls at the table had also been invited, so we were pretty sure we wouldn't get murdered unless the men had in mind some sort of killing spree, a *massacre* of sorts, in which case it would have just been plain bad luck that we got caught up in it, and nobody's fault, exactly.

We got in the car with the Englishman, Kevin, who joked about having enough cash to bribe the police if they stopped us, and even Joni was quiet as we wound up the cliffs in the dark, as if it was just sinking in that we were in a foreign country with strangers, being driven to an unknown second location by someone who, at the very least, was very, very drunk.

The villa was vast, but it was nothing compared to Ev's house in Eagle Hills, or even Joni's or mine in our own gated community back home. We all looked around, dutifully pretending to be impressed so as not to offend our hosts, but we split off from the tour as soon as we could. Joni went off with her girl, who'd also found herself at the party, and Ev and I surveyed the scene by the pool area, weighing up our options as I felt a wave of what I would later identify as existential dread. With uncharacteristic clarity, I knew that I would rather be anywhere but there, with those men who traveled in a pack and handed out drugs like they were chewing gum and who invited drunk teenage girls back to their villa high on the cliffs over the Aegean Sea.

Kevin was probably the most appealing of the men at the party after Pierre, who was in the shallow end of the purple-lit pool with a group of Speedo-clad men we hadn't met. Kevin poured us vodka oranges at the outdoor bar, and I figured he couldn't be too much of an asshole because he didn't make them too strong. I could hardly taste the vodka in mine, could perhaps have done with a little more.

Ev and I perched on a deck chair, while Kevin encouraged us to dip into the glowing swimming pool as steam spilled off the surface. He took off his shirt and jeans before slipping gracefully into the water in his black Calvin Kleins. He was almost entirely hairless, like a seal. When he emerged again, he slicked his hair back and beckoned for us to join him.

"No, thanks," I said. "We have pools at home."

Ev pinched my arm and I scowled at her.

"What?"

"You're being super rude," she hissed.

"And you're being *super* American," I said. "Kevin gets it. He doesn't give a shit."

We watched as Kevin did a few handstands, possibly not knowing what else to do now that he was in the water and we clearly weren't getting in with him anytime soon.

"He's kind of cute," Ev said, and I pretended to be horrified.

"Evangeline Aetos thinks someone is CUTE. Someone grab a femidom, fast!"

Evangeline shook her head.

"Not for me," she said. "I meant for you."

I paused. "Me?"

"Sure," she said as Kevin emerged from the water in front of us. Excess water was trickling down his face, and he rubbed his eyes, blinking a few times. He definitely didn't seem like the sharpest tool in the box. Ev glanced slyly at me and then, before I could stop her: "Kevin, Bess thinks you're cute."

Kevin smiled, willing to play along.

"Thanks, Bess," he said dryly. "You're *cute* too."

Evangeline smiled triumphantly, like he'd just sealed the deal and we were now obligated to make out in a room upstairs at the very least.

"Which one of you is going to fuck my man Kevin?" Pierre called then from the other end of the pool, where he appeared to be doing balloons, throwing the empty canisters into the water when he was done with them. I smiled at him even as a feeling of unease swelled inside me. So much for his sobriety.

"Yeah, which one, Bess?" Ev asked.

"Come on. You know I'm not interested," I said irritably, and she frowned at me in mock confusion.

"Whyever not?"

"It doesn't matter why," I said. "And I think it's uncool that you're pushing this."

"Uncool," she repeated. "You think *I'm* being uncool."

"Just say what you want to say," I said. "I'm sick of this."

"Okay," she said slowly. "Well, *Bess*, not only did you hook up with my brother when I clearly asked you not to, but then I find out that you plan to ditch me for him, at the end of a trip I both invited you on and PAID FOR, after literally making my life miserable at every opportunity. Can you see why *that* might be seen as being 'uncool,' as you put it?"

Joni appeared then, putting her hand on the back of the deck chair just as Ev stood up.

"What's going on?" she asked warily. When neither Ev nor I answered, Kevin shrugged and launched into a final backward somersault before swimming off toward Pierre.

"I'm actually done," Ev said hollowly.

Joni looked between the two of us.

"Can you guys just sort it out?" she said. "You know we're better than this."

"No," Ev said. "I don't think we are."

"Ev," Joni said, and I could see how disturbed she was, even though Evangeline was just belligerent and drunk and might not remember any of it in the morning.

"She was going to leave us," Ev said. "This is already over."

"How did you find out about Milos?" I asked quietly.

"*That's* what you want to ask?" Evangeline asked, her voice incredulous. "After everything, that's the only part you care about."

I stared down at the ground, my cheeks burning.

"We're not going to last," Ev said slowly. "I felt it last night at dinner, when we were talking about college. Our friendship isn't going to survive what comes next, and honestly? There was a time when the thought of that would have killed me, but after this summer? I don't think I care."

Joni let out a strange sound, almost a whimper, but Evangeline just stared between the two of us. Then she turned and walked away, heading past the pool and toward the edge of the villa's grounds.

"Are you going to follow her?" Joni asked me, staring after her.

"Are you?" I shot back.

"You made this mess," she said bitingly.

"I don't know," I said. "Ev knows about me and Theo going away, and I know I didn't tell her."

Joni turned to face me slowly. "So?"

"So you must have told her," I said, because I already knew that whatever happened next, this was the end of it all. Not just me and Ev, but me and Joni too. And, in that moment, I told myself I didn't care.

"Ev was right about us," I said. "Leaving you behind would have been the easiest thing I ever did."

Joni's dark eyes flashed with fury before she reached out and slapped me so hard I thought my jaw might crack.

"Your darling Theo told Ev," Joni spat. "Not me."

Then she turned and walked back toward the villa.

I clutched my cheek as my eyes stung with tears, and I watched as Evangeline climbed over the row of shrubs lining the villa's grounds before heading across the rough path carved into the cliff. She was, in theory, following the incline that would lead her back to the main road, but she was also very much in no-man's-land— halfway between the rocky beach below and the road that lined the rim of the cliff above us. The floodlights of the new port were flickering in the distance, and she probably figured that it would be less hassle than walking through the villa and navigating the winding network of roads in the dark to get back down to the exact same destination.

"Wait," I called after her, jogging to catch up. Evangeline looked behind, her round face luminous in the moonlight.

"Leave me alone, Bess," she shouted. Even as I followed her, I couldn't help but wonder if Theo had mentioned Milos to her in passing, or if the guilt had been eating him up too much to keep it a secret for any longer.

I picked up my pace, kicking up dust as I climbed over the shrubs to join her on the rocky trail. The cliff curved ahead of us, and I saw exactly what she was thinking as she examined the drop down to the beach. We were about forty feet above a bed of shallow rocks, and the trail along the ridge consisted of a thick grit, some-where between sand and dust, embedded with larger rocks and shrubs. The route looked simple enough to navigate, and I watched as Ev took a tentative step onto the trail, seemingly satisfied when the ground was sturdy and unflinching beneath her weight. I turned longingly back to the party, the illuminated lilac swimming pool with the twinkling lights strung through palm trees, and then I followed her.

"Come on, Ev," I said, once I'd finally caught up with her. "Let's just talk about this."

"About what?"

"Theo," I said. "Let's talk about Theo."

"There's nothing to talk about," she said, then she stopped suddenly and fixed her eyes on me.

"Clearly there is," I said. "What's the big deal?"

"The 'big deal' is that you already have everything, so why do you need him too?"

"What are you talking about I have everything? You're the one with a black Amex, for God's sake."

"It's always just been me and Theo," Evangeline said. "You could never understand."

"I'm sorry," I say. "But you're the most privileged person I know. I'm not buying that."

"You don't even know what that word means."

I threw my hands up in the air, and she stared at me in disbelief.

"Bess, your parents worship the ground you walk on. They're obsessed with you and your brother—they live somewhere they literally hate, just so you guys can get a good education and get into the colleges you want, and you never even think to thank them for it. If you took a photo of a dumpster, your mom would still ask if she could blow it up and hang it over the fireplace in your house. If you got too drunk at a party, your dad would drive out to the Palisades at two in the morning to pick you up, no questions asked. You are literally the luckiest person I know, and still you want to take the only person I have away from me."

"Ev . . ." I trailed off because I noticed a gap in the path then—a thin but definite alternate trail leading down to the beach below. I figured that while it was potentially a more practical route because I could actually see where it ended, it would also add at least half an hour to the journey, so I decided not to point it out to Evangeline. It was better when she was slower, struggling, because then at least she couldn't get away from me.

"Have you ever seen my mom ask me how my day was? Or what book we're reading at school? Have you ever seen my dad so much as touch me when we're not posing for a photograph?" Ev asked, her eyes bright and furious as she glared at me. She was so close that I could almost touch her, and I reached out a hand, but she darted away, the dusty earth skittering beneath her feet. She carried on walking, and I followed her.

"I guess not," I said. "No."

"Exactly," she spat over her shoulder. "Theo is all I have."

"You know he was always going to meet someone," I said, more gently now. "If not me, then at college, or one day after that. You can't keep him forever, not in the way you want him."

Evangeline paused again, looking at me strangely.

"Maybe," she said. "But it won't be you."

I felt a cold snap settle somewhere deep inside of me. "Excuse me?"

Her gaze was unflinching.

"It's not going to be you," she said slowly. "It was a proximity thing. You were literally his only option in that house."

"Fuck you, Ev," I said, my cheeks burning.

"It's true, and you know it is," she said. "And I tried to warn you. Which is why it's so sad that you did it anyway."

I tried to arm myself against her, remembering the gentle way Theo had touched my waist his first night in Tinos, right before he gave me my gift. As if reading my mind, Evangeline smiled.

"Theo isn't going to Milos. He asked me to tell you that he changed his mind, probably so that he doesn't have to deal with your drama. It was one night, Bess. You need to get over it."

Each word hit me square in the solar plexus. "Why are you doing this?"

"Because it's true," Ev said simply. "And because you're the worst friend I've ever had."

Evangeline stopped then, and when I looked past her, I saw that the path had ended abruptly and that we had nowhere to go but up or down, or back where we'd come from. The beach was now less than thirty feet below us, but we were separated from it by a large body of rocks, almost prehistoric in their stature. Ev looked down at her feet, seemingly unsure about her plan, but then she bent over and slipped her feet out of her sandals before holding them in one hand.

I watched her, and I didn't tell her we should turn back and take the secret trail down to the beach, or offer her my hand to help her steady herself or offer to swap shoes, because in that moment I wanted her to understand that her life wouldn't always be so easy, that she wouldn't always be blessed and flawless and rich. As if reading my mind, Ev frowned and doubled down in both senses. Barefoot, she hopped down onto a rock below and looked up at me, eyes shining. "I really don't think you're a good person. I'm sorry, I wish I could lie to you and say I would be happy for you, but I can't."

"You need to grow up, Evangeline," I said as a hot and sticky shame flooded over me. "People might pander to you now, but it's only because of who your dad is. I know how much you want to control me and Joni so that we never realize you're nothing without us, because you're *boring* and you're *ordinary*, and you can't buy your way out of that one, however much money your daddy wants to throw at you to make up for the fact he doesn't love you."

I stood, broken from the effort of trying to hurt her as much as she'd hurt me, and I watched as, face crumpling, Evangeline continued to stumble down the jagged rocks that were getting smaller and looser the further down she got. The waves crashed below, but Ev moved quickly to get away from me, fueled by fury and self-righteousness, or perhaps just by some childish belief that nothing bad would ever happen to her.

I watched her for a moment, and then I turned away and left her.

TWENTY-EIGHT

2018

I LIE IN BED AFTER dinner with Steven and Nova, trying to erase the night from my memory in the hopes of catching even an hour of unbroken sleep. Perhaps worse than Steven's war room, worse than Joni inviting herself, was how Nova had refused to look at me as we were leaving, as if I'd already failed her.

I reach down and slide my laptop out from under the bed, angling it so that the glow of the screen also illuminates the keyboard. Then I type in "Bess Winter guilty" and instantly find a slew of results for the type of forums Nova was talking about, forums that I hoped beyond measure no longer still existed, nearly ten years on. I should, of course, have known better—every true-crime podcast, every low-rent reenactment I flick past on cable TV, all of it just whets the appetite for stories like mine, creating a generation of rabid, self-righteous consumers and armchair detectives desperate to feel needed and powerful, as if they're ever getting all the information, as if they alone would ever be able to solve a riddle that was never built to make sense.

I click on the link for the first forum, and I scan the first few posts, looking for any signs of Steven. I'd always thought that my brother was the one person in my life to emerge unscathed from what happened—on the surface he has excelled, finishing high school with a computer science scholarship offer from Michigan State before gliding through his degree and subsequent working life without any obvious anger issues or major personality deficits. He plays soccer on the weekend with friends and shouts the answers to *Jeopardy!* if he happens to catch it on TV. Unlike me, he seems genuinely relaxed around our parents and is always perfectly genial, if perfunctory, in our rare meet-ups. The thought that, throughout everything, he has been fighting against the tide, defending my actions and weaknesses to strangers on the internet, nearly destroys me.

The forum posts are confusing at first, users often referencing pieces of evidence by full serial number, and Joni and me only by our initials, and I almost can't believe that there are still people out there devoting this level of detail to the worst moments of my life. I scan through the messages, and it doesn't take long to find an account I think could be Steven's: IBelieveThem76. His last comment was posted last night, underneath a post from a user called Dadditch.

FRIDAY, MAY 18, 2018, AT 15:00

Dadditch: Didn't it always seem like there was something sinister about Elizabeth Winter? It was those fucking eyes, man. People talk about getting a bad vibe from Joni but for me it was Bess—those texts and emails? The way she humiliated any guy who'd ever tried to please her sexually? Idk she always seemed like an asshole to me. Frigid too.

SUNDAY, MAY 20, 2018, AT 20:03

IBelieveThem76: If being kind of an asshole was an indicator of guilt, you'd be serving life in San Quentin. Try sticking to discussing the evidence instead of your feeble-minded opinions. You're veering dangerously close to incel territory, my friend.

SUNDAY, MAY 20, 2018, AT 23:09

Dadditch: Whoa, chill out, man. This is meant to be fun.

TWENTY-NINE

2008

I NAVIGATED BACK TO THE trail opening, the one I hadn't even bothered pointing out to Evangeline. The path was much easier to traverse than the one it splintered from and, if I wasn't still so furious, I would have been smug that I would no doubt beat Evangeline back to the hotel and could make a scene stuffing my clothes into my backpack before storming out of the room. I figured I'd make a collect call to my mom, begging her to book me a flight home from Mykonos so that I didn't have to go back to Tinos for the final weeks of summer. I'd spend the next four summers working to pay off the cost of the change if I had to; I just knew that I needed to get as far away from Evangeline, from Joni, from my humiliating memories of Theo, as possible.

I was halfway down the trail when I saw it. At first, it was just a black mass in the distance, something blowing off the side of the cliff like a leaf, only that wasn't right because the proportions were off and the mass was too big. As it got closer to the ocean, the reflected light of the moon illuminated the form like a firefly and I understood then that it was her, that Evangeline was falling and her bare arms were flailing wildly, reaching to grab on to nothing, and that soon her body would pick up velocity only to crack onto the bed of rocks below.

The entire time I was watching, I didn't make a sound. And that's how I knew that Evangeline was right and I was rotten to my core.

For just a moment, I had wanted it to be her.

———————

I stood on the trail. I could see Ev's body on the rocks below, and although the tide occasionally reached her, the water wasn't deep enough to carry her away. She hadn't moved in the time I'd been watching, which could have been thirty seconds or could have been three hours. Either way, the sky stayed dark behind the blanket of stars, and Ev's neck stayed bent, her hair trailing into the water like a veil. I could hear my labored breathing as if it were someone else's breath, someone else's pure terror, and I crouched down with my head between my legs while I worked out if I was going to black out or vomit. In the end I vomited, the acrid taste lingering in my mouth long after I'd finished.

Joni, I thought, looking up at the villa in the distance where the party was most likely still going on despite the accident that had just drawn a line in the sand of Evangeline's very existence, as well as my own. An alternate universe with its own rules, its own timeline. I knew there was no way I could leave Ev alone to go back there for help. She was too small, too fragile, and I wouldn't be able to forget that part.

My heart was pounding, my mouth dry as I made my way down to the sand, and I realized at a certain point that I was humming loudly, had been for a while, and I recognized the tune as an old Sublime song Steven and I had memorized soon after we moved to LA in an effort to catch up with our new classmates, who seemed to have each word ingrained on their brains like a tattoo, loudly singing it at every party, every opportunity, like an anthem. I wondered whether I might have even imagined the fall, because how could I still be here if it had really happened? Still walking and humming, practically *singing* at points, and thinking about things like where Ev's shoes might have landed. The memory of her falling had already begun to feel like a sequence in a dream—slippery and vague on details, becoming less tangible the harder I tried to remember it.

By the time I reached the rocks, I had all but convinced myself that they would be empty once I climbed up. That all I'd lost was my mind, which was better than having lost someone like Evangeline, who was good and kind and loved by everyone who knew her. Including Theo. *Theo.* I stopped in my tracks, barely noticing when the black foaming water washed over my feet. I tried to imagine explaining to Theo what had happened. And that's when I knew that I hadn't been dreaming, because even my dreams couldn't be that cruel.

Joni found me sitting on the rocks next to Ev's body, my forehead resting on my knees as I murmured something unintelligible, something even I can't remember, over and over again. "It was like you were praying," she would tell me later. "But in tongues."

Pale-faced, Joni told me that she had noticed we had been gone awhile, and had followed the trail Ev had taken to its natural end. And then she'd looked down, and spotted us both on the beach below. Joni had called my name, and when I looked up, she'd understood everything she needed to just by seeing my face. She had hopped down the rocks in the way that Evangeline had attempted before her, and within moments she was next to me.

"Oh fuck, oh fuck, oh fuck," Joni said when she touched Ev, her body still and broken, and I knew then that if Joni lost it, I would too, and I would never come back from it. I buried my head in my arms and I squeezed my eyes shut. For some reason, I thought of my mom, of the smell of sunscreen on her skin as she spun me around in a swimming pool as a child, maybe in Spain, or France, and the memory made me cry even harder. When I looked up, Joni seemed to have gathered strength, her eyes burning with intensity as she gripped my shoulders tightly, her fingers digging urgently into my flesh.

"Bess, listen to me," she said, processing it all even as she spoke. "You need to give me a minute to figure this out, okay?"

I shook my head, not understanding what she could mean. Evangeline was dead. There was nothing to figure out. I could feel my teeth chattering, but I didn't know how to make them stop.

"We need to back each other up on what happened," Joni said quietly, almost as if she was convincing herself. "That's all that matters right now."

"What?" I said, still not understanding. I thought that Joni seemed eerily calm until I noticed her hands, which were writhing around each other like snakes as she talked.

"Everyone at the party saw you and Ev fighting, and you following her out here," Joni said. "And now she's gone."

I shook my head, my body racking as I shivered. Joni wrapped her jacket around me, and I flinched at her touch. I saw one of Ev's sandals then, peeking out from under a rock just inches away from her body, the green jewel glimmering in the night.

"But she was alive when I left her," I said. "I swear she was still alive."

"I know, I know," Joni said, but I figured that she didn't believe me.

"I'm sorry, Joni," I said, burying my face in my knees. "I'm sorry I was going to leave you."

"Listen to me, Bess. We have to tell them we were with Evangeline when she fell," Joni said then, her breath damp and sour on my face as she leaned close.

I shook my head again, still not understanding. *No, no, no, no, no, this isn't happening.*

"We were so cruel," I said, so softly I wasn't sure if Joni heard me.

"Listen to me," she said again, even more urgently this time. "It's the only way. We have to pretend that this has happened right now, this very second, and that we were all together. We were walking home, and Ev just tripped. She was climbing down the rocks first, and she fell."

I looked up at her, my terror only growing. I wanted her certainty to ground me like it always did, but I couldn't submit to it this time.

"Come on," she said. "Bess."

"Why?" I whispered.

"Because otherwise, you're the only person to back up your story of what happened," Joni says grimly. "And because they have no reason to believe you, and a thousand reasons not to."

I swallowed another wave of bile as she began to quietly count: "One, two, three . . ."

Joni took a deep breath as she looked once more at Ev's body. Then she started to scream. After a moment, I joined her.

Someone at the party heard our screams and called the police. They arrived twenty minutes later, and by then, Joni had made sure that our story was straight. Joni had heard that Evangeline and I had already left the party to walk back to our hotel, and she had raced to catch up with us. We had all reached the end of the path together, and Evangeline had suggested we climb down to the beach. She had lost her footing almost instantly.

A female police officer who looked devastated when she saw Evangeline's body and the two of us huddled next to her, voices hoarse and eyes swollen, took statements from us on the spot, and then, in good English, told us she would follow up with us at the police station the following day. There would need to be an investigation, she said, but it would be more a formality than anything.

"Who . . ." Joni started, then she cleared her throat. "Who informs her family?"

The police officer put her hand on Joni's shoulder, and I watched as Joni winced. "We will do it, but, if you can endure it, it will be best coming from you first. From people who knew her."

Joni nodded gravely.

I have thought often about the officer's use of the word *endure*—an unusual choice, perhaps, but one that would prove to forecast the rest of my life. I had probably once believed that I had endured my time in Calabasas, or that Joni and I were enduring that listless summer in Tinos, or that I just had to endure the trip to Mykonos until Theo came back. The truth was, up until that moment, I had no idea what it really meant. Not only would I have to endure the next six months in Greece, but I was about to find that the rest of my life would become one long endurance test—an exercise in clinging on, in showing up, in wanting little and expecting even less.

As the sun rose, Joni and I walked back along the beach to our hotel, hand in trembling hand. I didn't tell her all the things Evangeline had said to me, because they were too shameful to relate, even to Joni. I don't remember either of us saying a word at all, because nothing would ever be enough to fill the looming chasm in our lives, left by Evangeline. The good one who had seen all the way through me to the monster I was inside.

THIRTY

2018

I T TAKES ME LONGER than it should to realize I'm being followed in Whole Foods.

The photographers have been back at Joni's house for a while now, cameras hanging by their hips as they casually update each other on their wives' pregnancies or house purchases, and even though I know it was never personal, just the sight of them can bring back a flood of memories so visceral I start to shake. Sometimes I imagine what would happen if they came after me—whether I'd raise my chin stoically as the flashes consumed me once again, or if some long-buried carnal side of me would be awakened and I'd bite back like a ferocious dog. I tell myself that it would be highly unlikely, almost impossible, for any of them to recognize me when they don't even know I'm here.

And yet, as I browse the grocery store looking for the exact type of tamarind paste Joni has requested, I notice a man around my age staying five steps behind me, a backpack slung casually over one shoulder. I deliberately circle back on myself, striding up and down aisles before looping back once more, but I still can't seem to lose him. I drop my basket of food in the middle of the floor and leave the store, panic building in my bones. I speed walk across the parking lot in the searing sunshine, pausing a few times only to see if the shadow behind me stops too. By the time I reach the car, my cortisol levels are so high that I think I could bite someone's ear off if they got too close to me.

"Bess Winter?"

I turn around. The man is now standing less than ten feet away, with a camera on his shoulder, and he's already filming. The red light blinks as he moves closer, and I hold one hand up to shield my face as I use the other to search for the unfamiliar car key in my bag. In an instant I'm transported back to nine summers earlier, when the news reporters and camera crews circled closer, pretending to be on my side even while they were ripping my life apart. *Tissues, wallet, flashlight, dumb citrine crystal from Joni, gum, flashlight again, lip balm, are you fucking kidding me where is this* key.

"I heard you were back in town to support your old friend," the man says, stepping closer still. "Does it feel a little like déjà vu? A reunion tour?"

"Leave me alone," I hiss as I claw in my bag some more until, finally, my fingers land on the leather key ring, tucked into the deepest fold underneath the pack of tissues. I open the car door, slamming it shut behind me, then I instantly start the engine and release the parking brake. My breath feels ragged, and I know I need to catch it before it devolves into a full-blown panic attack, but more urgently than that, I need to get away from this man. For a split second, I imagine pressing my foot on the gas and driving straight over him, his bones crushing under the weight of my fury. I picture a river of blood flowing beneath him, the final gasp of breath as he realizes exactly what I am capable of. In the end, the only thing that stops me from doing it is just how good it would feel.

"You should get used to this," the man shouts through the window, oblivious. "Word is out that you're home, *Elizabeth*."

As I drive away, his words echo in my mind.

Home, I think as the palm trees and billboards slide past my window and the ocean reveals itself in the distance. I haven't had a home in a long time.

I speed past the mass of bodies waiting outside Joni's house, before pulling into the neighbor's driveway. As I move through the linked garages, adrenaline still firing through my veins, I finally understand that I need to separate myself from Joni before it's too late. Willa has been missing for fifteen days now and, for whatever reason, hubris or self-preservation, Joni is refusing to play the game we've already lost once. I am suddenly furious that she has exposed me like this, that she actually believed either of us could outrun our past. Instead, I feel like I'm sinking back in time, like I could reach out this second and grab a handful of fine Mykonos sand from under the crescent moon.

Inside Joni's house, the back doors are open, and Joni is sitting in the middle of the deck in a butterfly pose, her hands resting on her bare feet as she tilts her chin toward the sun. She looks so calm, so without conflict, that for just a moment, I want to strangle her.

"What's wrong," she says, without opening her eyes.

"I was followed in the store," I say. "By a reporter."

Joni is still, the only sign that she heard me a slight flicker, a tug, between her eyebrows.

"Did you get the tuna steaks?" she asks eventually.

"Joni," I say. "I can't do this."

"Can't do what?"

"Will you open your fucking eyes?" I say. "It's like trying to negotiate with a corpse."

Joni opens her eyes, smiling slightly. She points to the lounge chair next to her, but I stay put, leaning against the doorframe.

"Tell me," she says. "What you're thinking."

"I'm *thinking* I need to go home," I say, my voice tight. "Me being here is only going to make this worse. We look like . . . it's going to look like we've got something to hide, and I don't know about you, but I won't survive it again."

"You're stronger than you think," Joni says. "But if you believe that hiding will solve everything, then by all means leave. That's worked out really well for you so far, hasn't it?"

"I know I haven't made the best choices since we got back from Greece," I say slowly. "But your way didn't exactly work out either."

"Well, I guess you were right all along," Joni says.

She smiles infuriatingly again and we're veering onto dicey territory, so I take a deep breath and adapt my approach. "Look, we're really making the same point," I say. "The closer we bind ourselves to the past, the more chance there is of our story gathering momentum again."

"I don't see it like that," Joni says. "But I appreciate your concern."

I want to shake her.

"Although, Bess—I do have one thing to tell you," Joni says. "Before you leave."

"Okay," I say.

"I haven't been totally honest with you," Joni says matter-of-factly. "Or rather, I lied."

I already feel untethered.

Joni tucks her hair behind her ears and nibbles her bottom lip so hard that I see a small bubble of blood appear.

"Joni . . . just say it."

"Willa was cheating on me. And she had been for a while."

I stare down at the top of Joni's head, at the same parting I

186

used to carefully drag a finger through before pulling the lengths of her hair into French braids.

"Why didn't you tell me?" I ask finally, when words come back to me, even though I know why she didn't tell me. She didn't tell me because it meant that I would have questioned her a little more about the lie she needed from me. She didn't tell me so that she could convince me to do what she wanted, because even if the Joni I knew back then didn't lie, maybe she does now, over and over again, to get what she needs. And she's telling me now because she thinks it might throw me off-balance just enough to make me stay.

"Bess," she says, but then she trails off because there's nothing she can say that will make up for her walking back into my life only to blow it up all over again. Joni might have tried to pass off what she was asking of me as a casual lie, a half-truth to cover up a silly, career-damaging transgression, but I see now that the rot went deeper than she ever wanted me to know.

"Who is she?" I ask, and Joni tightens her jaw.

"His name is Lucien," she says mechanically. "He's a high school English teacher. I'd known about him for a while."

"So what happened that night, Joni?" I ask. "The night Willa disappeared."

"Nothing spectacular," she says.

"Joni . . ." I say.

"I already told you," Joni says. "Willa saw a photo that Zoey sent me of herself in bed, and she lost it. And even though I felt this was particularly rich coming from her, I denied that I was still seeing Zoey because I didn't want Willa to know that I'd been so desperate, so in need of *validation*, that I'd stooped to her level. We argued about the photo and then I told her I was driving to see you."

"You didn't find out about Lucien that night," I say, and Joni shakes her head.

"Let's just say it was an ongoing discussion," she says.

"And where is Zoey now?" I ask, since she's possibly the only person other than Willa who knows the real timeline of that night.

"I need to keep her out of this," Joni says. "She doesn't deserve to be dragged into my mess."

Unlike me, I think, with a swell of resentment, because the writing was already on the wall for me after I sold my soul to Joni on a beach in Greece ten years ago.

"Why didn't you just tell me about Willa's boyfriend at the time?" I ask.

Joni chews on her bottom lip, unable to look at me for a moment, and I think she might finally break. Of course, she recovers beautifully within seconds.

"It wasn't relevant," Joni says. "And it would have complicated things."

I sit on the chair, exhausted suddenly from having to navigate the twists and loopholes in Joni's narrative—the deception and bluster, all the ways she's still trying to save face in front of me. I think about what she's actually telling me, and I figure it's probably true. I don't know if I'd have been so quick to cover for her if I'd known how badly Willa had hurt her in the first place, but Joni's right—what does it really change? Willa is still missing, and I have to believe that my friend doesn't know any more about it than she's saying.

"We're not eighteen anymore, Joni," I say. "Aren't we past this yet?"

"I wish you would trust me," Joni says.

I don't even trust myself.

We stare at each other for a moment.

"I need to go home," I say.

Joni blinks a couple of times.

"Joni," I say softly, but already she's recalibrating, and when she meets my eye again, her armor is firmly back in place, one eyebrow raised as she assesses me witheringly.

"You know it won't reflect well on either of us if you say the wrong thing to a reporter, or if someone photographs you looking like a disaster in the middle of fucking nowhere. It will seem like you have a reason to hide, which, by extension, looks bad for me too."

I feel a sting of shame that I work to hide from her.

"I'll be okay."

"Fine," Joni says finally, before she stands up. "But take my neighbor's car. And don't do anything stupid."

I ignore Joni's advice, climbing down the steps to the beach and walking south for a mile or so before booking an Uber to take me back to the cabin. I don't want to owe Joni any more than I already do, particularly if it means she'll just cash in the favor when I least expect it. No questions asked, just an eye for an eye. Blind support in return for blind support, regardless of the consequences.

THIRTY-ONE

2008

I WAS STILL SHIVERING WHEN we got back to the hotel. While Joni had a shower, I mechanically began to prepare my bed on the floor again, even though I knew I would never be able to sleep. It felt as if the entire top layer of my skin had been ripped off and I was left exposed, oozing everywhere if anyone cared to look. I was still staring down at the blankets on the floor when Joni came out of the bathroom. She was wearing an old Garth Brooks T-shirt, her makeup smeared down her face as she stared at me in disbelief.

"What are you doing?" she asked, in the way an exhausted mother might speak to her toddler if she found him flashing for attention. "You can sleep in the bed."

"No," I said. "I can't."

"She's not coming back," Joni said, her voice harsh now. "You know that, right?"

"Someone needs to call her family," I said, and I realized I was still shaking.

"Theo?" she prompted.

I shook my head as we locked eyes, and I silently pleaded with her.

Joni stared at me as if she'd just seen inside my soul and discovered just how decaying it was. I felt certain that she was going to say something, something so cruel and so true that we would never be able to come back from it, but then she stopped herself.

Her eyes flicked over the empty bed instead.

"Okay," she said, her voice soft in a way it had never been before or since. "I'll do it."

I sat in the locked bathroom with the shower on while Joni made the call to Theo. I didn't want to hear what was said.

We were driven to the police station only a few hours later to make our formal statements. We'd both taken showers, but nothing we'd packed for the week seemed even slightly appropriate for the occasion. I ended up wearing a pair of jean shorts and a white cotton shirt with baby blue embroidery I found in Evangeline's bag, to avoid having to give my statement in either a crochet bikini top or a minidress, or, even worse, the Ronaldo jersey Theo had given to me in another lifetime.

"Do you think we should ask for a lawyer?" I asked Joni as we got into the car, and she shook her head, pressing her finger to her lips.

"We'll be out of there within the hour," she said.

The police station was the same clean white as most of the other buildings in Mykonos, decorated with the same blue shutters and trim, and, at any other time, I would have sailed past it without a second thought, assuming it was a restaurant or another moped rental spot. Instead, Joni and I were separated and led into different rooms as we gave a more detailed account of what happened. It wasn't the female police officer doing the interview, but it was a young guy who seemed nice enough, although his English wasn't as good, so we used a translator to communicate any terms he didn't understand. It meant that the conversation felt even more jarring and formal, particularly when, as a witness, I had to take an oath before I gave a statement. As the interview progressed, however, I found the lie somehow made it easier to talk about what happened, like I was just retelling a story that happened to somebody else's friend. "She fell while she was climbing," I said simply. And when they asked me how she'd fallen, I replied, "Backwards."

Joni and I had decided to repurpose our conversation from dinner the night before—the one about writing each other letters in college—transporting it instead to a drunken walk across the cliffs of Agios Stefanos thirty hours later. I hadn't fully understood Joni's insistence on pretending that we were all together when Evangeline fell until I heard how much better this version sounded, how much less ashamed it made me feel to give Evangeline the final moments she deserved. Lying to the police didn't feel good, but it did mean that I didn't have to remember what she had actually said to me, or the vile things I'd said to her, and how undeniably cognizant she had been when I left her, and must have been in the final moments before she fell. I just imagined it was any other night, when we hadn't been so deliberately and unfathomably cruel to one another, and she'd just tripped in the middle of a conversation about something immemorable and benign.

When I mentioned how long we'd been drinking, the officer's expression shifted slightly.

"Fifteen hours," he repeated. "How do you remember what happened, then?"

"It's not something I would forget," I said. "I wasn't blackout or anything."

"Black out," he repeated, studying me.

"You know, blacked out. Too drunk to remember."

The translator explained it to him in Greek, and he nodded.

"How drunk were you?"

I thought about it for a moment, unsure how to quantify it. "Drunk enough to go back to a party when we didn't know anyone there. Drunk enough to think it was a good idea to walk home from the party. Unfortunately, not quite drunk enough to forget it happened."

The officer stared at me, and I smiled at him uncertainly. I knew it was an odd thing to do at the time, but I was more intrigued by how I felt like I was watching myself from above, like I might slip away from it all if I disassociated hard enough.

"You're making a joke?" he asked me, after a long pause.

"I haven't slept," I said, swallowing hard. "I barely know what I'm doing at this point."

"Still," he said, looking over his notes. "Your memory is very perfect for fifteen hours of drinking."

"Not perfect," I said quietly. "I can't remember the last thing she ever said."

I watched the officer write something down in his notepad, silently willing him to let me leave. He caught my eye again.

"Your cheek," he said curiously. "Is it sore?"

I touched my face where Joni had slapped me less than ten hours earlier, and I shook my head, fighting a fierce wave of nausea.

"The car ride to the party was bumpy," I said. "I must have banged it on something."

He frowned briefly at my answer but, to my relief, ended the interview then, telling me I would be free to leave the police station once I had given a written statement of everything we'd discussed.

"Do you have any questions for me?" he asked, and I paused.

"Just one," I said. "When can we go home?"

He glanced at the translator and smiled quickly.

"Not just yet. But it won't be much longer."

I was disoriented and jittery by the time I signed my formal witness statement, and I waited for Joni on a plastic chair in the lobby, my thighs swimming in a pool of my own sweat. I felt winded with relief when I finally saw her striding out of the questioning room with her trademark swagger, sunglasses still pushed up on her head, and she grabbed my arm and instantly pulled me up and out of my stupor. We stood, foreheads nearly touching as Joni touched my cheek to check I was okay. I shrugged in response because I was still there.

Someone had called a taxi to take us back to our hotel, and we waited indoors until it pulled up outside. When we finally walked out of the station, arm in arm, we found two photographers and a journalist waiting for us.

"How are you girls doing?" the journalist asked.

"Okay," I said instinctively, at the same time Joni muttered, "Just fucking peachy, how do you think?"

"Were you with Evangeline Aetos when she died?" the journalist pressed, and I felt Joni's arm clench my own.

"Come on," she hissed as she pushed me into a taxi.

"Joni . . ." I said, once we were inside. I looked at the driver quickly. He was a kindly-looking older man who was listening to a talk radio show, which he turned up when he saw me looking.

"It's only because Stavros is so rich," Joni said. "That's why they care."

"Maybe," I said, slipping away from myself again. Already the shock had set in, and I felt as if I were playing a part, one I wasn't entirely equipped to commit to in the way it required. I found myself wondering when this might be over, when I could return to being myself again, and then, with a crushing thud, I remembered that Evangeline was dead and that nothing would ever be the same again.

"Hey," I said quietly. "Did you say anything I should know about?"

Joni shrugged. "We didn't really go into any detail. They were too busy grilling me about the party and my debauched lesbian lifestyle."

"Oh," I said, so relieved that she hadn't got carried away, or, even worse, crumbled, that I didn't process what she said. "Okay."

"Fuck them all," she said, looking out the window. I looked up briefly, catching the eye of the taxi driver as he watched us in the rearview mirror.

THIRTY-TWO

2018

I MAKE THE UBER DROP me half a mile from my house, and I know that the familiar hypervigilance, my own desperate attempt at control, has taken hold again. As I walk down the track leading up to my cabin, I notice an intricate pattern of tire tracks weaving through the dust, and I think that perhaps Joni wasn't lying to me about the reporters at least. It's a barbed sort of consolation, and sweat drips down my temples as I round the final bend to find nothing but my ancient Saab parked outside my cabin.

I can hear the house line ringing as I climb up the steps to the porch and, once inside, I press the phone against my ear, half expecting it to be Joni calling with some magical, fabricated reason I need to come back to Malibu right this second. Possibly worse, it turns out to be my mom calling from Spain.

"Steven said you'd moved out for a while," she says, sounding even further away than usual.

"He's being dramatic," I say, already on the defensive. It's classic Steven to tattle on me to my mom, even though she's six thousand miles away and we're both the wrong side of twenty-five.

"He's worried about you," she says.

"He really shouldn't be," I say, and we've been on this carousel long enough that I no longer have to say the words *I'm fine.*

"I'm sorry to hear about Joni's friend," my mom says then, and I wonder now how closely my parents have been following the case, and whether this has brought back a flood of traumatizing memories they've had to repress. Other than the odd slipup, my mom hasn't mentioned Joni to me in years, and I realize now that it's late in Barcelona, nearly midnight, and my mom might actually be drunk on sangria or something.

"Friend?" I repeat.

"Girlfriend," she corrects herself.

"I've never met her," I say.

"But Joni?" she asks. "Steven mentioned you were back in touch."

"Did he ask you to check up on me?"

"I'm not checking up on anything. I just wanted to see how you were both doing. We're overdue a conversation, anyway."

"Well, I'm okay," I say irritably. "And Joni's okay. And Steven really shouldn't have bothered you."

"I told you, he's just worried about you," she says. "Whatever happened to Ivan, by the way?"

"God, Mom," I say. "We broke up eight months ago."

"Good," she says decisively, and I wonder again just how much she's had to drink. "He was joyless. Just one of those joyless people."

"Okay, thank you, Mom," I say, but I'm smiling a little now because she isn't wrong.

"You must come visit," she says. "You'd love Barcelona."

I don't say anything. We both know I haven't left California in nearly a decade, but she still insists on keeping up this charade.

"How's work?"

I wince thinking of how meager my paycheck is going to be this month. I've probably managed thirty, forty cases in the past two weeks, which would equate to between fifteen and twenty dollars.

"It's fine," I say.

"And have you been writing at all? Creatively?"

I feel my cortisol levels rocket at her words.

"I haven't written anything *creatively* since I was fifteen," I say. "When we moved to Calabasas, funnily enough."

My mom exhales. "I knew that place was a cultural vacuum the moment I saw it. I should have pushed harder for the Columbia position."

"I don't know if Manhattan would have been much better for my grand writing career," I say. "I think I was just at that age where you get distracted by other things."

There is a silence where we both realize that one thing at least would have been different if we'd moved to New York instead, and then I think she might pass the phone over to my dad so that he can ask me about the desert heat and the awful air quality, and when California lawmakers are going to treat the Salton Sea like the environmental emergency it is, and whether they even deliver newspapers out here and how Rupert Murdoch is still ruining the world and did I know that he saw one of his sons on a plane once (commercial!) and who the hell would waste their money paying for first class and why air miles are a total crock—

"Mom," I say, every nerve in my body willing me to stop talking. "Do you like Joni?"

There's another long pause, this time because this isn't what we do in our family—we don't talk about *what* happened because then we might also have to examine *why* it happened: why it was so easy for strangers to hate me.

"*Like* isn't the right word," my mom says after a long pause. "I've always felt sorry for Joni. She just seemed so lost, even before that summer."

"But do you . . . do you think she's capable of doing something bad?"

I hear her take a sip of something, and the thought of my own mother having to drink to fortify herself for a conversation with me makes me feel lonelier than ever. I angle the phone slightly away from my mouth so that my mom won't hear how labored my breathing is, how much I'm depending on her answer to comfort me.

"I don't know, sweetie, I really don't. And luckily it's not my job to know. My job is to support you."

"I feel like I don't know her anymore," I say quietly. *And maybe I never did.*

"I always thought that Joni was insecure, like she was just waiting for the bottom to drop out, even before what happened," my mom says. "It was almost painful to watch you girls together sometimes, she needed so much from you."

I frown at my mom's choice of words. "Insecure? Joni?"

"You wouldn't have seen it because she covered it up with that bravado. But she was so vulnerable. And she'd already been through a lot. I don't believe that her dad ever got in contact after she got home, even after everything. That does things to a girl, particularly one so young."

"But that was after," I say. "Before that summer, it always felt like I was chasing them both."

"Memory can be a strange thing," my mom says. "From where I was standing, it seemed like both of those girls adored you. I'll admit I found Joni a little intense at times, and at first I was relieved when you seemed to be drifting apart, but I could never deny how much she cared about you."

I grip the phone tightly, sweat prickling my palms.

"Steven doesn't like her."

"Steven was young when it all imploded. He doesn't understand the nuances, the ways girls can hurt each other without meaning to—death by a thousand cuts? I think that phrase must have been written about teenage girls. Your brother thinks that you were an innocent, and that Joni dragged you down with her. And you know, maybe in some ways he's right. I could never reconcile all those stories about you with the girl I raised. I still can't."

I can hear the stark grief in her voice, and I hold the phone a couple of inches away from my ear again, as if it might somehow blunt the edge of her next words.

"Sometimes I wake up at four a.m. and I wonder what would have happened if I'd never taken the job at Pepperdine. I wonder who you might have been, what you might have achieved, and it feels like I'm mourning someone I never got a chance to meet."

Each word shatters through me like an expanding bullet, ripping me apart from the inside out. And that's how it always is with my family—some sentimental remark, some otherwise throwaway comment, can plunge me right back to being eighteen and sick with guilt and needing my parents to tell me that I'm a good person, despite the bad things I've done. I try to plug the rising shame, but it's too late. It's always too late.

"This is why I left," I say, just before I hang up. "This is exactly why I had to leave."

THIRTY-THREE

2008

A FEW HOURS AFTER WE gave our statements to the police, Joni suggested we go down to the beach. We'd been locked up in our hotel room, forced to stare at Evangeline's belongings—her clothes hanging in the wardrobe (because of course only Ev had insisted on unpacking), her glittery makeup scattered across the bathroom, and, worst of all, the cuddly white elephant toy she slept with every night peeking out from between the pillows. I couldn't think of a single reason not to leave this room, preserved as it had been since before Evangeline died, so I agreed.

We walked down to the ocean, and I remember looking at the other people, a mixture of local families and sunburned tourists, and marveling that they had no idea what had happened just a few miles down the road. Those who had heard about Ev's death had probably muttered a short prayer at most, a throwaway *what a shame* before it was instantly forgotten. Nobody else was locked in it like I was: trapped in a nightmare somehow born from both a senseless accident and the culmination of every single choice I had ever made.

Joni was quieter than I'd ever known her to be, and I wondered if she was already regretting her offer to lie for me. I couldn't bear the thought that I was making losing Evangeline any harder for her, even if it meant going back on the pact we'd made on the beach.

"Joni," I said quietly. "You know we can always go back and tell the police the truth."

"But we've already given our statements," Joni said, frowning at me.

"I know, but maybe we could say we were traumatized and confused?" I said softly. "I'm sure it's happened before."

Joni shook her head.

"It's too late for that," she said, slipping her hand in mine. "And I would never do that to you."

I felt a swell of gratitude for her, mixed with a lingering dread.

————————

At some point we were approached by a man selling ice cream from a large cooler hanging around his neck. Joni looked at me and I shrugged. We hadn't eaten for over twenty-four hours, and ice cream wouldn't have been my first choice, but I couldn't exactly imagine sitting down for a meal without Ev either, choosing whether to have sea bream or calamari and communicating with a waiter like it was any normal day. Like yesterday never happened and Evangeline was just hungover in the hotel room like she should have been—unable to face the world yet.

"Cornetto, please," I said, pointing at the picture on the cooler. "Mint chocolate chip, efcharistó."

"Oreo sandwich," Joni said.

"Oh, can I have that instead, please?" I said, pointing at the cookie in question. "Two Oreos?"

"God, you literally want to be me," Joni said half-heartedly. "Make it more obvious, why don't you."

I smiled weakly and swatted her on the arm as she handed over the money for the ice creams. I appreciated her effort at normalcy, even if I knew we would probably never feel normal again, or not in the same way at least.

As we walked back toward the hotel, the sugar revived us slightly. We spoke about our childhood ice cream traditions and, for a moment, it almost felt like nothing had changed. When the sand burned the soles of our feet, we ran down to the ocean to cool them down, kicking water at each other accidentally at first, then on purpose. I was so absorbed by savoring that feeling for a few seconds longer, that *pretense* that nothing had changed, that I didn't even notice the photographer capturing it all.

We didn't go back to the hotel for hours. In our shared room, it was impossible to pretend that nothing had happened because the ghost of Evangeline was right there with us, asking us to check a mole on her back or insisting on sleeping in a full pajama set like a Victorian ghost because the air-conditioning was too intense. At one point I started to cry in the middle of the street, and Joni steered me away from the crowds, wiping my tears with her hands, her face filled with a level of concern I couldn't even comprehend. At another point, we tried on the ugly fisherman hats that Evangeline had pleaded with us not to buy at a tourist shop only two days ago, and we laughed a little at our reflections, because we looked just as bad as she'd told us we would. Then Joni grabbed my hand and quickly pulled me out of the shop, but she wouldn't tell me why we had to leave right at that moment, even though she'd nearly crushed my bones with her grip. Later, I would find out it was because an English girl had been secretly taking photo-graphs of us in the mirror.

When we finally walked back into the hotel lobby around sunset, Theo was waiting for us. I felt a lightning bolt to the pit of my stomach, and it was so strong that I had to bend over slightly to absorb the blow.

"Theo," I said softly, and as I took a step toward him, he took a step back.

"That's Ev's shirt," he said, staring at me strangely. "You're wearing her shirt."

The woman sitting behind the reception desk pretended not to hear us.

THIRTY-FOUR

2018

THE CABIN FEELS LIFELESS. Endless hours stretch ahead of me as I try to recall how I once filled a single minute here, let alone an entire day. I keep the blinds down and curtains closed, shuffling around in the gloomy light as I make myself instant noodles whenever I remember I've missed a meal. I spend the rest of my time resolving as many 5oulm8s cases as I can to make up for the two weeks I barely worked, skimming across the complaints lightly, trying my hardest not to linger for too long in the darkest chambers of a stranger's mind. I think of Joni often, and I remind myself that this life isn't an accident. This is what I wanted.

On my third morning in the cabin, I wake up with the uncanny feeling that something has changed. A strip of sunlight steals through a crack in the curtains, and I can hear not so much a specific noise but rather an absence of the overture of silence to which I've grown accustomed over the years. When I peek through the yellow curtains, I spot the silver nose of a strange car parked outside the front of my cabin.

I search frantically in bed for my phone before realizing it must be on the sofa where I fell asleep watching *Storage Wars* last night.

With a growing sense of dread, I throw on the same hoodie and sweatpants I've been wearing since I got back, and I creep into the living room. Through the flimsy curtains covering the door, I count the silhouettes of at least ten reporters at the end of my porch. When I finally locate my phone, I have seven missed calls from Joni, and a text that reads: **Please come back**.

I hold the phone tightly in my hand, savoring the unfamiliar feeling of being needed by someone, but then, just seconds later, I find myself wondering whether Joni tipped off these reporters herself, because we both know I can't stay here now. The landscape is too barren, my cabin too exposed, for me to allow it to become my prison. I think maybe I'll drive to Steven and Nova's instead, even though just the idea of exposing my brother to these people again fills me with a bone-aching dread.

I take a few breaths as I steel myself to face the waiting reporters, pulling my hood down to hide as much of my face as possible. As I unlock the door, I wonder if some sick part of me gets a thrill out of being hunted, or at least believes it's what I deserve.

The moment I open the door, the reporters move toward me as a mass—not quite the overwhelming surge of ten years ago, but still a dozen strangers, mostly men, all needing something amorphous from me before they leave—some humiliating display that will mean they've done their job for the day. As I move through them, the cool metal of cameras and microphones pressing against my skin, I work to drown out the discordant chorus of shouts for a comment about the news, about Joni Le Bon's involvement in the case, about what happened in Greece. And then?

About Willa's death.

I drop into my car as the words shouted at me by a reporter with short blond hair reverberate in my mind. The flashing cameras are now poised in front of my windshield, capturing every moment that passes, and I'm still here as I search for her in the crowd. We lock eyes and, after a moment, the reporter nods once, confirming my silent question.

Joni, I think.

Battling alternating waves of nausea and pure panic, I reverse out of the drive and weave my way across the network of desert roads and freeways to the coast, pushing my ancient car so hard that it is steaming and spluttering by the time I turn onto Joni's street, every warning light now a violent red on the dashboard. The crowd of reporters outside her house has tripled, and two men are unloading equipment from a KTLA 5 news van parked on the curb opposite. I hurriedly enter the code to Joni's neighbor's garage and keep my head down as I drive inside, my hands shaking long after the door has closed behind me.

I find Joni sitting on the sofa watching the news, but she doesn't turn to look at me. Instead, we both watch wordlessly as an aerial view of a beach south of Redondo fills the screen, police swarming as a crowd gathers at the perimeter. In a grave tone, the newscaster reports that Willa's body washed up on this strip of coastline earlier this morning. In an even graver tone, she states that an initial statement from the Los Angeles County Sheriff's Department indicates foul play.

I stand frozen to the spot. Somehow, despite the thoughts and prayers that have been demanded at the end of each juicy piece of coverage on the news, each discussion of her disappearance and the night it occurred, each interview with a panicked loved one or friend, Willa will never come home.

"Fuck," I say as I finally move toward Joni. "I'm sorry, Joni. I'm so, so sorry."

Joni stares at me like she didn't even know I was here, and her expression is so raw, so bewildered, that all I can do is sit on the rug at her feet and take her hands in mine.

The news is like a lightning bolt through the heart of the story, and the press step up their interest with electrifying fervor. The aftermath of the retrieval of Willa's body is filmed from both the ground and the air as crowds of mourners gather to pay their respects, carrying single white candles and hastily made signs protesting the violent and senseless slaughter of another young woman. Willa's existence is combed over, her friends interviewed, and the internet scoured for fresh content, but I can tell already that it isn't as easy for the media to categorize her as they did Evangeline. Evangeline's story wrote itself: she was a child still, a literal and metaphorical virgin when she died. But Willa? Willa was a twenty-three-year-old woman, with an indelible and colorful footprint in the form of thousands of social posts and videos available for anyone to devour. The word the media seems to have landed on for her is *fighter*—Willa was a fighter, as fearless as she was tough, and I wonder how much of her has been flattened to fit into this box, although of course she will never know what they're saying, will never think or feel anything again at all. The news reports show photos of her at various protests, or camping in Yosemite with friends, but the one that seems to be becoming the lead shot used across every network is a portrait of Willa throwing her head back and laughing, probably taken by Joni. When I see it for the first time, I have to close my eyes. There is no doubt that, up until eighteen days ago, Willa Bailey was full of life.

Joni and I sit in silence as the sky darkens outside, and somehow I know what comes next.

The winds have picked up and the past is coming back for us both.

We watch hours of coverage, flicking between the supposedly reputable channels and the trashier networks, with anchors already throwing out wild theories in an effort to make their own mark on the case. At around midnight, we watch the first outright reference to our old case, initially mentioned by a particularly malodorous pundit but soon by many more, each report punctuated by the same collection of the more incriminating photos—the ones where Joni and I held bottles of vodka or bongs, and pouted into the camera with arched eyebrows and glossy lips, like the mini killers everyone wanted us to be. They remember the emails, the leaked evidence photos of our handwritten notes (even just the sight of my childish handwriting sickening to me), before resorting, as expected, to the old classic: a dissection of the timeline of my and Joni's odd behavior in the days before we were arrested. On one channel, above a scrolling banner that reads TRAGIC EVANGELINE AETOS' LINK TO WILLA'S DEATH, my ex-boyfriend Ivan is interviewed on the doorstep of his house, rubbing his ginger mustache with a trembling hand and wearing the corduroy shirt I gave him for his birthday moments before I clamped his hands around my neck while we were fucking, gripping them tighter and tighter long after the horror had already filled his eyes.

"Bess was very private," Ivan says now. "We didn't talk about it, but of course I knew who she was. Now I think I understand why she didn't want anything to do with her past. Lightning doesn't strike twice, does it?"

The way he asks it sounds like a genuine question, one that the anchor ignores back in the newsroom.

"Are you okay?" Joni asks me, and I nod without taking my eyes off the screen.

At a certain point, around 1:30 a.m., someone leaks the information that Willa had sustained an injury to her head before her death by asphyxiation, implying that someone had tried to knock her out before strangling or smothering her and then had carelessly deposited her body into the ocean. According to the criminal law professor interviewed on CNN, without an ironclad alibi, it is now almost inevitable that Joni will be considered the number one suspect. *A crime of passion,* he called it. There are *astonishingly* few truly random attacks, he assures us.

I can't look at Joni, and I realize that I'm not breathing properly, my gasps inaudible at first, then becoming overwhelming the harder I try to fight them, until soon my body is racking with their force. Joni stares at me, her eyes wild and unfocused, and she looks just like she did that night. My best friend's person is dead, and I understand that she knows more than she's saying. Another young woman is dead and somehow I am involved again.

"Let's go down to the water," Joni says. "We have to do something."

The tension has built up inside me, and I need to release it somehow, to feel expunged after hours of hearing other people talk about a version of me that I can't quite access, perhaps never could. *Overprivileged, ungrateful, callous, unruly, rebellious, impulsive, reckless, indecent, Machiavellian, depraved*—the words are swimming around my mind, forcing their way back into my sense of self. I try to protect myself, but the tide is too strong, the consensus still ruling unequivocally against me all these years later. I don't remember the girl they're describing, but I can also feel her inside me, screaming and pummeling as she tries to get out, tries to explain herself and justify her existence. I think of all the stuff they didn't find—the diary entry where I bemoaned a boy from school's public rejection of my hug after his uncle's death (*I get that he's in pain, but did he have to embarrass me in front of everyone? I wish he'd die*), or the way my body still sometimes pulses with fury at Evangeline for dying, not because I miss her in those moments but because it meant that all my dreams of a future with Theo died along with her. In moments like this I think that releasing me at all was a mistake—that I am even *worse* than they said.

"Okay," I say to Joni.

We wordlessly shed our clothes on the deck until we're down to only our underwear. Like mine, Joni's body has changed over the years, but I focus on the similarities instead—the shallow line tracking down the center of her stomach, the birthmark on her left thigh, her long toes gripping the decking as she walks. Not the simple "W" tattoo above her hip, or the jagged scratch on her chest that I can still see faintly in the light of the skinny moon—a moon almost as lean as it was the night Ev died.

The paddleboard Joni hands me is lighter than I'd expected, but it's still awkward to maneuver down the steps as I numbly follow her to the water. My brain has been so saturated by the twenty-four-hour news cycle that I can think only in splashy headlines of faux concern or outrage—JONI LE BON TAKES MIDNIGHT DIP WITH FRIEND AFTER WILLA'S BRUTAL DEATH. Or even worse, THE HOLLYWOOD HEATHENS REUNITE JUST HOURS AFTER BODY IS DISCOVERED.

The tide is so far in that the bottom third of the stepladder is entirely submerged in water. It means that I can't acclimate gradually to the cold and the only option is to plunge straight in as if I too am made of steel. I push the paddleboard into the water before closing my eyes and jumping in after it, the icy water sending shock waves through my body. When I surface, I make sure not to gasp, because I know Joni will be watching, judging, comparing my fortitude not only to that of her dead fiancée but also to the old Bess, the one who would never show weakness because she thought that being brave and pretending to be brave were the same thing.

We swim out together, and then I mirror Joni, pulling myself up onto the board like she does once we're over the choppiest waves. I can taste salt water in my mouth, and the light of the moon flickers on the ocean as someone lets off fireworks a couple of miles down the coast. Joni's body tenses as she stands up on the board with her knees slightly bent, the paddle gripped lightly in her hands, and then she visibly relaxes. Shakily, I stand up too, testing out my balance and adjusting my weight until I'm nearly fully upright.

"Breathe," Joni shouts, and I nod, taking a deep breath in, and then out.

My legs shake as the tip of the board dips beneath the water, but I shift my weight backward to balance it out.

Joni and I move together in silence for a while, silently daring each other to be the one to say stop even when her house is just a flicker of golden light in the distance. The water is rougher out here, and eventually, as always, I'm the one to call it.

"We should go back," I say, and Joni nods. I use the paddle to turn, hoping that she'll follow me, and, sure enough, I can hear her behind me, the paddle thrusting gently against the waves. As if in a dream, I realize that I was worried, being out there alone with her. There is something unspoken in the air, some shared notion that we're both on the edge of something.

The water is choppy by the shore, and it takes me a few attempts to get any sort of grip on the steps up to Joni's house. I almost lose my footing when a wave crashes against my back, but there, I have it, and my hand tightens around the metal. I won't let go. I pull myself up and lift the board out of the water, climbing until I can maneuver it over my head and slide it through the open gate to the deck. I can feel Joni's presence behind me, and I am suddenly breathless with dread, more afraid than I would ever admit.

Once we're both on the deck, Joni throws me a large striped towel. I wrap myself in it and sit down on the chair, shivering in the breeze as I try to stay calm. Joni lights the fire pit, and we both watch as the flames dance across the glass beads.

We lock eyes and she blinks a few times, water trickling from the blunt ends of her hair and down into the towel tucked under her armpits. I can feel now that everything is changing, in the way that I felt it ten years ago, as soon as we left that house in the hills above Agios Stefanos.

"You told me the pink paddleboard was Willa's," I say.

Joni stares at me, her eyes, black in the moonlight, unreadable.

"Hers was blue," I say. "I found a photo."

"You didn't find anything," Joni says. "You were snooping."

"Not snooping," I say. "Checking."

"What exactly are you asking me, Bess?"

I feel sick, like I'm hurtling through time in the wrong direction. *I'm asking if you went out in the water with Willa that night and left her there,* I think. *I'm asking if I've aligned myself with a monster.*

"How could you do this to us again?" I ask instead. "Why did you have to take so much?"

"What was the alternative," Joni says. "Be like you?"

Her words sting, but I steel myself because I know the worst is yet to come.

"How did you get that scratch," I say, my voice low.

Joni looks down at it and then back at me.

"Willa," she says simply.

Everything feels wrong.

"Bess," Joni says calmly. "We don't know anything yet. There's no point playing detective when everything we do know has already been distorted by the media. Even if they did come for me again, remember that I'm older and smarter and wiser this time, and I'm going to do everything in my power to protect myself properly. But I need to know I can still count on you when I need you."

A white-hot fury surges through me as I think about how careful I've been, how contained my life has become because I built it to be. Perhaps Joni believed she was living enough of a life for us all, but freedom always comes at a cost—somehow, Evangeline had understood that even before we landed in Greece, and I learned it soon after, but Joni was the one who always chose to ignore it. She thought she could outsmart whatever it was that caught us, and now she wants me to set fire to the little I have left, all to protect this shallow kingdom she has built for herself.

"Please," I say. "Don't ask me to continue lying for you."

"Do you think I'd ask if there was any other way?" Joni asks. "You know what they'll do to me. Do you think my life would even be worth living anymore? I would lose everything. Not just Willa, but *everything*."

"Did you do it?" I ask, my voice low. "Did you do something to her?"

Joni won't meet my eyes over the fire, the light of the flames dancing across her face.

"Just tell me what happened that night," I say. "Tell me the truth, Joni."

"We fought," she says eventually. "Willa and I fought."

"About Lucien?" I ask.

"That's how it started," Joni says. "We'd been . . . trying to work through some things for a while, and I thought we were getting stronger. But then I saw this . . . this photo that he sent her, and I lost it."

"Fucking hell, Joni," I whisper. "Did you take her out to the water?"

Joni stares at me, confusion momentarily eclipsing her fear.

"I threw a rose quartz flame at her," Joni says. "And it caught her above the eye, and it looked worse than it was so I knew she'd use it to derail my entire fucking life. But I don't know where she went after that, I swear to God, and I certainly never touched her again. I locked myself in the bathroom, took a shower to cool off, and when I came out she was gone, and I figured she'd maybe gone out on the water to calm down, but then she sent me this shitty text and I panicked because I knew she was going to make me suffer if I stayed. I had to leave, and I had to know that you would cover for me if Willa went public with what I'd done to her. Honestly, I wouldn't have put it past her to have cut herself deeper just to make it seem worse than it was."

I swallow a rising tide of panic as Joni leans toward me, her face imploring.

"Can't you see why I came to you for help?" Joni asks. "Not only did Willa break my heart, but she was blaming me for it."

My mind is racing, trying to keep up. If the neighbor had spotted Willa seemingly happy and injury-free at seven p.m., then all Joni needed to prove was that she had left the house before then. Enter me, blithely promising that Joni had left Malibu at six p.m. to make it to mine.

"What did she say in the text?" I ask slowly.

Joni sits for a minute, blinking.

"Show me," I push, when she doesn't respond.

After a moment, Joni gets up and retrieves her phone from the living room. When she's close, she swipes across the screen and holds it up for me to read.

WILLA ♥ @ 9:05 PM: Soon the whole world will know exactly who you are.

I read it a few times, adding it to the timeline of events I'm assembling in my mind. Willa texted Joni at 9:05 p.m. on Monday, and Joni turned up at my house just after midnight. At that time, it would be around a three-hour drive between us, which would mean Joni had left her house around the same time she got Willa's text. The existence of the text means that Willa presumably can't have been sinking into the middle of the Pacific as a result of her injuries, and the content of the text makes Joni's panic about what she might do more believable. It would also explain why Joni had left her phone at home when she came to me, and why she had seemed so unsettled. Somehow, despite all the ways in which Joni has betrayed me, I still feel a faint tug of relief. Texts are concrete. Texts aren't something you can lie to the police about, unlike memories.

"You know the police will read this," I say. "They probably already have."

Joni nods, her jaw tense, eyes grim.

"And where is it now?" I ask. "The rose quartz."

Joni's eyes flick toward the ocean, and my heart sinks.

"Bess," Joni says softly, but I can't quite meet her eye now that I know why she needed me after all this time. Joni didn't need me to cover for her affair in case Willa ever found out. What Joni needed me to cover up, to shield the rest of the world from, was her own violence—the vicious streak that has lived in us both since we were kids.

"You never had an affair," I say. "There is no Zoey. It was only Willa."

After a pause, Joni meets my eyes and nods once.

"Why did you lie?" I ask. "Not to the police, but to me?"

"I lied because I needed you here," Joni says, so quietly I don't know if I've heard her correctly. "And I didn't want you to doubt me, even for a second."

I stare at her, the light of the flames flickering across her face.

"Was there a moment when you wished she would die?" I ask, my voice raw.

"Did I ask you that when I found you with Evangeline?" Joni asks.

I think about everything that happened after that night, and I shake my head.

"No," I say.

"Then you shouldn't have to ask me either."

I want to tell her to stop treating this like it's a game, but instead we just stare at each other for a moment. Underneath the sound of the crashing waves, you could almost miss the echoes of everything left unsaid.

––––––––––––

Later, when I climb into bed, still damp from the ocean, I finally ask myself whether I believe that Joni is capable of killing Willa. For the idea of Joni as I once knew her, eyes burning with fury and mirth and the weight of being smarter than most people, attacking someone isn't *entirely* outside the realm of possibility (it wasn't like asking whether *Evangeline* might hurt someone, or even me, at one time), but would she ever lose control so badly she would take away not only someone else's life but also her own? Because why would she kill Willa when she would have known it would also destroy everything else she valued—her career, her reputation, and surely her own mental health? If nothing else, Joni is too smart, too ruthless for that, and even though it's not the most reassuring defense I could make for the person I have lied for, the person sleeping one room over from me, it has to be enough.

I run the scenario in my mind where I take Joni's story at face value. Say she had fought with Willa about Lucien sometime around eight p.m., a fight that ended abruptly when Joni threw the crystal at Willa's head. Then, after hiding out in the bathroom, Joni had emerged to find Willa gone, and a text from her saying that she was going to expose her. So Joni had dropped everything and driven out to see me so that I could cover for her, constructing a story about her own affair to avoid having to tell me about their fight. She went back to the house the next day, waiting for Willa to say whatever she was going to say, only Willa never came back. And instead of helping Joni, that made her story infinitely more complicated, as well as my own.

If Joni had killed Willa before she left, surely she'd have known that coming to me for an alibi wasn't enough—that I would ask questions, that the police would look into it with increased manpower and precision, particularly once they saw the final message from Willa on Joni's phone. And, for that matter, if Willa had still been close enough for Joni to *kill* her, why would Willa have texted Joni to threaten her? No, Joni must have received the message from Willa and left the house almost instantly, which means when Joni came to my cabin, she was asking me to cover up only Willa's injury, not her death. A messy situation, but not a fatal one.

This is the thought I cling to like a life raft as I close my eyes— the promise that Joni had dragged me into her nightmare only half-cognizant of just how much she was asking of me, even though I also realize just how low the fucking bar is at this point.

THIRTY-FIVE

2008

THEO FOLLOWED US UP to our hotel room in silence. He stood in the middle of the room blinking back tears, and I didn't know if I wanted to throw my arms around him or throw myself off the balcony so that I never had to see that look on anyone's face again, least of all his. I felt furious, suddenly, that Evangeline had done this not only to herself but to all of us, and that, after all my countless hours of dreaming, this was the only reunion I would ever get with Theo. I already understood that none of us would emerge from this unscathed.

"I don't understand," Theo said, over and over again until it was almost impossible to bear. "She should be here."

"I'm so sorry, Theo," I murmured, and I felt a clawing at my chest that would never truly leave.

Joni was pacing up and down the room as if she could outrun the claustrophobic weight of Theo's grief. It reminded me again how callous we were to have nearly forgotten for a moment, how willing we'd been to push the accident out of our minds for a few hours.

"Bess," Theo said, his voice splintering slightly. He sat on the bed and, after Joni shot me a look, I sat next to him. I was careful not to touch him, leaving a couple of inches between us to show him that I had received the message before Ev died and didn't expect anything from him, but particularly not now.

"Did she . . ." he started before breaking off. He took a deep breath and tried again. "Did she know? Did she know it was happening?"

I closed my eyes, and when Theo took my hand in his, my heart still fucking leapt and I felt mortified, beyond ashamed of myself. I let my hand go slack, and eventually he released it.

"We were all pretty drunk," Joni said.

"I know," Theo said. "She tried to call me earlier in the night, but I missed it. I don't even know what I was doing. What the fuck could I have been doing that was more important than answering her call?"

I closed my eyes for a moment, wishing I were anywhere but in that hotel room with Theo's grief and my own heartache.

"Please," he said. "Whatever happened, it would be better for me to know. I want to know what she was thinking at the end."

I sat frozen, feeling the wet trickle of shame again. I knew I could never tell Theo what I was thinking in that moment—that it was his fault as much as it was mine that his sister wasn't here, because if he'd never told her about Milos, we'd never have got into a fight that night at all. I looked helplessly at Joni, but her face was unreadable and I felt the room begin to shift, closing in around me, when Joni stepped toward us both.

"Theo," Joni said, in a gentle but firm tone I'd never heard her use. "We know you've just lost your entire world, and I promise that one day we will sit down with you and tell you everything we remember about Ev, but we just can't do it right now. We are right on the fucking edge."

Theo looked between the two of us, and the grief on his face was one of the purest things I'd ever seen. I knew that he was trying to convince himself that Joni was right, that we'd been through too much to relive it so soon, but also that he'd never understand that we'd lost something too, not really.

"Another time," he said, and then he started to cry. I forced myself to place my hand on his arm, and we sat like that until the sky darkened outside the room, and I already knew that this would be the last time I ever touched him.

After he left, I threw away the jersey he'd bought for me.

If Joni noticed it in the bathroom trash, she never mentioned it.

"Mom?" I said later, my voice cracking. I was calling her from the phone in our hotel room while Joni napped, so I had to keep my voice to barely above a whisper.

"Oh, sweetheart," my mom breathed down the phone, and then she burst into tears. I felt something in my chest wrench open.

"We're going to come," she said. "We're going to come and get you."

"There's no point," I said, crying now too. "We'll only be here for a couple more days. Mommy, there's no point."

"I'm so sorry," she said, blowing her nose through her tears. "You shouldn't have to handle this alone."

"I'm not alone," I said, looking over at Joni's back as she pretended to sleep. "I have Joni."

We were called back to the police station once more before we understood that they'd decided Evangeline's death wasn't an accident. We thought it was just more red tape—that we were going back for them to ask all of their remaining questions before they closed the case and released Ev's body back to her family in the US. We wouldn't have left without her, even if we'd been allowed to.

We were separated again as soon as we got to the station. As I filled a paper cup of water from the cooler, I saw Theo being led out of another room, his eyes hooded and downcast. His skin had a greenish, sickly tint to it, and, in the moment before he saw me, I felt his pain deep in my core. When he finally looked at me, I tried to smile, but he just nodded grimly back. It was like the spirit had left his body along with his sister's, and I thought of their devoted closeness: all the private jokes and secret languages I'd observed and envied because I felt my brother pulling away from me at the same time. I wondered where everything went after Evangeline died and if Theo's brain would soon kick into self-preservation mode, repackaging their life together not in fully rendered, devastating detail but in broad strokes only, to protect him during the endless years and decades looming ahead that he would now be forced to endure without his other half.

My interview was with the policewoman from the scene, Eleni. There were two other people in the room too—the same translator as last time and a man I didn't recognize, somber with dark curly hair. He wasn't in a uniform but a gray suit, and he seemed more imposing than anyone I'd spoken to before because of it. Eleni briefly introduced him, but I didn't catch either his name or his title, and I didn't ask. This time, as I took the oath, swearing on a Bible written in a language I couldn't read, I wondered briefly whether I should have asked to bring a lawyer in with me. My mom had asked me the same question the night before, and I had scoffed at her and the implication that anyone might think that Evangeline's death had been anything but the most tragic accident. Getting a lawyer would take time, I told her, and all I wanted was to get back to California.

"Thank you for coming back," Eleni said curtly, and the way she wouldn't meet my eye made me feel less comfortable than I had expected, which, in turn, rendered me indignant—she wasn't being nearly as sympathetic as she should have been, considering my best friend had just died in a foreign country and I wasn't allowed to go home to my family.

"Of course," I said tightly. "Was something wrong with my statement?"

"No, no," Eleni said before letting off a flurry of Greek to the translator, a spidery-looking woman with wispy hair. The woman shrugged and said nothing.

"But a few things have come to our attention that we wanted to ask you about," Eleni said carefully.

I nodded even as my apprehension steadily grew. Eleni and the man exchanged a look, and Eleni made a quick note on her notepad before sitting down opposite me, her palms flat on the table between us. Her nails were unpainted, her nail beds flat and round.

"The house you were at before Evangeline fell—whose friend was that?"

"We met them at the bar," I said. "I only know two names, Pierre and Kevin. That's in my statement already."

"Hmmm," she said, checking her notes. "What do you know about Pierre Lauvin?"

"Literally nothing," I said, and when she stared at me like she didn't believe me, I shrugged. "Why?"

"He's a suspected sex trafficker," she said. "As of three days ago, Mr. Lauvin is wanted in Paris on charges of modern slavery, controlling prostitution, as well as class A drug and firearm offenses."

"Okay . . ." I said. "Well, funnily enough none of that came up."

The curly-haired man looked at me sharply, and I reminded myself that it wasn't Joni I was talking to.

"Funny?" he repeated.

I shook my head.

"Now remind me, what were you and Evangeline arguing about at the party?" Eleni started up again.

I felt a rush of panic.

"We weren't," I said, after a moment. "Arguing."

"We have multiple reports saying that you were arguing. What about?"

"And you think that has something to do with this Pierre guy?" I asked, trying to understand where this was going.

"Answer the question, please," the man said sternly, and I felt something give way in my stomach.

"We were arguing about dumb stuff," I said, unraveling now.

"You don't mention any argument in your statement," Eleni said, looking down at a piece of paper in front of her.

"Because it didn't mean anything," I said. "We'd been away together for a month and a half, and we were drunk and tired and ready to go home."

"Well, we know that *Evangeline* wanted to go home. We know this because she sent a text to her brother at eleven saying you were dragging her to a party."

"No, it wasn't like that. Evangeline wasn't a pushover. If she thought that Joni and I were forcing her into something, she would have complained about it. Going to that party was a group decision," I said, and I realized then that they had no idea about any of us.

"Not Joni and you," Eleni said. "Just you. Evangeline told her brother that *you* were the one who coerced her."

"That's bullshit. I couldn't force Ev to do anything," I said, my voice loud. "She's the most stubborn person I've ever met."

Eleni said something in Greek to the translator, who nodded before turning to me.

"Evangeline was clearly frightened enough to take a photo of

224

the driver's license plate," the translator said, her voice less animated than Eleni's. "She sent it to her brother from the car."

I paused, horrified at the thought of Theo talking to the police about me.

"She wasn't scared of us," I said quietly. "Of me. She was just cautious."

"And you weren't," Eleni supplied. "Cautious of these strangers, these grown men."

"No," I said, as I felt my grip on reality shift slightly.

"I wonder why that is," she said.

I shrugged, hoping beyond measure that this marked the end of the interview, that I could get out of the sticky windowless room and call my mom and tell her I'd changed my mind, that I did want her to come and hug me and stroke my hair until we could fly back to California together and forget any of this ever happened.

"Now, when Evangeline fell," Eleni said. "Was she distressed?"

"Distressed?" I repeated, swallowing. "No, not distressed."

"And while you were walking, did you notice anything else different about her, her general demeanor or appearance, that could be of note?"

I remembered Ev's face, pale and wretched in the moonlight as I walked away from her.

"No," I said, my eyes filling with tears. "Other than that she was happy."

"Was Evangeline a virgin?" the man jumped in, and I flinched at his question.

"Excuse me?" I asked.

"Evangeline was less sexually experienced than you and Joni, correct?"

"I guess," I mumbled, shame pouring over my every nerve.

"How many sexual partners have you had, Elizabeth?" The man leaned toward me, and I could smell the coffee on his breath.

"I want to go now," I said. "I thought you were just tying everything up. I didn't know . . . I had no idea that you'd ask me stuff like this. Am I free to leave? I can just walk out?"

Eleni and the curly-haired man exchanged a look. The man cleared his throat before speaking, his voice grave: "You're free to leave, Elizabeth. But you should know that from this point, you are no longer a simple witness in this investigation. You are considered a suspect, and you will be wise to have a lawyer present in all future communication with either us or the prosecutor assigned to the case. We will need to take a new statement with your lawyer present, and then we will inform you of how the case will progress."

I felt the blood rush from my head as I stood up and pushed my chair back. The interpreter was watching me with barely concealed pity, and it made everything even worse.

"How could you think I'm capable of being involved in this?" I asked Eleni, and she looked away.

"It's not my place to judge your innocence," she said. "I present the facts, and it is for someone else to judge you on them."

I didn't wait to find out if she was talking about a judge, God, or the rest of the world. Maybe she meant a combination of all three. I ran out of the room, tears blurring my vision as I searched for Joni.

Joni was waiting for me, ashen-faced, in the lobby, and I knew she'd had a similar experience. She grabbed my hand and we walked grimly toward the exit of the police station, where there was a crowd of thirty or forty men, journalists and photographers from the mainland and other territories in Europe, all shouting our names. Blinding cameras flashed and microphones were shoved in our faces as strangers yelled questions we couldn't begin to comprehend. "Don't cry," Joni muttered to me as we fought our way through the crowd toward our waiting taxi. "Just keep walking."

Word was out that Stavros Aetos's daughter had died and that her best friends were implicated.

"We need to tell them the truth," I said, whispering underneath the jaunty music blaring from the speakers in the taxi. "This is fucking insane."

Joni shook her head, frowning and gesturing toward the driver.

"We have to," I said. "Joni, we have to tell them."

"We can't," she said then, so quietly I had to lean in toward her to hear.

I shook my head, my eyes filling with tears as I understood just how much of a stupid mistake we'd made at the exact moment I also understood that Joni was right, that it was too late to rectify it without casting even more suspicion over ourselves.

We had made our choice, and now we had to live with it.

Later, in the hotel room, Joni stood in the bathroom, washing her underwear in the sink, her cheeks red and mottled as she rubbed hand soap into the crotch of a Calvin Klein thong.

"Is there anything you need to tell me?" Joni asked. "From today's interview."

"Like what?" I asked.

"Like did they ask you about any details I should know about?" Joni asked. "That you forgot to tell me."

"What are you talking about?" I asked, and Joni looked up then, her eyes flashing with fury in the reflection.

"We need to take this seriously, Bess," Joni said. "I'm the one who's risking everything here, so the least you can do is be fucking transparent with me, since it's obvious this isn't ending here."

"Joni," I said then, trying to be braver than I felt. "If you want to back out of this, say it now, and I'll understand. I swear I'll always understand."

"It's too late for that," she said. "You really don't understand anything."

We stared at each other, and I debated asking whether Joni actually had any idea what we were doing or if she was just better at pretending.

"I said everything we planned," I said finally. "Broad strokes with few details."

"Broad strokes," Joni repeated. "So no more details about your walk, or the last moments before she fell, or what she was wearing, or exactly how she screamed."

"I told you," I said testily. "I wasn't there when she fell."

After a moment, Joni nodded, but she still looked unhappy.

"I just hope I didn't get anything wrong," she said, wringing out her underwear.

After that, we finally had the presence of mind to call our parents and request a lawyer for our follow-up interrogations. We both held the phone away from our ears as our mothers cried and screamed, and we had to be the calm ones, comforting them and pretending everything wasn't as bad as we now knew it to be. Later, we snuck down to the hotel computer in the dead of night to trawl through the growing list of articles about us—inflammatory headlines printed below angelic photos of Evangeline, or photos of us stolen from our (apparently more public than we thought) Facebook profiles that showed us drinking or flipping off the camera or looking generally depraved. There must have been a leak at the police station, because the connection had already been made between us and Pierre Lauvin, a well-known figure in the hospitality scene in Europe, most notorious for securing girls to grace the decks of wealthy men's yachts for the summer, and God knows where else. We found out from an article in the *Daily Mail* (headline: AETOS ANGEL'S DEATH LINKED TO PARIS SEX RING) that Pierre had dined in the same Italian restaurant as we had the night before, something the press and prosecution would fixate on for months, even though there was no evidence to prove we were even there at the same time.

"They want us to be guilty," I said to Joni as I flicked open another tab.

"I know," she said.

"Are we really as bad as they say?" I asked, squeezing my eyes closed in an attempt to stem another wave of nausea. The new headline described us as cold and unflinching, emotionless as we left the police station hours after Evangeline's death. *Numb,* I wanted to scream. Emotionless isn't the same as *numb.* Emotionless isn't the same as willfully disassociating from the real world because it's too fucked up, too illogical for you to even try to comprehend. Already a portrait of us both was being painted, however tentatively at first, a little shading here and there, a few words like "outgoing" or "wild" thrown into an otherwise neutral article, but it wouldn't be long until the broad strokes began painting Joni and me as sex-crazed jezebels. The kind of girls who wouldn't think twice about luring their friend to her death just so that they could carry out their depravity, their feral agenda, with no fear of judgment or fallout.

"No," Joni said, but she seemed as uncertain as I'd ever known her to be. "They're just scared of us because they don't understand us."

THIRTY-SIX

2018

I PRETEND TO READ MY book in the living room while Joni holds an emergency meeting with her lawyer in her mezzanine office. I hear snippets of their conversation—legal terms that bring back a flood of unwanted memories (a cramped room in a police station, my lawyer's concerned face as she translated page after page of police reports for me, the strangers who took one look at me and decided I wasn't built to be free)—until eventually I clamp Joni's noise-canceling headphones on and listen to the sound of blood rushing in my ears instead, like I'm swimming in my own panic.

At around noon, they come downstairs and Joni introduces me to Kelly, a diminutive woman with RBG glasses and a huge Hermès bag, who looks me up and down with barely concealed disdain, and whose handshake grip is featherlight, as if she can't let go fast enough. I watch Joni closely as she ties her trench coat over her jumpsuit, but she won't meet my eye either.

"Where are you going?" I ask, unable to keep a note of desperation out of my voice.

"I have to go to the police station," Joni tells me calmly, and it feels like she's just kicked me in the gut.

"It's all going to be okay," she says. "I promise."

"You're going with her, right?" I say to Kelly. "You have to be in there with her."

"I'm going in voluntarily," Joni says, her tone still infuriatingly even. "As a witness."

"Come on, Joni," I say, panic rising in my voice. "Seriously?"

"It's a matter of optics," Kelly says tersely, clearly the type of intelligent person who doles out sparse information only to get frustrated when others can't keep up.

"It's not like last time," Joni says to me. "I'll be back in time for dinner."

"Is everything going to be okay?" I ask the lawyer, but she pretends not to hear me. Joni grabs my hand, her eyes drilling into mine.

"I'll be back for dinner," she repeats. And then she smiles at me.

"Why can't you just pretend to feel something?" I ask then.

Joni drops my hand. "Excuse me?"

"Just for me," I say. "Just pretend to be normal for me. You're making it so hard."

Kelly watches warily as Joni takes a step toward me, but I hold up a hand to stop her.

"You loved Willa, I know you did. So whatever happened, however badly she hurt you, this should all still make you feel something. And if it doesn't? Just fucking pretend like the rest of us do."

Joni shakes her head.

"I know it might sound callous, but I've already grieved the future I thought Willa and I would have together," she says. "And

231

I'm not going to put on some histrionic display just for you, Bess, of all people, especially not in my own home."

Her almost clinical conviction is so familiar to me that, as I listen, something close to relief weaves its way through me because it actually makes sense, in a way that only works with Joni's logic. I feel something, some fear or resentment, deflate inside me. I'm not entirely sure what I expected coming back here, when Joni has never done what people expected of her. She has always been volatile and odd, honest to the point of brutality. It was part of the reason I was drawn to her in the first place and the reason I most feared her—Joni can't pretend to feel something she doesn't, or be someone she isn't. Joni would never tell you she missed you if she didn't, or pretend to care about someone she didn't. Because, up until the past three weeks, I have only known Joni to lie once. And it was to protect me. I think of the aftermath of Evangeline's death and how life could feel almost normal in the pockets of time between grief, but then how the air would suddenly turn to stone around me and it felt like I might never breathe again, and I choose to understand what Joni is saying, even if nobody else would.

"I have nothing to hide, Bess," she says, and I let her familiar confidence soothe me.

"Please come back," I say, and Joni smiles before turning away from me.

"Everything needs to be *beyond* watertight," Kelly reminds Joni on their way out, and we all know exactly what she means. I need to keep my shit together if I want to protect her.

———

Somehow I fall asleep on the couch, waking up around six p.m. to the vast gray marine layer rolling in outside the window. I stare out at the sky, trapped in that slippery in-between place that isn't quite a dream but isn't consciousness either, and, once the room has darkened around me, I move into the kitchen. Trying to keep my panic at bay, I carefully chop chilies and cloves of garlic before sautéing them like my dad taught me when I was a teenager. On another gas ring, I heat a pan of water, adding a pinch of salt and half a pack of spaghetti that I found gathering dust at the back of another cupboard, perhaps because Joni believes carbs have "bad energy." Once I've drained it, I mix the pasta in with the garlic, oil, and chilies and I pour it all into a large bowl, decorated with lemons and olive leaves, that reminds me of Evangeline.

I carefully set the table for two, and then I sit in a chair facing the front door with my bowl of pasta untouched, waiting for Joni to come home.

It's after eleven when the front door finally opens and Joni stands silhouetted in the frame, a stream of bright flashes punctuating the shouts of reporters behind her for just a moment before she slams the door shut.

"Sorry I'm late," Joni says, grinning as she strides toward the table, flicking on the overhead lights as she does. At the last minute, she detours via the kitchen to pick up a bottle of red wine and two glasses, then I stare at my friend as she sits down opposite me and messily serves herself pasta, nonchalantly twirling the spaghetti around her fork.

"What did I miss?" she says, once she's swallowed a mouthful.

"Joni," I say. "What did they want from you?"

"I already told you," Joni says. "They just wanted to run through the timeline again."

The timeline, I think, with a thrum of dread.

"Did they ask about me?"

"Only insofar as confirming where I was that night," Joni says, careful to avoid the word *alibi.*

I nod wordlessly.

"It's all going to work out," Joni says firmly. "You just have to trust me for a little longer. It's nearly over."

Joni takes another mouthful of spaghetti, smaller this time, and I stick my finger in the pile of oily noodles in front of me. The food is cold, practically congealed.

"You don't have to eat this," I say.

Joni smiles at me. "I want you to know how grateful I am to you for still being here. It means everything to me that I don't have to be alone right now."

"Oh," I say, awkward in the face of her sincerity. "Well, being alone has never really been your thing."

"I don't know," Joni says slowly. "I've had to get pretty good at it over the years."

I feel a pang of anger, because whatever she wants to believe, Joni has no clue what it's like to be truly alone. And not alone because you're built that way, but because you don't think you're worthy of anyone else. As far as I can tell, Joni rebuilt her life so that she was surrounded by people right up until the night Willa disappeared.

"After we got back from Greece?" Joni says quietly, sensing my skepticism.

"You weren't exactly *lonely*," I say. "You adjusted pretty well, from what I remember."

Joni looks at me strangely.

"Not lonely, Bess. *Alone*," she says. "For a while, I had no one. Ev was dead and you were . . . disappearing. I could feel you slipping away day by day."

I'm about to correct her when I realize that I'm doing exactly what was done to us back then—I'm judging her interior life on the self she presents to the world. I'm also engaging in a pissing contest with the only person who might, underneath it all, actually understand how I feel right now, how I've felt since the day we got back to California. I try to ground myself in the present, letting old resentments soften, begin to break down inside me.

"Didn't you ever want to disappear too?" I ask, and Joni opens her mouth to say something, probably to indignantly inform me how hard she has worked to rebuild her life from the ruin, no, the mere *rubble* that was left for her to work with, but then she also catches herself.

"Sometimes," she says softly. "Recently, I've had this . . . I don't know, this thought that I could just get on my paddleboard and swim out as far as I can without turning back. And maybe I drift on to somewhere else, start some other life far away, or maybe I just stay out there in the middle of the ocean, floating on the waves. Leaving nothing of myself behind. Either way, I'm not frightened, Bess. I'm not leaving because I'm scared or because I'm being driven away or anything. I'm leaving because it's time. I'm leaving because it's the only way I'll finally be free."

"Joni," I say. "You're scaring me a little."

"Not like that," she says, smiling. "And it's not like I'm . . . I'm not *ashamed* of anything I've done or how I've tried to help people, and I don't know how I could have done things differently, but it does sometimes strike me how . . . *cruel* it is that my only way out was to bind myself to my worst moment for the rest of my life. And that's just a fact. There will never be a single interview or talk I give where I don't have to reference what happened to Ev, and to us, before I say anything else. Where I don't have to pretend that we were the lucky ones. And now it will be the same with Willa."

I reach out and take her hand, smoothing my thumb over her cool skin. Joni always did have cold hands and feet, like an amphibian.

"Maybe I was always destined to climb over the bodies of those I once loved to get where I needed to go," Joni says, smiling weakly at me. "But some days, I just don't have the stomach for it."

Later, I open an email from Steven with a link to a not-so-blind article on a celebrity gossip website. The photo shows me fleeing Whole Foods with my hand obscuring most of my face, alongside a photo of Joni taken from behind as she walked into the police station earlier today. As dread builds inside me, I read the accompanying words:

THE SIRENS' SONG

Which late-aughts gruesome twosome seem to have reconnected over yet another tragedy? The echoes of the past are as indisputable as this podcast host's God complex after another young woman meets a tragic end in a luxury oceanfront locale. And in yet another twist? Rumor has it this duo's alibis are even more entwined than they are...

Every single one of the 360 and counting comments guesses the article is about me and Joni.

THIRTY-SEVEN

2008

WE WERE ARRESTED TWO days later, hours after the local newspaper printed the photos of us smiling and eating ice cream on the beach, splashing around in the water like we had not a care in the world less than twelve hours after Evangeline's death. We had already been caught on camera leaving the police station, heads down, eyes burning, and Joni's "just fucking peachy" would be replayed over and over, the f-word bleep somehow making it even harsher and less appropriate for the circumstances. It was after the taxi driver claimed on TV that he'd heard us rehearsing our stories in the back of his cab, in the same segment that saw the hotel receptionist describe how horrified poor Theo had been that I'd rifled through his dead sister's wardrobe like a vulture. The press had already decided that Joni's smile was cunning, that my wide-set, icy blue eyes were unsettling as we left the police station the second time, after "refusing to cooperate." The police were open about the fact that they didn't think we were acting appropriately considering our best friend had just died (smiling, *laughing* even), and their darkest suspicions about us would soon be confirmed over and over again with each unofficial character statement that came out, embalmed for years to come.

We were still staying in the hotel, so I'm not sure if the adult film we'd watched for all of ten minutes had been discovered yet, or the vibrator that had languished forgotten in the secret compartment of my backpack since I'd landed in Greece, but that would all be found eventually, spurring hundreds of conspiracy theories about Joni's and my plans to sexually corrupt and dominate our friend. It was after they'd searched the house in Tinos, finding the notes Joni and I had sent each other, but before those notes leaked to the press. Nobody knew about the text message Evangeline had sent Theo on our way to the villa, but it would soon be printed on the front of newspapers across the globe, and by that point there was no way of arguing back, no way of telling the world that *obviously* it had been a joke, that Evangeline was just falling back into the easy roles we'd carved out for ourselves—Ev as the angel, Joni and me as the bad influences—when actually it was always more complicated than that.

Kevin had already told a local news channel that Evangeline and I had been arguing just before she died, implying that we had been in the middle of some sort of love triangle, but it was before they came up with the nickname "Hollywood Heathens" or the connection to Pierre Lauvin, who they conveniently then forgot when he turned out to be just another red herring in a seemingly endless string of them, just six months later. They had, of course, already trawled through our Facebook accounts and selected the most incriminating photos (Joni and me in matching bikinis at a party in Woodland Hills, posing with empty bottles of Hennessy in a hot tub with another girl from school; me on the back of an already forgotten classmate, my legs wrapped around his waist as I lined up a beer pong shot, my cheeks glowing and eyes demonically red from the flash), making sure to reference our photo albums with dumb titles taken from song lyrics, like "Bona fide hustler making my name" or just "Lick me like a lollipop," but it was before they hacked into Joni's account and found the messages we'd sent each other, cruelly and mechanically dragging our sexual conquests, people with dreams and parents and feelings who would then be approached for a statement. That reveal would come later, once we were already in prison and didn't have access to the internet, along with the video of me blind drunk in Evangeline's house, rolling around on her cherry-print bedspread and telling her I wanted to fuck Leonardo DiCaprio's brains out.

There were hundreds of eyewitness accounts of us being drunk and slutty (or sloppy and careless, or standoffish and snobby, depending who was remembering) the day Evangeline died, and CCTV footage of us brazenly doing shots at the bar as she looked on. The words to describe Evangeline were already predictably anodyne: *shy, beautiful, reluctant, sweet*; the inference being that we had dominated and corrupted her, that her only mistake had been in getting in with such a callous and sadistic crowd. This was around the time the international media caught up with the story too, that Stavros Aetos's American daughter had died in suspicious circumstances abroad, and by that point it was out of anyone's hands— everyone had their own theory about who we were and what happened that night. The coroner said it was impossible to determine whether Evangeline had fallen or been pushed, and, just like that, the demand for our blood had begun.

Everyone always talks about things being taken out of context, but in our case, it felt like the exact opposite—every single thing we'd ever done or said was now viewed only through the prism of Evangeline's untimely death. We were depraved, evil, and nobody had to look far to confirm it. We had dug our own graves years before we set foot on that plane, and, in the end, I couldn't even blame the police for what they did to us. They were receiving too much attention, too much pressure, to be seen to be taking it easy on us just because we were young and privileged, from "good" families and affluent homes. And the worst part was that it was all true—the messages and photos and witness accounts maligning us. Other than the story of what happened to Evangeline on that particular night, everything was true.

Joni and I waited in the damp hotel room, taking turns pacing the length of it. We both understood what was coming, and we could barely look at each other for fear of this worst of suspicions being confirmed in each other's faces. My body trembled as panic coursed through my veins, and Joni had to all but force me into the shower after she noticed the dirty black soles of my feet. She didn't need to tell me it would probably be my last hot shower for a while, and I sank to my knees under the burning water, covering my eyes as I begged for it to all be over soon.

They arrested us at our hotel in the middle of the day, making sure there were plenty of photographers around to capture it. Our parents were due to arrive in a matter of hours.

"Don't cry," Joni said to me again as we were led out of the hotel in handcuffs. "Never let them see you cry."

THIRTY-EIGHT

2008

WORLD NEWS TODAY

IF I DIE TONIGHT

By Alexa Huber
August 6, 2008

A teenage joke or a final plea for help? In the case of
Evangeline Aetos's death, nothing is as it seems . . .

Ask Elizabeth "Bess" Winter and Joni Bonnier, and they'll tell
you that Evangeline Aetos's death was a tragic accident. One
misstep after a wild night in the hills of Mykonos, and the
beautiful heiress's life was extinguished in seconds. The girls
were celebrating their high school graduation with a summer-
long trip to the Greek Cyclades Islands when tragedy struck.
And it sounds simple enough, until you scratch beneath the
surface of the story. Then you'll find that behind the gloss of

privilege and those steadfast claims of sisterhood lies something altogether much more sinister. For the first time, we can *exclusively* reveal the final text message sent from Evangeline to her beloved brother, Theo, along with a chilling photo of the license plate of the car that would ultimately deliver her to her fate. Words that will haunt Theo, as well as Bess and Joni, forever:

If I die tonight, you know who to blame.

It was only hours later, in the early hours of July 31, that Evangeline fell to her death from the hills above Agios Stefanos—an idyllic, sandy beach just over two miles from the main town of Mykonos Island. She'd been at a debauched party with Bess and Joni at the house of disgraced French playboy Pierre Lauvin, but how did someone like Evangeline, someone exclusively described only as a perfect student, a perfect daughter, a perfect friend, as being fundamentally opposed to cruelty in any form, as having judgment well beyond her eighteen years, end up at a party like that in the first place?

Joni Bonnier grew up in the affluent suburb of Calabasas, California, with her cosmetic surgeon parents, Sara and Michel. According to a friend of the family, Michel Bonnier had left the family home for good less than two months before the girls left for their fated trip to Greece. "Joni wasn't dealing with it well," my source tells me. "She lost her temper a lot, smashing photo frames and even punching through a wall in the hallway. Her own mother was terrified of her." Michel, now back in Paris with his new partner, would say only: "I haven't spoken to my daughter in months and I have nothing to say about what has happened in Greece. I'm as shocked as anyone."

Bess Winter grew up in the suburbs of England before her mother's academic career brought the whole family to

Southern California. Jennifer Liu, a former classmate of Bess's (now a freshman at Stanford), called to tell me about her. "Bess kind of flew under the radar at Calabasas High. She was quiet but not in a self-conscious way like most of the other girls. You know the movie *The Talented Mr. Ripley*? It felt like she could have been like the Matt Damon character, you know? Like one day she might just turn around and do the perfect impression of some mistake you'd made in English lit two years ago, something even you'd forgotten you'd said."

Another classmate recalls his horror when Joni and Bess flicked pieces of a dissected sheep's eye at each other during a biology class ("The other girls were *crying*, and here are Joni and Bess acting like it was the funniest thing they'd ever seen"), and yet another recalls the time a furious Joni broke a girl's ankle on the soccer field with a nasty tackle, all because "she was embarrassed the girl had kicked the ball through her legs to score." Then there are the persistent rumors of blood rituals between the friends, where they would streak their faces with their own menstrual blood and proclaim themselves blood sisters. The stories like these are plentiful—people who always suspected something wasn't right with these two girls and their friendship, however solid it looked from the outside. As another source puts it: "Evangeline was the outlier in that group. She always seemed sweet, kind of shy and even a little nerdy. But obviously she was loaded. It wasn't hard to see what the other two saw in her, if you know what I mean."

So what went wrong? From the moment the girls arrived in Evangeline's childhood haven of Tinos, Bess and Joni appeared dissatisfied. In notes written to each other on Stavros Aetos's own stationery, the girls plotted their escape from the island, likening Evangeline to their prison keeper. However beautiful the setting, they clearly had something darker, something more depraved in mind ...

Evangeline was uncharacteristically inebriated when she left the bar in Mykonos that night. She followed her friends because she trusted them, and they led her right into the lion's den. The press has been speculating about what they were doing at Pierre Lauvin's party at all—maybe Joni and Bess had concocted a sickening plan to sell Evangeline's virginity (a plan they might well have shared with Pierre himself at dinner in town the night before), or maybe they planned to get Evangeline drunk enough that they could coerce her into a compromising position with a mind to blackmail Stavros Aetos with the photographic evidence. The grim possibilities are endless, and, for now, all we know for certain is that three people went to that party in Agios Stefanos, and only two left alive. And only two were photographed the next day, laughing on the beach as their friend's body lay in a morgue.

So we return to that haunting message, sent hours before her untimely death: *If I die tonight, you know who to blame.* In a final act of bravery, Evangeline wanted everyone to know that whatever happened next, her best friends had already betrayed her loyal, trusting nature. All Evangeline had wanted was to share a cherished part of herself and her history, and, in return, these two disturbed young women had led her down a twisted and dark path that ended, ultimately, inevitably, with her death. Blame may be a meager consolation for her grieving friends and family, but, in a final gift from Evangeline herself, at least in this case it is unequivocal.

THIRTY-NINE

2018

AFTER ATTEMPTING TO SLEEP in restless, trippy stints, I'm woken up for good at six a.m. by my phone buzzing on the floor beside my bed. I groan when I see that it's my brother calling, as I figure he'll be in full panic mode at this point, reading God knows what about me on the forums. I ignore his call, knowing I won't be able to reassure him. Moments later, he texts me a link that appears on my home screen.

WILLA'S LOVER ARRESTED BEFORE DAWN

Ignoring the three dots indicating Steven's still writing a message, I scramble instead to open the link, my heart in my throat as I think that it's happened again—that Joni isn't at home at all but is locked in a cell somewhere, silently waiting for strangers to devour her existence and dismantle every choice she's ever made. I am almost blindingly relieved to find it's not Joni who stares back at me from the lead photo but a lanky man wearing a jean shirt and a yellow baseball cap, smiling as he poses with a rifle against a bruised violet sky. I scan the article, reading about the case the police have been building against Lucien Miller: a secret meeting spot with Willa in the rocky bluffs over Malibu; a surface blow to her temple consistent with an uneven, sharp object; a coroner's ruling of death by strangulation; and finally, what has become the key piece of evidence against him—traces of Willa's blood on the inside passenger door handle of Lucien's car, a blue Toyota Camry, suggesting she had been trying to escape from him the night she was killed. Once I've finished reading, I stand up so quickly I have to steady myself on the wall.

"Joni?" I call, moving across the bedroom and out into the living room. "Joni—have you seen?"

Joni is sitting on the sofa in a pair of reading glasses, taking a photo of the Lorrie Moore anthology in her hands. She raises an eyebrow and places the book on the arm of the couch as I stand in the doorway.

"They've arrested Willa's boyfriend," I say. "They're saying he was the last person to see her that night."

"I know," Joni says calmly. "Kelly rang me half an hour ago."

"Why didn't you wake me up?"

"The news is still news whether or not you're awake to hear it, Bess," she says, sounding mildly bemused.

"I'd still like to have been told," I say, and Joni smiles at me before turning back to her book. I stand uselessly over her, waiting for her to say something else. Anything else.

Everything is a choice, I remind myself. *Trusting Joni is a choice.*

"He was clay pigeon shooting," Joni says after a moment.

"What?"

"The photo they've used with the rifle," Joni says. "They've made it look like he was hunting, but he was just shooting clay disks."

"How do you know?" I ask.

"Willa took me to the same place for my birthday," Joni says, without looking up from her page. "But I was smart enough not to be photographed."

Hours later, I watch on the local news live as Joni stands less than thirty feet away from me on the other side of the front door, making a statement to the waiting press. On the screen she wears a pair of oversized sunglasses, and she is as tragic and beautiful as a Cindy Sherman self-portrait.

"There are no words to express the depths of grief I'm feeling at the news of Willa's death," Joni says hoarsely. "We have lost someone so bright, someone so deeply *cosmic*, that it seems almost inconceivable that we were lucky enough to have had her for as long as we did. Please respect both my own and Willa's family's privacy during this devastating time."

When Joni comes inside, she throws her sunglasses across the table, and we both flinch as they clatter to the floor.

FORTY

2018

THE REPORTERS ARE LEAVING for the night for the first time in weeks, and even though another young woman is dead, this alone feels like a miracle.

Joni and I stare at each other as the steely sky darkens outside. When the final journalist has gone home, Joni asks me where I would go if I could go anywhere in the world, and my answer feels both impulsive and inevitable as soon as the words have left my mouth.

I tell Joni I want to go to Evangeline's old house.

At the back of the Aetoses' Eagle Hills house is their private golf course. When we were younger and had stayed out later than our curfew, we'd get our friends to drop us off behind it so that we could sneak across the grounds to crash in one of the Aetoses' many guesthouses without waking anyone up. There is still a small gap in the bush we used to slip through, and Joni and I squeeze through it now, careful not to snag ourselves on any stray branches.

"You know her mom wouldn't have noticed if she didn't come

home at all," Joni says as we walk toward the house. "I think Ev just wanted to fit in."

When we reach the edge of the golf course, we both stop automatically. If we go any further, we will cross over into the grounds of Evangeline's childhood home, and it's as if there is a force field that prevents us both from doing it. The house is as isolated as a chateau, and we both stare up at it, instinctively feeling for each other's hands in the dark. I always wondered whether it would live up to my memories of it if I saw it again or whether, like Ev, my memory of the house had been transformed by the tragedy and I'd return only to find it diminished somehow, without the turrets and sweeping arches and the hundreds of flowering cherry trees Stavros once planted in an attempt to placate his wife after yet another business trip that went on for too long.

"Is that her?" Joni asks, squeezing my hand, and I follow her eyeline up to a room on the east wing of the house. Inside the bay window, I can see Evangeline's mom in a dressing gown, her white blond hair wrapped in a peach towel. From here, she looks the same, perfectly preserved in her Marie Antoinette bedroom like a doll in a dollhouse. I hold my breath as she moves around the room slowly, picking things up and putting them down. I wonder if we're spying on her bedtime ritual as she stares at herself in a mirror for nearly a full minute, and I realize I never had any idea how she spent her days, or any of her time when we weren't sticking our heads around her bedroom door to assure her that Evangeline was in good company.

"This is weird," I say as I exhale. "This is a weird thing to be doing."

"You wanted to come," Joni reminds me, because, as always, she's making me *own* my decisions, my darkness, and the truth is that I'm grateful she doesn't let me slip out of any of it and pretend that I want to leave, because I don't want to stop watching. It feels like we're looking into a window of a past life, and before I can stop myself, I remember how Evangeline would walk in each night to dutifully kiss her mom good night, one light peck on each cheek, a formality neither of them seemed to enjoy. My chest feels tight as Joni and I stand hand in hand, waiting for something.

"I'm jealous of her," I say, finally giving words to the nebulous feeling that has rippled through me since Evangeline died. "I'm jealous that Theo and her parents still get to think she's perfect, that she'll never screw up her life and be unable to blame anyone else for it. I'm jealous that she never felt ashamed, or lonely, or scared of who she might become."

"How do you know she didn't?" Joni asks.

"Come on, Joni. Ev is still the most well-adjusted person I've ever met."

"Only when she got what she wanted," Joni says. "She needed to be in control of everything to feel okay. Look, it's human nature to want to believe that there is sense in the senseless, like all that shit about how she was too pure for the earth, and how only the good die young. But you know that's just stuff people tell themselves to give meaning to something that is meaningless, right?"

I shake my head. "But she wasn't like us."

"So, where does that leave us, then?" Joni asks. "You think we should carry that burden for the rest of our lives?"

"However you want to look at it, we set it into motion," I say quietly. *I set it into motion.*

"Bullshit," Joni says, her tone fierce. "You can talk to yourself however you want, but I have too much other shit to deal with to feel guilty about being eighteen and kind of an asshole. We were just learning who we were, we weren't fully formed or even half-formed. We were just kids."

I feel a wave of uncertainty, like Joni has cracked the smallest opening inside me.

"Ev made some choices too. Good and bad. Like the rest of us."

I close my eyes for a few seconds. When I open them, Joni is staring at me gently.

"You're doing her a disservice," Joni says. "Ev was so much more than an angel. She was a teenage girl."

I've already turned away to leave when Joni grabs my arm and makes a soft whooshing sound as if she's been punched in the stomach. Behind Mrs. Aetos, the bedroom door is opening slowly, and I find that I'm holding my breath, willing it to be Evangeline.

"Oh shit," Joni breathes, and I can see that it's not Ev but Theo who has walked into the bedroom. It's Theo who is now standing next to his mother, but it's not the Theo I saw in the magazine spreads or the corporate portraits, it's Theo as he was in Greece— Theo in a T-shirt and shorts, his hair a little too long and messy, his smile wide and untouched by tragedy or loss. I blink a few times, and as he approaches the window to draw the curtains, I notice the changes in him—the thicker arms, the shadow of facial hair. For just a moment, I imagine that he sees me, crouching in the bushes and watching his everyday tragedy, but then the thick curtains fall across the window, and I realize that he wasn't looking for me at all.

As Joni drives us back to Malibu, I close my eyes and think again about what she said about Evangeline. I know that I, along with the rest of the world, have been guilty of mythologizing Ev after death, but I also know that I brought out the worst in her that summer, and that, without me, she would have lived past her nineteenth birthday at least, perhaps would still be here today. Or maybe not here, in this car with me and Joni, but somewhere far away, because the Evangeline of my creation drifted away from us after that summer, throwing herself into life at Brown before moving to New York to become a food stylist after college, like she'd always wanted. I can almost picture her now—frowning slightly as she moves a sprig of rosemary one millimeter over for the fiftieth time, training a team of juniors who adore and envy her in equal measure, and I wonder if her quiet determination might have grown into a worldly confidence the moment she was away from the slippery trappings of her childhood.

Tentatively, I wonder who I might have been in this same universe, and whether Theo would be in it with me, but I keep drawing a blank, like even my subconscious has put its foot down and placed a limit on my capacity to self-harm.

FORTY-ONE

2008

AFTER OUR ARREST, WE were held in a police cell in Mykonos for twenty-two hours. Both my parents and Joni's mom had flown out, and between them they had found us an Athenian lawyer, Nikki, who explained the complex judicial process to us. The statements we had given as witnesses would be inadmissible now that we were suspects, so we would have to give another statement, no longer under oath. When Nikki asked if I'd had any of it explained to me by either the police directly or through the translator, I didn't know what to say. I'd had so much information hurled at me in both English and Greek over the days following Evangeline's death, and I hadn't known how to process it—how to separate it into categories of things that were normal procedure and things that might destroy my life. All I'd known was that guilty people hired lawyers, and while I was guilty of many things, pushing Evangeline wasn't one of them.

Nikki explained that we would be escorted to the prosecutor's office in Syros, where we would appear first in front of an investigative judge and then before the prosecutor assigned to our case. These two people held our future in their hands—between them they would decide whether the case would be dropped and we could fly back home with our parents, or if our nightmare would continue.

From a holding cell in Syros, I scanned over the lists of evidence and translated witness testimonies that the police had gathered to support the charges against us, unable to focus for too long because I still didn't believe any of it was happening—not only that Evangeline was dead but that these adults, these experts, these people I had actually *met*, somehow thought Joni and I had planned it. I saw references to Pierre Lauvin, to Joni and obviously Evangeline, but also some names I didn't recognize who must have been either guests at the party or associates of Pierre. Nikki explained that Pierre had made a career out of securing young women to accompany wealthy men on yachts, and that there was reason to believe this was more than just an escort service, that it was used to traffic women. It seemed so outlandish that anyone would believe that Joni and I had got caught up in some sort of sex trafficking scandal that I almost felt relieved when she said it. Surely any judge would understand that Joni and I had no idea about any of it and that our biggest mistake had been buying into the lies that had been sold to us—that we would ever truly be sexually liberated, that the summer after we graduated high school had to be unforgettable, that we would be friends for the rest of our lives. At any rate, I figured that my parents' presence in the country would somehow restore some sense of order, of normalcy to our lives.

I had one supervised visit with my parents in Syros, and my knees buckled when I walked into a windowless interrogation room to find them waiting for me, so incongruous to the setting I was now worryingly used to. When I sat down, I noticed that my mom's roots were pushing through, the gray hairs wiry and star-tling, and my dad's hand trembled as he pressed his cup of water against his lips. They both had a constant supply of tears, enough for us all, that leaked down their cheeks throughout the meeting.

"I shouldn't have let you come," my mom kept repeating. "I had a bad feeling all along."

"I'm so sorry," my dad said. "Love, I'm so sorry."

I never asked what he was apologizing for.

"This is preposterous," he said too. "They must know this is entirely preposterous."

I thought of Evangeline's pale face when I left her on the rocks.

"I don't know," I said.

"Is it true what they're saying?" my dad asked before I left, and my mom clenched her hand around his arm as a warning. "In the press?"

"Which part?" I asked.

"The bad parts, Bess," he said, already looking older than he had before he'd asked me the question.

"Most of it," I said. "Yeah."

Soon after, Nikki gravely told us that the authorities were going to push for a charge of murder. Not death by negligence, loosely com-parable to a manslaughter charge (where we might have turned on our friend in a drunken haze), but cold-blooded, premeditated first-degree murder. While the transcripts of Joni's and my initial police interviews were now inadmissible in court, someone at the police station had leaked them to the press, and outside scrutiny on the case had only intensified. It seemed almost absurd to me at first, this sex-cult-gone-awry angle—the idea that Joni and I had tried to initiate Evangeline into Pierre's sex ring, and, once she refused, we decided she was worth less than nothing to us. They were supporting this claim by presenting the Tinos notes—that stupid, unfunny trash we'd written purely to impress each other, which now counted as evidence, however flimsy, that getting rid of our friend was already in the forefront of our minds. They would imply that we were sick of feeling judged and cloistered by her, of always feeling so envious of her wealth and popularity and her goodness, and had decided to exact the ultimate revenge. Theo Aetos had, after all, received that final text from his sister, forecasting her own death. If I felt sick reading Theo's name and the message that lost any nuance, any humor when you knew what came after it, I felt even worse when Nikki told us that a devastated Stavros Aetos supposedly wanted every avenue not only pursued but ransacked in the hunt for justice for his only daughter.

"The country has been crippled by this recession," Nikki told us sadly, as if it were some sort of logical explanation for what was happening. "There's a lot of anger and frustration."

I thought about the things I'd been reading about Greece's fate in the same newspapers that tore Joni and me to shreds, how unemployment and financial rot were already threatening to ravage the infrastructure of the entire country, and how they'd known it was coming for months, even as the hotel staff and restaurant servers had forced friendly smiles and pretended for us that nothing was wrong, and a heavy knot formed in the pit of my stomach.

"It would be unfortunate if they decide to proceed with the charges," Nikki said as we were escorted through the courthouse by armed local police officers. "But stranger things have happened."

Unfortunate, I thought, rolling the word around my mind as I weathered another thick wave of nausea. Unfortunate is dinging your rental car when you're on your way to return it, or planning a barbecue only for it to rain the entire day. Unfortunate is not being detained in a foreign country for killing your best friend,

and understanding that while you may not be guilty of that specific crime, there are a thousand other ways you need to feel ashamed
of yourself.

"And what happens if they do that?" Joni asked. "How long
until we would get to trial?"

"We wait. Six months, a year, up to a maximum of eighteen
months while we build our cases," Nikki said apologetically. "It's
a long time."

I sat next to Nikki in the prosecutor's office in Syros, stricken
and numb. I listened to the translator's gentle tone as Nikki presented an initial defense, first to the investigative judge, a dispas-
sionate older woman who made sure to meet my eye as she asked
me to confirm parts of my statement I barely remembered, and
then in front of the prosecutor, a young woman with close-set eyes
and a hard mouth who fired off a stream of questions that I answered falteringly. As Nikki tried to persuade these strangers that
my only crime was being reckless and young, I figured that everyone was probably right, that the person they were talking about
didn't sound like she deserved to be free at all. After a conference
with the prosecutor that lasted less than thirty minutes, the judge
took one final look at me and ordered my pretrial detention at
Korydallos Prison. As foreign nationals, Joni and I were automatically considered flight risks.

———

Joni and I were handcuffed and bundled into separate police cars
that would take us to our home for the foreseeable future. Korydallos was the only prison with a women's wing that could accom-
modate us, and it had been gleefully described as one of the most
notorious prisons in Europe in the media coverage I'd read. As
Joni and I stood on the empty top deck of the ferry, under police
custody, the engine rumbling beneath our feet as the incongruous

crystal ocean unfolded behind us, neither of us said a word. After a while, I squeezed my eyes shut because I understood that it was the last time I'd see anything so beautiful, so uncomplicated, and I figured knowing it was the worst part.

I thought about my parents flying back to Los Angeles and having to pick their lives back up without me. I thought about my place at NYU—how, any moment now, some other student would be called up off the waiting list and she'd be the one taking my place in a week, shyly joking after class with people who were never destined to become my friends. I thought about Ev's body being transported back to Calabasas, where she would now never leave, and of Theo, boarding a flight back home without his sister, and then I decided not to think anymore. Instead, I let a strange sense of disassociation wash over me as we reached the mainland, as if I had floated out of my body somewhere over the Aegean Sea. I figured this couldn't actually be happening to *me*, not really, because I would never have turned and hugged my parents calmly after our fates were sealed, nor would I later be able to withstand being screamed at like an animal as I was led into a stinking, roach-infested cell fit for two people that was filled with five strange and hostile faces I would soon have to know and understand. There was no way any of this was actually happening, because I simply wouldn't be able to survive it, and the fact that I could still taste the salt on my skin from the ferry ride from Syros made it all the more surreal.

Every day I woke up, shocked that I hadn't faded away in the night, and every night I somehow found myself still there, closing my eyes in the vain hope of getting even an hour's sleep amid the sickening heat and the shrieking and the crying and the yelling that was so loud it felt like the walls were vibrating. I retreated further into myself, avoiding eye contact and dutifully doing anything that was asked of me, eating whatever was given to me, until I could barely remember what I even used to do or say, or like or dislike. Joni would sometimes kiss the top of my head or take my hand in hers, but even she knew not to demand anything from me. And somehow, that's how it worked. I just kept on surviving, even when I wished I wasn't.

FORTY-TWO

2008

WHAT ELSE IS THERE to say about prison?

Prison is your best friend's voice in your ear, telling you every-thing is going to be okay.

FORTY-THREE

2018

IDREAM OF EVANGELINE FOR the first time since she died.
We're in a parking lot on the edge of Venice Beach, and she is
finally learning to skateboard. I watch as she scoots herself along
slowly at first, barefoot in the smocked dress she bought on Olvera
Street, before carefully placing her second foot on the board. She
sails across the tarmac for about thirty feet before jumping off, the
board skittering from beneath her feet and landing in the sand.

"Bess," she calls, waving me over. Her cheeks are glowing with
pride as she redoes her ponytail.

"You just have to pretend," she says, once I am close enough
to hear her. "I never understood, but that's all it is. You have to
pretend like you can do it before you can."

I'm chiseling away at an ancient jar of instant coffee when something catches my eye through the window. A black car, low and
silent, creeps slowly past, stopping for just a moment outside the
front of Joni's house before quickly pulling away. As soon as it's

gone, I move toward the window and close the shutters. I'm still standing there when Joni walks into the room.

"I've now seen the same black Tesla drive past twice," I say. "And that's just the times I've noticed. It can't be a journalist, right?"

"In a Tesla?" Joni says. "Unlikely."

"Okay," I say, grateful once again for her infinite well of confidence.

I try to work for a few hours while Joni has a meeting with her publisher, but I find that I have the concentration of a hoverfly, staring at threads and threads of messages and somehow being entirely unable to decipher what is happening, as if I'm trying to read a language I was once fluent in. Do people really send harshly lit photos of their most vulnerable body parts to a stranger they met five minutes ago? Do they really bring up their dead wives, dead brothers, dead parents so soon, trusting someone on the internet with their most damaged selves? This time, when my brother calls me, I answer it.

"Hey," I say.

"Where are you?" he asks irritably. "Mom said you were back in the cabin, but I'm outside and it looks even more desolate than usual."

"I'm at Joni's," I say. "You should have called first."

"Bess, I really think you should leave Malibu," he says. "Just until this is all over."

"It's already over," I say slowly. "Didn't you read the article you sent me? Willa's boyfriend was arrested yesterday."

"I know that he was arrested," Steven says tersely. "But Nova has a contact at the sheriff's department, and it sounds like even they know they're reaching. This guy's saying the blood in his car was old, that he hadn't even seen Willa in over a week when she disappeared. He just fucked up enough in the interview to secure the charges against him, and I don't think I need to remind you how that can happen, Bess."

There's a pause, where I don't say anything.

"Will you please just be careful?" he asks, his tone softer now.

"Steven," I say. "You don't need to like Joni, but you can at least accept she isn't a murderer."

"I'm not saying Joni did anything," Steven says. "Or even that this boyfriend of Willa's definitely didn't. But I know I don't like you being there alone."

"I have been alone since I was eighteen years old," I say. "I don't know how it's slipped your memory, but you weren't exactly desperate to be around me when I came home."

"This isn't about that," Steven says after a moment.

I let out a loud snort to show him what I think about that.

"That woman is like a hurricane, Bess," he says. "She breezes through the world entirely on her own terms, not caring when she leaves mass destruction in her goddamn wake."

"Listen to me," I say, my voice barely above a hiss now. "Joni is the only person who's ever even *tried* to help me rebuild everything I lost, instead of treating me like some hideous monster to be hidden away or, more specifically, unveiled only once you're engaged and it's too late to bolt. So you need to drop it and let the police at least attempt to do their job, Steven. It's over."

I hang up the phone without waiting to hear his reply.

FORTY-FOUR

2009

AFTER SIX MONTHS IN Korydallos with no trial date in sight, our lawyer, Nikki, informed us that while she was still working on collecting enough evidence to apply for a review of our case, we had also been held for long enough that the judicial council, the dikastiko symvoulio, would be legally obliged to review our case regardless. They would decide whether there was enough existing evidence to continue to detain us or whether the case should be thrown out, in which case we would be released and free to fly back to the US.

When Nikki said we had a good chance of being released, I didn't believe her. I couldn't imagine a world outside this rotting cell with the flickering light I had memorized the patterns of within the first week. I was eating less and less by this point, causing my parents to panic when they last visited and saw the bones jutting out of my T-shirt; my lips too big, jaw too angular for my face. They complained that I wasn't being looked after adequately, and, as a result, I received the occasional visit from a harried doctor who would sit and watch me make one biscuit last an entire hour. It meant that my cognitive abilities were diminished, my thoughts lumbering and heavy. Daily tasks like reading or going to the bathroom took extra focus, extra effort, and even though I felt Joni's frustration with me, I also knew that I would never have to explain it to her, how much of a relief it was to regain control over even one aspect of my life again.

In the end, Nikki was right. The judicial council ruled that the charges against us should be dropped and we should be released. Pierre Lauvin's own case in Paris was languishing without any concrete evidence to prove his trafficking charges other than the testimonies of a few women who were even less likely to be believed by a jury than Joni and me, and it was likely that he would be given less than a three-year sentence for the firearm possession charge. It made everything else too circumstantial, and, in a way, Joni had been right from the start—without a conspiracy charge, it was impossible for anyone to know what had happened on the cliffside, particularly since we had both been up there, obscuring any unequivocal identification of one perpetrator. It was suggested that the initial investigative judge and prosecutor had both adopted the same attitude as the police force, pressing charges based not on hard evidence but on instinct and emotion alone, the hunch that there was something not quite right about me and Joni, as if punishing us and locking us up would keep their own daughters from drinking and partying and from believing they were owed the world.

A police source suggested to the *Athens Times* that Stavros Aetos himself had also waded in to request our release, but this was never corroborated by anyone else, nor by Stavros himself, whom we never heard from once. It was generally accepted that the police had been tough on us, tougher than they perhaps needed to be, but they found a way to blame us for this too. If we hadn't behaved as *brazenly* as we had the night leading up to Evangeline's fall, if we hadn't been so *consistently* foolish and reckless with our own safety, if we hadn't acted so very *strangely* after our friend's death, then the police would have left us alone. Instead, we had all but railroaded them into pursuing us—it would have been an open-and-shut case if we hadn't implicated ourselves so heavily just by being our unsavory, humiliating selves. And so, six months after Evangeline's death, we were released back into a different world, one in which the paparazzi waited for us at every turn, and where every stranger on every corner of every street had an opinion about our innocence.

My parents and Joni's mom met us at the prison, where we had the final rounds of paperwork to fill out under Nikki's supervision. In hushed tones, knowing our time together was limited, Nikki told me that, under Greek law and the terms of res judicata ("a matter decided"), there was no way they could overturn the ruling in a year, or ten years, or twenty years, or if someone somewhere changed their mind one day. When I didn't believe her, she explained that anyone whose innocence had been asserted by the judicial council could not be punished or prosecuted again for the same crime, except in two specific circumstances—bribery of a judge or forgery of evidence. Neither of which would ever apply to my case. I knew that she was trying to instill in me a sense of relief, of security, but, as my parents looked on, cheeks still streaked with tears, I felt anything but safe.

I was silent as I waited for our possessions to be returned to us, but I nearly broke down when they handed me back not my phone and passport but the daisy friendship anklet they'd cut off me when I was being processed. The final item they handed over was the striped T-shirt dress I'd hastily thrown on when the police turned up at the hotel, now immortalized by the thousands of photos that were taken as Joni and I were led, stone-faced, from the police car into the station. I held it out to my mom, tears streaming down my cheeks as I shook my head, *no*, and she took it gently from me and handed me a tote bag instead. Somehow she had already considered this and packed a change of clothes for both me and Joni, as well as deodorant and a sugary breakfast pastry each. I put on the sweatshirt and jeans, and, as I pushed a pair of gold hoop earrings through my ears, I tried to imagine my old self returning to my body. I felt nothing.

Joni's mom had hired a minivan with tinted windows, and we were bundled from the prison and into the waiting car, through the thick crowd of journalists and news anchors in bright suits, all of whom innocently wanted to know how it felt to have our "freedom" back, whether we felt vindicated by the judicial council's decision, as if they hadn't played any part whatsoever in what had happened. Even as we ran to the car, I remembered to widen my eyes to make them look less steely, less unflinching than I now understood they looked naturally.

The driver sped away, and the outside world felt too bright, too potent, too beautiful to last, so I kept my eyes closed for most of the journey, my hand tucked inside my mom's. When the prison was no longer visible in the rearview mirror, Joni wound down the window and stuck her head into the void, her tongue dangling in the wind, and I had to look away.

There were more photographers and journalists waiting for us in a clump at Athens International Airport. They filmed from the moment the car pulled up to the curb, following us as we walked through the terminal, my dad's arm wrapped protectively around my shoulders as he tried to shield me from the attention. We moved as one in the end, a large mass of bodies walking together with opposing agendas, and I could hear the photographers laughing, joking with each other about something unrelated even as they took the photos that heralded my freedom. I understood then that it was just a job for them, one small sliver of their day, and yet it was to become my entire reality as the world tried to work out how to place us now that we were free—were we victims or masterminds? Women to be feared or girls to be pitied?

My parents started sobbing the moment we were inside the plane, their grown-up, substantial bodies racking with relief that the nightmare was almost over. I felt too stunned to cry, but when the wheels left the ground, I finally allowed myself to look out the window. I pressed my forehead against the warm, rattling plastic and watched as the city of Athens grew smaller and smaller below us until it was all but consumed by blue. I imagined the other prisoners below, the prison reduced to the size of a pack of my former cellmates' cigarettes, and instead of feeling better, I felt like I couldn't breathe. I knew then that I could never return to California as the same Bess who had left it, because I knew too much. I understood something that nobody else on this plane, not even my parents, would understand: I had learned how fragile it all was—that my entire life could be reduced to something smaller than a matchbox in the blink of an eye.

I looked away from the window and caught Joni's eye across the aisle. She smiled thinly at me, and I knew that she was thinking the same thing.

FORTY-FIVE

2018

ON THE WEEKEND, I spot the Tesla drive past the front of the house again. I mention it to Joni, but she dismisses my concern with a roll of her eyes as she hands me a cup of black coffee.

"I don't know if you've noticed, but those cars are rife around here," she says. "Malibu is riddled."

I nod, but I can't quite shake the feeling that it's more than a coincidence.

"Have you thought about what you want to do with your own car?" Joni asks. "As in, are you willing to accept that it's clinically dead?"

"I'm working on it," I say, thinking of my Saab collecting dust in the neighbor's garage. When I tried to start it a few days ago, it sputtered and wheezed for a few seconds before giving up any pretense of being a functioning vehicle.

"Can I loan you the money for a new one?"

"Joni," I say. "I'll figure it out."

Joni pulls up a chair opposite me and starts signing a pile of her own books while I go back to my cases. They are all fairly straightforward until I get to one in which the female complainant has reported a male user for verbal abuse. With a feeling of dread, I scan the messages for anything out of the ordinary before coming across a wave of language so graphic in nature that it instantly makes my stomach turn. I push my laptop away, as if the extra few inches of distance could ever protect me from the knowledge that humans like this exist in the same world as us, that they could be the person checking out our groceries or at the gas pump next to us, offering a polite smile.

"What is it?" Joni asks, noticing my discomfort as she looks up from the book she's signing.

"It's just work stuff," I say, struggling to keep my tone calm. "A particularly rough interaction. I guess I'm out of practice."

Joni nods and puts the lid back on the Sharpie she's been using to write the same note over and over again:

Dream big and choose YOU! Joni Le Bon xo

"Don't you think that's a good thing?" she asks me curiously. "Do you really want to be desensitized to that shit?"

I shrug. "It's the only job I've ever had."

"And why did you choose it?" Joni asks. "Because you love sifting through the dregs of humanity every day? Or because it means you can work alone, at home, without having to communicate with another soul, even those whose behavior it is you're judging. Instead, you can just dole out these judgments in the few seconds you have to decide, and you can feel like you're contributing to society in some way without ever having to risk anything by actually participating in it."

I pretend to be focusing on the screen in front of me as I reopen the same case and, without reading any of it again, immediately click on *block*. It doesn't make me feel better, since I know that this guy will be back under a different name within hours, and even if our software catches him, he'll just move on to one of the other apps, and then on to Reddit or the dark web, where he can spew his hatred all over again once the next woman unknowingly triggers him.

"Who would you be if you could be anyone in the world?" Joni asks then.

"Like a celebrity?"

"No," Joni says impatiently. "What is the best version of Bess Winter you can imagine?"

I pause, still unsure what she's asking me.

"Think about what you want from life," Joni says. "Because it's not just going to fall into place unless you fight for it. Remember you came here because you needed something to change."

"No," I say slowly. "I came here because I couldn't stay at my cabin. It was too exposed."

"If you believe that, then you're lying to yourself," Joni says. "You came here because you knew you wouldn't get away with whatever it is you've been doing in the desert all these years. You came here because you knew you couldn't hide from me. And, if we're really being honest about it, that's also why you lied to the police. I think it's the bravest choice you've made in ten years, so I'm going to make damn well sure you own it."

I wonder if she could be right.

Joni smiles at me gently, and, after a moment, I smile back.

"You know I dedicated this to you," Joni says. "The book."

She flicks through the copy in front of her before holding it up so that I can see the dedication page. Sure enough, there it is in print:

A long-winded, self-indulgent appeal
for B. W. to be fearless

"The book's about the choices we make every day, often without realizing it," Joni says, her eyes flicking over a table of contents she must have already read a hundred times. "And how if these choices are only made to avoid some imagined worse fate, we end up losing trust in ourselves. And, you know, self-trust can be a slippery fish to win back."

I feel a crack of gratitude in my chest as she closes the book.

"I don't know if you win a fish," I say eventually. "It feels like you didn't fully commit to the metaphor."

Joni finally looks at me.

"Santa Barbara Fair 2006," she says. "I won a fucking fish, Bess."

As soon as she says it, I remember it—a tiny orange thing that was nearly translucent. It puffed up like a pine cone one day, and then disappeared from the tank shortly afterward.

"Think about the last time I told you to trust me," Joni says. "It worked out in the end, didn't it?"

Sitting here, opposite Joni, as the warm sunlight streams through the windows, it almost feels like it did.

"I guess so," I say, before adding, "with a slight blip in the middle."

Joni smiles at me, and I realize it's the first time I've ever turned our past into anything resembling a joke.

"But that was because we were so shockingly depraved, don't you know?"

"Well, here's to being a depraved heathen," I say, a smile creeping across my lips too, and I can tell that I've finally shocked Joni by the way she chokes a little on her coffee. She wipes her mouth with the back of her hand, leaving a smear of clear gloss on her skin.

"To shameless heathenry," she says, holding her mug of coffee up to mine. "May they know us, may they loathe us, may they fear us."

I meet her eye and I grin at her, and, for just a moment, we're back to the land of the before: the place unmarred by regret or death or penance, the place where our immature jokes could be forgotten the second they left our mouths and we leapt down steps and careened around corners without dreading what was ahead because we were free to be as weightless and shameful and alive as we wanted, without thinking for a second that we would ever have to temper it, or that any of it would catch up with us in a million years.

———————————

I resolve a few more cases, but the next time I see one that makes me flinch—an older woman sending graphic photos for cash—I close the platform altogether. Then I email my manager to ask him for a couple of weeks off. It will be the first holiday I've requested since joining the company eight years ago.

Because maybe Joni's right.

Maybe I deserve more than this.

———————————

Later, when Joni sends me into the depths of the garage to find her KitchenAid mixer after I mentioned I was craving her banana pancakes, I lift the corner of a large waterproof sheet to find a pile of old paddleboards and oars. There is a red board—smaller than the others—a slightly moldy-looking green one, a deflated kayak, and there, right at the back, is the ocean blue board Willa was holding in the photograph I stole. When I run my finger down it and find that it has a large crack in the middle, I feel almost sick with relief that Joni wasn't lying to me about one thing at least.

FORTY-SIX

2009

B EING BACK IN THE Calabasas house was surreal, but I didn't feel relieved. I realized when I saw it looming above me through the windshield that I hadn't dreamed of it once when I was in prison, and there was little to remember or miss about it. I told myself to be grateful for the security at least, manned gates that kept the reporters from swarming around the house like locusts, and uniformed men who denied entry to the macabre true-crime aficionados lingering outside, desperate to catch a peek of a potential psychopath.

My parents had watched me for the entire journey home from LAX as if I were liable to disappear again at any given moment, and even Steven eyed me suspiciously in the rearview mirror as he drove, like the sister he knew had been replaced by an imposter he didn't entirely recognize.

Almost as soon as I walked through the door, I announced that I needed a nap, and my parents looked at each other helplessly as I walked up to my bedroom alone. Once inside, I flopped onto my bed and clamped my cuddly toy dog tightly to my face as I breathed in his familiar, slightly musty smell, tears stinging my eyes.

After a while, Steven walked in and stood over me.

"Hey," I said, sitting up.

"Hey, sis," he said, and I noticed then that he'd grown two or three inches in the time I'd been gone.

"How's life in Calabasas?" I asked, and when he only shrugged in response, I wondered not for the first time how it had been for him to have my private life made so public, my rotten core ripped open for everyone he knew to gleefully devour.

"I'm sorry about Evangeline," he said, sitting down next to me. "As well as everything else."

I blinked back tears, unexpectedly touched by his words, and I realized that, in the chaos of everything that followed, nobody had actually said that to me yet.

"Do you need to, like, talk about it?" he asked, already wincing slightly in case I said yes or, worse still, began to cry.

"Not really," I said, and he nodded, relieved even though it meant we were fresh out of conversation.

"Did you know that there's a disease where maggots hatch under your skin and no one knows how they got there?" he asked eventually.

"Please do elaborate," I said, settling back down on the bed and closing my eyes.

My conversation with Steven that day was the last time anyone in my family would address Evangeline's death outright. It was as much my fault as it was theirs—I knew that I could never reveal all the horrors I'd learned about the world when they weren't there to protect me, so, instead, we skated around the topic with the grace of a corps de ballet. Evangeline's death became "the accident," and the media train wreck that followed just "what happened to me." My incarceration was often defined as "when you were away," and the entire sorry affair was summed up simply by the term "in Greece." It was a shorthand that we would all have adopted seamlessly by the end of the year, until we stopped referencing it altogether. The atmosphere in our house became heavy with the weight of everything left unsaid, my parents circling me uneasily as Steven spent less and less time at home, often staying with a friend or girlfriend for days at a time to avoid being anywhere near me.

Outside the house was a different story. Everywhere I went, someone wanted to talk to me about what had happened. My dad's lawyer friend had advised us to get out and about as soon as possible in an attempt to defuse the interest, but I still felt exposed, like I had been stripped down naked for strangers to scratch their opinions onto my bare skin. Each whisper, each frown, each polite smile offered up like a compromise in exchange for their judgment of me felt like a direct indictment of my lifestyle. I wondered if the checkout girl at Macy's who avoided meeting my eye had memorized the evidence against me—the guys I'd fucked or hurt, the callous things I'd said—or if she too had just been offended by my general demeanor: the ruthlessness in my eyes or the set of my unsmiling mouth.

The news articles and TV reports kept coming, often oscillating wildly between sympathy and suspicion even within a single segment or piece. The author would express a basement-level display of compassion that we had been falsely accused, but the rest of the piece would still pit us against Evangeline, would still be dripping with the implication that we had brought it on ourselves by behaving so badly. As the guy delivering my Chinese takeout put it: "Damn. You're either the luckiest or the unluckiest girl in the world, right?" I wanted to tell him that I was neither. That it could happen to him too, when he least expected it, and that I doubted his slate would be entirely clean when it did—that he'd never written a text that could be misinterpreted, or wounded someone who had liked him, or captioned a photo with song lyrics that might come back to haunt him. Instead, I gave him a five-dollar tip and closed the door.

My parents went back to work part-time, but when they were home they continued to wait on me like I was fragile and in need of extra care, while Steven carried on with his junior year of high school. I tried to venture out like I was told, but I grew to despise leaving the gates of my estate. Instead, I would walk around the neighborhood at night, all too aware that any person I met, even looked at, could fixate on something seemingly innocuous about our interaction to fit their own narrative instead of the truth, whatever that was. I had no control over what other people believed about me, and I barely even knew who I was anymore. As a result, I mainly stayed locked up in the house, a feeling of pure, icy terror gripping hold of me whenever I thought about starting at NYU the following fall.

Joni was, of course, the opposite. Within three weeks of being home, she had somehow secured an internship in New York at *Dollface*, a burgeoning website and monthly zine known for its razor-sharp wit and feminist politics. Joni informed me that she planned to move to the city for the five months before she was due to start at Berkeley, in a vigorously breezy manner that implied she knew I would take it as a blow, since I was the one who was supposed to be in New York, and she was supposed to be the one staying in California.

"But you hate New York," I said. "You're always bitching about the East Coast."

"Plans change, Bess," Joni said, as if I hadn't already discovered this when I was staring at the peeling white bricks of a prison cell instead of walking through Washington Square Park with a cup of coffee and a Meg Wolitzer book tucked under my arm. "Why don't you come with me?"

"I can't," I said, and by that point I could barely muster up the energy to care about anything for too long. Everything seemed deeply and unsettlingly insignificant compared to the fact that Evangeline was dead, and my secrets would never be my own again.

By all accounts, Joni thrived in her new city, the city that was once supposed to be mine. She still got tailed by the paparazzi occasionally, but I could see in the defiant way she dressed (ripped jean shorts and cutoff vintage tees, crystal headbands and cowboy boots), and the way that she glared into the camera one day and grinned the next, that it didn't bother her. She called me every week to beg me to come and stay with her, but I always found a reason not to. Then, in her second month at *Dollface*, Joni was given a fifteen-minute weekly segment on their radio show, doling out friendship and life advice to callers, somewhat ironically at first and then more earnestly as she grew in confidence. She used to send me clips of her favorite episodes, and it frustrated me that she didn't know she was being used—that the only reason she was getting all of these opportunities was because of the publicity having Joni Bonnier attached would generate.

"I'm going to change my name for the radio stuff," she told me one day as she walked to her favorite East Village spot, Cafe Mogador. I held the phone slightly away from my ear so that I wouldn't have to hear the new composure in her voice, the aura of confidence she'd somehow spun out of dirt. "What do you think of Joni Le Bon? It still feels like me, but also an upgrade. Like I'm simultaneously putting on a pair of couture wings and also giving a giant 'fuck you' to my dad, which I obviously don't hate."

I thought it sounded like pretentious bullshit, but I didn't comment.

"Does anyone ever mention what happened to us?" I asked softly instead, and I could hear Joni suck on her rolled-up cigarette (another new habit she'd cheerfully adopted). "In New York, I mean."

"I don't let them," she said. "Because I always mention it first. I don't want anyone feeling sorry for us. That would be the worst thing of all."

I thought about how the list of everyone I'd ever hooked up with was emblazoned across the internet for anyone to read, and how most of the world knew the color of my first vibrator. I thought about the website I'd stumbled upon the other day: BessandJoni AreGuilty.com, which detailed every piece of circumstantial evidence against us, every single accusation and judgment ever made by either someone we knew or a random journalist with no skin in the game other than to sell copies or ad space so that they could make some rich asshole even richer and they could keep their own kids in private school and the newest Jeremy Scott shoes, and how the website also had a forum, where people could share their own theories about what happened that night, and people still wrote in to drag us even now, nearly nine months after it happened.

So no, people feeling sorry for us wasn't the worst thing of all. Not by any stretch.

Where did you go, Joni? I thought as we hung up.

FORTY-SEVEN

2018

T
EN YEARS," JONI SAYS, staring into her wineglass when we're halfway through dinner, a couple of weeks later. "In six weeks, it will be ten whole years she's been gone."

For the first time, I don't feel panicked when she says the words.

"Do you think we should do something?" Joni asks. "Nothing big. Just me and you, honoring her in some way."

"Maybe," I say, thinking about what that would look like. For some reason, I'm imagining us aboard a small boat in the Pacific, struggling to keep a candle alight in the wind, like Ev was fucking Princess Diana, and the image makes me smile. Maybe it would be okay to remember Evangeline as she was, now that the dust has settled.

When the doorbell rings, Joni and I look questioningly at one another before smiling again in quiet recognition. Of course neither of us invited anyone over. We don't have any other friends, and even the most dogged reporters packed up and left weeks ago, turning their feverish attention to a teenage boy who poisoned his family in San Pedro.

"Possibly a delivery," Joni says, when I'm already pushing my chair back from the table. "Would you mind?"

I open the door a few inches and my breath dies instantly.

Theo Aetos is standing on the doorstep.

"Bess," Theo says evenly, and I turn around to look for Joni to ground me, but she seems as lost as I feel. I stumble backward, and in doing so implicitly invite Theo inside. As the door closes behind him, I spot the black Tesla parked across Joni's driveway.

"I saw you on the security footage outside my mom's house," Theo says, his eyes flashing with something I can't identify.

"And you've been following us since then?" Joni asks, her eyes narrowed.

"I haven't had much luck getting hold of either of you," Theo says, his voice rougher than I remembered.

I walk numbly back to my seat and Theo follows, sitting in between us, at the head of the table. I try not to think how the last time we were in the same room was at the police station in Mykonos days after Evangeline died, when I thought he might split open from grief and confusion. I wonder if Theo remembers that too, or if the faces and memories became hazy and blurred in the weeks after Evangeline's death. If I became interchangeable. I look down at my ripped jeans and hoodie and think that this is how Theo will remember me forever now, replacing the golden eighteen-year-old with lemon-bleached hair and a Sharpie heart drawn on her foot.

Joni recovers first, offering Theo a choice of drink. As she's reeling off expensive whisky and mescal brands, he listens in a way that only reminds me of Ev, before asking for a glass of water. While he's interacting with Joni, I allow myself to study him, even though doing so feels almost bone-shatteringly painful because Theo looks even better than he did ten years ago, his face weathered in a way that implies a life filled with wholesome outdoor pursuits like kitesurfing and camping, as opposed to other markers of aging that come from overindulgence or extended periods of depression. His eyes are still a piercing green, and he has filled out somewhat, but overall he wears the past decade well, the only signs of tragedy being an intensity where there was once a boyish levity, as if he were somehow in on the joke of his own appeal.

While Joni is pouring the drinks, I feel Theo's eyes on me in return. I wonder what he sees, whether he feels embarrassed for me and the ways I've changed, or whether he still sees the same catlike eyes, the same sharp teeth set within a mouth he once deemed attractive enough to kiss. I smooth my jeans, and when Joni hands him his drink, I'm the first to look away.

"Thanks," Theo says as Joni takes her seat, opposite me.

"I've tried to get in touch with you," he says to me. "Did you get my emails?"

I just stare helplessly at Joni until she swoops in to rescue me.

"We're sorry we went to your mom's house," she says. "With everything that had been happening with Willa, and the anniversary of losing Ev coming up, we just wanted to remind ourselves of better times, but we weren't thinking straight. We shouldn't have gone there."

"No," Theo says. "You shouldn't."

"It's been a strange time," Joni says, studying Theo quickly. "I'm sure you'll understand."

"I heard about your fiancée," Theo says stiffly. "I'm sorry for your loss."

"Thank you," Joni says, after a moment in which we're all at pains to be quiet, paying our respects to the dead sisters and fiancées and child beauty queens. Then: "Fucking men."

Theo only shrugs in response in a way that feels unfamiliar, even though this shouldn't surprise me as I know nothing about him as he is now—this new version of Theo with a rose gold wedding band resting against his tanned knuckles, whose eyes I can barely bring myself to meet. He takes a sip of water as I search for the warmth, the compassion I remember from that summer.

"What exactly . . ." Joni starts. "Can we do for you?"

"I want to know—" Theo says. "I need you to explain why you never got in touch."

For just a moment, my heart is suspended in the air, waiting for him to reach out and grab. But then he frowns and starts again, and this time I can hear the bitterness simmering beneath everything he says. "You were with her when she died, and you never for one moment thought I might have some questions. Instead, you come back to LA, and you pretend like nothing happened. You pretend like I didn't lose the single most important person to me and that I might want to, you know, hear about her last days, or moments, or even talk about why the rest of the world was so happy to believe you killed her."

I stare down at my hands, unable to look at him.

"Theo," Joni says. "I understand that you're angry about what happened, but there is no happy ending to this story. There's no meaning, there's no closure that we, or anyone, can ever give you. She's just gone."

"You," Theo says, turning his focus on her. "You have built a career on my family name, and still you never think to check in on us? What happened to radical honesty? To healing past wounds? To open communication? Where the fuck do I fit into all of that?"

Joni sits back in her chair, stunned, and I try to absorb it all, the rawness of his grief. I remember now that Evangeline may have hero-worshipped Theo, but, in return, she was both his anchor and his safety net. As well as the sheer, unimaginable grief, the loss of his opposing force must have left Theo so stunningly unbalanced that it would have been impossible for him to continue along the path he'd once assumed was set in stone. I feel a sudden crushing sadness for him and everything he lost that night too.

"What is it that you want to know?" I ask, surprising both myself and Joni, who shoots a furious look at me. Theo takes a deep breath.

"Everything," he says. "For you, Evangeline is just one chapter among many more, but for her? The three of us? We were it. We were the whole book for Ev."

Joni stands to get a bottle of wine, and I slowly lift my eyes to meet Theo's.

You can do this, I tell myself. *It's time to remember.*

Tentatively, we land on the good stories first—memories that capture Ev's humanity, her innate hatred of cruelty and injustice, because these are the qualities we've internalized despite our best efforts, the ones we made ourselves remember because *only the good die young.* Then, little by little, as the wine bottles empty and Theo softens slightly, we open it up wider, inviting in the half stories, the ones without a perfect arc or lesson learned, the forgotten one-liners that captured Ev's immaturity or snobbery, and others that showcased her surprising sense of humor.

Once the stories have dried up and my face hurts both from smiling and trying not to cry, Theo drains the last drop of wine from his glass in a decisive manner that makes me think the night is over and somehow we have all survived it. I wait for him to stand up and leave for another lifetime, but instead he leans in toward me, so close that I can see the cabernet stains in the grooves of his lips.

"And the end?" Theo asks then, his green eyes landing on mine.

I try to catch my breath, but I am frozen, blindsided even though of course this was coming, of course we couldn't distract him only with shiny stories about when Ev was breathing and fallible, ignoring the moments before her young bones shattered on the rocks.

I meet Joni's eyes, and, almost imperceptibly, she shakes her head.

"I wish there was more to tell you about that night, but it just happened," Joni says. "There was nothing remotely special about it, other than that was the night we lost her. It doesn't help to try to give it some profound meaning now, Theo. Believe me, I've tried."

"You know, I think a lot about the last time I saw her. That last night in Tinos," Theo says then, his eyes still on me. "Bardo said she cried. Were we cruel to have left her?"

I feel a wet trickle of shame down the back of my neck.

"She seemed really happy," Joni says after a moment. "In Mykonos . . . You know that Ev was too good, too happy to hold on to anything dark for long."

After a moment, I nod my agreement.

"She was happy," I say quietly. "I remember her being happy."

Theo swipes at a tear, and we sit in miserable silence until he regains his composure.

"I should get going," he says, pushing his chair back. "I'm staying at my mom's for the week. Not that she'll notice if I'm not there."

"Of course," Joni says, the relief on her face enough to make me wince.

"Is it okay if I leave my car in your garage tonight?" Theo asks, and when he stretches, I can see a line of his bare stomach, softer and hairier than it had been ten years ago. I look away quickly so that he doesn't catch me comparing him to a boy, really, who doesn't exist anymore.

"How will you get back?" Joni asks, a note of irritability in her tone.

Theo looks down at his phone. "Embarrassingly, my mom's driver is always on call. In case she runs out of anything, I guess . . ."

He doesn't say what "anything" is, but we all know that he's talking about whatever it is that wraps her in a cloud of numbness, whatever it is that cut the cord between her and the rest of the world. Whatever it is that made him and Evangeline cling to each other like orphans when they were kids.

"You didn't drink that much, did you?" Joni says, even as she eyes the empty bottles of wine on the table, the telltale deep red rings of our glasses sinking into the wood. I shoot her a look to tell her that she's being rude, that if Theo wants to leave his car in her garage, she should let him, and not because it means I might get to glimpse him one final time tomorrow but because it's the least we can do for him.

"The only life lesson my old man has ever deemed worthy of passing on is to avoid cars, water, and heights if you've been drinking. Needless to say, after what happened to my sister, I avoid all three."

I peel a clump of green candle wax from the table to avoid looking at Theo.

"I'm sure it will be okay on the street," Joni says. "This is Malibu."

Theo and Joni stare at each other for a moment, and I feel as if I'm witnessing a battle of wills I don't fully understand.

"I'm sure it will be too," Theo says after a moment, and even though he's now acting like he's embarrassed to be making a fuss, I know that people like him, people who have been raised to feel entitled to the big things, people who have been taught that others exist to serve them, don't get embarrassed by their wants, not really. "But the car was a birthday present from Sophia, and I'd appreciate it if I could use your garage for the night."

After a long, heavy pause, Joni wordlessly takes her car key and walks out the front door to move her car out of the garage. Once she's gone, Theo reaches out to touch my arm. I glance down at his hand, and then up at his face, and I feel a kick of desire deep in the pit of my stomach. For just a moment, I allow myself to wonder if Theo had always wanted to get me alone, and whether Joni had sensed it.

"Bess, did I do something to you?" Theo asks then, his voice low as Joni starts the engine of her car in the garage. "Is that why you don't want to be near me?"

I want to tell him that the reason I don't want to be near him is that even though he was never mine, I still felt the loss of him like a bomb going off inside of me, probably still would if I let even a crack of light into the place I hid him when I was still just a kid.

"Theo," is what I hear myself saying instead. "It was so long ago."

"I guess it was," he says. "But if I did something back then, I would still want to know."

So that's what this is about. I force a smile to let Theo know that he's off the hook, that he didn't force himself on me or push me too far, and didn't he see all the stuff written about me, anyway? Doesn't he know that I was the one who let random guys finger me before I screwed them over publicly and forced them to change schools and release statements saying they'd never met me? That I would have deserved anything he inflicted on me anyway, just by being a certain type of girl? I bare my teeth at him to let him know that he is free to dwell on the right side of history as the type of man who is an ally, who would never hurt a woman and who holds himself accountable for any weak moments or blind spots in his past, but he still is unsatisfied.

"You changed your mind," I blurt out, before even I know I'm going to say it.

Theo frowns at me. "Changed my mind?"

"About Milos," I say, feeling ridiculous even saying the word with all the connotations it has for me, as if it isn't just an island but an entire alternate existence with infinite outcomes that are all better than the one I ended up living.

"What about Milos?" Theo asks, the look on his face one of pure confusion.

"You changed your mind about going," I say, averting my eyes. "With me."

"Bess," Theo says slowly. "I'm sorry we never made it to Milos, but my sister died, so obviously it wasn't the best time to go fucking island-hopping. Are you being serious?"

My words catch in my throat as Joni appears in the doorway, holding her car key.

"The garage is all yours, Theo," Joni says, looking between the two of us. "And your driver is here."

After a moment, Theo tears his eyes away from mine and, perhaps realizing Joni isn't leaving us again, he moves toward the front door.

"Thanks for tonight," he says once he's there, a lone silhouette against the black night.

"Of course," Joni says smoothly, curving her lips in a way that only I would know isn't a real smile.

"Look, I'm thinking . . . I'm thinking of doing a dinner next month, on the anniversary of . . . on July thirty-first. Just to say goodbye, you know? It will be ten years, and it feels like it means something. My dad won't even say her name anymore, and my mom doesn't get out much, so there aren't many people to invite, but if you two could come . . ." Theo breaks off, pausing to take a deep

288

breath before saying simply, "I would appreciate it if you both came."

I stare at Joni and eventually she puts her hand on Theo's arm.

"That's a nice idea, Theo," Joni says mildly, but I notice she doesn't commit to anything.

Once he's gone, and it's just the two of us left, I find I can't quite look at her.

FORTY-EIGHT

2009

JONI RETURNED TO LOS Angeles on the July Fourth holiday. She still had more than a week left on the room she'd rented in New York, and had planned to celebrate with her new friends at Brighton Beach, but, much to her irritation, she was having to fly home early after her mom had flat-out refused to spend another holiday alone. "It's hardly fucking Thanksgiving. And it's not *my* fault she couldn't keep my dad around," Joni spat down the phone to me as she walked through JFK. "And maybe if she hadn't been so vain about losing her figure, she'd have had another child instead of cursing me to be her only progeny."

I made a few sympathetic noises, but my mind was elsewhere. My mom had asked me to run a rare errand for her that morning, and I'd bundled myself up in layers and layers of clothes before taking her car to pick up some melatonin from Rite Aid at the Commons. The whole time I was in there, I was waiting for the shouts to start, for camera flashes to momentarily stun me, but instead something even worse had happened: I'd bumped into Mrs. Aetos. She had looked tinier than ever, skin papery and limbs so brittle she seemed far older than her forty-five years. She'd cupped my face in her cool hands and stared blankly into my eyes.

"Poor, poor girls," she'd said, and then she dropped her hand as if my face were burning hot, and she'd walked out of the store. I'd hyperventilated in the vitamin aisle for a few minutes, and then, in a blind panic, I had called Joni, who was already on her way to the airport.

"Should we have sent something?" I asked. "To the Aetoses."

"What, like a 'sorry we took our eyes off your daughter for one second and she died' card?" Joni said, her voice rough. "'Sorry you couldn't get out of bed for long enough to know how cool your daughter was' flowers?"

"Joni," I said quietly.

"Lighten up, Bess. You know it's true," Joni said, but I refused to be drawn back into our old games.

"I have to go," I said. "Have a good flight, Joni."

After we hung up, I drove home and checked Theo's Facebook page for the millionth time. He had been unnaturally quiet on there since Evangeline's death, quieter than I'd known anyone else to be since the day we'd all discovered that we could shout about our thrilling lives and dreams for everyone we knew to see at once. I'd heard he'd gone back to Providence in January, but other than that I had no idea how he was coping, or if he thought of me at all.

———

I opened my door early that same evening to find Joni standing there with one hand on her hip, eyes squinting in the dwindling sunlight as she stared at me. She was wearing a curious pink linen suit, unbuttoned with only a lacy black bandeau underneath. Her hair was shorter and slicked back, and she seemed so far removed from the girl I had trusted at my very lowest, who had coaxed me back from the breaking point on more than one occasion, that for a second, I couldn't remember anything about her other than her name.

"Fuck, Bess," Joni said. "What happened to you?"

I looked down and tried to see myself through her eyes. I'd lost even more weight since I'd been home, and I knew that it made me look unwell, but I didn't know the scale of it until I saw it on Joni's face. Now Joni was standing on my doorstep, and she was expecting an answer from me, as if she weren't the only person in the world who should have known. I imagined falling to my knees and screaming at her how lonely I felt, and how seeing her blossom only made it worse for me.

Instead, I closed my eyes and told her I needed to take a nap.

The next time Joni came knocking for me, I asked my mom to tell her I was out.

———————

On July 31, the first anniversary of Evangeline's death, I broke it to my parents that I wasn't going to New York. We were eating Chinese takeout around the marble dining table, and my mom had been talking cheerfully about a cute bedspread she'd seen at Target that might be nice for my dorm room, while we all pretended not to know what date it was or that this time a year ago my life was just about to shatter into pieces.

The media interest had started up again, the anniversary of Evangeline's death seemingly scaffolding enough to hang a story on, even when the truth was far less salacious than the lies about us had been. They had realized a while ago that Joni and I were the most interesting piece of the entire affair, more interesting than sweet Evangeline's tragic death, and our experience, our *plight*, became the focus of most of the pieces, disingenuous stories that pretended to sympathize with us even as they regurgitated old facts about our odd behavior that summer, and that still included all of the incriminating evidence against us as humans. During those hot, bottomless summer days, my parents watched me warily as I read through the news stories in silence, my head bowed as I absorbed the blows, one after another, because at least I felt more in control that way.

"Oh, I've been meaning to tell you, I'm not going to NYU," I said casually as I reached for another wing. "I called the admissions office today to let them know."

My parents looked at each other helplessly, as if I were perishing slowly in front of their eyes. Steven paused, his egg roll suspended in midair, halfway between his plate and his mouth, as he stared at me.

"I just think it's all still too high-profile for me to be alone in a strange city," I said carefully. "At least for now, anyway."

This was part of the truth at least. The press were still very much around, albeit more sporadically, snapping photos of Joni when she was in Starbucks after a run, or waiting outside the gates of our estate, and I could feel that the interest in us was still bubbling under the surface, just waiting for a reason to explode all over again. Someone had leaked that we were starting college in the fall, and, after that, it was mentioned in every article written about us and our return to the US. When I thought about having to wade through a pack of paparazzi just to make it to orientation or enrollment, an easy win for a tabloid to print on the second or third page, I wanted to scream. When I pictured walking into a dorm room and seeing the look of recognition on some girl's face, or worse yet, on the face of her *dad*, who was about to say goodbye to his baby for the first time, I felt like I was going to vomit. There was no way I could sit down in a creative writing class and trust that the other students weren't going to skew everything I wrote through the lens of the tragedy in Greece, maybe even "acciden-tally" leaking a passage or page to the press or on their own Face-book pages, a glimpse inside the tortured mind of Bess Winter. It wasn't that I had any delusions of grandeur or that these were particularly outlandish fantasies I was having; I just understood that we were unfinished business as far as both the media and the public were concerned—we had wronged in thousands of differ-ent, reckless ways, but we were never fully punished for it.

"So you'll stay here," my dad said slowly. "In Calabasas, with us."

"That's the plan," I said. "Maybe I'll apply somewhere next year, but I think it's best for me to be here for now. I'm safer here than anywhere out there, realistically."

My mom nodded, her mouth pursed as she tried to work out what to say. I didn't need them to like the decision, I just needed them to skim over it in the way we'd learned to skim over every-thing significant for the past year. I knew they'd never in a million years dream of demanding I leave home or even get a job, particu-larly not on a date as significant as the anniversary of Evangeline's death.

"Okay, sweetie," my mom said finally. "If you're sure that's the right decision."

Steven threw his half-eaten egg roll onto his plate and scraped his chair back abruptly. The look on his face was fierce, the vein on his temple bulging as he stared at us all in horror.

"What the fuck is wrong with you all," he said loudly.

"Steven," my dad said, his tone a warning.

"No, Dad, fuck this," Steven said, his anger making him seem older and far less lackadaisical than he had become. He looked down at me, and I saw an unfiltered fury in his eyes that made me feel sick. "Why are you punishing us like this?"

"I don't know what you're talking about," I said quietly.

"Steven, *please*—" my mom said.

"No, seriously, someone needs to say this to her, and it clearly isn't going to be either of you," Steven said, before turning his gaze back to me. "You're even more selfish than I thought if you can't see what you're doing to us. I sometimes think it was actually better when you were in jail because then at least we had somewhere to direct all this fucking rage and sadness, instead of having to tiptoe around you while you lose your mind, acting like your entire life is over when it's just fucking starting."

I felt my cheeks burn with recognition and closed my eyes so that I didn't have to see the hatred on his face. If my sadness was contagious, then perhaps so was his anger, and I didn't want to carry something so powerful. I didn't know if I was strong enough to bear it.

"Mom and Dad are miserable. Look at them. Mom hasn't been back to work for a full week in an entire year, Bess. Do you understand that? She's so scared of what you'll do that she's refusing to start up her life again. Have Mom and Dad been out to dinner or seen any of their friends since you got back? No, because they're so terrified that you're going to have some meltdown that they'd rather stay home with you, just in case. Have you even once thanked them for it? No. You know that I'm too embarrassed to have any friends over here because I don't know how you'll react or what state you'll be in, and I feel guilty as shit every time I go to a party or on a date because I know that you're just here, wallowing in your misery and whatever else it is that's keeping you here. Bess, they'll never say it because they're scared of what you'll do, so I'll do it for them. You are sucking the air out of this house. You are slowly killing us all, and you don't even care."

I sat frozen, my eyes on the tablecloth as silence descended over us like a weight. I could hear the refrigerator humming and the sound of my mom crying, but nobody said anything to refute Steven's claims or to make me feel any better. My parents were unable to look at me, their eyes clinging to each other like it might stop them from drowning. And that's when I knew that, if I cared about any of them at all, my brother was right. I had to leave to save them.

I cycled to Joni's house in the rain, and when I shouted for her, she opened her bedroom window. I hadn't seen her since her first day back in California, and I didn't know if she was even talking to me at this point, or whether she'd finally given up on me. Joni disappeared from the window and, after a moment, opened the front door, her expression cautiously hopeful. I didn't want to go inside because I couldn't handle the thought of facing Joni's mom and her blunt questions, so Joni grabbed two yellow ponchos instead, the type you buy at a theme park when it's raining, before joining me in her front yard. When I didn't take the poncho she held out for me, she draped it over my soaking shoulders.

"I'm not going to NYU," I said as the rain came down over us, partially obscuring my words. "But I can't stay here."

"Why aren't you going?"

Because New York isn't for people like me, I thought, but I didn't tell her that.

"I want to come up to Berkeley with you in the fall," I said instead.

Joni was silent while she thought about it. I wiped my tears away even though my face was already soaked from the rain.

"We could get a place together, still close to campus but a little more grown-up. We're hardly like regular freshmen, why should we pretend to be? It could be like how it used to be, before last summer."

"I'm not going to Berkeley, Bess," Joni said, avoiding meeting my eyes. I realized then that she had been the only person willing to actually look at me after Evangeline died, but now she couldn't bear the weight of me either.

"I'm going back to New York," Joni said then, unable to keep a small note of excitement from her voice. "*Dollface* offered me an editorial assistant job and my own radio slot. Permanently."

"No," I said. "You hate New York."

Joni frowned but said nothing.

"What exactly are you trying to prove?" I asked, my voice jagged. "How fine you are? How little you care about any of it?"

"Bess, what do you want me to do?" Joni asked. "Do you want me to be like you? To stay frozen in time from the moment we lost her?"

I stared at her.

"You're being selfish," she said. "You need to move on."

"*I* need to move on," I repeat slowly. "Joni, you're the one who's building an entire fucking universe on the ashes of our friend's death. So don't talk to me about moving on . . ."

Joni stood there for a moment, and I thought she was finally going to lose it, unleashing her trademark fury at me, giving me a sign that she wasn't as happy as she seemed, that inside she was decaying too but she was just better at hiding it, and I actually felt something close to relief as I waited for the blow to fall. But instead Joni just looked down at her rain-soaked shoes.

"I wrote about it," she said then, and, for just a moment, everything stopped.

"You did what?"

"I wrote about what happened to us for *Dollface*," Joni repeated. "Evangeline. Me. You. Our friendship."

I stood there blinking, my vision blurred from my tears. My nose had started to run, but I didn't wipe it, I just stared at the only person in the world who could have understood me but who had chosen to do the opposite.

"How fucking dare you," I said.

Joni met my gaze defiantly. "I didn't talk about the lie, if that's what you're worried about."

"You need to pull it," I said. "I don't want any part in it. Just fucking delete it, Joni. I'm sure they'll still give you a job."

"It's not your call, Bess," Joni said, her tone gentle but un-yielding. "It's in the print issue next week."

I felt a wave of fury. Not only had Joni gone against every-thing we'd been told—that no media was good media, that any words we uttered would be twisted and severed only to be used against us at some unknowable later date—but she had done to me exactly what everyone else had since the moment we lost Evange-line: she had taken away my voice. Once again, I was powerless, entirely at the mercy of someone else's opinion of me. And the worst part was that she knew it too. That was why she'd done it behind my back, and that was why she'd been all too happy to let me avoid her since she'd been home.

"Haven't I already done enough for you?" Joni asked, and her voice was raw and broken as she reached out to me. I looked down at her fingertips laced around my wrist, then back up at her.

"Actually," I said coolly, "all you've ever done is ruin every-thing."

"Bess, please."

"It was your idea to lie," I said. "Don't ever forget that. What, did you just want your dad to notice you?"

Joni pinched my wrist hard, but I still didn't stop. "Did you want to pretend we were both there just so that you could build your career out of it? Did you already know what you were going to do from the moment you saw Ev's broken fucking body on those rocks?"

"Fuck you, Bess." Joni stepped in closer to me, the rain streaking down her cheeks. "Do you think you'd actually feel better if the world knew this whole thing only happened because you broke Ev's heart until she couldn't bear to be anywhere near you?"

I felt a vicious relief that she had finally dared to say the words out loud—words that I knew to be true in the same way that I knew I was allergic to penicillin, or that my mom would never love me in quite the same way again.

"That's not why you feel like this," Joni said. "The reason you feel so fucking shitty is that you're too scared to forgive yourself, because it's all you know. You're ashamed of who you are, and I can see it in every single thing you do. Every choice you make and all the ones you don't. You're so scared of opening yourself up that you'd rather miss out on everything. You don't know who you are without this, so don't come at me accusing *me* of capitalizing on it."

"You never lie," I said slowly. "You never lie, and yet you did that night. Why is that?"

I could see that she was furious now too, her hands balled into clenched fists and her body vibrating like a coil, as if she had too much rage and adrenaline coursing through her and didn't know how to expend it.

"I know why you did it," I said. "You did it so that I would be indebted to you for the rest of my life."

"You really think that?" Joni said, her eyes burning with fury. "Tell me right now if that's really what you think about me."

I realized then that I'd never seen her cry. Not when her dad left her, not when she found me and Evangeline on the rocks, not when we were arrested or detained, not when she was headbutted in the nose in prison over a phone card, and not even when we missed Ev's funeral. I met her eyes, and I didn't back down.

"That's what I think," I said. "You tricked me into needing you."

Joni stood there, her arms dangling by her sides as she tried to unpack what I had just said. She opened and closed her mouth a few times and then she stopped, her eyes filling with tears.

"Now we can never go back," I said, just before I left. "You're free."

FORTY-NINE

2018

SOMETHING FEELS WRONG. SOMETHING feels wrong, but I can't tell Joni.

I type out ten versions of the same email to Theo after he's left, but I don't send a single one. It's one thing reminiscing about Evangeline with him, but it feels infinitely more dangerous talking about what did or didn't happen between us, pushing on a fracture that never quite healed in the same way. Still, as I lie in bed with the sky lightening outside, I can't help but wonder if Theo is lying in his childhood bed thinking about me too.

When it's too late to pretend I'm going to get any sleep at all, I dress in a white T-shirt and a pair of jean shorts—casual enough for it to seem like I haven't made an effort when Theo comes back to collect his car, but a definite improvement from the night before. I apply a few quick swipes of lip gloss and mascara, as if there's a chance in hell that Joni won't notice the extra effort I've made, then I brush my hair so that it falls over my shoulders like a shield. *It's the hope that kills you,* I remind myself as I walk into the living room.

Joni is already gardening out front, repotting succulents and cacti in a pair of thick black gloves. When I offer to help, she tells me that gardening is a form of meditation for her, and that she needs to be alone to focus on her breathwork as well as the task at hand, since the reporters have been trampling all over her plants for the past month. Chastened, I leave her out there and pretend to read my book on the deck, positioning myself so that the golden sunlight falls across me in a way that I presume is flattering for when Theo comes back.

At lunchtime, when I venture back outside to ask Joni if she wants tacos, Theo's car is gone from the open garage.

"Where's the Tesla?" I ask slowly, and Joni looks up at me, visibly hot and crabby from the exertion of whatever she's doing to the rock garden lining her driveway.

"Oh," Joni says. "He's been and gone."

I feel a hardening in my chest.

"Why didn't you tell me he was here?" I ask as Joni takes off a glove and pushes her hair behind her ear.

"You seemed upset last night," Joni says, as if it should be obvious. "I thought you'd want me to get him out quickly."

"I was upset because our first real conversation in a decade was cut short," I say. "Because you didn't seem to want to leave us alone for even a few minutes."

"What are you talking about, Bess?" Joni asks. "I was trying to protect you."

"You knew about Milos," I say. "You were the only person apart from Theo who knew about Milos."

Joni studies me carefully.

"Until he told Evangeline," she says, her voice cool. "Which is how the whole thing started, if you remember."

I clench my jaw so hard I'm surprised my teeth don't crack.

"Are you still this hung up on him?" Joni asks then, tilting her head to one side as her voice drips with faux sympathy. "I'm sorry, I really had no idea you felt this way."

I stare at her, reminding myself of how she'd brought me back from the edge more than once in my life. Maybe she's just scared that I'll leave her again, or, most probably, she's still trying to protect me. I shut down any other possibility on the spot.

"Did he ask about me?"

Joni looks down at her glove, using her bare hand to pick a sharp cactus spine out of it.

"Sorry," she says, throwing the needle on the ground beside her. "No."

I turn around and go back inside.

I open my laptop and open another blank email, thinking of all the things I could ask Theo. I could ask him what he meant when he said he didn't change his mind back then. I could ask why he didn't fight harder to find me after it happened, or why he waited ten years, until he was already married and I was already broken beyond repair, to show up. I could ask him a thousand questions, but I know that they would still make no actual difference to my life. Theo would still be with Sophia and I would still be exactly who I am: a twenty-eight-year-old woman, hiding out in her best friend's house, mourning a life she never deserved, anyway.

Later, Joni flings open my bedroom door without knocking. I glance up from my phone and can tell that something has happened from the way she is practically glowing with self-satisfaction as she sits on the foot of my bed.

"I've been speaking with my publicist," Joni says, breaking into a wide smile. "And they've rescheduled my book release for next month."

"Oh yeah?" I say, looking back down at my phone.

"Yeah. It's coming out on July thirty-first."

I feel a shift deep inside my bones. *July 31.* The tenth anniversary of Evangeline's death, to the day.

"Joni . . ." I say.

"I'm not in control of the release date, Bess," Joni says, her tone sickeningly casual. "It has something to do with it being a book club pick, anyway. All good things, I'm promised."

All good things.

"My publicist is also setting up an in-depth TV interview to talk about . . . everything," Joni says. "Here, at home."

"Everything," I repeat.

"Willa," Joni says. "Evangeline."

I finally meet her eye. Her cheeks are flushed now, and she looks irritated that I'm not behaving exactly how she wanted.

"And, Bess? She thinks it's a good idea for you to be a part of it too," Joni says, and I feel sick to my stomach because suddenly I'm standing in the rain in Calabasas, finding out about the *Dollface* article all over again.

"And if I don't want to be?" I ask, and Joni's face contorts into a frown before she recovers.

"It's obviously not mandatory," Joni says. "But we're going to be talking about you, so your absence would be noted."

Joni smiles in a way that sends chills down my spine. And that's when I remember her words from weeks earlier:

Maybe I was always destined to climb over the bodies of those I once loved to get where I needed to go.

I wake up hours later drenched in my own sweat, a memory rattling on a loop in my mind.

I'm in Mykonos, sitting on a toilet in a locked stall in the bathroom, trying to catch my breath after an embarrassing epiphany on the dance floor, and then I'm walking through the bar as the palm leaf canopy rustles above me, and Evangeline is watching me with a deadened look on her face as Joni whispers in her ear, one tanned arm snaked around her tiny waist, and I'm getting closer and closer, until they finally have to stop talking and face me.

I think about my favorite refrain, my unbreakable assertion that Joni never lies, based on the scrappy, straight-talking teenage version of her I first met, and I ask myself whether that's become the greatest lie of all. What if I constructed that narrative only to protect myself, to give meaning to the bad choices I've made when it comes to her, and the worse ones we've made together. I think of the lies she's told me even in the past five weeks, the omissions, the distortions, the outright myths, and I feel suddenly, blindingly stupid. What if the truth is that Joni lies constantly, over and over again, even to the people she is supposed to love? Especially to the people she's supposed to love.

FIFTY

I WAIT FOR STEVEN OUTSIDE the Starbucks on Ventura Boulevard. He seems visibly wary as he takes a seat opposite me, and I remember how, the last time we spoke, I accused him of hiding me away like a monster.

"Steven," I say, pushing a venti black Americano across the table. He takes it from me and removes the lid to let out some of the heat.

"I'm willing to accept that there might be more to this story," I say slowly.

Steven says nothing, taking a sip of his drink.

"And I think that you're right that I should . . . be a little warier than I have been. That maybe I need to gather as much information as possible about it."

Steven raises his eyebrows. "*It?*"

"About Joni, Steven. Okay? I'm worried about Joni."

Steven nods.

"I heard Lucien made bail," I say.

"Yeah," Steven says. "A bunch of parents at the private school where he teaches pooled their money, apparently. He must either be a *really* good English teacher, or not the kind of guy you want to believe could do something like this."

"Or rich people just love a project," I say, not wanting to think about it too much. "Look, do you think Nova could get in touch with him somehow? Maybe one of her mutual friends with Willa might have met him. Or even through his lawyer?"

"Because all lawyers know each other," Steven says dryly.

"I don't know," I say. "I thought it could be worth a shot."

Steven opens a sachet of sweetener and pours it into his coffee.

"Please, Steven," I say, and when he looks back up at me, his expression has softened somewhat.

"I'll see what I can do," he says, as if he finally understands how hard this is for me.

Three days later, Steven and I meet Lucien in a condominium in Sherman Oaks, not far from where Steven and Nova live. The walls are covered in a raspberry floral wallpaper, and the furniture is both decaying and decadent—a threadbare crushed velvet sofa, an electric fireplace so bright it's almost neon.

Lucien himself is tall, at least six foot five, and rangy, wearing a corduroy baseball cap and light jeans. He seems almost willfully awkward in his grandmother's condo, all limbs and childlike clothes and stooped shoulders, as if he wants you to know that he's all too aware of the inconvenience his presence causes. Steven shakes his hand warmly as if he's just come back from vacation, not the county jail. I, in turn, eye Lucien warily.

"My lawyer told me to stay somewhere I wouldn't be found," Lucien says, wincing slightly as he looks around, as if he's seeing it for the first time too. "So house arrest is a thrill."

"We got you a juice," Steven says quickly, wielding a tray

filled with three bloodred juices with a flourish. "I hope you're a beets guy."

The gesture, the entire futile attempt at normalcy, is so my mother that I have to look away.

"Thanks," Lucien says, smiling weakly. "It's good to meet you both."

"Likewise," I say stiffly, perching on the end of an armchair covered in wiry white dog hair.

"I've heard that our interests in this case being solved may overlap somewhat," Lucien says, and I just stare at him in response.

"I told Lucien that you have some concerns about Joni," Steven says.

"And I told Steven that you both need to be careful around her," Lucien says.

I try to read the flicker that crosses his face as he speaks. Is that guilt or something else?

"I just want to hear your side of the story," I say eventually.

"Well, before we start, I need you to know that I don't feel good about it," Lucien says, and I think he's talking about killing Willa right up until he adds, "the affair."

"How long was it going on for?" I ask, and Lucien shrugs.

"A while," he says. "Almost as long as I knew her."

"Which was?"

"Eighteen months."

Half the duration of Willa and Joni's relationship.

I must look as sick as I feel, because Lucien leans forward, his long hands clasped together tightly, as if in prayer.

"I could tell you that I didn't mean for it to happen, or that it was just some fun that spiraled out of hand, but in all honesty, that would be bullshit. I knew I loved Willa from the second I saw her, and I regret no part of it, even now."

"And Willa?" I ask.

"What about her?"

"How did Willa feel about you? Because it looks like she can't have felt all that much if you were together for eighteen months and she didn't do a thing about it. In fact, she got engaged to someone else while you were together."

"Yeah," Lucien says. "I guess if that's how you want to measure our relationship, that's a leap you could make."

"Willa was never going to leave Joni for you," I say.

"We don't think," Steven says quickly, and when I turn to look at him, he just shrugs. "I mean, she could have tried that night. The night she went missing."

I glare at my brother before turning pointedly back to Lucien, waiting for him to tell me about that night, but instead he looks wearily down at his feet, clad in a pair of beaten-up Vans, and I have a glimpse of the type of English teacher he must be—the kind who reluctantly cites the Kardashians and Instagram-famous poets in order to connect with his students, and who inevitably sleeps with the artsy and beautiful senior two weeks before graduation.

"Look," he says. "When I met Willa, she was already resigned to the fact that she had to manage Joni in a lot of ways. And while she would do whatever it was that Joni wanted from her, it wasn't in her nature to hide her resentment while she did it. Joni was obviously older and more established, but she also cared more than Willa. It was never an even balance, emotionally."

I had always assumed that part of Willa's appeal, part of why Joni had fallen for her in the first place, would have been Willa's adulation of her—this slightly older, accomplished woman who had already created a perfect universe for Willa to slot right into.

"And what are you implying would have happened if she hadn't done the things Joni wanted?"

"I think you wouldn't be here if you didn't know the answer

to that yourself," Lucien says. "Look, Joni had a temper. Once Willa showed up to meet me at a wine tasting and she had bruises all around her arm and shoulder. She wouldn't tell me what happened, but I figured it was Joni."

I swallow, suddenly reluctant to ask any more about it.

"And obviously there was the money thing," Lucien says.

I frown at him. "What money thing?"

"Joni paid for everything and everyone in Willa's life."

"They were together for three years," I say. "It's pretty normal to share money with your partner."

"It wasn't like that," Lucien says. "It was Joni's way of controlling Willa. Joni didn't just share her income or lifestyle or whatever, she actually *paid* her. Like, she'd reward Willa for not partying on a weekend by giving her a five-thousand-dollar bonus on the Monday. She wouldn't say that's what it was for, but Willa knew. How do you think Willa could afford to be so principled?"

I stare at him.

"Did everyone know about this?" I ask. "The money part."

"Anyone who knew her well," Lucien answers. "Willa would buy a round of drinks, and people would joke that Joni would kill her if she knew where her money was going. Joni didn't like Willa drinking or even going out that much. In all honesty, I felt sorry for Joni, because if she wanted a house cat, then she'd just clearly picked wrong. I could have told her from the start that Willa was going to be impossible to tame, but wanting that level of control, it's not healthy. Being indebted to someone isn't a reason to stick around, you know?"

And you never know when she's going to cash it in.

"But you must have believed Willa could be tamed once," I say. "To have waited for so long."

"I wasn't waiting for anything. I never put any pressure on her," Lucien says, stretching his palms out to me. "I made it clear from the day we met that I'm never going to be the superhero-perfect husband. I was happy with how things were. Willa was the one who decided she wanted out of what she and Joni had."

"So did she tell her?" I ask, and Lucien frowns at me. "That night. Did Willa tell Joni it was over?"

"Joni knew she wasn't getting the best of Willa, and she hadn't been for a while," Lucien says, and I can see that even Steven is getting frustrated with him now.

"But that was probably the plan, right?" Steven prompts. "The night she went missing."

"It was Willa's plan, yes," Lucien says slowly.

I swallow a knot in the back of my throat at the thought that Joni might have lied to me yet again. Because isn't this what I've feared all along, that Joni only found out about Lucien the night she turned up on my doorstep?

Lucien closes his eyes briefly, his eyelids fluttering as he thinks about what he wants to say next. "Willa used to say that it would kill Joni if she ever found out about us."

"That's not what happened, though, is it?" I ask. "It didn't kill *Joni*. And if you actually mean what you're insinuating, then I don't understand how you can be so indifferent about it. The woman you loved from the second you saw her isn't alive anymore."

"I try to be as philosophical as I can," Lucien says after a long pause. "Like, we're all dying right now, you know? But still it feels pretty definitive—the loss but also the contrast. That she was here one second, then gone the next. I'm trying to capture that starkness in my writing, but it's pretty elusive. That's why so many of the greats relied so heavily on nature imagery."

I stare at Lucien, unimpressed. I imagine how much the police interviewing him would have hated his faux cerebral smugness, his meandering, self-indulgent way of answering questions, and I can understand exactly how he ended up where he is, with a murder charge seemingly light on actual evidence. I can understand it because I was once where he is now: guilty of being unpalatable and strange before they even got to the actual crime.

"And you're fine with your face being on the front page of every newspaper, every news outlet? You still think it was worth it?"

"The truth will come out," Lucien says. "If not now, then once my trial starts."

"The truth," I repeat. "You haven't actually said what you think happened."

"Like I told you," Lucien says. "Willa wasn't the type of woman who could be tamed. And Joni couldn't handle the thought of setting her free."

I can hear my own heartbeat in the silence that follows.

"You seem pretty set on that idea, but any human can be tamed," I say, my voice slicing through the air. "If you take enough away from them. It's not a sign of weakness."

"Maybe," Lucien says, clearly thinking the opposite.

"So what did Willa say when you saw her that night?" I ask, and Lucien stares back at me like I'm being deliberately obtuse.

"Bess, I'm sorry, I should have made something clear from the start," Lucien says. "I didn't see Willa that night."

I glance over at my brother, who is watching me closely.

"Her blood was in your car," I say, but did I really believe he might drop the act for me, that he would just lie down and reveal himself to be the monster I so badly need him to be?

"Oh, *that*," Lucien says. "That is bullshit, and they all know it. I told everyone I spoke to that Willa caught her hand on a gnarly branch at a climate march weeks ago. I have about two hundred eyewitness accounts to corroborate that too, but obviously no one wanted to hear it. They're just buying time."

He leans in toward me, enlivened suddenly.

"Do you know what the entire case against me really hinges

on?" Lucien asks. "Three text messages Willa and I supposedly sent each other that night. Three text messages that conveniently place me with her before she disappeared. Three text messages that will never stand up in court in a million years, whatever the district attorney wants you to think."

I swallow hard as Lucien smiles at me, his eyes unblinking and clear, teeth shining.

"But the thing is," he says, "those messages weren't from Willa."

FIFTY-ONE

2018

"YOU KNOW THE AIR-CONDITIONING can't work with your window open," Steven says, while he drives me back to Malibu. I ignore him and close my eyes, Lucien's words still whipping through my mind like a tornado.

Lucien said that Willa had always been militant about deleting all forms of digital communication between the two of them, to the point where he often had to send the same text twice if it contained an address or venue name. This was relevant, insofar as whoever had sent him the message on the night Willa disappeared would presumably have been working from a blank slate.

At around nine p.m., he received a message from Willa's phone saying **I need to see you. Can we meet at the beach?** followed by a black heart emoji, but instead of the message reassuring him, Lucien grew suspicious. In the entire time they'd been seeing each other, Willa had never once sent him an emoji, knowing how he felt about them. In the first class of every academic year, he would hand out letters sent between Simone de Beauvoir and Jean-Paul Sartre to his high school English students, comparing their notes to teenagers' texts today as an example of digital communication being the death of intellect, of passion, of nuance, as if any number of acronyms and pizza emojis could ever encapsulate as much emotion as the human language, which has already lasted over a million years, for fuck's sake. Willa, while still demonstrative in her emoji use with Joni, for example, would never dream of sending Lucien an emoji, let alone one of a black fucking heart.

His spidey senses firing, Lucien wrote back: **OK. Our spot?**

As long as it's me and you, I'm there.

Another emoji—this time the three droplets of water, suggestive and crass.

Lucien didn't leave his house until the following morning, when he drove himself to work.

Steven pulls up at the end of Joni's street, the engine still running.

"I know we don't know anything for sure," he says carefully. "But I still think this is for the best."

I stare out the windshield as a dying wasp crawls across the glass.

"Do you want me to come in with you?" he asks, and I shake my head.

"She's at a meeting with her agent," I say, and then, because I can't believe where we've ended up, I add, "Look, I'm not doing this because I believe Lucien, okay? The guy hid an affair for eighteen months, so he's hardly the most reliable source, and he's also obnoxiously pretentious. I'm doing this for you, because I can see how stressed you are about this and I don't want to hurt you . . ." *Any more than I already have.*

Steven nods, but he's gripping the steering wheel so tightly his knuckles have turned gray.

"Just grab whatever you need, and get out of there as quickly as possible," he says. "I'll be waiting."

I enter the security code and open the door to Joni's house. I listen for any sign of her, but the house is still, the faint crashing of the waves outside the only signs of life. With my heart pounding, I grab my duffel bag and pack it with everything I brought over to Joni's, back when I was a different person. Laptop, jeans, striped T-shirt, 5oulm8s hoodie, and my book on emotional resilience with the photo of Willa still tucked inside.

I'm nearly at the front door when I notice that Joni's bedroom door is open a couple of inches. Checking my phone for the time, I figure Steven can wait another few minutes. Before I even have time to decide if it's a good idea, I've dropped the duffel bag and I'm inside Joni's room for the first time since I arrived here.

Her bedroom is typically tasteful and orderly, decorated in muted desert shades with dusky pink walls lined with photos of Joni at various events—one of her clutching the hands of Melinda Gates, another of her being awarded an honorary membership to a prestigious women's-only space in New York. There are no photos of Willa, no signs of Joni having any friends other than those to whom she's paid tens of thousands of dollars for the privilege of being in the same room.

I open the top drawer of her dresser, which reveals surprisingly simple underwear—the same thongs in various shades of nude and black, Joni's A-cups never having had any real need for bras. I'm about to close the second drawer, filled with neatly balled socks, when I spot the corner of something yellow underneath the second layer. A leather journal.

Hands trembling, I open the book to find Joni's familiar cursive scrawled across each page. I'm almost sickeningly relieved when I find that it's filled with to-do lists—deadlines and massages and facial bookings, and phone calls with her editor—each of Joni's days planned down to the nearest five minutes up until the moment Willa disappeared. These aren't the possessions of a stranger by any stretch, and the thought soothes me more than anything as I bury the diary back underneath the socks. I think about Steven waiting outside and how meeting Lucien might have triggered some delayed-onset PTSD over what happened to me in Greece, and how maybe I should tell him to talk to someone. I'm about to call him to say to leave without me, that I'll be fine here for a few more days, when I see something that makes my heart drop down, down, into the bed of the ocean.

In the third drawer, under a pile of old magazines and press cuttings about Joni's stellar career, I find a slim phone in a cream case. Embossed on the back of the case in gold are the initials *WB*. I drop the phone and, before I can think about it, I am moving, stumbling to get out of the house before Joni gets home, heaving my duffel bag onto my shoulder and running to find my brother to take me away from whatever has happened here, from whatever I've understood or misunderstood or known all along.

FIFTY-TWO

2018

A MESSAGE FROM JONI: **Where are you?**
I ignore it, turning over in the bed Nova made up
for me. I'm allergic to goose feathers, but I don't mention it. When
Steven hangs by the door to ask me if I'm okay, and what I'm planning to do about Joni, I just stare blankly back at him until he
leaves. The feathers are already making my eyelids itch.

There's a commotion outside the window just after sunset. I crawl
along the wooden floor and peek through the blinds. Joni is trying
to come inside, but Nova and Steven stand like rottweilers at the
perimeter of the yard, telling her to leave. I try to feel something
as I watch her drive away, but I fall short. My blood has turned to
stone.

When I decline Nova's invitation to come downstairs for dinner,
Steven delivers me homemade gazpacho in bed. He presents it to
me with a proud flourish, but the soup is unsatisfying, frigid in my

mouth, and I have to force myself to swallow it, like I'm learning how to eat again after a stroke. There's an old-fashioned radio in the room, and it's already tuned in to the same golden oldies station that our mom used to listen to while she made us breakfast before school. The jangling guitars and dulcet tones of the presenters' voices fill the room, and I wonder how many times she's stayed here without telling me.

Steven has left a copy of *Vogue* on the bedside table for me, and I stare at it for a while, trying to work out who he thinks I am.

"You need to come downstairs," Steven says, standing in the doorway of his own guest room the next night. "Just for dinner. Seriously, this is unacceptable behavior. You're not a kid anymore."

I groan and pull my eye mask up, squinting to focus on him in the low light.

"Bess," he says quietly. "This is getting bad again."

I'm about to snap at him that I just need more time, a couple more nights to lie in a darkened room and let time devour me, when I recognize the look on his face. My brother is begging me to be okay, and the only thing I know is that I can't do it to him again.

"Fine," I say. "But it better not be cold fucking soup."

Steven looks so relieved it makes me want to claw my own eyes out.

Over dinner, Steven and Nova make polite conversation as if they're on a first date, a setup presumably, sticking only to the safest of topics like I'm a nervous-minded child. When Steven asks Nova what her favorite subject was in school, I think that they must be doing it for my benefit—surely they must already know this about each other. I drink a glass of wine too fast, and I hate myself for not being the person they need me to be, the type of person who would know exactly what to do if they thought their best friend might have done something so awful it was almost inconceivable. I think of Lucien, rotting away under house arrest in his grandmother's condo while Joni swans around Malibu, preparing for her book release, and I feel sick to my stomach.

"Bess?"

When I look up, both Nova and Steven are staring at me expectantly. I look down at the unidentifiable food on the end of my fork and try to remember what it is that I'm eating.

"So good," I say. "Eggplant?"

"Nova was asking about your job," Steven says, and I shrug.

"I'm taking some time off," I say. "I need to recalibrate."

"Joni's idea, I assume?" he asks.

"Mine," I say. "It gets pretty tiring only seeing the worst in people."

After dinner, Nova whispers something to Steven, and he shakes his head.

"Come on," she says. "Stay with us."

"I'm with you," he says, stooping slightly to give her a kiss on the head, the quiet intimacy nearly winding me. "I'm always with you."

"So stay in the real world," she murmurs.

"One hour," Steven says, shooting a quick glance at me before he disappears up the stairs. And that's when I realize it must be Sunday.

Steven sits in his war room on an ergonomic office chair, in headphones, frowning at the screen. I stand in the doorway as he scans the list of new posts before typing something into a search box.

Soon, I see multiple *Besses* highlighted on the screen, and Steven rubs the back of his neck before getting started. I begin to feel weird watching him like this, so I step across the room and touch him on the arm, understanding as I do that he would have already seen my reflection in the monitor.

Steven takes his headphones off and looks warily up at me.

"You can pretend I'm not here," I say, my eyes scanning the screen for any mention of my name.

GalacticDetective34: If E was that drunk, why did they even bring her to a party? It all seems suspicious to me. Where is Pierre Lauvin now anyway? Has anyone investigated his digital footprint? Could there be a link to J and B?

"Does it make it harder?" I say softly as Steven types out a response. "How you feel about Joni?"

IBelieveThem76: If you look at the blood toxicology reports, it was clear that they had all been drinking, and by all accounts E was there by her own free will. I'm not saying it was a good decision, but who hasn't made a dumb choice the summer after high school? Especially when alcohol is involved. B + J + E did the right thing by going home together. What followed was a tragic accident.

"I don't think of it like that when I'm in here," Steven says, once he's finished. "I'm an analyst by nature, so all I do is focus on the evidence and learn how to work with it. I'm not actually here to make any moral judgments on Joni's character or even yours, regardless of what I think—the most I'll ever do in my responses is to remind people that we're all fallible. I'm here to present the facts to people who, for whatever reason, are desperate to bend them to fit their own framework, or fantasies. Like this guy here—GalacticDetective—I've seen him around other forums, and he mentioned once that a drunk driver crashed into his four-year-old when she was skipping on the sidewalk. The driver survived, his daughter didn't. So maybe blaming you for what happened to Evangeline gives him some comfort that things like this aren't always just bad luck, or being in the wrong place at the wrong time. And I get that, I really do, only that's not the story here, that's just what he wants to be the story. So my job is to point people back to the evidence. To remind them that, really, that's all we ever have."

"The truth," I say softly, and Steven shrugs.

"Even better," he says. "The facts."

I nod, watching as his fingertips fly effortlessly across the keyboard.

"I have to tell you something," I say, and Steven nods but doesn't stop typing.

"No, Steven," I say, my voice cracking slightly. "I really have to tell you something."

After a pause, Steven slowly turns around to face me. He looks young and unsure, and I nearly change my mind.

"We lied," I start, my voice shaking as I say the words out loud for the first time. "Joni and I lied to the police in Mykonos."

FIFTY-THREE

2018

"IT WAS MY FAULT Evangeline fell," I say. "But I wasn't there."

Steven stares at me, and I have to watch it dawn on him that this might all be much, much worse than he ever thought. That all the Post-its and transcripts and evidence photos could never have prepared him to discover that Joni and I took less than five minutes to make a mistake so big it would define the rest of our lives.

I tell him the story from the beginning. The tension, the power struggle that began in Tinos, the night I spent with Theo and what Evangeline said to me, how Joni had manipulated us to get to Mykonos, the night we spent discussing our futures, the calm before the storm, the day drinking in a beach bar, the MGMT song we thought was written for us, the way Joni left us and Ev turned on me, and how hurtful the things she had said to me were but also how true they were because I would have ditched her in a second to spend even one more hour with Theo. I even tell Steven what I said to Ev in return, the last words she'd ever hear, and how I decided not to mention the path down to the beach that turned out to be hauntingly easy to traverse. I tell him how I saw her body fall like a paper airplane, and how, for just a moment, I wanted it to be her. Then I tell him about how Joni found me down there, and how she made a promise to protect me, at whatever cost to herself. When I finish talking, Steven is grim and uncomprehending, his eyes flitting from Post-it to Post-it as if he can't quite compute this new version of events when the facts were already seared so deeply into his mind.

"That's impossible," Steven says. "That makes zero sense."

"Steven. It's the truth," I say. "I'm giving you the facts, just like you wanted."

"No," Steven says slowly, his mind clearly still reeling. "It makes zero sense why Joni would tell you to lie. She placed you both at the scene of the crime when you weren't there. That makes no sense."

"It was so stupid," I say. "I know this now."

"I'm not thinking that," Steven says, and then he turns back to his computer screen. He opens a folder and scans the contents before clicking on a pdf. What looks like a transcript fills the screen, and my stomach sinks at the prospect of being pulled even further back in time.

"You know, I always figured you were covering for Joni for something," he says. "Not the other way around."

"No," I say. "That wasn't it at all."

"But it's weird," Steven persists. "Joni's initial police interviews always felt more detailed than yours. The ones that were leaked, I mean. They were more vivid, somehow, even though I couldn't put my finger on how."

"I remember I was so scared of saying something that she might have missed that I clammed up," I say. "Maybe she did the opposite?"

"Didn't you work out what you were going to say before?" Steven asks.

"We said to stick to big strokes, few details," I say. "Look, it was hard enough talking about it with Joni, let alone the police."

Steven shakes his head. "I don't know, Bess. If there's one thing I know about Joni Bonnier, it's that nothing she does is selfless."

I stare at him as a sense of dread creeps across my skin.

He stands up. "Maybe take a look for yourself."

I look at the document on the screen, lines and lines of words that fell off my tongue in seconds and were somehow enough to seal my fate.

"Joni's is in the folder too," he says, then he bends down and kisses me on the head. "I'll leave you to it."

When Steven's at the door, he lingers for a few more moments. We lock eyes and I think he's going to crumble, but then he rallies.

"You know I didn't mean for you to leave and never come back," he says, clearing his throat. "It wasn't what I meant at all."

"I know," I say, my voice tight as I nod. "I know."

FIFTY-FOUR

2018

WHEN I CLOSE THE transcript of my second police interview, the memory of the cramped white room is so vivid that I can almost smell my own sweat, can almost feel the paper water cup disintegrating beneath my panicked, fumbling fingers. And all I want to do is walk out of this room, out of this house where my brother now knows exactly who I am, and go somewhere there is no trace of that naïve teenager who had no idea how much worse it was about to get. Except I'm so close now. I can't turn away.

I take a few deep breaths, and I open the transcript of Joni's interview from the same day.

The line of questioning is similar to mine until her interviewer begins to ask about the specifics of the walk, and even on paper I can tell that Joni is panicking at this point, trying desperately to keep up with the lies we told and the scant details I was able to give her.

CHRISTOS PANAYIOTOU: So you left the party to look for your friends, who were walking along the cliff.

JONI BONNIER: Yes.

CP: And were they difficult to find?

JB: Not really, I found them pretty quickly. There was only one obvious path.

CP: And when you found them, how did they seem?

JB: Good. They seemed OK, like they were excited to get home.

CP: And who was leading the way?

JB: That was Evangeline.

CP: And was that usual? For Evangeline to be leading the way?

JB: Not really, no. But she wanted to go home more.

CP: And why was that, Ms. Bonnier?

JB: I don't know, I guess she was tired. We were all tired.

CP: I thought you said your friends were excited when you found them.

JB: I made a mistake. We were all tired by then.

CP: Did you walk in silence? Did you argue? What was the conversation?

JB: I don't remember exactly, but I think we were talking about college. How we'd all be leaving each other at the end of summer but that it wouldn't be the end.

CP: It was a calm conversation?

JB: It was a happy conversation. We felt happy about what was to come.

CP: A big conversation for that time of night.

JB: We didn't know how to have small conversations.

CP: Would you say that Ms. Aetos was the ringleader of your group?

JB: What? No.

CP: But she was a risk-taker?

JB: No. God no. Evangeline was . . . almost always scared.

CP: But she went first that night. Down the rocks. She climbed down first.

JB: I—I don't know.

CP: You don't know if she went first?

JB: No, I mean I don't know why. I don't . . . it wasn't like her. I—I can't remember too well.

CP: Perhaps she wanted to get home most of all.

JB: We all wanted to get home.

CP: And while you were walking, did you notice anything else different about Ms. Aetos, her general demeanor or appearance, that could be of note?

JB: Oh . . . you want . . . Wait—what?

CP: We don't want anything, Ms. Bonnier. We just want the truth. I will repeat the question. While you were walking, did you notice anything else different about Ms. Aetos, her general demeanor or appearance, that could be of note?

JB: Do you mean her shoes?

CB: Her shoes?

JB: Yes. She was holding her sandals in her hand. As she walked. She had blisters, so she took off her sandals to . . . to walk home. Or maybe—maybe that was another night or maybe I dreamed it or something. I don't . . . I don't think I understand why this is important? Haven't you got everything you need already?

CP: Wouldn't you say Evangeline must have been in some distress to attempt to walk all that way, even with blisters on her feet? Wouldn't you say she was running from something?

JB: I don't know. We all just wanted to go home.

CP: How much time elapsed between Ms. Aetos's fall and you following her down?

JB: I'm not sure, we were . . . we were extremely upset. I think about five minutes?

CP: That's not a long time to leave your friend alone?

JB: We were . . . we were destroyed, but we knew we had to get to her. Bess went down a path a little further back, and I climbed down the rocks after her.

CP: But you already knew she was dead.

JB: Yes.

CP: I can tell that you want to tell me the truth, Joni, but something is stopping you. Is it your friend? Are you protecting her? We know Bess and Evangeline had been arguing and that they left the party before you. This isn't the time to protect your friend; this is the time to protect yourself and tell us what really happened that night. You owe it to Evangeline, if nothing else.

JB: This is the truth.

I stop reading because, by now, all my nerves have started to tingle and the feeling that something is wrong is growing stronger with each passing second. I reread Joni's answers over and over again, hearing the words spoken in her voice as it was back then, before I figure it out.

I had forgotten that Evangeline had taken off her shoes while we were walking along the cliffside. I can remember them now as clear as anything, the large green gems still glittering under the sliver of the crescent moon when they landed only feet away from her. But how would Joni know that Evangeline had been holding her sandals before she fell if I had never told her? We had, of course, constructed a story together, but we stuck to broad strokes, the order we walked in, the general content of our conversation, figuring we could attribute any vagaries or inconsistencies to our drunkenness. But I had never once told Joni that Ev had taken off her sandals before I left her, because I hadn't remembered it myself.

Steven appears back in the doorway, and we stare at each other for a moment. He is gripping his phone, and I understand that he was in the other room, doing the exact same thing I was doing in here.

"The shoes," he says. "Why would she make that up?"

"She didn't," I say.

I remember back in the hotel room when Joni asked me if I'd remembered anything in the interview that I'd forgotten to tell her. She must have been trying to coax the same detail out of me so that she could pretend that's how she knew it, jumbling the timelines. But why? Why would Joni have been with Evangeline at the end, and why would she have lied to me about it?

"Why didn't they pursue it?" I ask, my voice thick with emotion. "If they thought that something didn't add up, why didn't they question it?"

"For the same reason you never did," Steven says quietly. "Joni is a fucking good liar."

FIFTY-FIVE

2018

I WAIT UNTIL STEVEN AND Nova have gone to bed to leave the house, taking the key to their Prius from the hook by the front door. The roads are almost empty, and I arrive in Malibu around one a.m., knowing that Joni will still be awake.

As I drive, one word snakes around my mind: *liar.*

I enter the code into the keypad at Joni's front door, aware of a familiar, bone-shattering fury building inside of me. Only this time I know I need to give it an outlet before it consumes me.

When will it end?

Joni is standing in the kitchen in a silk dressing gown, watching the black ocean through the windows. The moon is full and glowing on the waves, just how we used to like it.

"You were the one who told Evangeline about Milos," I say. "Not Theo."

Joni turns to face me, her mouth already opening, searching for the perfect words to reassure me.

"Don't lie to me," I say. "Not now."

After a moment, she nods.

"Why did you do it?" I ask.

"Why did *you?*" she asks me softly.

"Answer my question, Joni. You've had enough time to figure it out."

Joni's eyes flick over mine.

"I told her because I knew that nothing would be the same again if Theo came back," she says after a long pause. "And not because I thought you'd get married or anything, but because it was so *obvious* he was going to break your heart. Things would get weird between you and Ev, and then you'd slowly pull away from me too until we had nothing left in common, no shared references or jokes that weren't from high school, and soon it would just become easier for you to miss my calls or pretend you hadn't seen my emails, and maybe we'd check in with each other once or twice a year after that, congratulating each other when we got notified about a job promotion on fucking LinkedIn or Facebook, but it would never be the same. I could see it all from ten miles off. You were lost the moment Theo arrived in Tinos."

"Didn't you ever think that maybe our friendship was never meant to last past that summer?" I say.

Joni frowns at me, uncomprehending.

"When my dad left . . ." she starts, her voice buckling under the strain. "When my dad left, the worst part wasn't that he was gone, it was that I couldn't trust any of my memories of him anymore either—like he'd just been pretending to be charmed by me but all along he was waiting until the first moment he could get out of there. I felt like I didn't know who he was but, even worse, like I didn't know who I was. Like everything up until then had been a mirage. And then, without even knowing it, you and Ev picked me up and put me back together, like you always did. So the thought that you two were not only leaving me to move across the country but that we might fall apart even before that felt . . . it felt impossible. Like my entire world was slipping away from me again. And the worst part was, I was the only one who knew it was happening."

"Joni," I say slowly. "What exactly did you think would happen if you told Ev like that, wasted in a bar, thousands of miles from home? How did you think she'd feel if she didn't hear it from me or Theo?"

"I thought if Theo knew how much it was hurting Ev . . . I thought he wouldn't come back for you. He didn't care as much as you did," Joni says. "We could all see that."

I try to ignore the cruelty of her words.

"You followed us to make sure she didn't tell me it was you," I say. "You were scared that I'd find out what you'd done. You were there at the end."

I watch Joni's shoulders slacken, and I know that I've finally relieved her of her worst secret, the one that comes for her at night.

"I didn't want her to fall," she says softly. "You believe that, don't you?"

"What did you want?" I ask.

"I wanted her to stop saying it was all over," Joni says. "To stop trying to leave."

I consider this for a moment. A lie?

"Her foot got stuck," Joni says, her voice cracking. "In between two rocks, and instead of dropping her fucking shoes and grabbing hold of something, she panicked. I tried to get down close enough, but she had already gone. She was already falling."

Joni flinches, and I watch as it plays out all over again behind her closed eyes.

"Did she know?" I ask, my voice barely above a whisper.

Joni opens her eyes and takes a moment to focus on me and what I'm asking, and then she just nods.

"Was she scared?"

Joni nods again, and I have to fight a blistering urge to reach out and comfort her. All this time I blamed myself for what happened when Joni could have put me out of my misery by telling me one single truth—that it wasn't my fault. *Everything*, I think, everything that happened was because of her. That we were even in Mykonos instead of playing Scrabble at the Tinos house, that Evangeline knew about Theo's and my plans in Milos, and that she was so furious and heartbroken that she tried to climb down a rocky path that wasn't made to bear our young bodies. And all Joni has ever done is lie to me about it.

"You were so scared we were going to fracture that you broke us first," I say.

I watch as Joni's face crumples, and I think she knows that I finally see her.

"You know, you had been Ev's best friend for six years, Joni," I say. "You should have protected her, but instead you made it so much worse. You told her that two of the people she cared most about in the world were planning to leave her behind, and then you made her promise to keep it quiet. We were never meant to leave that night with our friendship intact, but somehow you still made it work for you. You watched her fall, and then you let me think it was my fault."

"I know I messed up," Joni says. "I promise I know."

I close my eyes.

"Do you believe me?" Joni asks, and she sounds more vulnerable than I've ever heard her. "You believe I would never hurt either of you, don't you?"

Something ingrained in me, some long-established instinct or capacity to forgive and excuse Joni, makes me want to go over and comfort her, to tell her that it wasn't her fault and any of the countless other messages she's tried to instill in me this summer. Only now I understand more. I understand why she's dedicated her entire life's work to helping people like me. It wasn't because she'd discovered some magical secret to the universe, it was because of what she did to me on that beach in Mykonos. For not only pulling me down with her but making me feel grateful for the privilege.

"How could you do that?" I ask quietly. "Make me think you were saving me?"

Joni closes her eyes for a moment.

"I had nothing else left," she says. "I couldn't lose you too."

Stop, I think. *You were saving yourself.*

"So then you wrote about me in a fucking article," I say. "Maintaining our friendship was *clearly* a major priority for you."

"You never read it," Joni says slowly. "After everything, you've never even read it."

"Of course I didn't," I say, and when Joni just stares sadly at me in response, I feel another burst of fury.

A silence follows while I gather my strength to do what I have to do next.

"I met with Lucien," I say, and, when I look at her, I see that Joni's face is ugly and contorted, and, for just a moment, it is the easiest thing in the world to believe this person killed someone she loved.

"He said that you were controlling. That you used money to control Willa."

"You ask my dead fiancée's lover about my relationship and you think that could ever define it? Consider the source, Bess," Joni says, her voice tougher now, serrated. "I'm shocked that I have to explain this to you out of everyone."

"Will you tell me the truth, then?" I say, struggling to keep my voice even as I give her one final chance. "Just tell me what happened the night Willa died."

Joni turns her focus on me, and the full force of her betrayal is written all over her face.

"You're trying to decide whether I'm worth what you might lose," she says. "But that's not how it works. You can't flatten the people you love into equations, Bess."

As I watch her outrage grow, I wonder if Joni has deflected and distorted for so long that she's forgotten how to be accountable for anything.

"No, no, Joni. This isn't a theoretical question," I say, speaking slowly and carefully. "I'm actually asking it. Did. You. Do. It?"

Joni is trembling, and despite a voice inside me telling me to stop now, that I'll never get what I want from her, it's like something has been unleashed and I can't help but push ahead.

"Was Willa trying to leave you too?" I ask, my voice low and barbed. "Is that why you killed her?"

"Fuck you, Bess," Joni says quietly, and something inside me explodes, because I can finally see her now, as clearly as I'll ever see anyone, and I can taste blood.

"Wasn't it enough to ruin me once?" I ask, and suddenly it feels as if every nerve, every inch of skin on my body is ablaze. "Isn't it enough that I can barely look at myself in the mirror because of how vile, how vicious and unworthy of anything *good* I am? Isn't it enough that I think every day of my life that it should have been me instead of Evangeline, and that most of the time I wish it had been? Don't you think I know full well that I'm wasting my life being so scared of everything, but that it's still better than the alternative, which is to build something so bright, so *beautiful*, that it can be ripped out from under my feet again in a matter of seconds? Why did you have to come back for me, Joni?"

"I already told you," Joni says, her eyes shining in the dim light. "When I asked you to help me, I didn't know Willa was missing."

I shake my head.

"I need you to believe me," Joni says. "I need you to believe that I didn't mean for this to happen."

"I found Willa's phone," I say hollowly.

Joni's head snaps up, and then her body deflates like someone's pulled the rip cord, and I find that I can't look at her anymore.

"You were looking through my stuff."

"How did you have her phone?"

"I found it buried in the sand," Joni says. "Later. Much later."

I shake my head. *Enough,* I think. This is enough now.

"I think you knew exactly what you were doing that night on the beach," I say, each word forming a barrier between us that she will never pass again. "And the sad thing is, I probably would have covered for you back then, if you'd only told me the truth. Because at least it would have been my choice—a choice made for the right reasons, like you always say. But this time? You've lied to me one too many times for me to believe you, and this has to end somewhere."

I look at her one final time, the sharp line of her jaw, the sad curve of a mouth I once knew as well as I knew my own, and I shake my head. "I can't save you anymore, Joni."

I'm turning to leave when Joni finally lifts her head, her eyes glossy with tears. I watch as she swipes at her nose with the back of her hand, the telltale slick of blood she tries to hide from me. She looks as exposed as I've ever seen her, like her flesh has been stripped back and I can finally see her bloody heart beating in her rib cage.

"It's too late, Bess," Joni says flatly. "Don't you see that? Whatever you do now, we'll always be bound together."

FIFTY-SIX

2018

ONE WEEK LATER, WHEN the inevitable happens and Detective Frost's navy car pulls up outside my cabin, there's still a part of me that wants to protect Joni. It's the first day of July, the month that always ends with Ev's death, and I can already feel myself offering up excuses about Joni's abandonment issues or her fierce loyalty or any number of extenuating circumstances that still can't quite explain why she couldn't stop lying to me. Instead, I force myself to think of Willa, the photo of her now propped up on my mantelpiece to remind me that this isn't about me or Joni, it's about two young women who will never get to be alive or needy or imperfect ever again.

Detective Frost sits down, and this time she accepts a cup of tea when I offer. I'm looking for the box of decaf tea bags when I come across a bag filled with suspicious-looking gray dust instead. *Fucking Cordyceps,* I think, pushing it to the back of the cupboard as Joni's voice rings in my ears: *The only cure for . . . for whatever the fuck this is.*

"I need to tell you something before you ask me anything," I say, my hand trembling only slightly as I pour the boiling water over the tea bag. I shoot the detective a glance over the counter, and she is sitting with her notepad and pen in hand, poised to re-cord the words I'll never be able to take back.

"It's about Joni," I say, the calmness in my voice belying the terror I'm feeling inside.

"Have you heard from her?" she asks curiously, and I pause.

"I was staying with her up until recently," I say.

"And when did you last speak to her?"

"This isn't what I need to talk to you about . . ."

"Ms. Winter," Detective Frost says, a certain gentleness to her tone now. "Joni's been reported missing by her lawyer."

Another rip in time. My stomach plummeting.

"Missing like she's in Tijuana, or missing like Willa was miss-ing?" I ask slowly.

"We're not sure," she says. "Nobody's heard from her in com-ing up on a week. We thought you might be able to help."

"I think she's trying to get my attention," I say, hoping it's true.

"Maybe," Detective Frost says carefully. "But it seems a strange time to disappear."

"A strange time," I repeat.

"Given that she's a key witness in the case against Lucien Miller," she says.

"What do you mean?" I ask, and I can barely bring myself to say the next words out loud for fear of her answer. "You don't think—you still don't think she had anything to do with it?"

When I look up, Detective Frost is watching me unflinch-ingly, and I think she's about to tell me more about the case when she changes direction, her face now filled with the type of earnest sympathy that makes me feel awkward in my own skin.

"You know, for what it's worth, what happened to you both . . . it wasn't fair. I was a few years older than you, but I remember it because I was . . . Well, let's just say we all did things we weren't proud of when we were that age. I think sometimes people get scared of how quickly the world is changing and they look for someone to hold up as an example. And back then, they chose you and Joni."

I nod, avoiding her gaze because I don't think I'll be able to bear the pity in it.

"I know what those friendships can be like," she says. "The intensity is . . . it's unlike anything else."

You don't know the half of it, I think. When she seems to have finished talking, I try again, unwilling to let either myself or Joni off the hook just because this person once had a friend she idolized too.

"Have you read the text Willa sent Joni before she went missing?" I ask. "I think it might change things."

Detective Frost stares at me for a moment.

"We can't build an entire case around a text message, Bess."

"But isn't that exactly what you're doing with Lucien?" I ask, and she frowns instantly at the mention of his name.

"Lucien Miller lied to us from the moment we started questioning him. And he's still lying, even though his alibi fell clean through as soon as we applied the slightest pressure to it," she says, her voice now tight with something I can't identify. "The finer details of the case are confidential, for obvious reasons, but we have reason to believe that Lucien would have stopped at nothing to prevent the details of his affair coming out. At this point, you can rest assured that we are doing everything in our power to make sure that Lucien Miller never hurts anyone again."

I think of the rose quartz crystal now languishing at the bottom of the ocean, cleansed of Willa's blood, and close my eyes briefly.

"Are you sure?" I ask quietly. "Joni couldn't have . . . ?"

"Now, obviously this is still between me and you, Bess," she says. "But the thing about a murder investigation compared to a missing person case is that certain members of the general public become much more willing to help, to *remember* what they saw once there's a body. So some things have changed with Joni's situation, even not accounting for Lucien."

Detective Frost flips through a few pages of her notebook.

"We already had the neighbor spotting Willa alive and well at seven p.m. on her deck, and now we get two surfers spotting her sitting alone on a nearby beach between eight and nineish," she says. "And from there, critically, we have the neighbor who got back from vacation and alerted us to their security camera footage of Willa leaving her house on foot, from the front this time, at around 9:35 p.m."

"So Willa could have messaged both Joni and Lucien while she was down on the beach," I say slowly, thinking about how I'd dismissed Joni for trying to suggest something similar. "Not paddle-boarding, but hiding." *From Joni,* I add silently, a heaviness lingering inside me.

"Off the record, that would fit the timeline we're working with," Detective Frost says.

"Where was Willa going?" I ask. "At 9:35?"

"That's where Lucien Miller comes back in," she says, more carefully now.

"And Joni?" I ask tentatively. "Where was she?"

"There's a pawnshop in West Adams, around thirty-five miles from Malibu, that's had some expensive break-ins, to the point where no insurance company would touch them unless they installed some state-of-the-art surveillance equipment. We have Joni on their cameras, driving past at 9:45 p.m. We figure she would have left Malibu around 9:00 or 9:10 p.m., latest, to come over this way, exiting the 10 for a couple blocks to miss the traffic building up behind an accident that occurred at 9:41. Whoever was in that wreck has hand delivered Joni her alibi, so when she turns up, I hope she covers their medical bills."

I try to focus, the numbers and locations flying behind my eyes like sparks. I think of Steven and can almost hear his voice in my head, telling me, *Think of the facts. The ones that count.* Willa left the house alive at 9:35, and at 9:45 Joni was already thirty-five miles away from her, on her way to my house in the desert.

"I must have got the times confused," I murmur, my mind reeling. "When we first spoke."

The detective raises an eyebrow at me.

"It happens more often than you'd think," she says. "Time can be funny like that."

I nod wordlessly, my eyes prickling with tears.

"Now, is there anything else you might have misremembered?"

"I saw . . ." I start, before forcing myself to finish. "I saw Willa's phone. At Joni's house. She said she found it later, but I thought . . . I guess it doesn't matter what I thought it meant."

Detective Frost nods before making a final note in her pad.

"Do you think Willa was running to the wrong person?" I ask when she stands up to leave.

"It looks that way, Bess," Detective Frost says. "Lucien Miller's wife is just devastated."

Once she has left, I slump on the sofa, reeling from the revelation that Joni wasn't lying about some things at least. I can feel my fury slipping further away from me each second, and I'm terrified to find out what's underneath it. Why couldn't Joni have just waited for the truth to come out? Why after she fought with Willa couldn't she have gone anywhere else in the world other than here? Why was it so important to Joni that, even after all this time, even after everything she'd already taken from me, I was still the person to lie for her?

FIFTY-SEVEN

2018

WHEN JONI HAS BEEN missing for a month, I start to wonder what she has done. At first, I assumed she disappeared to get my attention, or to punish me, or maybe both, but wouldn't she have reappeared by now if that were the case? Now that Lucien has been outed as having had both opportunity and motive to kill Willa—a secret double life as a devout Catholic with a beautiful wife and a baby on the way, and an unpredictable girlfriend who was threatening to blow it all up?

The first reported sighting of Joni came hours after the story of her disappearance broke. I sat on my couch and watched as a trucker in Bakersfield said she saw someone fitting Joni's description at a gas station on the 5, buying a burrito and a can of Diet Coke. The CCTV was broadcast on every news channel, but I knew instantly that it wasn't Joni because of the posture—this woman was stooped, cowed as she walked out of the kiosk clutching her purchases. Sure enough, a local teacher came forward as the mystery woman within hours. She was interviewed outside her home, blinking as she gripped a can of Diet Coke at six a.m. and talked frankly about the calls she'd already received from friends and family after they saw the footage and recognized her. "If my experience is anything to go by, Joni Le Bon isn't going to get far," she said, like she'd seen a brief glimpse of Joni's life and felt sorry for her.

The next sighting was more believable, a woman in a hooded jacket and Gucci sunglasses spotted lurking in Fred Segal at LAX, but once she was detained by airport police, she turned out to be the mother of young twins, flying home to Berlin after a work trip.

Part of me believes that Joni won't be able to keep away for long. The fact that she didn't find a way of saying goodbye, that she never sent me some overwrought, guilt-inducing message before she disappeared, makes me think that she has to come back. Most nights I wait for her to appear on my front porch dangling a bag of adaptogens to show me she's decided to forgive me, as if we haven't both scarred each other in a thousand senseless ways.

A week before the anniversary of Evangeline's death, I rent a car and drive myself to Joni's house. I enter the security code and push open the familiar front door, my heart racing in my chest. The house feels lifeless as I walk around it, searching for any traces of Joni. I hold my breath when I walk into her bedroom, not because I'm scared that it will smell like her but because I'm scared it won't. Her bed is undone with a half-drunk glass of water still on her bedside table, but it only smells like dead air. I look for a note with my name on it or, better yet, some sort of filing box or envelope, filled with evidence of our shared history, that Joni will no doubt instruct me to open only when I'm appropriately drunk and nostalgic and missing her the most. Instead, I find nothing.

When I walk into the kitchen, I spot a rioja-tinged wineglass still in the sink—another room preserved at the last sign of life.

When I find no note, no postcard hidden in plain sight on the fridge, nothing at all to suggest that Joni is planning to come back or that she's starting over or is even still alive, I start to really worry. Before I leave the room, I reach up and take the photo frame from the shelf next to Joni's fridge—the photo of the three of us during our first week in Tinos. I drop it into my tote bag because I don't know what will become of it if Joni never returns. Where will all of our shared memories live if I'm the only one left?

Next, I open the doors that lead out to the deck. All the furniture is in the same position as when I was last here, although the cushions are now streaked with seagull shit. I walk to the edge of the deck and look out at the water, as if Joni might have left a sign somewhere out there for me. I wonder if I'd even know if she tried—if one night a specific type of firework might light up the sky and I'll instinctively know it's Joni telling me she's okay. When all I see now is cornflower blue stretching all the way to the horizon, I turn back around. I'm about to walk back into the house when I notice something that stops me in my tracks. One of the paddleboard racks is empty. Joni's black and yellow board is gone, and only the pink and silver board remains. I remember asking Joni if she ever wanted to disappear, and I wonder now if it was the most honest conversation we will ever have and Joni has left nothing of herself behind, not even for me.

I think of Joni as she was back then, the way we danced on the beach like wild summer creatures, the feeling of her hand in mine as she instructed me not to cry when we left the police station, and the Joni of this summer—the woman who drove me to face my fears at the Aetoses' house, who wanted me to dream bigger and live better, who dedicated a *book* to me—and I know that it will never be as simple as Joni asking me to lie for her because we'd made some Faustian deal all those years ago. No, Joni came back for me because she had to know if, given the choice, had I known everything back then that I know now, I'd have stood by her. She wanted, probably needed, to believe that even if she'd told me the truth that night, I'd have pulled her up off the sand and promised to protect her with everything I had inside me, and that I'd have gone through it all over again for her. She was testing my loyalty, yes, but she was also trying to make herself feel better about destroying my life. She wanted to fix me at the same time as she needed to test me. She came back for me to find out if she could be enough for me.

As messed up as it is, a small smile forms on my lips. It's pretty fucking Joni when you think about it.

FIFTY-EIGHT

2018

FOR THE NEXT FEW days, I think of Joni constantly. I remember when she told me that I had only come back to her because I needed something in my life to change, and I think now that she was right. Maybe I knew that I wouldn't be able to pass as a ghost for long in the place that shaped me, the place where I was someone's sister, someone's best friend, and some days I can almost understand what she wanted for me.

Three nights before the anniversary of the moment that changed everything, once Steven and Nova have gone home after a long dinner where none of us felt the need to apologize anymore for not trusting each other to endure our darkest moments, and as chunky droplets of rain fall outside and my favorite MGMT song plays from my laptop, I dig out the framed photograph I took from Joni's house. I promise myself that I will at least try to understand how Joni could have been so fixated on outrunning our past while being desperate to preserve it. Perhaps I owe it to all of them: Evangeline, Willa, Joni.

I stare at the photo—a posed shot of the three of us, arms linked under defiant grins—and I try to remember what it meant to be that girl on a beach in Greece, standing in between my best friends with the rest of our lives hovering in front of us. I think of the five weeks we spent alone in Tinos, lazy and sunburned as we navigated the never-ending politics of being a group of three: blazing with fury one moment, then dancing on tables the next, arms wrapped around each other and foreheads touching as we screamed the lyrics to the songs I'm still playing now. I think now that I've been doing a disservice to us all in blaming only myself for how things fell apart. Sometimes we could be cruel for sport, yes, but most of the time we hurt each other to hide our own gaping wounds. To find out not just if we were enough for each other but if we would ever be enough for anyone.

I'm about to put the photo away when I notice a glossy white corner peeking out from the back panel of the frame, as if there is another photo tucked behind this one. I open the back of the frame, and the photo I find makes my breath die in the back of my throat.

We are back in the damp hotel room in Mykonos, and Joni is stuffing a slice of leftover pizza into her mouth, and next to her on that stupidly small bed, Ev is throwing her head back, her mouth wide open as she meets my eye above the camera, laughing at something either Joni or I said. I try to remember how I felt when I was taking the picture, but I can't summon anything other than a blinding sense of relief at seeing them like this, as if I'm holding a piece of evidence that proves that things weren't always how strangers made them out to be afterward, but that sometimes we were good for each other too. I wonder whether, if we'd all boarded our flight back to LAX at the end of the summer, Evangeline would have regretted having invited us, and I figure that the answer is probably both no and yes, but that the memory, the sting of it all, would have soon faded either way. I think that it's these other moments, the spaces in between the drama and the intensity, that Joni had wanted me to remember all along. I swap the photos so that this is the one facing out, and then I place the frame on my kitchen table.

When the rain stops, I sit on the porch for a while, thinking about how Joni has slipped out of her own life, and I wait for the shame to hit as I remember the cruel things I said to her before she went. When all I feel is sadness, I know it's not as simple as it could be. Perhaps Joni walked out of her life to protect me, yes, but she also did it because of the things she'd done—the lies she'd told and the people she'd hurt—and while I can no longer hide from the things I've done either, I figure that the potential of starting over, of being reborn, is there every single day if I can just learn how to take it.

And then, weightless underneath a stretch of stars so beautiful, so shameless that I could still be in Tinos, I realize something.

Nine years after she wrote them down, I'm finally ready to read Joni's words on the summer that defined us all.

FIFTY-NINE

DOLLFACE, AUG '09 ISSUE

HOMEOSTASIS

By Joni Le Bon

Yesterday I read a quote by Yevgeny Zamyatin that reminded me of last summer: *Those two, in paradise, were given a choice: happiness without freedom, or freedom without happiness. There was no third alternative.* Now, obviously Zamyatin wasn't thinking about three privileged teenagers from Calabasas when he wrote it, but I do believe that, without even knowing it herself, my best friend Evangeline had been trying to offer us the same choice before we left each other for college. As immature as she could be, Ev knew that all of the opportunities and networks and pathways that would make up our futures would also inevitably let in something rotten and impure, and she just wanted to hold on to the simplicity of childhood for a while longer. She wanted to let time trickle past slowly in sun-soaked hours, re-creating all the lazy summers she'd spent in Tinos as a child, because for Ev, in the stone house on the hill we were safe. In some ways, we already knew that it would be our last summer together like this (just the three of us, no jobs, no serious partners or new friends we had more in common with, no rent to pay, no money worries of our own), but in trying to hold on too tightly to our childhood innocence, we ended up losing something even more precious along the way.

Evangeline wasn't perfect, like they say. Yes, she spent hours learning dance routines alone in her predictably frou-frou bedroom, and, yes, she was fundamentally *allergic* to cruelty, and, okay, it is true that she once missed a party to sit with a homeless man outside a Jamba Juice all night because he told her it was the anniversary of his wife's death, but she was also just *Ev*, our sports-hating, Jackie Collins–loving friend with the surprisingly stinky feet and vicious pinch. She could be as insecure as Bess and as stubborn as me, and she was both entitled and babyish to boot, and, maybe worst of all, she resisted change at any cost, including the good kind. The kind you need to grow.

Ev saw the world in black and white, which made her an excellent ally to have in your corner, but not someone you'd ever want to cross. Because while Ev could be loyal, she was also fierce. But we were all fierce in our own ways. We had built fortresses to protect ourselves from our parents, our classmates, the world, before shyly inviting each other in by the front door. We loved each other more than anything, but the flip side of love isn't hate—it's the power to destroy. We were experts in each other's weaknesses, blind spots, barely healed wounds, and, very occasionally, we used this insider knowledge to hurt each other.

In many ways, Bess and I *were* as bad as they said. Or as bad as the avatars they created of us—Bess and Joni 2.0, recognizable instantly by the shit-eating smirks and unbecoming behavior. We partied hard, we bitched and complained, we hurt people, we thought we knew everything about sacrifice and loyalty and how the world worked. We had casual sex a little and we talked about it a lot, we exaggerated stories to impress each other, and we almost always pretended we were tougher than we were. We wanted to be fearless. And we wanted Evangeline to want to be fearless too.

A lot has been said about how Bess and I behaved both in the weeks before Ev died and in the days that followed, but few people have tried to understand us. The truth is that our trip was doomed from the start. We were on the brink of independence, of womanhood, and yet we were still playing our old parts, clinging to an idealized version of our friendship because we were too scared to move forward, which served none of us in the end. Bess and I pretended we were resisting change for Ev's sake, denying the natural order of things so that she wouldn't feel left behind, but it was also to soothe and protect ourselves. The fact that Evangeline died was a senseless accident made all the more tragic because it occurred at the end of a summer that should never have happened in the first place. It was a summer in which we all made poor choices for each other, for ourselves, for the wrong reasons and the right ones, and we all ended up paying for it in the most unfathomable way.

Since coming home, I've had to accept that, for now at least, both my best friends are lost to me. Bess is a hologram flickering in front of me, and even though all I want to do is reach out and grab her, I also know I have to let her find her own way out. I will find comfort in knowing that an invisible force will connect us for the rest of our lives, and sometimes I even imagine that this force is Evangeline herself, stretching her arms so wide that she can touch each of us on different coasts. All I can do is wait and hope that, one day, in a week or a year or maybe even ten, I'll show up on Bess's doorstep and maybe we'll achieve Zamyatin's elusive third alternative—happiness *and* freedom—because we'll both have changed in a million necessary ways, but also none at all.

Whatever I do next, people will know who I am. I will probably never be a famous actor like I always planned, but I will always be infamous in the way nobody wants for themselves. So I have a choice—I can either join Bess in the shadows, hiding out in case even the California sunlight turns out to be a spotlight once again, or I can step back out into the world. I can adapt and survive, choosing to tell my story, *our* story, in a way that might just save someone else's life one day, as well as my own. Because while it's not a happy story, it's not only a tragedy either. It's the story of three perfectly imperfect women who hurt each other in all the most obvious ways, but who loved each other enough for a lifetime. And it doesn't end here.

SIXTY

2018

THE DRIVE UP TO Theo's house in Oregon is predictably beautiful, winding through lush fir tree–lined streets, the velvety scenery an unexpected relief after the arid landscape of California—the blues and dusty beige of the dust embedded under my nails even now.

I pull up outside a two-story glass and wood terrarium overlooking Lake Oswego, and I park my rental car behind a Land Rover with two matching silver bikes strapped to the roof. My hands are shaking as I check my face in the mirror, and I look as nervous as I feel—my complexion pale and slick in the high noon sunlight.

Theo's wife, Sophia, answers the door in a broderie anglaise maxidress. When she sees me, she tilts her head to one side in gentle recognition before she reaches out and pulls me in toward her. She holds me for what feels like an inordinate amount of time, and I'm already blinking back tears when I feel something brush against my leg. I look down to find two German shepherds circling us, creating a living barrier between us and the rest of the world.

"Bess," Sophia says. "I've heard so much about you."

"Thank you for having me," I say awkwardly as I follow her inside. I find myself comparing the house to the set-dressed *Vogue* spread I devoured, sprigs of dried eucalyptus and colorful bowls of dragon fruit and physalis now replaced by gnawed dog toys and a bowl of half-eaten overnight oats balanced on the arm of a sofa. Looking around now, I realize that this is the home of two humans with full and complex lives, who have probably fallen in and out of love with each other countless times in the years that have passed since the moment I kissed Theo in Tinos.

"Thank you for coming," Sophia says. "Theo isn't close to his parents, so I know it means the world to him that you're here, especially today. This is never the easiest day in our house."

Sophia speaks in a way that denotes a certain reverence to Theo's past, and I wonder how her life has been impacted by this girl she will never know, and if Evangeline is the ghost between them too.

Sophia offers me tea while I wait for Theo at the reclaimed wood table in the kitchen. One of the dogs lies at my feet while the other stands guard, watching me through narrowed eyes. The industrial windows lead out to a backyard with a tasteful hammock and a lemon tree, and a jetty out onto the vast lake.

"It's probably too warm for tea," Sophia murmurs once the kettle has boiled, perhaps in response to the sweat trickling down my temple.

"I grew up with English parents," I say. "That concept doesn't exist."

Sophia smiles and, a few moments later, presents me with a glass of hot water and lemon, along with two sprigs of fresh mint, a stick of cinnamon, and a small glass dish of honey on a bamboo platter.

"Thanks," I say as I stir some of the viscous honey into the water.

Theo walks into the kitchen then, and I think he will be embarrassed by the fuss Sophia is making, but instead he purposefully leans in to kiss his wife on the cheek, lightly touching the small of her back, and I have to look away. When he hugs me next, I freeze and try not to smell his neck in case Sophia is watching us, but of course she isn't; she is checking something on her phone while also stroking one of the dogs and nudging a tennis ball with her foot for the other.

"Bess, I've set up one of the guest rooms for you in case you decide to stay over," she says when she catches me staring.

"Oh. I actually have a hotel room . . ." I say, realizing now that this dinner I've agreed to, this celebration of Ev's life, might just be the three of us, and I don't know whether to feel relieved or horrified about that. Perhaps it doesn't matter. Either way, I'll still have to face up to the same truth.

"You don't have to decide now. See how you feel," she says warmly, and her quiet insistence reminds me of one person only. I look up to find Theo watching me as I force a smile.

"Thanks, Sophia," he says then, in a warm but firm way that we all understand means it's time for her to leave. I don't catch her expression as she closes the door, and I wonder if this is how she spends her life, making hard things seem perfect and effortless for her husband.

"I know," Theo says to me once she's gone, and he's pretending to hang his head through his smile. I wonder what he means, whether he's telling me that he knows how charming his wife is, how well he chose, or whether he understands how much she reminds me of Evangeline.

"She's perfect," is all I say as I take a sip of tea. He smiles again in the same self-effacing way, and I want to tell him he can drop the act, that we both always knew he would find someone like this.

"Have you heard anything from Joni?" Theo asks then, and his bluntness almost makes me smile because I'd forgotten how, despite being perceived as easygoing, neither Evangeline nor Theo was ever any good at small talk. They both wanted to get down to the important stuff—what it was that made you cry with joy, and what had the power to destroy you. *This is why I came,* I remind myself. *Because I can't run away anymore.*

I shake my head and meet Theo's gaze.

"Not since the night they say she disappeared," I say slowly. "We had a fight."

Theo nods and is about to say something when Sophia sticks her head around the door, iPad now in hand.

"I just noticed how sticky it's getting, and I remembered we have iced tea if you'd prefer?" she says. "Just as an option . . ."

"Really, everything's perfect," I say.

Sophia closes the door again, and it makes me feel strangely powerful to think that my presence might cause a woman like this concern, after everything.

"How is your wife running a magazine and making seventeen different types of tea while also being ridiculously chic and charming?" I say, because I understand now that this is what is expected of me—something Theo can relay to Sophia once I've left, to put her mind at ease that I'm not the type of ghost from his past that will try to reclaim him. Theo looks relieved, as if a part of him was also worried I might still expect something from him, some alternate ending to our love story, and I try to absorb the blow with dignity.

"You have to let me say it," I say. "You know you married your sister, right?"

Theo's about to deny it, then he just nods and we both start to laugh. We only stop when our eyes meet over the spider plant, and I can see the tears glistening in his eyes.

"I miss her so much," he says, and the grief is so raw that I instinctively turn away before forcing myself to look back at him, because however hard it is for me, Theo lost more than any of us that night.

"Ten years," I say softly, and he nods.

"It feels like ten seconds," he says.

"And ten lifetimes," I say, and our eyes meet again in mutual recognition.

"Theo," I say quietly. "I'm ready to talk about that night. The truth this time."

Theo exhales heavily, as if he's been holding his breath since it happened.

"Before . . . before it happened. Did you mention our Milos plan to Ev?" I ask.

"I don't think so," Theo says slowly, frowning as he tries to remember. "I thought it was better to tell her when I got back. We were going to tell her together, weren't we?"

"And you never . . . changed your mind?" I ask, mortified by how vulnerable I sound.

He shakes his head. "You said that before, at Joni's. Why would I have changed my mind?"

I remember Evangeline's flinty cruelty that night, and how much I must have hurt her that she would want to make me feel like that. Only it wasn't just me who was going to leave her, it was Theo too. It had been Theo's plan from the start, so why don't I blame him like I've blamed myself? *Because neither of us did it to hurt her,* I think now. We did it for thousands of reasons, and not one of them was to break Evangeline's heart.

"Is that what you wanted to tell me?" Theo asks now, bringing me back to the present. I feel an odd, almost nostalgic embarrassment at the thought of explaining it all to him, but I force myself to carry on, to dwell in the darkness of my own memories and discomfort for once.

"Ev didn't think we were good together," I say, and then, because I'm still softening it: "Ev didn't think I was good enough for you."

Theo's eyes spring to mine, and it feels like my chest is in a vise.

I take a deep breath and continue: "She took a dumb route back to the hotel because we were arguing, and she wanted to get away from me. I followed her, but I didn't tell her we should turn back. I wish I had more than anything, but I didn't, and she fell."

Theo nods.

"Was she scared at the end?" Theo asks then, his green eyes swampy and darker than I remembered. "It's like if I can picture it, then I might have a better chance of letting her go—does that make sense? I just want to understand."

"That's the thing, Theo. I wasn't there," I say quietly, allowing myself to feel the full force of the discomfort, of the pain in Theo's eyes now that I'm doing what I should have done ten years ago. "Joni was there, but I wasn't. We lied to make it sound better. We lied to make ourselves feel better. I don't know why we lied, but we did."

I hold my breath, waiting for Theo to berate me, to tell me how irresponsible and cowardly it was to divert an investigation in that way, but he doesn't say anything.

"Our fight wasn't about you," I say. "Not really. It was about us."

As I say the words, I realize their truth—it never was about Theo. It was about the power the three of us held over each other as best friends, as chosen sisters—the power to cleanse, heal, and lift each other up, yes, but also the power to hurt each other, maybe even to destroy.

"I'm sorry we lied," I say. "I'm sorry it wasn't the three of us together at the end, like we said. But most of all I'm sorry that she's gone, because she would have been so proud of the life you've built, Theo."

Theo studies me, his eyes scanning my face as if he doesn't want to miss a tiny detail, and my heart twists in my chest, but it's only for all the possibilities that were lost that night too, all the ways in which we might have been happy.

"Thank you," Theo says. "I know."

And then he smiles at me in a way that reminds me of Evangeline, and it feels like my chest is finally splitting open, a brilliant light illuminating some long-buried part of me, some capacity for hope or yearning or forgiveness, and the light both hurts and terrifies me but I'm still smiling as I think of my younger self, because at least I know it means she's still here, after everything.

SIXTY-ONE

2018

THEO SHOWS ME AROUND the grounds of the house after sunset, fireflies darting as we stand side by side next to the lake in comfortable silence, both lost in our own memories. The three of us eat outside at a farmhouse table lit with church candles as tasteful music plays in the background. Sophia is as funny and accomplished and likable as I knew she would be, and for dessert she's made a lemon meringue pie decorated in glossy maraschino cherries that somehow manages to be both nostalgic and cool at the same time, which she presents with a self-effacing laugh that reminds us all she's in on the joke.

"To Evangeline," Sophia says, holding her champagne glass over the table. "Not an angel, but even better."

Theo and I meet each other's eyes and then lift our own glasses.

"To Evangeline," I say softly.

After we toast, Theo tells a story about Evangeline failing her driving test three times because she refused to admit she needed glasses, a story Sophia has no doubt heard countless times before, but she still looks as open and encouraging as if she were hearing it for the first time, and I try to be pleased that Theo found someone like her, someone so frustratingly perfect, the kind of woman he always knew he'd end up with, but it still feels bittersweet, even though most likely whatever we had would have faded the moment we left Greece. I was about to start a new life in New York, and he was about to knuckle down for his senior year, anyway. *How many couples get together just after high school and make it for the long haul?* I think as I watch him tease Sophia about her unending love for her Hôtel Costes playlist.

After dinner, Sophia hugs me goodbye, and Theo walks me to my car. It's dark now, and the chirping crickets remind me of lazy nights in Tinos, and both of these things embolden me enough to finally ask the question that's been on my mind since the moment Detective Frost turned up at my cabin.

"Where do you think she could be?" I ask as I lean against my car. "Joni."

Theo shakes his head, his expression grim in the moonlight. "I don't know."

"I think she was trying to save me from going through it all again," I say. "But she never said goodbye."

"Joni's an adult, and she can make her own decisions," Theo says. "We were kids back then, but we're grown now."

I feel his generosity like a balm. We were all so young, just trying to keep our heads above water, trying to stay alive for another day, another week, perhaps a whole lifetime, if we were lucky.

"I think I'd know if she was dead," I say. "Like I'd be able to feel it. But I also don't think Joni is capable of disappearing, and that scares me."

"I don't think any of us know what someone else is truly capable of," Theo says. "Even when we love them. That's part of the thrill of being alive."

Theo's face is now only inches from my own as he holds open the car door, and for a moment I just stand there, remembering how it felt to be young and hopeful and so in love with the world it felt like I could burst. The air between us is thick, and all I can hear is our jagged breathing as I scan Theo's eyes and wonder if he's thinking the same thing as me, that maybe if we kissed we would open our eyes and be back in another life, back in that olive grove under the moon, our mouths bruised from needing so much from one another. I know that we would drop each other's hands as soon as we realized where we were, and we'd race through the night back to the stone house, shouting the whole way for Evangeline to get out of bed and bring her camera so that we could all watch the sun rise together from the cove.

I'm the one who breaks the moment when I turn my face away from Theo, smiling gently. He breaks into a rueful grin too as I slide down into the car seat, and I wonder briefly if he's done this before, or if I've awakened something latent in him—some darkness he'd forgotten about. *It doesn't matter,* I think. None of that matters anymore, not really.

"See you around, Ronaldo," he says as he closes my car door.

"Bye, Theo," I say, and, as I drive away, I think that maybe it's okay if it doesn't turn out to be Theo at all, and that maybe this feeling, this cavern inside my heart that is filling and bursting, maybe that's the thing that matters. Maybe Joni was right and life is about being fucking terrified and still showing up and turning yourself inside out because you know that loving someone gives them the power to break you, but that maybe, one day, you might just be lucky enough to stumble across another human who recognizes you exactly as you are and who will spend the rest of their life learning how to strike a match to fill your darkness.

Whatever Joni's motivation, however flawed or deluded her thinking could be at times, she never wanted either of us to be defined by our shame. It makes me sad to think that, all this time, we were always both just muddling around in the dark, reaching for a new existence or at least some way we might be able to forgive ourselves. I wonder whether Joni knows I'm thinking of her, wherever she is.

One day, I will find a sweet longing where I now feel sorrow, like when I'm walking down St. Mark's Place and catch a glimpse of a teenager in a fringed leather jacket with a rolled-up cigarette between her teeth, or if I hear a filthy pun that I know could have made Evangeline snort with laughter. In those moments I think I might even find a way of telling our story—the one where we were just three teenage girls living in the spaces between the labels the world gave us, existing in relation to each other but also in a state of flux as we figured out who we wanted to become. Later still, I'll start to recognize our teenage mannerisms in my own daughters, in flashes of their fearlessness and kindness but also in the way they expect the world to change for them because they don't yet know any different. And only then will I understand what Joni left behind for me the day she disappeared.

The knowledge that I will never be the one to tell them otherwise.

ACKNOWLEDGMENTS

Thank you to my editor, Jen Monroe, and my agent, David Forrer. I'm sorry you both had to read quite so many words to get to this point, but I'll be forever grateful that you did and that we ended up here.

Jen—once again, I've so appreciated your intelligence, wit, and frankness, and your commitment to getting the best out of me. You always understand the women I write, and I can feel your respect for them from the very start. There's also no feeling quite like getting that first *DAMN* from you in the comments of a draft.

David—thank you for your steady grace and humor throughout everything, and for making it feel like there isn't an ocean between us! I look forward to many more years of your generosity, your positivity, and (best of all) your wonderful stories.

Thank you to everyone at Berkley—Jin Yu for your marketing magic, Candice Coote for your incisive edits, Craig Burke and Chelsea Pascoe, Hannah Engler, Jeanne-Marie Hudson, Claire Zion. I so appreciate everything you do. Thank you also to my brilliant copyeditor Angelina Krahn for your talent and for saving me from myself, and to Colleen Reinhart and Emily Osborne for designing yet another beautiful cover.

Thank you to the team at Inkwell Management, and to Julia Silk for being the first agent to tell me I could do this. I'll always be grateful. And to Dana Spector for all things "Hollywood," and for the macarons.

Thank you to every Greek legal expert who generously took the time to educate me on the Greek justice system: Kriton Metaxopoulos, Irini Daroussou, Katerina Nikolatou, Stella Mitili, and Niki, as well as one more kindly defense attorney who asked to remain anonymous. Any errors or inconsistencies are entirely my own (and hopefully for the benefit of the story).

My CBC writers' group—thanks to Rachael Blok for reading nearly every word I've written since 2016 (sorry!), and to Jodie Chapman, Ailsa Caine, Clare Mcvey, Julia Andersen, and Louise McCreesh for your always insightful reads (either past or present), and for being such inspiring and supportive company.

Thank you to everyone in the reading community. Booksellers and librarians—I'm in awe of your tireless work to get books into the hands of readers, and I appreciate you. Thank you to the Read with Jenna and Book of the Month teams for changing the course of *The Comeback*, and to all the podcasters and content creators who use their platforms to celebrate books, writers, and booklovers everywhere. To the readers who send kind messages of support—hearing from you is undoubtedly the best part of publishing a book. To the other authors I've "met" over the past couple of years—thank you for your words of encouragement, or just for writing books that have inspired (and educated) me.

Thank you to Athina Andrelos for everything Greece-related—I hope I've done a few of your (and now my) favorite places justice. Thank you to Chris Olin, Paige Duddy, and Amanda Kaplan for the insider LA high school / Calabasas tips. And thank you to Tom and Claire Byrne for the solid life lesson that I borrowed and gave to an infinitely less loving fictional father.

A special thank-you to Tilda, James, Jackson, and Jeanne—it feels wonderful to be so unconditionally backed by you all. And to Jazzy and Athina (again!) for the dinners and moral support and the check-ins when I've slipped off the radar. To Sophie, Ben, Emily, and Paul—our message group has got me through some DAYS. Thank you to my other friends and family (some mentioned in my acknowledgments for *The Comeback*, some missed!) for the incredible support / enthusiasm / jokes / generally stunning behavior over the years.

Thank you to Lola for the lifesaving walks, your constant encouragement, and for always challenging my perception of things. Somewhere in between us may be the perfect person, but I never want to meet her.

Thank you to Sophie for being the best big sister I could have ever wished for, and Dan for being my favorite brother and neighbor. We're so lucky. But both of you, mostly thank you for my best friend Jesse, whom I adore.

Thank you to James for calmly guiding me through multiple meltdowns and crises in confidence over the course of the past couple of years, and also those even stranger glimpses of delusions of grandeur (what is that?). All I know is I love you madly and am so very lucky to have you (and Rocky) by my side.

And thank you to my parents—I love you so much there are (almost!) no words for it. But how clever I was to have "chosen" you as mine! *"All the time in my heart."*